ECHOES IN THE WIND

THE SHEPHERD'S OVERWATCH

BOOK 1

ROGER MARSH

Chiselbury

Published by Chiselbury Publishing, a division of Woodstock Leasor Limited, 14 Devonia Road, London N1 8JH

www.chiselbury.com

ISBN: 978-1-917837-55-2 (paperback)

ISBN: 978-1-917837-56-9 (epub)

A CIP catalogue record for this book is available from the British Library

First published in 2018 by Barrallier Books, Victoria, Australia

AUTHOR'S NOTE

The well informed reader will realise that there is no such place as Murruwa, and no such unit as the Second Recruit Training Battalion. Both of these fictitious, as are the people and events depicted in this novel. However, what I have written is intended to be a true echo of the lives of those who serve in the Australian Army. I dedicate this novel to my friends who have not served, in the hope that we might get to know each other better again; and with grateful thanks to Kristy, Wendy, and my dear wife Anna, all of whose encouragement, wisdom, feedback, and editorial skills gave this story the life and shape I intended.

PROLOGUE

IRAQ, early 2005

From a vantage point a couple of floors up in a disused building, a sniper pair from 40 Commando, Royal Marines, carefully scanned the area around a market place, observing its various comings and goings. The light of day was beginning to fade; however the changing colours in the sky did not draw a second glance from the watchful men. Inattention during an overwatch task could lead to deadly trouble, so they maintained their vigil without letting the presence of some more colour in the sky distract them. There would be other times to enjoy the Iraqi sunsets, but when they were on the job, distraction and complacency were deadly enemies; as deadly as the insurgents themselves.

More and more people began to emerge from their homes; and as this was a market day, a real crowd was starting to build, thronging around the various stalls that had been set up in the bazaar. Like all middle-eastern markets it sold a wildly diverse range of wares; from aromatic spices to poorly pirated movies. Watching the bazaar was exacting work, requiring an eye for the shifting details inherent in a press of broiling humanity; and reading those shifting details truly could mean the difference between life, and sudden, violent death.

Snipers are best known for the excellence of their marksmanship, but however important this might be, there are a number of other skills that are needed before ever a shot is fired. Beyond their skill at arms, what sets them apart from other warriors is their ability to observe and see, and to keep on observing and seeing, long after the average person would have given up out of sheer boredom. Humans beings usually only notice what they think should be in a particular place, and are very happy to leave out those things that do not quite make sense. However snipers are trained to see not what they think should be there, but what is actually there, and also those things that want you to think that they are something else.

The need for invisibility is another one of the demands on these special marksmen. Often this means keeping still for extended periods, regardless of the call of nature, or the invasion of biting insects. Consummate camouflage skills are required to maintain this invisibility, and the demands of camouflage change according to the terrain. In Iraq it is not useful to try and look like a clump of bushes when much of the landscape is a washed-out brown sort of colour.

The pair passed their time in quiet talk about the comings and going of the market, as the mercurial and unpredictable locals went about their business. No stiff upper lip on show amongst these people, but bare-knuckle, bare-blade passion, whether it be in their opinions of the various factions vying to exert political and military influence, or in the way they bought and sold goods. This bazaar, like all others in the Middle East, was a mad cacophony of humans in the furious pursuit of commerce and commodities. Yet somehow it represented a sliver of normality to them in a country that had well and truly been turned upside down. It was integral to the life and viability of the local community, and protecting this little piece of normality was vital to the success of the mission the Marines had been given.

During their time of observation so far, the pair had seen nothing that would indicate that this was going to be anything other than a normal, boring overwatch mission; if watching the place could ever be said to be normal. Yet both of them could not shake off the feeling that all was not well. Much is made of experienced soldiers having a 'sixth sense' of when things are going to go wrong. However both of these men had learned long ago that the senses could take in more information than could be passed on to the conscious mind. Yet with proper training the mind could be taught to note these small pieces in the jumbled jigsaw of reality.

Something about the atmosphere of the evening did not bode well; yet try as they might, they could not discern any ripples of abnormality in the human terrain. Down below, a Troop of their fellow Marines was patrolling the area, trying to maintain security in the ebb and flow of the crowd; a demanding and unpredictable task.

'Taff, we've hardly been here any time at all,' said Corporal John Blakeney, his broad Yorkshire accent still plainly evident even though he was talking in hushed tones, 'and already we're starting to get a bit jumpy like.'

However the man he referred to as Taff made no answer. Instead, he continued looking out over the scene through the telescopic sight of his rifle. However, after a bit more scanning of the area, he made a noise of realisation.

'Hey Johnno, have you seen our friend who is normally selling vegetables in the far corner of the bazaar?' asked Taff, his soft Welsh accent explaining the inevitable nickname. Johnno narrowed his eyes as he looked through the spotting scope, intent on the area that Taff had indicated.

'Well I'll be buggered,' said Johnno, noting the absence, 'first time he hasn't been there.'

'Can't be too careful, can we now?' mused Taff. 'Complacency will kill us both; we want to get back to Taunton in one piece.'

The pair of them continued to scan the market for threats. The absence of that particular vegetable seller may not be anything sinister; he could just have a head-cold, Johnno reassured himself. However, it could also be the prelude to big problems.

As the minutes wore by, the two of them maintained their patient vigil, fighting to bring maximum concentration on the little world that was laid out before them. It took a special kind of mind to maintain such concentration; one that was both relaxed enough to endure the boredom, and sharp enough to maintain focus through the inactivity. No words passed between the pair for a some time, however Johnno soon became absorbed in a radio conversation, before he turned to Taff with more information.

'Looks like our instincts were on the money,' said Johnno, 'I-COM[1] chatter warns of a suicide bomber in the area. They seem to be targeting the bazaar. The lads on the ground are aware. All indications are for a VBIED[2].'

'Acknowledged,' replied Taff. He too had heard the news over his headset, but was so focused on watching the world in front of him that he left concentrating on the radio to Johnno.

They could both hear the Marines at the check-point, out of sight on the other side of the market talking urgently as a white

---

1. Intercepted communications
2. Vehicle Borne Improvised Explosive Device

sedan approached their position, and then orders to open fire were given as the vehicle refused all instructions to stop. Moments later the shuddering concussion of a blast was felt, followed soon afterwards by a column of smoke going up into the air from the far side of the market. The vehicle had been stopped before the explosives inside could kill people, other than the driver; but the blast went off regardless, sending a pillar of dust, debris and black smoke high into the air. The noise and falling debris dismayed the crowd of people, and they started to mill about shouting and gesticulating, whilst some began to gather up their goods and leave.

Neither of the sniper pair said anything in response to the explosion. Another day, another blast; it had all become so routine. However the change in the mood of the crowd did give them cause for comment.

'That's stirred things up good and proper,' muttered Johnno, as people started to move in all directions.

'Yeh, no kidding Sherlock,' muttered Taff.

'Ay-up, what's your caper?' Johnno continued, looking at a couple of people he had just noticed talking in a nearby side street. A man, and a boy of about twelve were in conversation. The lad was wearing a new-looking white robe, but the view through the spotting scope indicated there may be more to the story. Both of them saw that the man was their absentee vegetable salesman. Yet it was not the adult who was causing them most concern.

'Shit; I'm sure that lad's got a suicide vest on, the shape under the robe is all wrong for a kid that size,' said Johnno in horror, 'better let the fellas know.'

He then spoke to the patrol, whilst Taff looked through the telescopic sight of his L96 sniper rifle. By some miracle, there were currently no people in between them and the two individuals who had drawn their interest. They were standing just out of view of the main market, and would have to cover about seventy yards before they reached the bazaar proper.

'If that lad moves toward the market and won't obey orders to stop, they want us to engage him, if we have a clear shot,' said Johnno.

'Got it,' Taff said, 'and watch that bloody green grocer on the corner there, I don't want him getting away.'

The boy had just started walking toward the market, whilst the adult male took out a mobile phone with one hand, and held a camera in the other, apparently filming. A Royal Marine in the bazaar spotted the boy, guided by Johnno's instruction, and held up his hand, yelling in Arabic for him to halt. The boy did not. The question on the mind of both Taff and Johnno was: Who has the trigger to set off the bomb? Was the mobile phone held by the adult male the trigger, or was there another? What if they were completely mistaken and innocent people died? However, their hard won self-discipline drove the 'what-ifs' from their minds as these thoughts flew by in a fleeting instant. Eliminate the immediate threat first, said their training. Taff aimed carefully at the boy; reluctantly he decided on a head shot, lest the percussion of the bullet strike detonate the suspected explosives. It was not a long shot at all; it would hardly be a test of his marksmanship. It would be all too easy.

'*Bendigedig yw yr Arglwydd, fy nghraig ... ,*'[3] said Taff under his breath as he squeezed the trigger.

The rifle barked sharply, and the boy crumpled, his head shattered by the passage of a 7.62mm round. Working the bolt fluidly as he traversed the rifle, Taff acquired the erstwhile vegetable stall owner in the telescopic sight. The man had been momentarily stunned by the sudden demise of the boy, and was looking around dumbly for where the shot had come from.

---

3. Blessed are you, O Lord my rock.

However he soon recovered and started to use the keypad on the mobile phone, and from where Taff was sitting that made him a threat, as who knows what it could activate. So the watchful Welshman fired again, and the round thudded home, hitting the man square in the chest, throwing him against a wall. A trail of blood smeared down the wall as he slid down to the ground, and there was a pock mark that showed the bullet had passed clean through the body. The dying grocer groped for the phone that was lying on the ground nearby. Whilst he could reach the phone he was still a threat, so Taff fired again, and the blood stain on the wall grew, mixing now with other matter.

'... *ef sy'n dysgu i'm dwylo ymladd, ac i'm bysedd ryfela,*'[4] said Taff after the final shot.

Perhaps the dead man had been hoping for footage of a Marine from the market place shooting the child, or maybe he had hoped to film the carnage when the bomb went off, as well as sending the youngster on the road to martyrdom. Whatever the case, the sniper team had changed the end result decisively.

All the shooting had happened in less than ten seconds. By now the market had gone from restless to full uproar, and people were screaming and running to get away. Taff and Johnno watched the unfolding scene with no apparent emotion; there was no time for such niceties. Instead they had to maintain focus to see if any further threats presented themselves. The Royal Marine patrol in the market secured the area, and tried to calm the locals. However there was no way that things were going to return to normal that evening.

'Looks like the car-bomb may have been trying to distract us from the real threat,' observed Johnno.

'Or they thought two was better than one,' replied Taff.

As intelligence was gathered from the incident scene, it

---

4. who trains my hands for war, and my fingers for battle.

turned out that the sniper pair's instincts and training had been correct. The boy had been wearing a suicide vest, a verse of the Koran in a small pouch around his neck, extolling the virtue of martyrdom in Jihad. The vegetable seller's phone and person had yielded some very valuable information, to say nothing of what was on the memory card of the little film camera. It appeared that an emerging suicide bombing facilitator had met his end, though quite why he had tried to personally oversee this attack was not yet known. Perhaps he had wanted to begin destabilising the town, and film the results for the purposes of insurgent propaganda. Film footage of a Marine shooting the boy, or of the boy being blown to bits and killing others with him could have been useful to the jihadists. The first would portray the British as brutal invaders, the second would show them as incapable of providing the security needed for life to improve.

Taff and Johnno learned much of this when they were de-briefed after coming back to their patrol base; and they at least had the satisfaction of having their judgement confirmed. Straight afterwards they cleaned their weapons and ate a meal in relative silence, drinking a toast in Coca-Cola to their own survival, and to the fact that fewer people died that day than might have otherwise.

They were a great team, and through their memory and powers of observation, had already been responsible for a stream of useful intelligence coming the way of British forces. Johnno was a larger-than-life wit; and being a Yorkshireman of West-Indian descent, he tended to stand out in a crowd. Taff however was the quieter analyst, with an ability to remain invis-ible just about anywhere. They knew each other's moods well, and for that reason, on this evening, Corporal Blakeney was a bit concerned for his friend. He had seen Taff in a reflective, melan-cholic mood before, but that was normal. Normal behaviour did not bother Johnno. It was when one of his mates started acting unusually that he got worried. There was some deeper and darker Celtic clouds gathering in Taff's soul, that looked as though it would soon burst forth in a storm. Quite how strong the storm would be, or how it would blow itself out was not plain at this stage.

It was not the first time that either of them had killed. In the course of their deployments to Iraq, they had both taken lives on a number of occasions; it had almost become a matter of banal routine. Taff and Johnno had participated in the invasion of Iraq two years before, when their enemies had worn uniforms. Now, however, the enemy was often anonymous, and virtually indistinguishable from the local populace. It had become a war on a continual knife edge, never knowing who to trust; and having to have a plan to kill any Iraqi they saw, lest the Marines drop their guard and pay the ultimate price. Johnno had muttered that it was just like being in a warmer and more 'agro' version of Northern Ireland, but without the regular access to beer.

Not long after the events in the market place, they were again selected to conduct an observation post, this time over part of an oil pipeline that insurgents were trying to target. It would be another day of concentration, shared with other sniper teams. Johnno had resolved to question Taff a little more closely about how he was going, and see if he could draw the quiet Welshman out a bit; he had already tried a few times but he always seemed to get thwarted by something else happening.

'Spoken to your family at all lately?' ventured Johnno, as they made the drive to oil pipeline. He was planning on taking a long run up to asking more detailed personal questions. Taff was the master at not talking about himself, but Johnno knew how to get past his guard; and most of all it required time.

'No; I think it's easier on them if they don't hear from me too much while I'm over here,' said Taff blankly, his eyes continually roving.

'Things seemed to be quiet this morning,' said Taff, as he looked around him. There were definitely a lot fewer people about, and his and Johnno's senses began to hum with the heady arousal of one who was expecting imminent trouble.

'You're dead right there,' said Johnno, noting the change in the pattern of life. These streets were normally active, but not today.

'Bloody quiet round here isn't it? Too bloody quiet,' he remarked.

Taff had a word with the driver of the Land Rover Snatch wagon, who acknowledged the concerns, and everyone in the vehicle kept an even sharper lookout for anything that could indicate an impending attack. The convoy turned a corner, and came out onto a long, straight road. Open country was on a one side of them, whilst a row of decrepit residences occupied the other, but just as they had rounded the corner Taff and Johnno both saw the street ahead of them was deserted. Taff's eyes narrowed behind his ballistic glasses. Normally there were children out playing football around here, but instead not a soul was to be seen.

'Oh shit,' said Johnno quietly, and he grasped his SA-80 rifle a little more firmly. However at that moment there was a rush of dust and noise, and their view of the world was blown into many shades of brown. They felt the vehicle lurch, then roll onto its side, cascading the driver and passengers onto the rocky surface of the road. The barking thump of AK-47s firing soon followed, as the insurgents sought to exploit the confusion caused by the blast. However the enemy fire was soon answered by the crackle of SA-80s, and other heavier weapons. But almost as soon as it had began, the shooting stopped, and the insurgents melted away.

After briefly ensuring all vital appendages were still present on his body, Johnno looked around furiously for his friend, and then he let out a gasp. Taff was laying on the ground, motionless, and his face was a bloody mass.

'It's all right mate, hang on will ya!' Johnno said crawling over to him, trying not to think about the growing area of blood. Taff tried to get up, but he soon collapsed back again and remained where he was.

Johnno could see the rest of the patrol with whom they were working that day forming a secure perimeter around the site of the blast. Thankfully the explosion did not seem to have been large, but even a small bomb could cause big problems for a Land Rover.

'What kind of pillock thinks a thin-skinned vehicle like that is good for this fucking hole?' Johnno asked himself bitterly, as he watched Taff slip into unconsciousness.

'C'mon, stay with me you Welsh git!' Johnno said, fighting back tears and oblivious to the pain of his own wounds. Soon medical personnel began to work on Taff, until the thrum of rotors heralded the arrival of rescue, but Corporal Blakeney only remembered it as a blur, as he watched sullenly while the medics did their job and patched Taff up as best they could, and then attended to Johnno's wounds as well. Just as he was wondering how the rest of the day was going to play out, he too was ordered to board the Lynx helicopter that had come to pick up Taff.

'You need to go in too Corporal Blakeney,' said the troop sergeant of recce troop, 'The medics need to have a bit more a look at some of your injuries.'

'Okay, got it,' he replied and moved off toward where the helicopter had landed.

'I think he'll be okay, Johnno,' said one of the medics about Taff, as they moved toward the helicopter. 'He's pretty beaten up, and has concussion, but there were no arteries cut or anything.'

'What injuries does he have then?'

'He has some deep lacerations, a broken arm, and maybe some other broken bones.'

'Okay.'

'Blood spreads everywhere; he looked a lot worse than he actually is,' remarked the medic. 'He'll be pretty scarred-up though; and that's his tour of Iraq over I reckon.'

'He was never an oil-painting anyway,' muttered Johnno, drawing a laugh from the medic.

'Better be careful then, by the time the surgeons are finished with him he might be better looking!'

'That's sodding impossible!' returned Johnno.

He had got away from the blast far more lightly, as he had been on the opposite side of the vehicle to the point of detonation; apart from cuts, dirt, and bruises, he felt fine. Fine, that is, if he did not think about his Welsh mate. They completed the dash to the Lynx, and then took off in a tornado of dust and flew the short distance to the nearest medical facility. For the next few days Taff was fairly heavily sedated, before being flown out to a military hospital in Germany.

Taff himself did not remember anything clearly again until some days later when he saw bright lights and whites and blues mixing in a confusion of unaccustomed colour; then as his eyes focussed he saw the shape of a woman he knew.

'*Helô Mam, dw heb dy weld ti ers talwn*[5],' he said wearily. However his mother did not manage a reply; instead she let out a cry and then ran away sobbing. Taff sighed resignedly. About what I thought she'd do, he thought sadly, and then lay there, wondering what was going to happen next.

---

5.   Hello Mum, long time no see.

$$1$$

Australia: 2011

It was just past 0615, and the smell of steam permeated the air, as calm and meticulous hands forced the material of a Disruptive Pattern Camouflage Uniform[1] into flat, smooth, obedience. Not many people in the Australian Army took such trouble with the camouflaged uniform, but Chaplain Owain Robert Llewellyn, or Rob as he liked to be called, was not like many people.

The iron hissed and gurgled rhythmically as it passed over the material, sending urgent clouds of steam through the mottled greens and browns. Rob was grateful for the almost total lack of creases required in this uniform, though he did not find ironing creases especially taxing. In fact he barely even needed to think about what he was doing, and instead used the time to mull over the things he had been told before he came to Murruwa, because this was the first day of his first posting in the Australian Regular Army, after having served for a year in the Army Reserve.

---

1. Usually contracted to DPCU.

Rob was usually a very deep thinker, which proved to be both a blessing and a curse at times. Looming large in his active mind was that he was going to be working at a home of insane military perfectionism; the Second Recruit Training Battalion, or 2 RTB for short, which was located near the town of Murruwa, in southern New South Wales. Hence the attention he was paying to the appearance of both his uniform and himself.

Being the kind of person he was, Rob had done extensive research about his new posting, and everyone he spoke to in his old Regiment seemed to say the word "Murruwa" with a curious blend of awe and loathing. Judging by the way people had reacted to the word, he felt like there was some contrasting sense of both loss and gain that was driving their responses.

'Strewth, Padre! Murruwa!' one Sergeant had said, 'They reckon the word means "West wind" or something; and man was that wind cold! Best thing that ever happened to me that place, but it was the worst few weeks of my life. I had to grow up in a hurry!'

For that Sergeant, like the other people Rob had talked to, the word Murruwa seemed to sum up a sense of loss of innocence and freedom to the relentless demands of the military; but on the other hand a gain in confidence and camaraderie from shared experience, and in having together done what had been unthinkable before they joined. Not the only bunch for whom a place name carried so much weight, he thought. In his past, Rob had met United States Marines who had a very similar association with Parris Island. The words which in one sense were only a denoting a location, had gone beyond merely designating geography, and had somehow become a code for everything in their life that had changed when they left the civilian world behind; and a carefully crafted lament for the sense of alienation that they felt ever afterwards from the old life they had once known.

Rob sighed as he looked at himself in the mirror, caught between memories of his own, and examining his standard of dress. Satisfied at least that his appearance was unlikely to draw the ire or irony of a passing superior, he picked up his day pack and slouch hat, got into his car, and started the journey out to the base. It was a bright, hot and hazy morning, and Rob saw the countryside as a brown, shimmering immensity, unfolding out before him as he drove.

Soon after turning off the highway, Rob arrived at the security check-point, and after having his pass checked, he drove up the hill, and arrived at the Chaplaincy Centre at Morshead Barracks just before 0715 hours. Standing in the car-park, he carefully took in the sights and sounds around him, as was his long habit. Platoons of recruits could be seen marching around the base, like gigantic green caterpillars. From his vantage point four different groups were visible, moving from one lesson to another, in the relentless routine of the Second Recruit Training Battalion. The rhythmic 'left-right-left-right-left-right-left' of the marching cadence echoed through the summer air, as did the sound of the recruits calling the time in response. The new platoons lacked some of the polished coordination of those who were much further through basic training, and sometimes drew exasperated comments from the instructors as a result. Closer by a platoon came past, going up the hill in marching order[2].

'Head up Recruit Simmons!' barked a Corporal. 'People pay a fortune to back-pack all over this country, and here you are being paid to do it! Man I love this shit!'

This remark brought a chorus of groans from the recruits, and laughter from the Corporal. On seeing Rob watching, the Corporal called out, 'Thirty-two Platoon, eyes left!' and at his command the passing recruits turned their heads.

---

2.   That is, with rifles, webbing, and packs on their backs.

'Morning Sir!' said the Corporal as they passed, and Chaplain Llewellyn came smartly to attention and returned the salute with a slight smile.

Rob appeared to be a man in his early to mid thirties, and stood about six foot tall, with grey eyes, and close cropped hair of a nondescript colour. He was quite powerfully built, and had evidently kept himself in good shape. Army Chaplains, or Padres[3] as they are often known, are an unusual breed. They are all 'ordained' ministers or clergy of their respective faiths, however as they have to minister to all comers, regardless of faith or lack thereof, the job requires a person who is un-fazed by the breadth of human experience, or the depth of human folly. Humility, humour and compassion are also vital to the role, and the ability to keep confidences; for competent Chaplains are some of the most trusted people in the Army. Along with being ordained, they are also trained as Specialist Service Officers[4], as are the other professions, such as doctors, nurses, dentists and psychologists. In that sense Chaplains have a foot in two camps; having to maintain their credentials in their faith group, and in their military skills. Rob was a Presbyterian minister, and was only in his fourth year out of theological college when he had taken up the challenge of exercising his calling in the Regular Army.

As he finished taking in the world around him, Rob walked to the door of the Chaplaincy centre. He entered a central room, where he saw three other Padres gathered; including the coordinating Chaplain, Patrick 'Pole-Axe' O'Neill, a Catholic Priest who had previously risen to the rank of Bombardier in the Royal Australian Artillery.

---

3. The respectful and affectionate term "Madre" is often used for female Chaplains.

4. Or SSOs for short. Other officers are General Service Officers, usually abbreviated to GSO.

'Good morning,' said Rob.

'Rob is it?' Pat boomed as he lumbered over and administered a hard but friendly handshake, 'Pat O'Neill's the name. Mate, am I glad to see you!'

'Pleased to meet you,' Rob replied, in a quiet and gently accented voice.

'Now let me introduce you to rest of this motley lot; here we have Alan Deakin,' Pat went on, pointing out a genteel looking fellow in his early fifties, 'he's one of those Anglican types, likes playing a guitar, singing kumbayah, mucking around with his train-set and all that; and this is Steve Schwarz,' he continued, indicating a stocky balding fellow in his mid-forties. 'He's a Baptist. It'll be good for him to have another Protestant around, otherwise he tends to get a bit bitter and twisted. So you will make up the fourth member of the three musketeers.'

'Greetings d'Artagnan,' chimed in Alan, standing up and shaking Rob's hand, 'I suppose Pat qualifies as Porthos ...'

'And I qualify as the cynical mongrel,' cut in Steve, before Alan could go any further. 'Sorry mate, I was a copper for thirteen years; bitter and twisted is just my way of looking at life.'

'This admission is a usual part of Steve's introductory patter,' explained Alan. 'He feels that it saves misunderstanding later on when the bitter or the cynical makes itself frighteningly evident.'

'Interesting,' said Rob in reply.

Having exchanged greetings, Pat did not allow Rob to stand there talking to the others for long. Instead he showed Rob his office, and then took him on a brief tour of the Chapel precinct; which included Protestant, Anglican and Roman Catholic wings to a main building, along with prayer facilities for other religions.

'You got a wife and kids mate?' asked Pat as they walked down the stairs toward the chapel.

'That I don't,' said Rob.

'Girlfriend?' asked Pat, and Rob shook his head.

'Really? Not many Protestant pastors are single blokes.'

'True enough,' answered Rob.

'You don't want to become a Catholic Priest do you? You're already half way there mate!'

'I'll pass, thank you,' replied Rob.

'Bugger. Well, I could only ask! Anyway, as well as Sunday services, this building is used for Character Training,' Pat continued. 'So you'll be familiar with it pretty soon.'

Rob did not respond to this comment, but nodded as he continued to soak in the sights around him.

'I'll be kind to you to start off with,' Pat said to him, 'you won't be on-call Chaplain for a couple of weeks, but after that you'll be swimming gleefully in a sea of shit. Are you living in town somewhere?'

'Yes, I actually bought a small place,' Rob replied quietly.

'Not some cheap joint in Badhiyang I hope?' Pat asked warily, referring to one of the suburbs with a less than salubrious reputation.

'No, I was warned about that area,' Rob remarked, as they back up the stairs, 'so I bought a house with a small yard, close to town like.'

'Good stuff,' said Pat emphatically. 'Mind you, your house won't feel like much of a home. Sorry to harp on it, but you'll be flat-out here. On that note, d'you have any hobbies? You'll need something to take your mind off things, otherwise you'll go stark staring mad!'

'I have a few things I do,' said Rob, 'I'll be okay I think.'

'Good to hear,' said Pat, and slapped him on the back as they re-entered the Chaplaincy centre.

On their return, Rob saw a man carrying a pace stick, whom he assumed to be the Regimental Sergeant Major[5].

'Morning RSM!' said Pat, confirming Rob's suspicion.

'Morning Padres,' said the RSM as they entered, 'I take it this is your new arrival,' he continued nodding towards Rob.

'He is,' said Pat. 'Rob, the RSM offered to show you around and help you conduct your march-in. Pete, meet Padre Rob Llewellyn.'

'Peter Costigan,' said the RSM, extending his hand.

'Morning Sarn't Major,' replied Rob formally, shaking the RSM's hand in return.

'Righto sir, grab your docs[6] and come with me,' said the RSM, 'and I'll give you a good look at the place as we move around.'

Rob then left to conduct his 'march-in' process, a posting by posting ritual undertaken by Army members every time they move to a new location.

'So Padre, do you know much about Murruwa?' asked the RSM as they marched down the hill together. Being lower ranked than Rob, he was careful to walk on the left, so that the new Padre would have to give and return salutes as appropriate.

'Not much at all really, apart from its role,' was Rob's reply.

'Well that's a good start, but to get the vibe of this joint you'll need to know a few things. First thing is that a posting to Murruwa as an instructor is seldom sought after,' commented the RSM. 'The hours here are long, the scrutiny is high, and the work can be bloody hard and repetitive. For young officers, it is often a last posting before their promotion to Captain, or a last ditch attempt to try and fix a cluster.[7] The recruits are mainly

---

5. Mostly contracted to RSM.
6. Abbreviation of 'documents'.
7. Short for cluster-fuck; an incompetent person.

given their training by the Corporals, who command each section that makes up a platoon. There are usually three to five sections of about ten people in a recruit platoon, which can number up to around fifty or even sixty people. Each platoon also has a Sergeant, and is commanded by a Lieutenant. Recruit platoons can vary quite a bit, and tend to show a 'group personality'; but because they're basically a collection of mostly young people thrown together in a strange and stressful environment, the group dynamics can be pretty fucking volatile to say the least.'

'Are the girls trained in all female platoons?' asked Rob.

'No, we haven't done that for years,' said the RSM, in a slightly pained tone. 'Recruit platoons are often mixed, but sometimes all male.'

'Do the mixed platoons create many issues?' asked Rob.

'Not really,' replied Warrant Officer Costigan. 'We realise with the mixed platoons there is the risk of frat[8] taking place; but this happened with single-sex platoons as well. I mean the recruits are mostly late teens and early twenties, so you expect shenanigans; but the rooms they sleep in are never mixed guys and girls, and they have separate toilets and showers. We have four companies in 2 RTB, Alpha through to Delta.'

The RSM then halted, and pointed toward a building.

'A little bird told me that you'll be working mainly with Charlie Company; the lines where the recruits are accommodated are down there. You can just see part of it, downhill from Delta Company. Each floor of the building houses a platoon.'

That he was going to be working with Charlie Company was news to Rob; Pat had not mentioned anything about it as yet. As they continued their journey Rob caught sight of a Major walking up the hill toward them, probably on his way to

---

8. Fraternisation.

battalion headquarters. The RSM twitched a little nervously, wondering how the new Padre was going to respond to seeing someone of higher rank whom he had to salute. Warrant Officer Costigan had seen a couple of SSOs who seemed to be allergic to saluting, so he watched with interest as they walked toward the Major. However he need not have worried. As they came close, Rob gave a picture perfect salute.

'Morning sir,' he said in a clear voice as they passed.

'Morning,' said the rather preoccupied Major as he returned the salute, sparing Rob a brief glance as he did so, before continuing on his way.

Having delivered his personnel file to the main administration building, Rob and the RSM then got into a car, so the RSM could drive Rob around the rest of the barracks.

'Get a good look at this place Padre,' said the RSM as they arrived at the hospital. 'You'll get to know it very well. Besides the genuinely sick and lame you get an awful lot of lazy sods or people with heartilage[9] issues in here.'

Rob narrowed his eyes slightly, but said nothing in response to this piece of information. Evidently it did not surprise him over much, thought the RSM. Rob went inside to deliver his medical documents, and having done that, they drove back to the Chaplaincy centre together.

'So what brand are you Padre?' asked the RSM, when he had been seated.

'I'm sorry?' said Rob.

'I mean what denomination are you?'

'Oh, I'm Presbyterian; basic evangelical protestant if that

---

9. Heartilage is the fabled tendon that gives people the ability to persevere in difficult circumstances. For varying reasons, some people struggle with heartilage issues.

means anything to you,' he answered, now comprehending what the RSM wanted to know.

'Not really, sir, I'm a survivor of a Catholic education,' the RSM confessed, 'so I never really wanted to be part of it or any other organised religion again.'

'Not an unusual story,' said Rob.

'No it isn't really,' said the RSM. 'What made you join the Army, if you don't mind me asking?'

Rob considered the question for a moment before answering. Peter Costigan watched this pause with some interest. Padre Llewellyn evidently was a man who weighed his words carefully.

'I wanted something a bit different from the normal run of the mill thing of parish life,' Rob said eventually. 'Not much of an answer really, I know, but that's it in a nutshell.'

'What were you doing before you became a priest?'

'I was teaching music with my uncle in Sydney,' answered Rob, though he inwardly disliked ever being called a priest. 'He runs a music academy there.'

'Oh well,' said the RSM, as they arrived back at the Chaplaincy Centre, 'you'll get something a bit different here, that's for bloody sure.'

'Thanks for showing me around Sarn't Major,' said Rob as he exited the vehicle.

'Not a worry sir. I look forward to working with you,' replied the RSM, and then departed, questioning in his mind what it was that drove a former music teacher to end up in the Army as a Chaplain.

'Oh well, it takes all sorts I suppose,' he said to himself as he drove off, wondering how the newcomer was going to fit in.

Whilst Rob had been gone, the other Chaplains had gathered in the central lounge area, as there were not any other pressing tasks, and it was wise to take it easy while they could, because the peace was sure to be limited in duration. Pat sat down with a sigh, trying to evaluate their new colleague from what little he had given away, which gave him very little to work with.

'What's our new friend like, Pat?' asked Alan Deakin.

'Well, he seems all right. I reckon the RSM wants to size him up as well, which is probably why he insisted on taking him around,' Pat replied. 'Rob's not very talkative, but he seems friendly. I think he'll be okay. My bowels didn't lurch when I met him, and they're not often wrong; that last bastard meant that I didn't need to eat bran for a year. Rob's single though! Bit strange for a Protto. I wonder if he's queer?'

'Pat, you're the only man I know whose guts can read the weather; you're in the wrong job mate,' put in Steve Schwarz. 'I had a yarn to a couple of Presbyterian mates about Rob last week. They reckon he's a good guy; really smart, very good at counselling, though not inclined to say much unless he has to. Bit of a fitness nut too. He's never married, and they couldn't tell me much about his background before he went to theological college — apart from teaching music that is. Apparently his church was sorry to lose him, which is a good sign. We're just going to have to wait and see what he's like I reckon.'

'Bloody coppers,' said Pat, 'where do you get that information from?'

'Old habits die hard, mate.'

'Does he have an accent? He didn't sound like an Aussie,' said Alan, whose own very cultured English meant that he was frequently mistaken for an upper-class Englishman rather than a native of Traralgon in Victoria.

'Now I didn't even ask that, but you're right, he does sound like a Pom of some sort,' commented Pat. 'No doubt we'll find out soon enough. I've told the CO I'm going to put him with Charlie Company and see how he goes.'

'What? Anne Le Bon is OC[10] of that company! Rob's only a Captain, and you know how prickly she can be,' said Steve in surprise. 'Maybe you should put one of us in Charlie and move him over to Bravo where he can work with somebody who isn't going to give him a death stare from day one! We're Majors, so at least we can deal with her as a peer. The woman doesn't even shave her armpits!'

'Steady on now Steve; don't judge the lady by her follicle foibles! Besides, that is an unconfirmed rumour. Do you have intimate knowledge of her armpits perchance? Or have you merely been trying to look up her sleeve?' asked Alan with a playful smile, which only broadened when he saw the dark look on Steve's face. 'I know for sure she attended an Anglican Church in town, though she goes go somewhere else now. She has a very strong faith, and with any reasonably competent Chaplain she's going to be fine. But morons, whether they're Chaplains or not, are going to have a very hard time of it.'

'That may be, but will she ever recover from having had Dickhead attached to her company?' asked Steve, in a reference to the recently departed but certainly not lamented Padre, whose position Rob had taken over.

'Well it won't be the last time Rob has somebody tricky to work with,' Pat put in. 'Better he do it here when he has others who can help, than in a combat unit where he might get hung out to dry before anyone can intervene. Besides, Anne's fine so long as you're straight with her.'

---

10. Officer Commanding; usually a Major, in command of a Company or Squadron. They are referred to as sub-unit commanders. Unit commanders are Commanding Officers or COs.

'But is she straight?' asked Steve cheekily, referring to occasional rumours about her sexual orientation.

'Irrelevant,' Pat replied in a warning tone, 'whether she's a screaming dyke, or as straight as an arrow, the fact is she's someone I trust. I especially trust her to not stab people in the back, but if you upset her she will gut you fair and square. If Rob goes wrong with her, then he's going to go wrong sooner or later. He needs to learn to work with sub-unit commanders, and she's a good start.'

'So what you're saying is you're going to let him sink or swim with Anne?' asked Steve, a little alarmed.

'That's exactly what I'm saying,' said Pat. 'We can't afford to have fuckwits in our part of the Army, and if he is one, she'll weed him out.'

'How much ministry experience does he have?' asked Alan. 'He's the youngest Chaplain I've seen in a while.'

'The guys I talked to said he's only got three years full-time experience,' said Steve at this point, 'but they also said he was doing a lot in his congregation while he was at college; he had done some study before he arrived in Australia, so who knows how much time he's spent in actual face to face pastoral work. Apparently he performed out of his socks last year in the Army reserve, so they decided to let him go ARA[11]. Sign of the times I suppose; we need as many guys as we can get.'

'Whatever his background and performance history, our friend is going to have his work cut out for him,' said Alan. 'I'm amazed that they posted him here to be honest. There are other vacancies he could've filled.'

'Well, you know how it is,' said Pat, 'if there's a vacancy here, then it's filled as first priority; and now he's here, he'd better be up to the job, or he's going to get fried! I don't want any of you

---

11. Australian Regular Army.

guys to sugar coat it with him. He's under the gun from day one, and if he's no good there'll be no chance for a second chance.'

Pat said this with such an air of finality that neither of the other two felt like discussing the matter any further, so they resumed their previous conversation, and compared notes on the goings on of the previous year. Despite, or perhaps because of their disparate personalities, the group functioned well together. Steve was an occasionally grumpy ex-policeman, who had a boundless cynicism for human motivations, including his own. He had found pastoring a Baptist Church a bit pedestrian after years of collaring criminals, so he decided to exercise his ministry in the Army instead. He often joked that in the Army he was just working with a better class of criminal, but there were some days when he was inclined to wonder. Steve was a master at finding out information on just about anyone and anything, deftly developing a range of useful contacts everywhere he went. He could be hard, cynical, and sarcastic, but for those in real trouble he was also a resourceful problem solver.

Alan by contrast was a calm, caring, and scholarly fellow, with a well known skill for making scale models of various things, and some talent with a guitar. He had studied Classics and English literature at University, before doing a PhD in an obscure branch of Classical Greek. Despite having a strong inclination toward becoming a lecturer, he went into the ministry instead, studying a Ridley College in Melbourne, and then working as a parish priest, before entering the Army at the age of forty-two. He was now in his fifties, a very experienced Chaplain, and an excellent listener. Both Alan and Steve were married with children. Pat, despite being the team leader, at the age of forty-four had been the youngest member until Rob had arrived. He was 6'2", powerfully built, happy, loud, and a terror on the Rugby field, having earned the nickname Pole-Axe for the way he tackled people. Pat was the model of compassion with people in need, however with those who were lying or lazy his patience was slim, and few people who had witnessed his wrath ever wanted to see it again.

About an hour after he had left with the RSM, Rob arrived back from doing the various bits and pieces of administration he needed in order to properly march-in to the base. The process had been unusually short as by some miracle he had been able to find all the relevant signatories. Given the tone of the discussion whilst Rob had been out, Alan decided he might try and befriend his newly arrived colleague early on.

'Do you have any books or the like to bring down here?' asked Alan, leaning in the doorway as Rob looked around, sizing up the office that had been allocated to him.

'Yes indeed, they're up in my car. Are you offering to help me bring them down?' said Rob.

'Absolutely!'

The two of them promptly disappeared up to the car park, and returned with a box each, and disappeared again, reappearing with two more. As they began to impose order on the space, Alan decided to broach the question of Rob's origins.

'Where do you hale from Rob?' asked Alan. 'Are you English?'

'No, not at all,' he replied, with a rather pained expression on his face, 'A Welshman I am. I'm from a town North of Swansea called Ystradgynlais; my mother is from Australia though, and my sisters and I have dual citizenship.'

'Ahh, Archbishop Rowan Williams is from your part of the world is he not?'

'Yes, I believe he is, but I don't know him, if you're wondering. I'm impressed that you have heard of it at all!'

'Do you speak Welsh?' asked Alan.

'*Ydw.*'[12]

'I take it that what you just said means yes?'

'Not exactly, but it does the job. Welsh is my first language, but I don't get many opportunities to speak it these days. How about yourself? Where are you from? You don't sound like the average Australian.'

This last word Rob endeavoured to say, without success, in an Australian accent.

'Oh me? Just another Victorian. You don't happen to follow Aussie Rules football at all do you?' asked Alan, hoping forlornly for another fan of his favourite football code.

'Not at all, though I love Rugby, if that helps,' suggested Rob hopefully.

'Not really, though Pole-Axe will be pleased. Oh well, one can live in hope of some vestiges of civil society seeping their way North,' Alan remarked in a despairing tone.

'Civilisation! Rugby is how violence and brutality is turned into art and poetry! It is highly civilised,' said Rob, for the first time showing a degree of animation.

Alan rolled his eyes, resigned to another year without a fellow Aussie Rules follower amongst the Padres, and then took up one of Rob's books and read out the title.

'*The Children of Hurin!*' said Alan, examining one of the volumes. 'Are you a Tolkien fan?'

'Yes indeed,' replied Rob, and Alan began enthusiastically looking through the books as he took them out of the boxes. He was a big believer in not judging a book by its cover, but he did believe in judging people by the covers of their books. What a person read, or did not read was a window of insight that he felt too many ignored. Also, what looked well read on a person's

---

12. I do.

bookshelf, and what looked untouched, was also worth observing. In Rob's case all but the very newest volumes looked like they had been well read.

'What will Pole-Axe be pleased about?' asked Pat, shoving his head through the doorway.

'Our new friend loves Rugby, that weird cross-country wrestling sport you like to play,' said Alan.

'Really! What position do you play?' said Pat beaming.

'Well, I've usually played flanker,' explained Rob, 'but I can kick well, so occasionally I get used in the centres.'

'I'm liking you more already! Rugby tryouts won't be far away. Are you keen to have a run?' continued Pat, his enthusiasm increasing.

'Indeed yes,' said Rob firmly.

'Do you sing at all?' asked Alan, hoping to swing the conversation away from Rugby into an area he enjoyed far more.

'I do; a tenor I am. I got back into singing in the last couple of years.' Rob replied.

'Okay song birds, we should crack on and have our team meeting now, though there's not much to discuss just yet,' came Pat's voice from outside Rob's office.

They all gathered in the central area, and after a short devotional, they discussed the trends of the previous year, and things they may need to be aware of in the year to come. High on their list was the damage done by the chaplain Rob had come to replace, and the team took some time to explain

'Every Corps in the Army has its toss-bags and idiots who are just a waste of space, and the Royal Australian Army Chaplain's Department is no exception,' said Pat as he explained some of the events of the previous year.

'Absolutely,' agreed Alan, 'however, because the effectiveness of a Chaplain depends upon trust, discretion, and respect, when you have someone who breaks all three of those, you can end up with a tragedy of Homeric proportions. Thankfully it all ended when our former colleague blew well over the legal limit. These days any officer who does that is on very thin ice, and being a chaplain it meant the ice cracked and he fell through.'

'Some said it was just as well the idiot had blown over the limit,' said Steve dryly, 'as Pat here probably would've ended up beating him to a pulp.'

'Now, now,' remonstrated Pat, 'I wouldn't have beaten him to a pulp. I just might've made it hard for him to eat solid food for a while.'

'The adjutant said to me that he was offering odds on that very thing happening,' said Alan fairly, 'while 2iC[13] Charlie Company told me he offered to hold your shirt while the deed was done. Still others offered to hide the body, and provide a suitable alibi. Thankfully, in the end it wasn't necessary.'

At this moment Pat ceased the reminiscences, turned to Rob, and addressed him with great sincerity and seriousness.

'You might gather from this little discussion that you come here under a bit of a spotlight,' explained Pat. 'I'm sorry it's happened this way; they might have sent you somewhere else first and stabbed some other lazy prick to come here instead. But anyway, for a while people are going to watch you like a hawk, in case you're like the guy you've replaced. Not fair, I know, but life's not fair, so fucking deal with it.'

Rob did not show any emotion as he was being given these warnings; rather he sat opposite the other chaplains and took in the information he was being given with an utterly unreadable expression on his face. Only the occasional nod showed to the others that he was absorbing what they said. When Pat had finished talking, he looked at Rob, as if expecting some sort of

---

13. Pronounced as 2-i-C; short for second in Command.

extended response. However his only reply came in a single sentence.

'Thank you for the heads up,' he said.

Gathering that Rob felt the subject dealt with, Pat also brought him up to speed on the latest trends within the Second Recruit Training Battalion.

'Passing on trends in behaviour or complaints is an important part of how a Chaplain advises his or her chain of command,' Pat explained as they did this. 'Now because we're able to keep a high level of confidentiality, we're often entrusted with fairly sensitive information. One of the ways we pass this information on, whilst still protecting the people we talk to, is to present it as part of a trend, because complaints or problems often don't occur in isolation. They're sometimes part of a broader picture that needs to be understood if the problem is to be fixed.'

'They emphasised this sort of thing at the Chaplain's College,' Rob remarked.

'Did they now!' said Pat. 'I'm glad to hear it. But our role in Army isn't just advising command, as you know. Most of your time here will be spent in pastoral care; listening to people, comforting them and encouraging them and so on. Also, the instructors tend to call us when they have something a bit strange or out of the ordinary, and then we're often trying to point them in the right direction. Because of that, you'll get to know the psychs here pretty well too, because a lot of the recruits you'll talk to may need to see a psychologist for one reason or another. They're a good bunch, and the chief psych's got a stronger faith than most chaplains I've met. We all work together pretty well, and I want to keep it that way.

'We also are responsible for making sure the religious requirements of any recruits are taken care of; I don't expect you to be a spineless twat who has no convictions and who sprouts shit about all religions being one and stuff, but the Army expects us to respect the convictions of others, even if they differ from your own. So if a recruit says he wants the sacred text of the fucking church of the left-handed monkey god, then go and get it.'

'I prefer the text of the church of the flying spaghetti monster,' said Alan, 'it's got pictures!'

'You're more likely to win over somebody you respect,' continued Pat, with a furious look at Alan, 'so show the respect for freedom you'd want to be shown, okay?'

'Fair play, I'll make sure they're looked after,' said Rob.

'You better.'

Pat then went on to explain to Rob how his working week would play out.

'Now, every week we have responsibility for often two, sometimes three sessions of character training. That basically starts with teaching how a worldview affects values and behaviour, and then building from there. And for one week every month, you'll be on-call Chaplain,' said Pat, 'and what a fucking funky fun-filled lucky-dip of disaster that is! Whoever's on-call won't usually do character training, cause they won't have time to scratch their own arse-hole; but sometimes you'll have to do both. Too bad, so sad, you'll just have to suck it up and get on with it.'

Rob sat still, with the same thoughtful concentration that he had been using that whole morning, and still without much in the way of verbal response. Alan then took over the description of the working life of the Chaplains.

'With the new recruits, a lot of the time when they want to talk to a padre, all that's really the matter is that they're homesick, or missing their girlfriend of two-weeks, that sort of thing,' said Alan. 'Of course, you'll get a number with more serious issues, and some of them will end up in hospital awaiting medical or psych evaluation. On Sunday mornings is Chapel, which is very well attended because the recruits can get away from the instructors for a couple of hours.'

'You and Steve'll share the Protestant Chapel,' said Pat, resuming. 'We've found it best to divide up our responsibilities by taking a company each, so we're sticking you with Charlie Company. We all sort of share Echo; however most of your pastoral work outside of being on-call will be with Charlie. Major Le Bon, the OC from that company says she wants to meet you. Let me just say this; don't piss her off! She's a good operator, but she's got no tolerance for fools.'

Rob narrowed his eyes slightly as he took in this piece of information.

'What's the best way to avoid pissing her off?' he asked.

'Don't be a dickhead,' said Pat matter of factly.

'Apart from that?' Rob enquired, evidently wondering if there was anything more tangible he needed to be aware of.

'Well, tell her the truth about what's going on, especially if something big is happening, so she can brief the CO accurately, and has visibility of emerging problems. People don't like surprises in this job. Anne doesn't always come across as the most friendly person in the world, however don't let that put you off.'

'It's all right,' said Rob. 'I've worked with some prickly char-acters before; but I'll stand my ground if I have to.'

'And if standing your ground is the right thing we'll back you up,' said Pat, who was nonetheless a little concerned by the measure of resolve he thought he had heard in Rob's voice, 'but if you're in any doubt, get some advice before you dig yourself a hole. We bounce ideas back and forth here all the time, so don't go it alone.'

With this advice their conversation moved onto other matters, and it seemed like no time at all before it was time to go down to the mess for lunch. They all piled in one car together, with the windows wound down to save them from the heat that had built up inside it throughout the morning. Though he gave no outward sign of doing so, Rob was carefully thinking over everything that had been said to him so far.

'Was there a strong mess culture in your Reserve unit Rob?' asked Alan as they drove down.

'No, not really; it was a bit haphazard to be honest,' he replied.

'Well, the Officer's mess has been an important institution throughout the Regular Army, because aside from providing meals, it's a place of retreat from the business of the day. Actually it's often viewed as rude to discuss work there, though sometimes it's unavoidable. It also helps to build those relationships that help in a professional setting, and in many places it forms a pleasant social hub, that makes the demands of military life a little less pressing. Sergeants and Warrant-Officers have an equivalent mess system, whilst other ranks usually have a soldiers club that fills a similar role. Unfortunately the whole institution of messes is under assault from bean-counters and social engineers in Canberra, but we do what we can to keep it going.'

Having found a car park after the short drive, they wandered toward the entrance of the mess.

'Look out, it's the god-botherers!' said one of the Company OCs, smiling as he held the door open for them.

'Just wait till Rugby training starts, my son,' replied Pat with a broad smile, and then nodding toward Rob said, 'I have a new flanker for you by the way. Meet Rob Llewellyn.'

'G'day Padre, Major Sean O'Donnell, OC Alpha Company,' he said, introducing himself. 'So you're a Rugby player?'

'Yes sir, I play flanker,' explained Rob, 'though I've played inside-centre as well.'

'Can you kick?' Sean asked. 'We didn't have a reliable goal kicker in the Rugby team all last year, and it really cost us.'

'Well, I can, but it was never my top job. You might want to have a look at my form first.'

'Oh, we'll do that, don't you worry. Good to have you here; we'll be getting our money's worth out of you very soon. Come in and grab a feed.'

On this day all the OCs, the Commanding Officer (CO) of 2 RTB, plus a number of other officers were gathered. Rob was delighted to meet again Captain Anthony Jenkins, who had been his small group instructor during the SSO course at the Royal Military College, Duntroon. He had found Captain Jenkins a very capable and highly humorous individual. Anthony then took the opportunity to introduce him to Major Anne Le Bon, the Officer Commanding Charlie Company. She was a quite an attractive lady in her early thirties, with a tanned olive complexion. Rob estimated that she was around the same height as him, and noticed that she had eyes that were as dark as her hair.

'Pleased to meet you Padre,' she said in an even, confident tone of voice, that had the faint echo of an accent in it that he could not quite place. Major Le Bon then returned to the conversation she had been having when the Chaplains had arrived. As he watched her talking briefly, it seemed to Rob that on first impression she was a happy and extroverted person; however, a well-developed intuition in him formed the impression that she could probably change her demeanour rather quickly.

Before long they were all seated and eating their lunch together. Rob listened carefully to the ebb and flow of the conversation so that he could gauge the relational dynamics of this group. He sensed through the course of the conversation that Anne Le Bon was very much respected for her professional capabilities, whereas Sean O'Donnell was a man of infectious enthusiasm for anything military and all-things Rugby. He was a cavalry officer, and embodied the confidence and quick judgement for which officers from Armoured Corps are well known. However Rob was not left to his observations.

'You're very quiet there Padre,' said Major Le Bon, turning to him, an apparently friendly and disarming smile was on her face.

'Yes, ma'am,' said Rob smiling, 'often the best shortage is a shortage of words.'

'But he plays rugby Anne!' said Sean O'Donnell. 'Who cares if he talks or not!'

'Well, if all you want is somebody who grunts and drags their knuckles on the ground I guess that's not a priority,' said Anne tartly. 'But being a padre I hope he can talk; people may think it's important.'

Well, well, well, thought Rob, I'm dealing with an assassin!

'Anthony here tells me he was your Small-Group Instructor at RMC.' said Anne. 'You performed very well during the SSO course. Were you in the British Army?'

'No ma'am,' said Rob emphatically, 'definitely not in the Army.'

'Really?' she continued, her inquisitiveness far from satisfied. 'Anthony also said you shot an average group size of thirty-five millimetres. That's exceptional for somebody from a civilian background.'[14]

Rob noticed that this last piece of information grabbed the attention of everyone at the table, not least the Commanding Officer. Shooting a group that small was indicative of serious skill with a rifle.

---

14. Unlike some other nations, Australian Army Chaplains train on weapons, though they are not obliged to carry them afterwards.

'You should have seen him on the falling plate shoot, sir,' commented Anthony at that point, 'he won us the competition; which was just as well because the rest of the section were shit shots.'

'And you got one-hundred percent in all navigation tests,' added Major Le Bon, her head inclined to one side.

'My main sport is actually target shooting; small and full-bore rifle,' Rob explained firmly. 'I've been doing it for years. I also did orienteering at school.'

Major Le Bon was about to speak again, however this time the CO got in first.

'The Murruwa rifle range has full-bore, Padre,' said the CO, Lieutenant-Colonel Graham Ramsay. 'I'd think as long as Sean's rugby team isn't affected they'd love to have you come over.'

Rob thought for a moment that the CO's comments might have steered the conversation in a different direction, however Major Le Bon resumed her questioning.

'Are you married?' she asked.

'No; I have no romantic entanglements at all.'

'You seem very emphatic about that!'

'Well yes. I don't think I've ever had time,' Rob replied. Time to turn the tables he thought, so he fired out a question of his own.

'Have a background in interrogation do you ma'am?' he asked innocently, his grey eyes fixing her, and a sudden hush seemed to fall on the other people at the table, watching for Major Le Bon's reaction.

'Yes, indeed I do,' she replied, a small smile playing around the edge of her mouth. For a long moment the two of them looked at each other intently, her dark eyes seeming to strive with Rob, before she shifted back to more business like matters. 'I'd appreciate it if you could drop by this afternoon. If you and I are going to work together it'd be good if you knew what to expect from me. Can you make a meeting at 1400?'

'Yes ma'am, unless Pat has other plans for me,' Rob replied coolly, looking at his Coordinating Chaplain.

'No I have nothing for you; best establish a good professional relationship as soon as possible,' said Pat. 'He'll be there Anne.'

'Excellent, I look forward to talking to you some more,' she said. 'Sir, gentlemen, please excuse me, I have to take off. We're raising two platoons tomorrow and some details still need to be sorted. Come on Anthony, we'd better get a move on.'

With those words she left the mess, her 2iC in tow. After making sure she had left, Major O'Donnell turned to Rob and said:

'Mate, I don't know if you were meaning to be cheeky back there, but that was frickin' gold! You must be the first person I have ever seen wrong-foot her when she is after information,' but then he added in a quiet voice, almost as if he was scared she would be listening in. 'I think she realised she was coming on a bit strong, so she decided not to pull-out the thumb screws. Great person Anne, very professional. She is where she is because she's earned it, not because of being favoured because she's a chick. Don't push your luck though; she isn't known as 'Lethal' Le Bon for nothing.'

Everybody seems to be warning me about that, Rob thought; this could get very interesting before it is all over. Maybe the woman needs to learn not to push her luck with me!

With lunch finished the Chaplains drove back up the hill, for the moment lost in a mixture of their own thoughts, and post-lunch befuddlement.

'Well, you survived Round One with Major Le Bon, ... just,' said Pat grimly. 'Don't make a habit of looking at her like that though, it might piss her off, and we've warned you about doing that!'

'Pat, she was trying to press his buttons and see what he did,' said Steve. 'I did the same thing when I was interrogating suspected criminals.'

'However, Anne is still a bit touchy after the chaplain who shall not be named worked with her last year; and not just because of that,' added Alan. 'I have known Major Le Bon for some time. Best to be polite, if you can manage it.'

2

———

Major Anne Le Bon CSC[1], Australian Intelligence Corps[2], was an officer with a formidable reputation, who had attracted both admiration and envy in her fourteen year military career. A lack of opportunity within her own Corps, combined with a desire for something a little different, meant that she had taken a position as a Company commander at Murruwa when it had been offered, and at this moment, she was sitting in her office considering the platoon commanders she had for the year. One of them in particular was causing her some concern.

This young officer had a reputation for chaotic behaviour, and patchy performance, managing to earn himself a variety of derogatory nicknames; but a Drill Sergeant at Duntroon had called him Jar-Jar, after the hapless amphibian from the Star Wars movies, and this had stuck. Somehow it seemed to capture perfectly the individual's mixture of apparent ineptitude and over-flowing goodwill. Of the six platoon commanders she had

———

1. Conspicuous Service Cross.
2. Pronounced like 'core'. Pronounce it like "corpse" and we'll think you're talking about a dead body.

currently, four were very professional and pleasant individuals, another had struggled but was now coming along nicely; and then there was Jar-Jar, Lieutenant Chad Weston.

Anne sincerely wondered how it was that he had ever graduated from the Royal Military College[3]. Possessed of an incredibly pleasant manner, coupled with a seeming inability to think through the consequences of his actions, he was the kind of officer who caused nightmares for commanders. You never quite knew what he was going to do, or what possible damage his buffoonery could cause. Jar-Jar was an officer in the Royal Australian Electrical and Mechanical Engineers (RAEME), and Anne had tried several approaches the previous year in an effort to iron him out, but none had really worked. First she tried the friendly, 'I am here to help, and I'm giving you a fresh start' approach. This had gone well for a while, however a series of stuff ups resulted in Anne adopting her 'I am going to perform a vasectomy on you via the throat' persona. Many would have quailed in terror before such an onslaught, but Jar-Jar withstood her wrath with a philosophical attitude that Anne found to be at once disarming and infuriating. In the end she had decided to put him in a Platoon with a strong Sergeant. This would at least mean that any "clanger" he dropped would fall on a soft surface. Still, she was glad he would not be commanding either of the platoons that would begin training in that week.

Her reverie concerning Lieutenant Weston was broken by her 2iC knocking on the door.

'Come in, Anthony,' she said, and motioned for him to sit down. 'Interesting fellow our new Padre,' she remarked, recalling the lunch time conversation with a smile.

'Yes ma'am. He wasn't very friendly to you though,' replied Anthony.

---

3.   Often shortened to RMC.

'Noticed did you?' said Anne inquisitorially, wondering if her 2iC had taken some pleasure in the Padre knocking her off balance. 'That's all right, I can't give everyone the third degree and expect them to just sit there and take it. Anyway, I just wanted to see how he would react.'

'Well, with this guy you have to be ready for the surprises,' said Anthony.

'Like what?' Anne asked.

'Ma'am, I always had this funny feeling that he was holding himself back when he was on the SSO course, like he didn't want to shine or something,' Anthony explained. 'I mean it's cool if a Padre doesn't want to be top of the heap and stuff, but I felt like he had more in him; a lot more. But he was well-liked, hardworking, and never complained. When they found out he was single, some girls hung off him for a while, but the female attention seemed like water off a duck's back.'

'D'you think he's gay?' asked Anne, curiously.

'Don't think so ma'am,' said Anthony. 'He was friendly to everyone, but no one was really close to him.'

'Did he do anything unusual?' Anne asked, her curiosity about the new Padre growing.

'Sometimes he did,' replied Anthony. 'When he was duty student, he drove the trainee platoon around so well that the Drill-wing Sergeant-Major wanted to demote him there and then and make him a sergeant. I think he thought such a good parade-ground voice was wasted on a Padre.'

As she turned over these facts in her head, Anne thought it was as well to remember that not all clergymen fitted the inept and effete stereotype they were given in popular media; though I think he hates my guts already, she continued internally, before reminding herself that she was not paid to be liked.

Despite her own faith, Anne had met few chaplains she respected; Pat and Alan were two of those. Indeed, Alan was almost like a second father to her. Steve Schwarz she tolerated more or less willingly, but this new padre was going to take a while to figure out. With that thought she returned to her preparations for the next day. However she was soon disturbed.

'Afternoon Ma'am,' said Chaplain Llewellyn, after he had knocked at her door, and then fired off a picture perfect salute. His stealthy approach and sudden knock mildly startled her. This guy is very Regimental for a padre, thought Anne.

'Come in, take your hat off; close the door if you would. Please take a seat, relax,' she said, smiling, trying to be as disarming as possible. 'This isn't meant to be a formal interview. I just wanted to communicate a few things, and find out a bit more about the way you operate.'

She paused for a moment and briefly regarded Rob. He had sat down, he had his hat off, but he still looked like he was still internally at attention. If anything, he had been more relaxed in the mess, but this could just be his business face, she thought. Oh well, I can use a business face too if this is how he wants to be. She watched as he quickly scanned her office, like he was taking careful note of his surroundings.

'So what did you do before you went into ministry?' Anne asked, in an effort to engage in lighter conversation.

'I was a music teacher with my Uncle in Sydney,' Rob said simply, and Anne groaned inwardly. Just what I need, she thought, a muso; that explains the air of defiance at lunchtime. An artistic temperament and the Army could be a lethal combination.

'Okay,' she said in a voice that was far more pleasant than what she was thinking. 'Army's a bit of radical change then. Were you unhappy in a church?'

'Not unhappy, ma'am; I was just attracted to the kind of ministry in the Army. Here I get to relate to different kinds of people, not just church-goers,' Rob explained. Great, thought Anne, an idealist as well; this just keeps getting better!

On the surface however, she was nodding and appearing to be friendly, though Anne could not shake the feeling that Chaplain Llewellyn was somehow aware of her thoughts. It seemed to her that he looked like a dog watching a person it distrusted. Anne therefore decided to get right to the point she wanted to make in their conversation.

'The other padre's may have said to you that the guy you replaced wasn't competent, and in fact undermined me and my platoon staff with some of the games he was playing,' she explained formally and firmly, her dark eyes boring straight into his. 'I'm not making the assumption that you're the same by any means, but it does mean that the reputation of chaplains suffered in Charlie Company, and I hope that you'll be able to go some way toward restoring it. Now, when you're called to talk to someone about a problem, what do you do when they raise an issue?'

'Ma'am, that'll depend on the situation,' said Rob, 'but my basic policy is to solve a problem at the lowest level. If it's a purely personal issue, I'll deal with that person, and the conversation goes no further, unless they're a threat to safety, or if they want me to pass things on for them. In that case, I'll deal with the immediate chain of command, rather than taking things over their heads. If those relationships have broken down, I might have to do something different, and if I see an issue in this Company that looks like a broader pattern of problems, I'll brief Captain Jenkins, or yourself if you wish. What you do from there is your responsibility, and if your decision differs from what I think, then I won't try to undermine you, because you may be aware of things that I'm not.'

'If there is a pattern you think is significant then I'd like you to tell me personally,' she said, both relieved and surprised at the confidence with which Rob spoke. 'Even if you think I'm part of the problem, tell me straight. I value frank and fearless advice.'

'Yes ma'am,' he replied, eyeing her evenly with his serious grey eyes.

Anne considered his impassive face for a moment, and noticed for the first time what seemed to be scarring down the left-hand side. From where she had been sitting in the mess she had not been able to look at it closely. Anne then deliberately remained quiet for a few moments, interested to see what he would do; however Rob stayed quiet, seemingly immune to the usual human impulse to fill in a void in conversation.

'Where did you get the scars on your face, if you don't mind me asking?' she asked.

'Just a vehicle accident, ma'am; it's nothing really,' he replied.

'It looks more than nothing,' said Anne, with raised eyebrows. Rob just shrugged his shoulders.

'I hardly felt a thing.'

Major Le Bon looked at him again for a moment, before she decided to bring their meeting to a close.

'Thanks for what you've said; I'm happy with what I've heard,' she said. 'If I have a problem with something you've done I'll deal with you personally, and not stab you in the back.'

'I am quite confident in that ma'am,' he replied, still betraying no emotion whatsoever.

'I'm glad you are!' she replied, standing up and coming out from behind her desk. 'I don't want to rush you out, but I've got a lot to do. It'd be great if you could make it to staff PT[4] tomorrow morning. Thanks for coming down; and I hope we don't run you too ragged in the coming weeks.'

Rob rose and came to attention as she approached, and they

---

4. Physical training.

shook hands before he took his leave, and walked back up the hill to the Chaplaincy Centre.

Not long afterwards, Anthony Jenkins came into her office with some paperwork for her to sign.

'Your talk with the Padre didn't last long, ma'am,' he remarked as he placed the papers on her desk. 'How'd it go?'

'Well, I think,' she said reflectively, 'though it's a bit hard to get him to talk. Not very chatty, but he seems confident. A bit different to his predecessor.'

'Yep, that guy put the fuck back in fuckwit,' said Anthony, remembering the previous Chaplain with no pleasure.

'Indeed.'

'For pure essence of fuck in fucking fuckwittery, he knew no equal,' the 2iC continued, evidently enjoying both his word-play.

'I got the idea the first time,' said Major Le Bon, with more than a hint of warning in her voice, prompting Captain Jenkins to make good an opportunity to leave her office.

'Have you ever noticed the scarring on Padre Llewellyn's face?' she asked as he walked out.

'Yes, I have.'

'Did he tell you how or where he got that?' she continued.

'No ma'am, he never said.'

'Why doesn't that surprise me?' said Anne.

'As I said, he doesn't say much about himself,' commented Anthony, 'but what he lacks in talk he makes up for in action.'

Anne then mentally sorted what she knew about Chaplain Llewellyn into several pieces, and tried to get a mental picture of him. This was an old habit of hers, in which she took the various bits of information she knew about a person, and tried to get it to fit together, like some sort of jigsaw puzzle. She did not think she had enough of the main pieces to get an adequate idea about the man, and he certainly did not invite or encourage questions about himself. However, she thought, so long as he can do his job, nobody was going to mind much.

The rest of the day went fairly quietly for Rob and the other Chaplains, and they finished work in an up-beat mood. After the new-comer had walked out of the Chaplaincy centre, and headed home, Pat turned to Alan with a sober look on his face.

'The only question on my mind after lunch time is how we're going to stop Rob and Anne killing each other?' he said. 'But if he starts any bullshit with her I'm the one he's going to have to worry about.'

Alan nodded. He too had his concerns, and despite Anne's formidable reputation, there was something indiscernible about Rob that warned him not to underestimate the quietly spoken Welshman. Would two such personalities be able to survive one another?

'Who knows, Pat,' he remarked amongst the jumble of his thoughts, 'but I think we are going to be in for a couple of surprises before all is said and done.'

'What d'you mean?'

'I don't know exactly, but I can't shake the feeling that there's something lurking under Rob's quiet,' remarked Alan. 'Not anything nasty I think; but something.'

'Well thanks a lot mister vague generality, that's a real help,' retorted Pat.

'Don't mention it, I'm always happy to oblige,' returned Alan mildly. 'I wonder if it was a good idea telling Rob about how prickly Anne can be. I think we may have turned him against her from the start.'

'That's not my problem,' said Pat.

'Well as you're the Coordinating Chaplain, if it all goes south then it will become your problem,' said Alan. 'By the way, how did Anne react when you told her that her new padre only had a year of military experience?'

'Not real well, but I won her over in the end.'

'The age of miracles has not passed then,' said Alan, and then turned to go home himself. As he sat down to drive home, he took in a big breath. He was not sure that any of them could handle another conflict between Major Le Bon and one of the chaplaincy team. Briefly Alan wondered how someone with Rob's lack of military experience could tell if a person had a background in interrogation, before the many other things on his mind ushered that notion into the little part of the brain where insightful thoughts are lost amid the clutter of the every-day. Alan then himself left work, with the idea he should pay Rob Llewellyn a visit.

That evening Rob had just finished showering after his evening run when a knock came on his door. Rob had just got changed and was about to order Thai takeaway when he was greeted at the entrance of his house by the sight of Alan Deakin and a lady who was evidently his wife. They were both carrying containers of food.

'Good evening, I come bearing gifts of a culinary variety. Allow me to introduce my wife Jo,' said Alan, indicating the graceful lady at his side, who smiled at him warmly as they bustled in and placed the pots in the kitchen, which they found of their own accord.

'I'm afraid that I'm rather banking on you not having eaten yet. Is that correct?'

'Yes, it is,' answered Rob.

'Excellent. Sorry to barge in like this, but I couldn't bear the thought of you eating by yourself; our boys have all left home now, so we could use the company some days,' he said smiling, before asking, 'I say, where are your plates, brother?'

'Just in the sideboard there,' Rob replied.

'Capital!' said Alan, and busied himself with rummaging around the kitchen finding things with which to set the table.

'Alan tells me you are a Welshman,' she said as she set out the plates.

'Yes I am, and you must be English with an accent like yours.'

'I was born in Scotland actually; father was an officer on submarines in the Royal Navy,' she replied. 'However, I am far more English culturally, but don't hold that against me! Did you spend any time in England before coming out to Australia?'

'I lived in England for a while, though I went back to Wales as much as possible,' replied Rob. 'I came out here for a change, and also because my Mam was born here.'

'What brought her to the UK?' asked Alan this time, emerging with cutlery and placing it on the small dining table.

'Her parents were Welsh, and she met Dad when she came over to work for a year. They are both teachers,' Rob explained. 'She ended up marrying him and staying.'

'Where is that a painting of?' asked Jo, admiring a landscape painting on one of the walls of the lounge room as she served plates full of delightfully aromatic food on the table.

'That's a view of Pen Y Fan in the Brecon Beacons.'

'Have you been there? I think I've heard father talk about it before, though I don't think he ever went there.'

'Many times,' came Rob's economical reply. 'I actually grew up not that far away from there; not far in Australian terms anyway.'

'Righto, let's eat!' said Alan emerging from the kitchen, 'I hope you don't mind me commandeering your beer; it looked lonely there in the fridge.'

'No, that's fine,' said Rob, 'so long as you brought out one for me as well!'

For a couple of minutes they simply enjoyed the food. Rob's house was an attractive little place, though it looked a tad spartan to Alan's eyes. The kitchen, however, appeared to be well equipped for a single male.

'How did your time with Major Le Bon go this afternoon?' Alan ventured, as he continued to look around.

'Well enough,' said Rob, 'she just wanted to find out how I operate.'

'Was she happy with what you said?' asked Alan.

'Not my concern really,' said Rob with a shrug. 'I'll just do my job and she can evaluate whether my words are worth anything.'

Alan smiled weakly, as he tried to figure out the exact import of Rob's words, however he was not given any opportunity to follow up his question.

'So how did an Australian and the daughter of a Royal Navy submariner come to meet?' Rob asked, and Alan and Jo began recounting the tale of their relationship, which involved plenty of laughs, and so they spent some time telling stories of their life, before Rob prompted them to discuss the various doings of their sons. It was a happy time, and they left a couple of hours later, but as they drove away, Alan grew quiet and preoccupied.

'A penny for your thoughts, darling?' asked Jo.

'Interesting fellow my new colleague,' he said reflectively.

'I think he's lovely, and he listens really well,' said Jo.

'He is an *exceptional* listener! But what would you say you learned about him in our whole time there? Apart from the fact that he is Welsh!' said Alan.

His question was greeted by silence by Jo, who was apparently struggling to think of anything.

'Precisely!' concluded Alan, and they continued their homeward run in silence.

The next day promised to be just as warm as the one before had been, and it would be no time at all before those participating in staff PT were going to be in a lather of sweat. At about 0710 hours, Major Le Bon and Captain Jenkins walked out of Charlie Company Headquarters, and into the growing heat of the day on their way to the gym.

'So ma'am, d'you reckon Chaplain Llewellyn is going to turn up this morning?' asked Anthony.

'Not sure. He could be like Pat and fairly fit,' commented Anne, 'but he could be a slug like most other padres I've known.'

'Well it's going to be a kick-boxing circuit this morning, or so I'm told,' said Anthony.

Anne laughed out loud, for she was very skilled at kick-boxing. She then had the amusing thought that she might partner the former music teacher turned Army Chaplain to see what he was made of; and to make sure he knew what she was made of as well. However, when she expressed this idea to Captain Jenkins, his response was less than enthusiastic.

'I said yesterday to be prepared for surprises around this guy,' he said seriously.

'But he's a padre, Anthony!' said Anne, confidently dismissing his concerns.

'Well, how many padres do you know that can fight?' he replied.

'There are a few,' she admitted, before adding with a degree of sarcasm, 'but this one seems too quiet. Music teaching and boxing don't really go together, it might ruin the fingers!'

'He plays Rugby Ma'am, there has to be some thug in him somewhere,' argued Anthony.

'I think that's an anomaly, and he could just be talking big for Sean O'Donnell!' she said dismissively.

'I've never seen this guy talk big for anyone,' said Captain Jenkins quietly, however at that moment they both arrived at the gym and were mildly surprised to see Chaplain Llewellyn there waiting, along with the other staff.

'Good to see you here, Padre,' said Major Le Bon, walking up to him. 'It's a hot morning for PT.'

'Yes ma'am, it's redders again today,' said Rob, looking around as people arrived at the gym.

'It's what?' asked Anne in confusion.

'I just mean it's hot,' he explained.

True to her earlier thought, OC Charlie Company offered to be Rob's partner for the PT session, as the Instructors had told all present to pair up after the warm-up was complete.

'It's all right, Rob,' she said in a slightly patronising tone of voice as she put on the training mitts, 'I promise not to break you.'

'Thanks ma'am,' he replied quietly. A number of other people had noted with smiles and smart remarks who the new Padre had as a partner.

'Looks like Anne wants to sort this one out early, before she has any problems,' remarked Major Cliff Thomson, one of the other OC's. 'Good luck to her. Padres have no place in today's Army.'

At this remark Rob shot a quick look over in Major Thomson's direction, however Sean O'Donnell immediately spoke up.

'Don't be a dickhead mate, we'd be screwed without them

here,' said Sean O'Donnell, with concern. 'I just hope he can still play rugby by the time Anne's finished with him.'

As Anne saw Rob put on the focus mitts for her to punch, she found herself looking at his bare limbs. The new Padre was quite strongly built, with scars along his left arm, that were very similar to the marks on his face; there were even a couple of tattoos that were just visible where the sleeve of his PT shirt ended and bare skin began. Anne had a couple of discreet tattoos herself, but it was not quite what she thought she would see on a quiet music teacher like Rob. When the PTI[5] blew his whistle for them to start, she then began to punch the focus pads on Rob's hands in a polished and aggressive manner, and by the time her two minutes were up, both she and Rob had worked up a sweat. They then traded mitts, and it was now Rob's turn to punch.

'C'mon, show us what you can do,' said Anne with a note of challenge, and he nodded once in response without meeting her eyes. As Rob waited for the PTI's whistle, he settled into a comfortable fighting stance that indicated to Anne that he may not be a new comer to boxing. However, this observation did not prepare her for the furious and focussed assault that he launched, and it took all of Anne's great strength and fitness to be able to hold her hands in place. However, after a time the sheer force of his punches changed and he seemed to focus on speed instead.

Okay, so I've underestimated him, she thought, as she watched his hands fly in effortless combinations. Rob's face wore a look of remorseless, concentrated, cold aggression. In fact, Anne found it oddly frightening, and she was not an easy woman to intimidate. Were she to have made a judgement at that point, she would have said that he was a person who would

---

5. Physical Training Instructor

have killed another human being without hesitation. Yet when it came time to stop, his face softened and they prepared to do the next phase of exercise, which involved kicking strike shields.

So on through the various parts of the PT session the same pattern repeated itself, with Rob demonstrating a fearful and entirely unheralded capacity for fighting. From kicking they moved to using elbow combinations, before finally taking up punching again. His kicks were even better than the punches he threw, though the most alarming of all were his elbow strikes which impacted with jaw-shattering power.

Anne took it as a matter of professional pride that she maintain her position as Rob's training partner throughout the PT session, despite a discreet offer from Sean O'Donnell to change places. She had even chided Rob at one point when she thought he was holding back his kicks on her account, though he claimed that he was merely trying to make sure his technique was correct.

'Nice work, that was excellent,' she said to him when they finished, trying to be encouraging despite the shock she had received. 'You didn't say you were so good at kick-boxing!'

'No, I didn't ma'am,' agreed Rob, in a disconcertingly gentle tone of voice. He then nodded to Anne and Anthony, and made his way back to the Chaplaincy centre.

'Bloody hell, did you see that?' said Sean O'Donnell, coming over to where Anne stood drinking water copiously. 'Rob hits like the hammer of Thor!'

'Funnily enough, I think I may have noticed,' she said tersely.

'Oh, come on Lethal! Just chillax will you,' said Sean, 'even that big gorilla Scott Morgan would have had trouble with that onslaught; and I would have given serious cash to see him do that to Thomson!'

Sean's attempt at light-heartedness was lost on Anne at that point, and "chillaxing" was the last thing she wanted to do; and his use of her nickname did not help either. She felt anything but "lethal" at that moment. A little bit of over-confidence on her part was going to result in a good deal of quiet ribbing from her peers, and the news of Rob's prowess was going to spread quickly. *Oh well, I did put myself out there,* she thought resignedly.

'I told you to be prepared for a surprise, ma'am,' said Anthony reproachfully as they both made their way back toward Charlie Company.

'Yes, you did, and I wasn't,' admitted Major Le Bon, though her 2iC wisely steered clear of any further "I told you so" type statements.

There was an imperceptible something about the Padre; an arrogance even, she reflected as she showered after PT. Not the kind of loud obnoxious arrogance that was easy to see either, but a quiet "stuff you" sort that was much harder to spot until it snuck up on you and bit when you were not expecting. Anne had wanted to send him a subtle warning that morning, but instead she was the one who had been warned; and not subtly either. Chaplain Llewellyn had publicly and comprehensively bested her in a show of strength. As she put on her uniform, Major Le Bon wondered whether he was the kind of male who could not handle having a woman in a position of authority over him.

'Oh please God, not one of those,' Anne said sincerely, lacing her boots in a unusually vigorous manner, 'anything but that.'

Maybe he just doesn't like having people try to push him around, she thought fairly, trying not to allow any prejudice to develop too early. Whatever the case, the new pieces to the puzzle that was Chaplain Llewellyn did not seem to fit at all with those she had already. Time would tell if she was ever going to be able to make sense of them all.

Rob had little chance to enjoy the quiet satisfaction he had at giving Major Le Bon a shock, for on his return to the Chaplaincy Centre he walked into an emerging pastoral situation; unusually involving one of the other Padres. Steve Schwarz's wife had phoned in saying that their middle child had been admitted to hospital, and Steve had left in haste. The main complicating factor for the other Padres was that Steve was meant to take over as on-call Chaplain that day. Pat was just finishing his duty period, and was naturally reluctant to take the phone phone for two weeks in a row. Alan had taken the Christmas duty period, which meant that both pairs of eyes fell on Rob.

'You can say no and I won't hold it against you, mate,' said Pat, 'but it's going to happen sooner or later.'

'It's all right,' said Rob without hesitation, 'I'll give it a crack, yeah.'

'Fucking legend!' burbled Pat, 'no heroics though; if you need help, just ask. It's just as well really, as both platoons being raised today are Charlie Company, so you'll be on-call when your Company is going to need you most. We'll do handover after you've had a shower; best enjoy it because soon you'll be swimming in the fucking deep end.'

The rest of the day passed without incident before the new recruits arrived in two large coaches. It was an interesting experience observing the potential soldiers, Rob thought, as he watched them file off the bus. For one thing, the variety of clothing was stunning; everything from suit and tie to purple jeans, and something that looked like a male flamenco dancing shirt; and their facial expressions showed a similar variety. Some looked determined, others looked blank, and still others wore a look of shock or fear.

As Rob eyes moved over the ranks of the new-comers, he wondered at the transformation that was about to take place in those people. The other Chaplains had said that it usually took a couple of weeks to be able to adjust to the new way of doing things, though for some the adjustment could be too much. As he was turning these things over in his mind, all the initial briefings were conducted, and the recruits were taken to the places that would be their homes for the next eleven weeks, if all went well.

'If all goes well,' Rob muttered to himself. If all did not go well, they could be at Murruwa a lot longer, or not very long at all. As Rob was about to turn to go, he saw a young lady who stood out from the others in their ordered rows; for unlike every other new recruit she was standing there without any kind of bag or suitcase beside her. One to watch for later, Rob thought, taking very careful note of her appearance before he left.

'People who arrive at basic training without any bags are seldom lacking baggage,' he said quietly as he walked away.

For the rest of that evening the on-call phone maintained an ominous quiet. Everything the others had said caused Rob to eye it suspiciously as he lay down to go to sleep, however his mind was too full from the day's events to worry about it for long. The greater concern for him was how he was going to go relating to Major Le Bon. Whilst the prickly Major had probably learned not to underestimate him, Rob felt that the only way to keep himself out of trouble with that woman was by hard work; and with that thought he lay his head down on the pillow. For a brief moment his fingers ran over the cross that hung from a chain on the corner of his bed, and then he went through some mental exercises to relax his body and mind, before finally drifting off into a light sleep.

3

---

*The blast of an IED shattered the stillness of an Afghan summer
morning. The ASLAV[1] armoured vehicles that had been in overwatch[2]
on an Australian Army patrol, were simultaneously engaged by rocket
propelled grenades fired by insurgents, who were concealing themselves in a nearby corn-field. Thump-thump-thump, came the noise of
the 25mm cannon on the ASLAVs as they opened fire, and tore into the
Taliban. Vegetation and pieces of shattered humans flew through the
air, starkly visible though the sights in the turret. Thump-thump-
thump came the sound of the guns again, their steady rhythm the
bass beat beneath the rough music of battle. And when the sound had
died away, horrors lay upon the ground; dead insurgents in the corn-
field, but in the dust of the dasht[3] Australians lay, shattered into many
pieces by the force of the blast that had started the battle. Voices were
shouting. It was the dream again. And then he screamed.*

---

1. ASLAV = Australian Light Armoured Vehicle, an eight wheel drive armoured
vehicle. The gun cars have a turret with a 25mm gun.
2. i.e. watching over a position.
3. Term used for desert areas in Afghanistan, in contrast to the 'green zone'
where there is more foliage.

Thump, thump, thump; thump, thump, thump; Lieutenant Scott Morgan knocked on the door of the room of his good friend Evan Davies.

'Get up! Wakey, wakey, hands off snakey! Are you getting up or what?' said Scott, more commonly known as Morgs. Evan had agreed to go for an early morning run with him and it was unusual for him to not be up already. However, the noise he then heard on the other side of the door drove away any thought of running. It was a primal scream; a potent mixture of grief, pain, and memory made into noise. Morgs wrenched the door handle, and thankfully it was not locked, but even if it had been it would not have made much difference. He was a mountain of a man, and with his blood up he was like a demolition ball with legs; but what he saw when he entered the room chilled him to the core. Evan, who was normally the picture of cavalry officer self-confidence, was curled up on his bed sobbing uncontrollably, tears streaming down his face in ragged rivers.

Soon afterwards, Rob's sleep was shattered by the sound of the on-call phone going off. He noted the time as 0540 as he sat upright.

'On-call Chaplain speaking,' he said, his mind resentfully catching up with the fact that his body was now awake. He listened to the voice at the other end of the phone with growing concern.

'Okay, I'll be right there,' Rob said, and then changed into his uniform with a sense of clarified urgency, as it seemed a lieutenant was in great distress. Without asking for further details he had set out for the base, and arrived a short time later to find a powerfully built young man waiting for him at the agreed meeting place at the entrance to the Officers' mess.

'G'day Padre, I'm Morgs,' said the young officer. 'Come this way.'

Lieutenant Morgan led Rob up stairs and down a hall to a room about half-way along, which looked out over the officers' mess car-park. Inside was somebody he had not met as yet, who had obviously been crying, and Major Le Bon was standing near the doorway, looking mildly surprised to see Rob, rather than one of the other Chaplains.

'Hi Padre,' she said, 'could I have a word before you go in?'

Rob nodded his assent and they then moved a few paces down the hall.

'So they've thrown you in the deep end already!' she said as they drew aside. 'I thought they might've given you some time to settle in!'

'They were going to wait, but Steve's son fell ill, and Pat asked if I'd take on the on-call phone,' he said, but he added when he saw the expression on her face, 'I can ask one of the others to come if you prefer.'

'No, it's fine Padre,' she said, though Rob thought he detected a moments hesitation on her part. 'In that room is Evan Davies, he came to us late last year with a very good reputation. I think he's definitely going to need to see Psych, but I wanted one of you guys to have a yarn with him first. I'll leave now, but if you could drop past my office after you're done, that'd be great.'

'Yes ma'am,' Rob replied.

With that, she led him back to the room, and introduced him.

'Evan, this is Padre Llewellyn, I want you to have a talk with him for a moment, while we try and tee-up a time with the Psychs. It could take a while for one of them to get into work.'

Rob shook Evan's hand and took a seat, adopting as relaxed a posture as he could, and he quickly scanned the room, looking for things that might tell him more about the guy. Lieutenant

Davies was evidently a cavalry officer, as a model of an ASLAV was on his desk, and a pennant bearing the call-sign two-one in numerals, as well as the unit crest of 2/14 Light Horse Regiment were on the wall. Lieutenant Davies had been troop leader of 1 Troop, B Squadron, Rob told himself. A year in a Reserve cavalry regiment had come in very useful after all!

There was also some indication that Evan had been drinking in his room. A couple of empty bottles were visible on his desk. The question that ran through Rob's mind at this point was what significance should be given to the bottles: was this addiction, self-medication, or just somebody who was untidy?

'So what's going on mate?' Rob said gently, sincerely wishing for some other way to start the conversation, but deciding to just go with the obvious.

'Bad dream Padre, it's been happening more lately,' said Evan, 'but this morning was really bad, and Morgs heard me scream.'

'Do you mean this is a recurring dream?' Rob enquired, carefully checking his perceptions of what Evan had said.

'Yeah,' Evan replied nodding. Rob let this fact rest for a moment; a recurrent dream could mean several things, he reminded himself, but with soldiers who had been deployed it was usually possible to narrow down the cause.

'Is the dream related to an operational deployment?' said Rob eventually, continuing in a relaxed but direct manner.

Again Evan nodded. 'I was okay when I first got back, but over the last month or so, this dream keeps coming up, I'm not sleeping well at all. It's getting a bit fucking much.'

'Have you sought any help at all?' Rob asked.

'Nuh, none; I was trying to manage it myself, but that doesn't seem like a plan anymore,' Evan replied; and with that admission, he began to weep again, his knees drawn up toward his chin in the agony of his grief. Rob sat, not saying anything for a short while. Many people grow uncomfortable in the silences that arise around a grieving or traumatised person, and feel they must fill the void with something. Rob had learned differently; he thought of silence as a way of giving dignity to horrors that a person cannot yet describe in words.

'I won't ask you for details,' said Rob when he heard Evan's breathing become more even again, 'but I would bet that you've seen some truly horrible things. I've seen some bad stuff in my life too. In my experience it's normal to feel terrible at times.'

Evan looked up at Rob with watery and uncertain eyes, but said nothing.

'And it's normal for the subconscious to remind us of what's happened through nightmares and so on,' Rob continued in his quiet lilting tones. 'You're not strange or demented. You're a normal man who's seen some terrible things.'

'But this is going to finish my career!' protested Lieutenant Davies. 'I've seen it happen.'

'I think you're getting too many steps ahead of yourself there,' Rob replied reassuringly. 'It's important to get treatment for this as soon as you can. However, you mustn't assume that you've got some kind of zombie virus that's going to doom you forever. Perhaps you've tried to be too strong for too long all by yourself, and that'll need to change. We all need help sometimes.'

Rob then pointed to the bottles on Evan's desk, 'That can sometimes be a sign of trying to cope too long in isolation. Don't worry about your career for now, what is more important is that be healthy. I'll do everything I can to give you top cover with the OC. I won't tell you a lie though; this is going to take a while to work out, so you need to give yourself the time to do that. In the end a career is worth nothing at all if you don't have your health.'

Rob sat talking to Evan for nearly an hour before somebody

else came to take him to an appointment with the military psychologists. Lieutenant Davies had been deployed to Afghanistan on Operation Slipper, and had been through a very difficult time. Rob sat listening to the young man's story, and he was deeply impressed. It very much seemed like Evan had been able to carry on through an extremely taxing eight month deployment. However, in his apparent desire to not allow self-pity to take hold of him, he had found it very hard to admit that he was having trouble at all.

'Have you seen people recover from this kind of thing,' Evan asked eventually.

'Yes I have,' Rob replied thoughtfully, 'but it'll take time.' He then turned to the young cavalry officer and asked. 'Do you mind if I tell the OC what we've talked about?'

'No Padre, she's been a good boss,' he replied. 'And it's not as if I can hide it now; not since she saw me in a foetal position.'

'Well I must admit that does give the game away,' Rob admitted grimly.

Some time later, after Evan had been taken away to see a psychologist, Rob walked down to Charlie Company headquarters to brief Major Le Bon. It was good to feel the wind on his face after the stillness of that room. His mind was still humming with the concentration he had employed in his interaction with Evan; especially in choosing words with care. He had not wanted a careless comment to make the situation worse.

As he walked into Charlie Company headquarters he found the nerves inside him rising a bit more. Even though he did not anticipate this being a bad interaction with the Charlie Company OC, he was on edge; and only partly because she was intensely interested in Lieutenant Davies' welfare. Every time he had talked to her it seemed like she had been trying to trip him up in some way, and he was tiring of the mental games. In all then, it was a rather preoccupied Chaplain Llewellyn who arrived outside Major Le Bon's office.

'Come in Padre, take a seat,' she said as soon as he appeared, her face filled with concern. 'What can you tell me?'

'Well, I think that we are looking at a very traumatised man, who has tried to bottle up his feelings and memories for too long,' said Rob succinctly. 'Perhaps in more than one sort of bottle, mind.'

'Do you mean it looks like he might have been drinking too much lately? I saw the bottles on his desk and wondered the same thing.'

'Perhaps he has,' he said. 'Overall it seems like an accumulation of things, with a couple of particularly bad experiences thrown into the mix, and now it's just got on top of him. It might also be worth asking his friends how he has been going; if he's been withdrawn, drinking too much or just acting in ways that are different. I think it's also important to make sure he still has contact with his friends throughout whatever treatment he gets. Relationships are really important for recovery.'

'Do you think I'm right in withdrawing him from commanding a platoon for the present?'

'Without a doubt, Ma'am,' said Rob with conviction. 'He needs time and space.'

'Mmm, I think so too,' said Anne drily, before calling her 2iC.

'Captain Jenkins!' she said and he soon materialised in the doorway. 'Tell Jar-Jar to get his butt over here.'

Anthony's eyes bulged slightly.

'Would you like me to see if we can do some sort of drug deal with another Company, and get one of their idle L-Ts[4] to take 23 Platoon?' Anthony suggested helpfully.

'No, it's time for that crazy diamond to shine,' Major Le Bon

---

4. Pronounced el-tee; it is a contraction of Lieutenant.

commented, 'or burn,' she added under her breath. She turned to Rob at this point. 'When you are finished here, if you could just have a word with Anthony on the way out. He'll have a couple of questions he wants to ask you for a report.'

'Is there anything more you would like to discuss Ma'am?' asked Rob, sensing that this may be an opportune time to make an exit.

'No; not at the moment, thanks Padre. If you and the other Chaplains could keep tabs on Lieutenant Davies that'd be good; I don't want him disappearing into the bowels of the medical system without being able to maintain overwatch,' she said. 'The CO is going to want to keep a close eye on what happens to Evan. In the meantime if you could find time to drop in on Lieutenant Morgan that'd be good. Finding his best friend like that must've been pretty hard.'

Rob nodded and took his leave, relieved at having got away without too much interrogation. After he had finished a brief discussion with Captain Jenkins, he started to march back up to the Chaplaincy Centre. He had not gone half-way when the phone rang again; and in his mind he could hear Pat saying "Welcome to Murruwa!" all over again. Thankfully this one was not as urgent, but still, he had another appointment in an hour from the Rehabilitation platoon. When Rob finally made it back to the office he spoke to Pat and Alan about the situation with Lieutenant Davies.

'Crikey! You were called for Evan!' exclaimed Pat, 'The poor bugger! He's a good hand. Who's she going to put in 23 Platoon now?'

'Lieutenant Weston; I think his nickname is Jar-Jar.'

At this point both Pat and Alan looked at each other and burst out laughing; and it was a minute or so before they both regained their composure. Rob waited for their mirth to subside somewhat before carrying on. Eventually Pat and Alan recovered, though Alan was still wiping his eyes for a couple of minutes afterwards.

'Major Le Bon wants a watch kept on what happens to Evan in the medical system. Reading between the lines, I think she's a bit unsure that the right things are going to happen,' said Rob, eyeing their previous amusement uncomfortably.

'She's a wise woman,' said Alan more seriously, 'sometimes it can be hard to keep an eye on how your people are going. We don't want him left in limbo somewhere without support.'

'And of course there are some Doctors out there who couldn't find their own arse with both hands in broad daylight; with a fucking GPS,' added Pat sourly. 'Don't worry mate, you and I'll work out a welfare plan for Lieutenant Davies with Anne and we'll run it by the CO.'

'I'd better go now,' said Rob, looking at his watch, 'I got a call from the Rehab Platoon, and I need to be there in five minutes.'

'I'll take that one, I can hazard a guess who it might be,' said Alan with a knowing smile. 'We sometimes have a couple of frequent flyers from the Rehab and Remedial Platoon, and there's one who has racked up so many points he's currently in the running for a ticket to Los Angeles; one-way if I have anything to do with it,' he added ominously. 'On another note, I suggest it might be kind to call in on Lieutenant Morgan. He and Evan Davies are very close and this will've rocked him to the core. Please tell him that if he feels like he has mental health issues of his own, that it's best to deal with them proactively rather than reactively, if he can.'

'Thanks Alan, Major Le Bon asked me to drop in on him in any case,' said Rob, and left the building.

As Rob walked off, Alan turned to Pat.

'I think this week will let us know what our young friend is made of,' he remarked.

'Yes, and he'd better be made of stern stuff,' replied Pat. 'This week's going to be a mongrel, I can feel it in my bowels.'

'You really should have them looked at you know Pat. I know the Greeks used to try and tell the future by examining a chicken's entrails, but being able to read your own entrails seems a tad concerning,' replied Alan with a dead-pan face.

'Oh, fuck off!'

'Must you use that poor little word, when so many others are loafing about doing nothing?' said Alan, mildly exasperated.

'Well it's a lot simpler than telling someone to take a job involving sex and travel!' replied Pat, rolling his eyes.

'Oh really!' sighed Alan. 'An absolute E for effort and originality,' and with that the two friends got on with the work they had in store for the day.

Rob made his way down toward Charlie Company lines again. The momentum of that morning seemed to have no end, though he had always been able to maintain a cool head in a crisis. As Rob came close to the main building he passed three soldiers who were gathered together, and conversing intensely about something.

'Stand fast!' yelled the one who had been facing him, a lean Corporal of the Royal Australian Armoured Corps, whose surname Rob could see was Nguyen.

'Stand easy,' said Rob, as he returned the salute. 'Could you tell me if Lieutenant Morgan is currently in his office?'

'Not sure sir, but I reckon he is,' answered a Sergeant Maxwell, 'we're the Platoon staff for 23 Platoon. Lieutenant Davies was our platoon commander.'

'How is he sir? We heard a bit of what happened,' asked Corporal Schulz, the only female in the group.

'Well he didn't look great,' answered Rob, aware of the need of not giving away too much, 'and it'll be a while before he's back in action.'

'Is it true we're getting that fuckwit Weston?' asked Corporal Nguyen. However, before Rob could manage an answer, the Sergeant spoke.

'F-Bomb, if you survive this year without an insubordination charge it'll be a miracle! Now I told you before we're getting him. The CSM told me himself. That's that and we'll have to make the best of it and stop the fucking whinging,' he said in an exasperated voice. 'Sorry sir, we all like Lieutenant Davies, but the same can't be said of Mr Weston.'

'Think nothing of it,' Rob replied cheerfully, 'loyalty wasn't a crime last time I checked. Now I must excuse myself and go and find Mr Morgan.'

With a brief nod Rob walked off in search of the commander of 24 platoon.

'Some kind of Pom[5] by the sound of him,' said Erica Schulz after Padre Llewellyn had disappeared.

'Let's hope he's better than that piece of shit he replaced,' muttered the Platoon Sergeant.

'I wouldn't fucking count on it,' said Corporal Nguyen.

'Shut up F-Bomb,' said the Sergeant, and then the group resumed their discussion of how to manage a platoon with Jar-Jar Weston in charge.

---

5.   Australian nickname for a person of British birth; often derogatory.

Rob found Morgs in his office doing administration for the recruits under his command.

'Come in Padre, take a seat,' he said when he saw Rob at the door. 'The OC said she hoped you might come by.'

'Did she now? Sorry to disturb in any case, but I thought I should come by,' Rob said, 'it hasn't been the best of mornings.'

'You got that right,' rumbled Scott.

'It seemed like you and Evan knew each other well,' observed Rob.

'Yeah, we were at RMC together. He was my mate best there,' Morgs explained. 'We got posted to Brisbane about the same time, and we deployed together last year. It was a rough trip too.'

'How long were you back in Australia before you got posted here?'

'Only a couple of months actually; not the best idea in the world,' Morgs mused. 'You know, in the army we teach people to carry on with a can-do attitude; so it can be a bit hard to know when to stop carrying on and stick up your hand for help.'

Rob nodded in agreement.

'Knowing when to persevere, and when it's unwise is not an easy question to answer.'

'Got that right, Padre,' said Morgs. 'Where were you before coming here?'

'In a reserve Cavalry unit in Sydney.'

'Really? Oh well, at least you seem to understand the shit things of life pretty well.'

'You only have to live with your eyes open for that to happen,' Rob replied. 'The problem is a lot of people live life with their eyes tightly shut.'

'Ain't that the fucking truth,' said Scott.

'Question for you,' said Rob, recalling something on his mind. 'The staff of 23 Platoon seem pretty unimpressed at getting Lieutenant Weston. What's that all about?'

'Oh, Jar-Jar! He's a good bloke, but he tends to cook off and do random crap from time to time,' said Morgs. 'He drove the instructors mad at RMC.'

'Why did he do that?' Rob asked, but Morgs just shrugged.

'Fucked if I know,' he replied. 'You'd better excuse me now Padre, I really have to get back to this admin.'

'Not a problem, I'll get out of your hair right away,' said Rob as he rose to leave. 'I hope the rest of your day is a little less eventful.'

That remark brought a wry smile from Morgs, and Rob walked briskly out of the platoon lines, and back toward the Chaplaincy centre, thinking carefully about Lieutenant Weston. Now there's one I'll need to research, he said to himself.

That day there were a few more calls on the duty phone, but they were either recruits requiring reassurance to persevere through their first day of training, or else he was able to hand them on to one of the other Chaplains.

Later on, Rob went to the hospital, as was the daily responsibility of the duty-chaplain, making a point of spending some more time with Lieutenant Davies. Evan still looked very shaken and uncertain, so Rob was glad that he had taken the opportunity to visit him.

'I won't give you a lot of advice about how to work through your issues,' said Rob as they talked together. 'I've had stuff of my own to work through, and I've learned that each person struggles in different ways. But I'll be a listening ear; you've been through some very tough times.'

'Thanks Padre,' said Evan, 'it's good to know you guys are around. The Padre in Afghan was really good too; but you know, when you get back home people get posted out, and all the supports you had disappear. The only thing cheering me up at the moment is the thought of Jar-Jar taking over the platoon. I wish I could be a fly on the wall for that one.'

'It didn't seem to make the platoon staff happy,' commented Rob.

'No, it wouldn't,' said Evan. 'Jar-Jar's a good mate, but he just loves to flick the bird at authority; and after meeting his parents I think I understand why.'

'That makes sense,' commented Rob, and the two of them talked about Lieutenant Weston for a while before their conversation drifted back to the incident that caused Evan to have constant nightmares. It was a vivid memory that he had shared with few others, however as Rob listened to the tale he felt like a cloud slowly came over him, and memories of his own came stealing back into the present.

'Are you okay Padre?' Rob heard a voice ask, and shaking himself briefly, he looked into the rather concerned eyes of Evan Davies.

'Yeh, I'm fine. Why d'you ask?'

'You just had a full-on thousand yard stare on your face,' said Evan.

'Sorry, I must be getting tired or something,' said Rob shaking his head. He remained talking to Evan a little longer before leaving in response to the ongoing demands of the on-call phone.

That night as Rob sat at home, the phone kept an uneasy peace, and Rob sat reading and reflecting on the day. Whilst a bit tired, he felt satisfied with what he had done. He then went through his evening routine, trying to order his inner-world to prepare for what would come tomorrow.

4

———

Taff was sleeping, but only fitfully. He tossed and turned, until a vision grew in his mind, and scenes long remembered played again in the uncensored hours of his soul. The vision of a boy in white, a sense of hot urgency running through his body, the sound of a suppressed sniper rifle firing, and a boy crumpling in the grim finality of sudden death. At that point he woke with a start, sitting up in bed, his breath coming in rapid heaves, his heart pounding in his chest; his mind only gradually catching up with the present in place and time.

Taff desperately grasped for the cross beside his bed, and ran his fingers over it, before slowly leaning back on his pillow. He began to breathe deliberate, deep, breaths, all the while letting the solid reality of the metal object sink into his consciousness. As he ran his fingers over it he described it to himself, trying to bring his mind into the present and the real. It had been ages since he last had a dream like that; maybe this new life he was living was going to start dredging things up again.

'Mab Duw, helpa fi,'[1] he said quietly each time he breathed out, and eventually he drifted off to sleep again.

———

1. Son of God, help me.

Rob found that the next day was busier, as Pat and Alan were absorbed in character training, so he had to handle all calls from all the training Companies, not just Charlie. First off came a call from 23 Platoon, where a recruit from Corporal Schulz's section had been found in a foetal position under his desk.

'I don't know if there's anything you can do with this one Padre, but I thought it was worth a shot. If you think we need to call an ambulance from the health centre, we'll do that,' said Corporal Schulz, as she showed him where the recruit was sitting. Rob looked in the room, and the sight that he saw was distressing to say the least. The young fellow was on the floor, shivering as he hugged his knees; and he rocked back and forth, sniffing as he did so.

As he noticed Rob, he turned his head and said, 'I've gotta mellow out man, I gotta get out of here!'

Rob walked over and sat down on the floor near him, deliberately turning his body away slightly so as to present a less threatening posture. He looked sadly at the young man trembling, and the beads of sweat forming on his brow; and it was plain to Rob that the sweat was not caused by heat, exertion, or even a virus.

'How long were you on drugs before you joined the Army, my friend?' asked Rob quietly.

'Ohhh; you can tell?' the recruit replied, looking a little startled through his trembling and sniffing.

'I've seen it before now,' said Rob, trying not to sound sarcastic, 'and the sweating and shaking are a bit of a give away.'

'I wanted to do something, I wanted a clean start,' blurted out the recruit as another wave shaking took hold.

'Well, this is not a dry-out clinic, it's the Army,' said Rob in a firm but sympathetic tone of voice. 'What's your name?'

'Nick,' came the reply, and Rob held out his hand so the fellow could shake it. Rob felt a great wave and grief and pity at

Nick's plight, and wondered for a moment on the desperate resolution that drove him to try and join the Army and break from his destructive life. However, whatever respect Rob had for Nick's desire to make a new start was tempered by the sure knowledge that there was very little likelihood a fellow like this would be in Murruwa more than a week. The stress of basic training and the strain of drug withdrawal would be too much.

'I take it that you don't want to keep going through the training?' Rob said, though he had a pretty good idea what the answer was going to be; and in any case he was hardly going to recommend that Nick continue, for the recruit was not the only person whose welfare he had in mind. Everybody in this fellow's platoon, staff and recruits alike, would suffer if that young man were to remain in training; and ultimately the Army could not afford to have a person who was already so broken. Nick shook his head miserably, and continued to sweat and shake.

'Where're you going to go when you leave here?' Rob asked, though he found the prospect of what the young man would face on the outside rather sickening.

'Dunno.'

'Well, when they get you down to the hospital, I'll drop by. If you want to dry out properly from drugs, I know a couple of places that can help out.'

'I can't afford rehab, I'm not a fucking celebrity.'

'You won't have to pay, I promise; and I don't make promises lightly. You hang tight here, and we will get you to a safe place,' Rob said, before going to find Corporal Schulz.

'He's a fucking what?' she said in astonishment as Rob spoke to her about what he had observed.

'He's going through withdrawal; I think he's probably been on drugs for a few of years at least. I've seen it before now,' Rob said. 'He needs to be seen by a doctor.'

'Righto sir, we'll get on it. Thanks for coming over,' said Corporal Schulz.

Rob did not have any time to dwell on Nick's fate, for no sooner had Erica Schulz said that, than the duty phone rang again, this time from 24 Platoon. Thankfully it was not another drug addict, only a couple of home-sick individuals who needed encouragement to persist until they got used to the Army, and made new friends amongst their fellow recruits. So on through the day a progression of undramatic but nonetheless important pastoral issues presented themselves, and by the time he had finished, the clock had just passed 2100; so he decided to head home. As he was driving out the gate the security guard on duty came out of the guardroom and stood at the boom gate with a big grin on his face.

'Now are you sure you want me to let you out?' he said. 'They're going to call you again you know!'

'I'll take my chances,' Rob replied, 'my bed is calling me!'

'All right, if you insist,' said the guard, and lifted the boom gate, allowing Rob to exit. He headed in towards town, but no sooner had he turned onto the Olympic Highway than the phone went off again.

'Hi Padre,' came the voice at the other end of the line, 'Corporal Jamieson from 5 Platoon here. I have an issue that's a bit out my league.'

'What do you mean "out of your league"?' Rob asked, as calmly as he could.

'Try a recruit's ex-wife and new partner are on meth and are a danger to his kids, so he wants to do a runner and kill them both,' she explained to him.

'Well, that's fairly comprehensive isn't it!' said Rob, 'I'll be right in.'

'Thanks Padre.'

Rob turned the car around, and headed back.

'Where's my caramel latte?' quipped the security guard as he came back through the gate. 'Told you you should have stayed! Do you think you're meant to have a life or something?'

Rob just smiled grimly and drove on.

He was soon at 5 Platoon, which belonged to Alpha Company. The conversation with this fellow was never going to be short. In his own words, the recruit had married for looks when he was twenty, and four years and two-children later his wife had left him for another man, taking the children with her. The recruit, whose name was Daniel, had joined the Army about a year after the divorce came through, with the hope of being able to rebuild his life, and be able to provide for his children. Then the ex-wife had left her new guy and taken up with a person who Daniel described as a "drug-fucked loser", and it had all gone downhill from there. With Daniel's permission Rob took the step of writing notes on this one, partly so he could brief Alan, who was the Alpha Company padre. More work for tomorrow, he thought, and time spent with Alan and Major O'Donnell, OC of Alpha Company. Corporal Jamieson and Rob then both talked to Daniel and secured a promise that he would not attempt to go AWOL[2], while the Alpha Company chain of command tried to help him sort things out. Thankfully, that was Rob's last call for the night, and he was able to get to sleep by 0030.

When Rob's alarm went off in the morning, he found that waking up and getting out of bed contained an element of reluctance that he had not experienced in some time; however he was

---

2.   Absent without leave.

able to drag himself into an upright position and go through his usual morning routine before driving in to work again.

'How'd last night go?' asked Pat as Rob walked in, looking rather tired.

'Yeh, I got a few calls; most were reasonably straight forward, but a couple were more complicated,' explained Rob, 'Alan isn't in yet, is he?'

At that moment Alan walked through the door, and grinned when he saw the fatigued look on Rob's face.

'Burning the midnight oil?' he asked innocently.

'Yes, in fact,' answered Rob wearily, 'a recruit from Alpha Company meant I was here until after midnight.'

Rob then explained the situation, and his opinion that it was going to be necessary to talk to the OC of Alpha Company, in order to mobilise some more resources to help this recruit deal with the situation.

'I wonder,' said Alan, 'did this recruit mention anyone else with whom the children could stay if the mother is declared unfit by the Courts?'

'He did in fact; he said his ex mother-in-law was a trust-worthy person.'

'Did he really? There's a first time for everything I suppose!' said Alan in wonder. 'If you could just send me an email with the relevant facts, I'll handle it from here. You're going to have enough to do chasing after your own recruits without worrying about one of mine.'

'Thanks sir,' said Rob absent-mindedly, speaking with a measure of relief at having been able to hand on the case of the recruit from 5 platoon.

'What did you just call me?' asked Alan in surprise. 'American Chaplains might call other Padres of higher rank "sir", but we do not!'

'Sorry Alan,' said Rob quickly. 'I don't know what I was thinking.'

What he was actually thinking was that if last night was anything to go by, this was going to be a busy week. However Rob did not have to wait until the evening before things started to take a turn for the interesting. An hour after his conversation with Alan, a call came from 23 Platoon. Somewhat ominously it was Corporal Nguyen speaking.

'I've got a recruit down here who is demanding to speak with someone outside the platoon, and you're the first one I thought of,' he said sharply.

'Fine, I'll be there as soon as I can,' Rob answered, though with no great enthusiasm.

When he had seen Corporal Nguyen the previous day, Rob had formed the impression that he did not like Chaplains over much. With this in mind, he turned to Alan and asked, 'What can you tell me about Corporal Nguyen?'

'Ah the infamous F-Bomb,' said Alan, 'He's very competent, but also very rude and abrasive. He and your predecessor hated each other with a passion. Indeed, the Nameless Padre tried to have F-Bomb investigated for bullying.'

'Was it substantiated?' asked Rob.

'No. Corporal Nguyen was exonerated, and our lately departed colleague was investigated for making vexatious accusations.'

'Was that substantiated?' said Rob.

'Yes.'

'Ah,' he said, and without further comment walked out of the building and down the hill toward Charlie Company.

As he left the Chaplaincy centre, Alan and Pat turned to each other for a moment.

'Well, a busy night on-call and no obvious clangers,' said Alan, mildly relieved.

'That's a relief to be sure,' said Pat, 'but him calling you "sir" was a bit weird.'

'Oh well, he had a big night last night,' said Alan with a casual shrug of his shoulders. 'Fatigue has a similar effect to alcohol.'

'Does that mean somebody'd have to be pissed before he'd call you "sir"?' asked Pat with an evil grin.

'Now, now, Pat. Play nicely.'

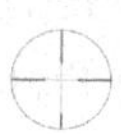

When Rob arrived at 23 Platoon, he was greeted in the foyer by the fabled Lieutenant Weston, whom he had not as yet met.

'Hi Padre, Chad Weston's the name, though everyone calls me Jar-Jar,' he said in a laid back manner. 'Recruit Adam Nancarrow is in the brew room ready to see you.'

Jar-Jar pointed in the direction of a room off to one side of the foyer. Rob ran his eyes quickly over Jar-Jar. It wasn't that he was wearing his uniform sloppily, but for some reason the young Lieutenant just looked a bit untidy.

'Was he the one Corporal Nguyen rang me about?' said Rob bringing his mind back to the matter at hand.

'Yep,' answered Jar-Jar.

'Can you tell me much about him?' asked Rob.

'Not really Padre; he doesn't like the training, and he doesn't like Corporal Nguyen either,' Jar-Jar replied as he turned around and started to slouch his way back to his office.

Rob paused for a moment when he saw the recruit in the brew room. Something about the sight of the fellow caused him to turn for a moment and speak to the retreating Platoon Commander.

'Lieutenant Weston,' he said quietly, and Jar-Jar turned to face him. 'Could you have someone have eyes on me when I'm talking to this guy?'

'Sure Padre,' he answered in bemusement, and Rob then went into the brew room.

The recruit inside was about an inch taller than Rob, and wearing a belligerent and unpleasant facial expression. Rob held out his hand to shake, but the recruit refused and simply stared at him.

'Who are you?' he asked, with a look of utter hostility.

'I'm a chaplain,' Rob answered steadily, 'I hear you wanted to talk to somebody outside the Platoon, so they called me. How can I help you?'

'I want to get out of here and they won't let me,' snarled Recruit Nancarrow, 'they say I've got to put in a fucking letter of resignation or some shit. I just don't wanna be here and get yelled at all day, especially by that Asian cunt. He said I'd failed to make my bed to the required standard; well I've never failed anything in my life.'

'Well, you have to write a letter of resignation ... ,' began Rob mildly, trying to hold back his rising annoyance, and remembering the discussion he had had with Pat about the process if a Recruit wanted to discharge from the army; however the angry young man cut right across him.

'Well, I want out of here now, and listen to you! You're not even a bloody Australian, just like my Corporal,' he said pointing a threatening finger at Rob, 'and I'll hit people to fucking get what I want, even a fucking god-bothering officer like you!'

This was too much for Rob, and his voice and face changed in an instant.

'You cowardly lump of antipodean misery!' Rob roared, taking a step forward, 'I ought to rip out your spine and use you as a wet-suit! You know nothing about me boyo, but if you take a swing you'll find out more than you ever want to know! And if you actually land one, I'll make your life a living hell!'

Having someone so apparently mild-mannered unleash in this way was quite beyond Adam Nancarrow's limited life experience. But Rob was far from finished, and continued his rather vigorous counselling session from within ten centimetres of the young man's face.

'Is this the way you always solve your problems? By threatening people until you find someone you can bully into giving you your way?' yelled Rob, the strident, ringing quality of his voice only increasing. 'Now you open that sewage pipe you call a mind and listen to me! It's time you grew a set and faced something hard, instead of throwing your teddy in a corner and having a tanty when things aren't just the way you like them. Your Mam isn't here to give you your bottle now! Did you think this was going to be easy, sunshine?'

The young man just stared at Rob stupidly, unable to find any bravado at all.

'Well answer me!'

'No,' replied the wide-eyed Nancarrow.

'No who?' Rob yelled, even louder than he had before.

'No, sir.'

'Well man up and do something with yourself, you numpty! You should be beyond the stage when you think you deserve a trophy just for turning up!' Rob went on, 'But right now I'm picking you for somebody who joined because they got fired from McDonald's for licking the hot plate! They make you make your bed to that standard to teach you attention to detail, because in this job details kill!'

With those words Nancarrow gave an involuntary squeak.

Rob's voice had continued to rise until it reached a tone that seemed like it could shatter reinforced concrete. His face had a hard, and fierce look to it and Nancarrow appeared as if he was sincerely wishing he could walk backwards through the wall, so that he could escape the anger of the Padre. Rob was completely lost in the moment, staring at the recruit in angry contempt; however he was brought back to reality when he saw out of the corner of his eye that he had drawn an audience amongst the Recruit Instructors for 23 Platoon.

'Your choice, sunshine; face hardship and learn, or run away and whither and die! Something else for you to chew on before I leave; not everyone who yells at you is your enemy, and not everyone who kisses your fat arse is your friend.

'Nobody here has the job of being a curator for your fragile ego! We're here to train you to be a soldier! And if you talk to a superior like that again, I'll turn you into a sock puppet!'

At that remark Rob turned on his heel and walked toward the platoon commander's office. He heard the sound of laughter and applause coming from where the Corporals were standing. He had to admit it, it felt good to have ripped into that appalling individual, though his heart sank at having done so. That wasn't meant to happen, he thought dismally, the animal had just leapt out!

'Fuck me,' said F-Bomb reflectively, as Rob walked away, 'the bloody Padre ripped him a new arsehole!'

'I'm using some of those lines, the one about the sock-puppet was fucking gold!' said Erica Schulz admiringly. 'What's a curator anyway?'

'A dude who looks after shit in museums and stuff,' said F-Bomb.

'I wonder if he's single?' she mused, eyeing Rob's well-built form as he walked away.

'Schulzy! He's a padre for fuck's sake!' blurted Corporal Nguyen in shock.

'Why should that matter?' she asked.

'He could be a Catholic Priest!' argued F-Bomb, 'And if you fuck a padre your tits will fall off!'

'Bullshit!' said Erica, but the argument stopped as F-Bomb walked over to the still stationary Recruit Nancarrow.

'Well, well, well!' said Corporal Nguyen in a low growl, as Nancarrow stood still, rooted to the spot where Rob had torn into him. 'Top effort mate. The only ally you had left here, and you pissed him off as well. If I hear you threaten anyone like that again, I'll cut off your balls and sell them to my uncle to cook in his take-away shop. What do you think we use to make dim-sums anyway?'

Nancarrow made no attempt to answer Corporal Nguyen; he just stood there, still trembling with the shock of Rob's face-ripping, and tears started to form in his eyes.

'Don't blubber about it! Padre had some fucking first-class advice for you,' continued F-Bomb. 'There's only one skin colour here, champ, and it's fucking green! I should have you up on charges of threatening a superior, but I'm going to give you a chance to change your mind. Now fuck off and stop using oxygen in my presence, you jack[3] piece of shit!'

Rob did not hear this little exchange, but guessed something

---

3. Being 'Jack' refers to a person who is just out for themselves and does not care about others. When used seriously, it is a word the conveys genuine contempt for a person.

like it may be happening. As he knocked on Lieutenant Weston's door a voice on the other side said, 'Come in.'

'Was it you yelling out there?' asked Jar-Jar as the Padre appeared in the doorway.

'I'm afraid so,' Rob admitted.

Jar-Jar looked at him appraisingly.

'Well F-Bomb will've enjoyed that,' he said enthusiastically. 'Do you want me to charge Nancarrow's arse for him?'

Rob shook his head.

'Let's give him the opportunity to learn first, shall we,' he suggested.

'I'm fine with that, but I'll make sure you're covered if the bastard makes a complaint,' said Jar-Jar. 'You seem to have cooled pretty quick after losing your shit.'

'It's a talent I have.'

'Right! Well is there anything else we need to know about dealing with Nancarrow?'

'I actually think he just needs to take himself a little less seriously,' said Rob.

'You could be right there Padre' said Jar-Jar. 'Most of the Army takes itself too seriously these days, that's why I like being a jester.'

'A jester?' asked Rob curiously, his interest sparked by this piece of information Jar-Jar had volunteered.

'Sure thing Padre, that's how I roll; see the way the crowd's going, and then go against the flow,' Jar-Jar explained, 'and if I can create havoc in the meantime, then it's a bonus.'

'You're in a strange organisation for a crazy individualist,' observed Rob. For a moment his mind drawn back to a friend from his past who did similar things, though Rob sincerely hoped Jar-Jar was not like him in other respects.

'Damn straight I am, but the Army needs me; it needs people

who can hold a mirror up to it, and show it how stupid and self-absorbed the whole thing is.'

Rob sat and listened, fascinated by this young officer. Everything Rob had heard about Lieutenant Weston had indicated that he was incompetent. However, these were not the thoughts of somebody who lacked competence as such. The question beginning to form in Rob's mind was whether or not he was just a smart-arse, or if there was something else driving his behaviour.

'So you like to play the fool so you can watch the real fools jumping up and down?' Rob asked.

'Damn straight!' said Jar-Jar, impressed. 'Just look at the Chief of Army. He gets up on TV, with a face that looks like the arse of a constipated cat, and talks up things like treating women with respect, and zero-tolerance for bullying. But it's all empty words for the politicians and feminists who fawn over him; his head's shoved so far up the arses of people like them that he doesn't have the foggiest about how completely out of touch he is with the rest of the Army. The worst bullies in Army are people above the rank of Lieutenant-Colonel who've been able to prosper because people like him have promoted them to higher positions, whilst he prances around pretending he's a hard man on unacceptable behaviour. Useless piece of shit!'

'You're very cynical for a young man!'

'You show me why I shouldn't be, Padre! And you're not much older than me!'

'No argument from me now, I'm cynical too.'

'I thought it wasn't allowed for Christians?'

'Read the Bible, have you?'

At that moment their conversation was interrupted by a knock at the door. Sergeant Maxwell entered, seeking after Rob.

'Hey Padre,' he said to Rob with wide smile, 'that was the most awesome fucking face-ripping I've ever heard!'

'Really?' said Rob, smiling weakly.

'Yeah mate, you're a real pro!' he said, 'We called you down here because that low life spat the dummy when he learned what the discharge process was. He called F-Bomb a yellow, slant-eyed bastard, and told him to go back to the take-away shop he came from. You can imagine how it went from there. He deserved every word you said, and you didn't even swear!'

'It took a lot of self-control, I can tell you,' replied Rob, with no apparent enthusiasm, 'he had me turbo-threaders, that's for sure.'

'What? What's turbo-threaders mean?' asked Sergeant Maxwell. 'Who on earth says 'turbo-threaders'?'

'I meant I was really unimpressed,' explained Rob.

'Oh, okay. Well, thanks for coming down and brightening our day anyway, Padre. I knew that fucktard'd be a special child the moment I saw him,' said Sergeant Maxwell. 'Quick question for you before I bust a move, are you a Catholic Priest?'

'No, I'm a Protestant,' said Rob a little confused.

'Are you single?' Sergeant Maxwell went on in his line of questioning.

'Yeh, what about it?' asked Rob, growing suspicious.

'Ahh, it's nothing Padre, just curious,' he replied, and left with a smug smile on his face.

Rumour of what Rob had done spread rapidly through Charlie Company, and was the talk of 23 Platoon in particular for some time afterwards. F-Bomb especially formed a new opinion of Chaplain Llewellyn, and a relationship of mutual respect grew between them from that point onwards.

'He's not Mr Fun Smiley Padre, but at least he won't back

stab the recruit instructors when some useless wanker tries it on,' F-Bomb said. 'And he gives a fucking awesome face-ripping.'

'I thought you said all Padres were bastards?' said Corporal Schulz, a slightly triumphant smile on her face.

'Sure they are,' said F-Bomb, 'but that Padre's a fucking good bastard!'

'F-Bomb,' she said, shaking her head, 'some days .....'

'Schulzy, don't get too cocky now you won the bet about the Padre being available!' he said evilly. 'And your tits will fall off, even if he isn't a Catholic.'

'Bullshit, F-Bomb!'

At that moment Sergeant Maxwell approached, his face serious.

'What's up?' asked Erica.

'A quick word with you crackers,' he replied. 'I don't want it getting out that Padre ripped that little twat, you got it? We need to give that Chaplain top cover in case shit for brains wants to *waaah* because he got yelled at.'

'Not much fucking risk of that,' said F-Bomb. 'I'm hardly going to let that get out. But the other recruits would have heard it too, unless they're fucking deaf, and Nancarrow is going to tell others for sure.'

'Good point,' said Sergeant Maxwell. 'Well, I might go and get in the ear of the CSM[4] first. That way we might have some top cover.'

'Fuck yeah! Jock would've bayoneted the little prick, not just yelled at him!'

The rest of the morning was relatively incident free, and the

---

4. Company Sergeant Major.

phone maintained an uneasy peace. Rob had been intending to avoid Major Le Bon if he could, however when they were both at the mess eating lunch, she asked him to drop by afterwards.

As Rob sat in her office later on, he tried to be as clear and concise as possible. After they had discussed what was going on with Evan Davies, he told her about the recruit called Nick who was going through drug withdrawal.

'I'm going to check in on him at the hospital this afternoon,' Rob explained.

'Thanks Padre, it'll take a couple of days for the discharge paperwork trail to catch-up, so he will be in the wards for a bit,' she said.

'Okay then; I've got some things to talk to him about in the meantime.'

'Like what?'

'What he's going to do on the outside and stuff like that.'

'Don't fall into the trap of trying to rescue these recruits, Padre,' warned Major Le Bon. 'Once they leave here they're no longer our responsibility. That is the sad reality, and there's nothing we can do about that.'

'I know that, Ma'am,' said Rob, bristling internally. 'I just know a couple of places he can go and get rehab for free. It's a small thing to pass that information on.'

Major Le Bon did not reply to his comment, but instead tilted her head to one side, considering him for a moment.

'So how's your first stint as on-call chaplain going?' she asked.

'Fine Ma'am,' he replied. 'Busy, but fine.'

'Really? It's a bit frantic usually. Do you feel up to it?' she asked, looking at him seriously. 'I'm surprised they sent somebody as inexperienced as you to this place. It's demanding enough for more seasoned campaigners like Alan.'

'Time will tell if I'm up to it or not, ma'am,' said Rob, with an unconscious emphasis on the last word of his sentence. You patronising cow, he thought, I'll give you something to think about before long! In his experience of life, when somebody asked if a person felt "up" to something, it was a thinly veiled implication that they should give up and try something else — an accusation of incipient incompetence.

'I'm sorry,' she said testily, 'I don't mean to be rude, but I'm pretty ruthless when it comes to looking after the interests of my soldiers; and I think having a capable chaplain is definitely in their interest.'

'Of course, ma'am,' said Rob, wondering where it was he could have been found wanting in his work that week. Not capable? So my work so far's been rubbish then?

'If you're unhappy with someone of my lack of experience, you can always take it up with Pat,' he added.

'I didn't say I was unhappy; not yet,' replied Major Le Bon tersely. 'I just expressed my surprise.'

'As you say Ma'am,' he said, now trying to defuse the rising tension, however it did not work.

'What do you mean "as you say"?' she asked, now sounding angry. 'I hope you're not being sarcastic!'

'Not at all,' said Rob, trying not to show his own annoyance, and for words to explain himself before the situation spiralled further. 'I was trying to admit that I misunderstood what you were implying.'

'Well why didn't you just say that?' she asked.

'With respect, ma'am,' said Rob, looking straight at her, 'I thought I was being clear.'

'Okay then. More experience of the military should make your communication more precise,' said Major Le Bon. 'However, I'm not happy with the way you're reacting to my questions. A fragile male ego and the modern Army will not mix. Do you understand me?'

'Yes ma'am.'

'Good. I hope for your sake that you're a fast learner.'

As Rob looked at her, it again seemed to him that a silent tussle was taking place, but Major Le Bon broke the moment by changing the subject.

'On a lighter note Padre, are you aware that in a couple of weeks we'll be having our first Yurali Patisserie run for the year?' she said with a calculating look.

'No, I wasn't,' replied Rob coldly.

'Well, the first one is going to have some friendly rivalry between companies, and I was hoping that you'd be there to do Charlie Company proud.'

'Yes ma'am.'

'And I don't want any of this grey-man[5] business on the run; I want to see what you're made of. Is that clear? Some of the fire in the belly you showed at PT would be good,' she said, a little imperiously, though Rob only nodded by way of reply.

'Okay then; well, I won't keep you any longer. Good afternoon Padre.'

'Afternoon ma'am,' Rob replied, and left the building as quickly as he could.

'*Ast!*[6] Of all the patronising ...,' he said sharply as he walked out of Charlie Company Headquarters. You'll soon see whether I'm "up to it" or not, he thought mutinously.

'*Llysnafedd gwyrdd!*[7]' he muttered as he continued walking.

It was not as if he had been found wanting in anything that

---

5. Grey-man: Army slang for somebody (of either gender) who hides in the background, never drawing attention to him or herself.
6. Bitch!
7. Green slime!

had happened, he brooded, so why would she ask if he felt up to it, and then get snarky with him?

'How about encouraging someone instead of holding a gun to their head? Now there's a radical thought for you!' he said as he reached the Chaplaincy Centre, wrenching the door open with a mighty heave.

It actually took quite a bit to earn Rob's dislike, but in a few short days Major Le Bon had succeeded very ably. He could feel a fire of rage rising within him. *If that woman is not careful, her ego is going to get more of my fragile ego than it can handle!* However as that thought came through his mind he stopped himself, and began to breath carefully and deeply, trying to calm his mind.

'Are you all right there Rob?' said Alan, who was gazing in the door of Rob's office.

'Yeh, I'm fine,' said Rob quickly. For a moment Alan just gazed at him, before he moved away looking a little doubtful.

When Rob had calmed down some more a resolve grew in him to only present cold formality to OC Charlie Company. *I won't give that woman the satisfaction of knowing that she's got to me,* he thought; *in fact, beyond the necessities of work, I won't give her the satisfaction of knowing anything at all!*

Rob said nothing of that awkward conversation to the other chaplains, or to anyone else for that matter. His feelings about Major Le Bon became another thing about him that was cut off from the knowledge of other people, and the thought that he may have misunderstood her did not enter his mind.

5

That evening 23 and 24 Platoon had their welcome barbecue at the Chapel. Pat led the presentation to the two platoons that told them about the role of Chaplains in the Army. The Padres then circulated amongst the recruits asking "home town" sorts of questions. As they sat eating together, Rob smiled to himself as he watched the interactions, as he thought he could see a few Recruits who were mourning the loss of the electronic security blanket of their mobile phones. Pat had told him earlier of the kinds of angst caused by the restrictions placed on mobile phone use. Seeing the new arrivals up close also gave the Chaplains a chance to gauge how things were going for the platoons, who were now into their second day of training since arriving at Murruwa.

No particular concerns came to the attention of the Chaplains or platoon staff for the rest of the time at the Chapel, and it was well after the recruits had left that the next incident occurred. 24 Platoon were going through their bedtime routine when a female recruit was corrected for the way she was moving through the lines.

'Stop! Steady there, Recruit Jefferson! You will move through the foyer area in the manner previously indicated! Go back and try it again!' barked Bombardier[1] Ian Stewart. However, instead of going back to the entrance of the foyer and trying again, she froze on the spot, and started to shake. He was about to increase the volume of his voice in an effort to get her to move, when he saw a damp patch appear at the front of her pyjamas and move rapidly down her legs.

'Shit,' he said under his breath, before yelling, 'Sarge, get out here now!'

The Platoon Sergeant, Tom Taylor, poked his head out of his office, looked at the girl and said, 'Shit! Over here now Recruit!', but the girl was still frozen to the spot.

They both then came to her side, and ushered her quickly into the Sergeant's office, laid a towel on a chair, and sat her down. Lieutenant Morgan had by this time become aware that something was wrong, and his massive frame loomed out of his office to assess the situation. After having what had happened briefly explained to him, he decided to call the duty chaplain; which meant he called Rob.

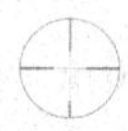

Once again Rob had been caught on his way home, but he did not even ask for a reason from Morgs. His passage back through the security gate was greeted with a roar of laughter by the guard. Upon arrival at 24 Platoon, he was briefed by the staff as to how the situation had developed. Bombardier Stewart was actually a bit taken aback by what had happened.

'I don't mind scaring the shit out of people, Padre,' he admitted. 'But causing that kid to piss herself has rattled me a bit.'

---

1.   Bombardier is the equivalent rank to Corporal in the Artillery Corps. Never call a Bombardier a Corporal. For some reason it really upsets them …

'Who knows what has happened in her past,' replied Rob. 'They don't come here with instruction manuals.'

'Wish they did though sometimes.'

Rob was then ushered into the Platoon Sergeant's office, where he found Recruit Tahlia Jefferson with Corporal Lydia Timoshenko, one of the other section commanders from 24 Platoon. Before Rob had arrived, Recruit Jefferson had showered and changed, and even though she was now in uniform, Rob recognised her as the recruit whom he had seen standing without any bag or suitcase beside her on the day she got off the bus.

'I'll leave if you like, sir,' said Corporal Timoshenko when he came in, but Rob shook his head.

'If it's all right with you and Recruit Jefferson, I'll get you to stay.' Both nodded their assent, and Rob then sat down opposite the two of them, looking at the troubled young lady.

'Could you tell me what happened, in your words?' Rob asked in the gentle, sing-song South Wales accent that was his normal speaking voice, rather than the ringing tones he had used on the aggressive Recruit earlier in the day.

Tahlia then gave her account of events. Rob saw no sign of her looking at Corporal Timoshenko for guidance, so he was fairly happy that what she had said was what she had felt happened, rather than having been coached into saying something to avoid scrutiny on the recruit instructors.

'Now, I'm not a psychologist, Tahlia,' he said after she had finished, 'but in my experience what happened to you tonight tells me that you have had some very bad things happen to you. Am I correct?' In response she nodded and began to cry, and Rob and Corporal Timoshenko exchanged glances that had the same thought in it: this girl is not going to make it in the Army.

'Do you feel like you can keep going with training right now? Everybody'd understand if you said no,' said Rob, trying to give her a dignified way out if she wanted one. He knew in his heart that this young lady had suffered abuse of some sort. Like a whipped dog she had urinated involuntarily in the presence of an authority figure who had shown a degree of aggression.

'I want to do this more than anything in the whole world, sir!' she replied, a mixture of desperation and anger in her voice. 'I want to get away from them, and show them I'm not a doormat. They don't know that I've joined yet! I kept it a secret. I just walked out of home and never came back.'

Rob was momentarily caught off guard by Tahlia's answer.

'You just off and left? How did you keep all the interviews a secret?' Rob asked.

'I told them I was going to job interviews in the City,' she continued.

'By "them", you mean your family?'

'Yeah, my step-Dad and Mum; then just a few days ago, I put on my best clothes, shoved my tooth brush and a change of underwear in my handbag, and went in to Brisbane — and now I'm here.'

'I'm actually in awe of you right now,' Rob admitted. 'You've got more courage and cunning in your little finger than most people have in their entire bodies! You're a brave woman. Now that fire in the belly's your friend. Use it! But I'm not going to lie to you; if you want to stay in training you're going to have some tough things to work through, and being in the Army can be tough in itself. Military training's not easy, nor is it meant to be, but you have to find a way of knowing that you're worthwhile, regardless of what's happened in the past.'

'I find that pretty hard sometimes, sir,' she admitted.

'Well, we'll talk more about that, but for now I'm just going to have a word with some of your staff. Is it okay if I share with them what we've just discussed?'

Tahlia nodded her agreement, so Rob went into the Platoon

Commander's office with Bombardier Stewart, and Sergeant Taylor.

'How do you reckon she'll go?' asked Sergeant Taylor.

Rob scratched his head thoughtfully.

'Look, I think she's very marginal to be honest, though I rate her basic courage highly,' Rob said, 'and she says she wants to continue more than anything. She's been abused, and will definitely need help from Psych; but if you can find some way of showing her that you're on her side, that'll make a lot of difference. I don't think she's had many decent examples in her life, so if someone shows her good, positive leadership, I think she'll follow them very willingly.'

The three members of the Platoon staff considered each other for a moment, before Sergeant Taylor spoke up.

'I think we can manage something Padre. Thanks for your help,' he said.

'Not a problem,' Rob said, 'and if you could find a time for me to catch up with her every week for the next couple of weeks, that'd be grand.'

'No worries,' said Morgs. 'I'm sure we can sort out something in the training program; I'll shoot you an email with a couple of options.'

'Magic! Much appreciated!'

With that remark Rob left the platoon lines, and the staff got on with the rest of the evening routine.

'The Padre sure seemed to know what he was on about,' remarked Lydia Timoshenko.

'Yep, he's got all his shit in one sock, that's for sure,' replied Ian, but his thoughts were interrupted by seeing Recruit Jefferson marching through the foyer again, and he promptly called her over. Looking her evenly in the eye Bombardier

Stewart said, 'Well done for showing courage, but I won't be going easy on you just because of what happened tonight. It's my job to train you to be a soldier. But remember, it doesn't mean I hate you or want to hurt you. You got that?'

'Yes Bombardier,' she replied.

'And one more thing Recruit, if the people who hurt you ever come near you again, just let me know. I'll kill them personally.'

'Thanks Bombardier.'

'Don't mention it. Now get out of my sight,' he said to her with a look on his face that was far more kind than his words.

'Yes Bombardier,' she said, and went on her way into the toilet.

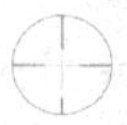

When Rob left 24 Platoon, he walked back up the hill from Charlie Company toward the Chapel, lost for a moment in the sadness of Tahlia's story. He was realistic enough about life to know that abuse of many kinds was regrettably commonplace, but that did not stop him feeling for those who were its victims. Having grown up with three sisters, he had known a couple of their friends had suffered abuse in different forms, and had seen the marks it had left. Not only that, he had once had to prevent one of his sisters suffering the same sort of thing; though hitting that teacher had got him kicked out of school! A brief flush of triumph coursed through him at the arousal of that memory, before Rob drew his mind back to the present.

The heat of the summer day had passed, and a cool evening breeze blew pleasantly as he walked, easing the melancholy of his mood. Rob thought that there was only one thing to do after dealing with something like that; go and seek solace in music.

Moving through the front door of the Chapel he went inside. Even Rob's relatively light foot fall seemed to echo loudly in the space of the foyer before he went into one of the wings and turned on the electric piano. He sat, eyes closed, breathing steadily for a time, before he began to play; he usually sang as well, but this evening he began instrumentally, improvising out his head chords that would tell the story of his feelings. What emerged was for him a lament to the betrayal of trust that was child abuse. On and on he played, unaware of the world around him; it was one of the only environments where Rob was not continually trying to remain attuned to his surroundings. So it was that he was unaware of a person leaning in the doorway, listening in amazement at what she heard.

Major Le Bon had come up to the Chapel to seek a break from her computer screen and the work that had been occupying her mind this late in the day. She loved the hushed stillness of the place, and would often come and pray, or simply sit and feel the blessed silence surround her. However tonight the silence was gone, and instead it seemed like the building itself sang with the music coming from the piano. Anne had learned the instrument as a child, and had been able to sweat her way through reading music and playing the notes that were on the page, but nothing she had ever done came close to what she was hearing now. Padre Llewellyn was making the piano come to life.

As she stood listening, the melody slowly began to change and then Rob shifted into song. Though she did not understand a word of what he sang, there was meaning beyond words in what was heard. It was a song in a minor key, that yet had within it a note of defiance, a lot like the man who was doing the singing.

'*Arglwydd Iesu arwain f'enaid ...,*'[2] he began, and the sound of his voice filled the building as he continued through the song.

---

2. Lord Jesus lead my soul

Rob's voice had considerable power, and the Chapel reverberated with the great waves of sound. Feeling like she was intruding into some moment of private sanctity, Anne left, and walked back down to her office.

'What on earth is he doing here with a voice like that?' she said to herself as she walked away, even more unsure of what to make of Padre Llewellyn. How does somebody like him make the choice to be in the Army instead of using all that talent? The answer to that question was another piece of "the puzzle of the Padre", as Anne was beginning to label it in her mind, and with that thought she set off back toward Charlie Company headquarters.

The rest of the week flew by, though the issues raised by recruits were less urgent in nature than they had been in the first couple of days. 23 and 24 Platoon were actually shaping up to be relatively happy and healthy groups of people, despite the inevitable rocky start. Rob reached this conclusion during the swim test for the platoons, for he saw that the recruits were beginning to encourage each other and work together well. Most of them were able to swim competently; with two exceptions. One of these was a young man of Chinese descent, who was an exceptional athlete in most respects, but seemed singularly unable to float. The other was a fellow of Sudanese background who likewise could run like the wind, but if anything, sank more quickly.

'Kick, paddle; try that,' said F-Bomb to Recruit Pubudu, the young Sudanese, trying to make the right sort of arm actions to indicate what the Recruit should do with his limbs.

'Fuck! That didn't work!' he said as Recruit Pubudu sank again. 'All right, down the shallow end with you, sunshine,' he said as they dragged him from the water.

'Yes Corporal,' said the recruit, spluttering water as he did so.

However with Recruit Cheng, F-Bomb was less kind.

'C'mon Cheng, if you want to be an Asian legend like me, then you're going to have swim better than that!' said F-Bomb as the recruit struggled desperately to tread water.

'That's the way, use those skinny legs of yours!' he continued. 'Thank fuck you didn't join the Navy!'

'It seems wrong doesn't it?' said Jar-Jar to Rob, hardly able to contain his laughter. 'Pubudu and Cheng can run like a hares, but when you put them in the water all their awesome is gone!'

'I think it's something to do with muscle mass,' said Rob, as Recruit Cheng narrowly avoided having his head go under water again.

'Well Pubudu there looks like he's made of lead, even though he can run 2.4 kilometres in 7 minutes.'

'F-Bomb doesn't have anything against Cheng does he? asked Rob, as Corporal Nguyen continued haranguing the young man.

'Nah Padre, he insults everybody in a very even-handed manner,' said Jar-Jar philosophically. 'He actually likes Cheng. That kid's got backbone; but if F-Bomb likes you, he'll just hang shit on you more than ever before!'

'Got it,' said Rob, smiling faintly, and moved on to his next task for the day.

That Sunday the Chapel services, as always, were well attended, with about one fifth of those who came actively engaging in the service. Pat had told him when he arrived at Murruwa that the Chapel was also a place of rest where recruits could meet with family members and enjoy some precious space before being thrust into the rigours of training again, and he saw that in action on that Sunday. Family members talked to him after the service as well as recruits, and it was very nearly lunch time before he left. Rob then had lunch at the mess, and went down to the hospital to do the daily rounds of the on-call Chaplain.

When eventually it came time for Rob to hand over the phone the following week, Pat asked him laconically, 'So whaddya reckon mate?'

Rob raised his eyebrows and gave a slight smile.

'That was an eye-opener, there's no denying,' he admitted, to general laughter and ribaldry from the others.

'What has just happened to you is actually a fairly normal week for an on-call Chaplain,' Alan explained, 'especially when there are newly arrived recruits on base.'

After he had handed over the on-call phone, Pat told Rob to go home and get some rest. When he had left, Pat turned to the others.

'I think I could warm to this fella,' he said.

'He doesn't say much,' said Alan.

'But he does a lot, and that's what counts,' concluded Pat, and they all went on with the work of the day.

News of Rob's work in the company filtered back to Major Le Bon through the ever watchful eyes of the Charlie Company Company Sergeant Major (CSM); Warrant Officer second-class, Donald McIntosh. Warrant Officer McIntosh had formerly been a soldier in the Black Watch, Royal Highland Regiment, when it had still existed independently of the Royal Regiment of Scotland. As the changes to his beloved Regiment had looked likely, he had laterally transferred to the Australian Army, and had ended up in an infantry battalion in Townsville. McIntosh was one of the most feared of all the CSMs on the base, though he could be just as ferocious in defending his soldiers as he could be in correcting them. For a lucky few, he permitted them to use the inevitable nickname of 'Jock'; the unlucky ones seldom got a chance to call him anything other than "sir". He and Major Le Bon made a formidable combination, and when Anne, ever the Intelligence Officer, had wanted news of how Chaplain Llewellyn was performing, she knew that the CSM would be a fantastic source of information, as he seemed to know everything his NCOs[3] were thinking about.

'Any news of our new Padre from your end, Jock?' asked Anne after they had sat for a while discussing the various other goings on within Charlie Company.

'Very good so far, ma'am, from what I can tell, and I did hear that he ripped a new arsehole for an unpleasant recruit,' he said in his glottal Clydeside accent. 'Not what you usually expect from a Padre. Apparently the little shit made racist remarks to both F-Bomb and Chaplain Llewellyn.'

Anne was stunned. To make racist remarks to F-Bomb was to invite death and disaster, if you were lucky, but she had not expected a response like that from the reserved Padre. Another piece of Rob's jigsaw had just been handed to her, but its place in the overall picture remained elusive. The flashes of annoyance that she had thought had come across his face in their last conversation sprang to mind, as did his devastating prowess at kick-boxing. However it was still hard to reconcile this with the quiet, serious man who had been in her office on the day they had met.

'Did he say anything inappropriate?' asked Anne, barely able to contain her confusion.

---

3. Non-commissioned officers; refers to Lance-Corporals, Corporals, Sergeants, and the two classes of Warrant-Officer. The post of company sergeant major is occupied by a Warrant-Officer Second Class, whereas the higher ranked Warrant-Officer first class will be a Regimental Sergeant Major.

'From what I heard he didn't even swear, though Corporal Nguyen was a bit cagey about what was actually said,' commented the CSM, evidently impressed. 'Apparently he went from quiet to breathing fire in an instant.'

'How's the recruit been since then?' she asked.

'Like a wee lamb, ma'am; very anxious to keep out of trouble.'

'Wow! That's unexpected!' remarked Anne. 'What else have they said about Padre Llewellyn?'

'They say he's been compassionate, but realistic; a good balance. The staff have really appreciated the advice he's given.'

'So you've got no concerns about him?'

'Professionally, I've got none at all,' he said.

'How about non-professional concerns?' she asked, curious as to why the CSM seemed to have qualified his endorsement of Rob.

'Well, I'll say this,' said Jock. 'People don't give a face-ripping like that without having done it before. F-Bomb said Padre Llewellyn just exploded, and then tore the recruit apart; he didn't even have to think about what to say. It's the mark of experience. I think our man was something other than a chaplain at some stage in his life.'

'He's only been in the Army for a bit over a year,' said Anne, 'and before that he was a music teacher apparently.'

'Well ma'am, if that lad hasn't been something else in the military, then I'm an Englishman,' he said categorically, which needed to be taken seriously, for Jock hated being called an Englishman.

Anne considered this remark for a moment. The very regimental way Padre Llewellyn conducted himself could point to that also; or it could point to someone who is nervous and finds Army formalities a good way of hiding. Could he be hiding something? For a moment she mentally arranged and re-arranged what she knew about the Padre, but the picture still did not make sense. Finding patterns in information was what she did for a living; and even when she was away from doing Intelligence work, she still used the same skills in her management of people. In an odd way Chaplains were similar, she thought, except that the information they gathered was used for a different purpose.

'You don't think he could be a fast learner?' asked Anne, who was still struggling to come to terms with the person her CSM was describing.

'I doubt it,' he replied, 'though I admit the quiet bit doesn't seem to fit with the fierce bit'

'Well, whatever the case,' she said eventually, with a note of satisfaction in her voice, 'I'm just relieved that he isn't like the last guy.'

'Too right,' said the CSM, 'that scunner was a disgrace to the uniform and his calling.'

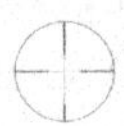

Later that morning Anne left her office and decided to do one of her routine inspections of training in Charlie Company. After a brief moment of consideration, she walked down to where 23 platoon and 24 Platoon were engaged in a lecture, and found that they were taking a break. Noticing that Rob was just finishing a conversation with a female recruit, Anne paused for a moment to allow him to walk away without noticing her, before she went over and talked to the young lady.

'Good morning Recruit!' Major Le Bon said with a smile.

'Stand fast,' squeaked the young lady, coming to attention, and causing everyone around her to brace up as well, though as she was not wearing her hat, she did not salute.

'Stand easy,' said Anne pleasantly, to everyone around, before addressing the recruit directly.

'What's your name?' she asked.

'Tahlia Jefferson, ma'am,' said the young lady shakily. She found talking to Bombardier Stewart stressful enough, but talking to the Charlie Company OC was terrifying. For Tahlia, Majors were a mythical creature that inhabited a realm well beyond her own.

'Having a chat to Padre Llewellyn, were you Recruit Jefferson?' Anne continued in her friendly tone.

'Yes, ma'am,' she said, 'he's helped me a lot. I found it really hard last week.'

'I'm glad to hear it,' said Anne. 'How's he helped you the most?'

'Well, he's mainly talked about how what I believe about myself and other things affects what I do,' Tahlia explained, 'then we talk about how that works with what I face in training. Bombardier Stewart has been great too, but he pushes me really hard.'

'That's not a bad thing,' said Anne in an encouraging tone. 'Well, you had better get back to it now, don't you think?'

'Yes ma'am,' said Tahlia, who then walked away relieved at having survived her first conversation with a Major.

When Recruit Jefferson had walked out of sight, Anne decided that she might head up to the Chaplaincy Centre and thank Rob for his work. Too often giving positive feedback was ignored in the Army; negative feedback on the other hand was usually quick in coming.

It seemed that with the troubled and the truculent, Padre Llewellyn was having an impact. As to what lay in his past, that was anyone's guess, and Rob was proving to be about the most closed book she had ever met. However, when Anne arrived in the Chaplains' office she discovered that he was not there; he had come back into the office briefly before heading off to the high-wire confidence course. Only Pat and Steve were in the building at the time.

'Morning Anne,' boomed Pat, as he walked across the room, 'how can we help you?'

'I'm chasing Chaplain Llewellyn actually, but I'd actually like to talk to you as well,' she said.

At this Pat stopped mid-stride, and the colour appeared to leave his face.

'He hasn't stuffed up already has he?' Steve said from where he was sitting, fearing that Anne wanted to have Rob removed from her Company for some failure or another.

'No, nothing like that; his performance this week seems to have been stellar,' said Anne, though she carefully omitted the reports of Rob having yelled at a recruit.

'Well that's good,' said Pat, relieved, 'some guys have an instinct for the job, and Rob seems to be one of them. But he looks utterly rat-arsed. He's been working hard.'

At that remark a look of concern came over Anne's face.

'Does he have anyone he can talk to if things get tough?' she asked; unbeknownst to Rob, her ruthless dedication to looking after her soldiers also applied to him, whatever the doubts he thought she had expressed.

'No idea Anne,' sighed Pat, 'I haven't thought about it. It's a bit hard to get much out of him other than talk of work.'

'He could just be a really quiet one I guess,' said Anne, 'but please keep an eye on him from your end. I don't want him to burn out!'

'We'll do that,' said Pat, though he was wondering to himself how on earth you kept an eye on somebody who moved as quickly as their new colleague.

The Wednesday after he had handed over the on-call phone saw Rob conduct his first Character Training session. The lessons last all day, and are designed to give recruits an insight into how character and belief systems drive ethics and decision making. This particular group of recruits were from Bravo Company, and had been at Murruwa for five weeks, and it must be said, were looking forward to a day under the less rigorous instruction of the Padres. However, those who were in Rob's group were in for a bit of a surprise; rigour was certainly not absent.

He had been told that during character training days, the recruits were usually given their mobile phones, with the understanding that they are only to be used during breaks. However one individual decided to use his whilst Rob was giving a lesson that highlighted the ethical dilemmas surrounding the use of deadly force.

'Recruit Bates!' said Rob in a terse voice. 'What corps of the Army are you going to again?'

'Infantry, sir,' said Tim Bates, who was startled into awareness by Rob's sudden interjection, which drew some laughter from his fellow trainees.

'Okay then genius, let's pretend for a moment that you're in Afghanistan,' Rob continued in deadly earnest, 'and you have a car that's driving headlong at your check-point. Your rules of engagement say that you have to shoot at any vehicle that doesn't obey orders to stop, and this vehicle has not obeyed orders to stop.'

'Ahh, I'll open fire, sir!' he said recovering, confident in being more warlike than the chaplain.

'Really?' said Rob, smiling faintly. 'You can see through your sight that the car contains a family. What are you going to do then?'

'Ummmm,' said the Recruit Bates, staring at the Padre in surprise.

'C'mon man, hurry up,' said Rob, raising his voice, 'there might be a bomb in that car! Your mates could die if you hesitate!'

'I, I, I'll open fire!' stammered Bates, his eyes widening.

'Will you now?' said Rob more quietly. 'Okay; you do open fire. You stop the vehicle, they all die, and your mates are safe. But when the EOD[4] team searches the car, there's no bomb; there are no weapons of any kind. Just very dead people. Seen a dead body have you?'

'No sir,' said Recruit Bates quietly.

'How are you going to feel then, Recruit Bates? You've killed "innocent" people,' said Rob, pressing home his attack. Bates was looking at Rob in mute horror, completely unable to wrap his mind around the situation Rob had set before him.

The whole class of recruits was also looking at Rob with facial expressions that ranged from surprised to truly terrified.

'Why are you all looking at me like that?' he said. 'It's happened before now you know! You have orders to open fire that you have to obey, but old mate driving the car is running late, or is high on drugs, or any of the other things that cause people to panic when an armed person tells them to stop. You ask any warfighter on this base and they'll tell you what can go wrong at a checkpoint!'

All the recruits were still staring at him, the stunned silence laying like a blanket over the room.

'Fighting a war is a nasty, untidy business, and if you go into a war zone, thumb in bum, mind in neutral, you might die, or

---

4. Explosive Ordinance Disposal.

you might lose your mind; this is not a game!' barked Rob. 'If you have no way of reconciling your conscience to the crazy things that can happen in a war, then you are going to have a very hard time of it. So, Recruit Bates, I suggest you pay closer attention. And if anybody else uses their phones while I'm giving a lesson, I'll drown the thing in the Baptismal tank; and it's four feet deep!'

'How do you reconcile your conscience to war, Padre?' asked another recruit, once Rob's ire had subsided a little.

'Well, sunshine, I suggest you shut your gob, and you'll find out!' he said, 'But the real question is not about me, it's about you. How're you going to reconcile your conscience to what can happen in a war?'

For the rest of the day the group was rather more attentive, and the Padre's vivid explanations and deadly serious manner made some aspects of character training the talk of those two platoons well into the evening. When some of the Corporals in those platoons heard what the recruits were mulling over, it led to some frank discussions about the reality of war. It also led some of the instructional staff to wonder what drove the new Padre to think the way he did. Rob was rapidly proving himself to be unlike any Chaplain they had ever met.

6

―――――――

When the weekend finally came around, Rob found himself
with the first substantial amount of free time he had enjoyed
since arriving in Murruwa He spent much of Saturday shooting
at a rifle range to the south of the town. It was wonderful to get
out into the country, and away from the base, and everything
else that had been occupying his mind over the past couple of
weeks. That evening he spent a long time in his music room,
losing himself in the joy of playing the piano. By the time he
went to bed, his mind felt a little more relaxed after the gathering tension that had taken hold. The next day Rob awoke
more reluctantly than usual, aware that attending church meant
breaking his blesséd solitude. He breakfasted and got changed
in something of a daze, before leaving his house and walking the
kilometre to where the service was held. Rob arrived a little
early, and sat quietly in a pew, content in the relative stillness of
the building.

A friend from theological college was the minister, and had
been delighted when Rob had said he was coming to Murruwa
with the Army. On this morning however, Rob still felt somewhat drained, and the thought of making small-talk with civil-

ians was not at all attractive; a week like his would have been incomprehensible to the average person in any case. So he was sincerely hoping he could come to church without getting entangled in any conversations, awkward or otherwise. It had been quite an introduction to work at Murruwa. One officer and multiple recruits had struggled with various issues, but so far everyone had been kept safe. So there he was, sitting in a pew, his eyes shut, and his head down. The duty phone was no longer in his pocket, with its treacherous ring threatening to throw the day into chaos. But he had to admit it, he was good at chaos; the more things got bent out of shape, the better he seemed to perform. That much had not changed over the years.

Rob became aware of a person sitting down next to him, and groaning inwardly at the thought of having to relate to people, he opened his eyes and to his horror he looked directly into those of Anne Le Bon; though it took him a moment to realise it was her. The tightly tied bun and DPCU[1] were gone, replaced by a simple blue dress, and her dark hair falling down on her shoulders. Rob felt like a cold frost moved over him, regardless of the summer warmth. The prospect of attending church with her did not thrill him at all.

'Are you okay Padre?' she asked softly, as she settled down next to him.

'I'm fine ma'am, just a bit tired,' he said firmly, kicking himself for giving the appearance of weakness to her. There is no escape from this woman, he thought despairingly.

'I bet you are, it's been quite a week from what I've heard,' she said looking at him with a slight smile on her face. Anne looked around at the building, and at the people who were steadily filing in. The congregation itself was a broad mix of ages, with all the delightful chaos that came from having a fair

---

1. Disruptive Pattern Camouflage Uniform.

number of young families involved. Two small boys, evidently brothers, had decided that the pews made an excellent assault course.

'I like this church,' said Anne, winking at the impish face of one of the boys as he peered at her over the top of the seat. 'Are you going to come here yourself?'

'I'm not sure,' he said in a non-committal tone of voice, making a mental note to try the other congregation of his denomination when he next had a free Sunday. 'I went to College with Pete Norman, the Pastor here.'

'I've been going here for a while now. It's been really good,' said Anne. 'Pete's very down to earth.'

At this moment their careful manoeuvring around each other was interrupted by Pete's wife Christine bustling up to them both. She was a short, cheerful, and currently pregnant lady; with a pronounced New Zealand accent. Rob also remembered her as a person who was very frank, and quite unconcerned about others' opinions of her; a useful quality in a Pastor's wife.

'Rob! You actually arrived!' she said embracing him. 'Good morning Anne! Pete insists that you both come over for lunch today! He has been dying to catch up with Rob, and I thought it'd be great if you came too Anne, since you're both in the Army and everything! Are you able to come over?'

'Thanks Christine,' said Anne pleasantly, 'that'd be lovely.'

At this moment Rob felt like a caged wild animal. He wanted to keep his interactions with Major Le Bon clear, concise, but above all, brief. However, now he felt like he was caught by the demands of being polite to his friends and a professional colleague.

'Sure,' said Rob's mouth, quickly jumping in before the rest of him could think up an objection.

'Great! Do you like Indian food?' asked Christine.

'Love it!' said Rob, his eyes lighting up despite the trepidation he was feeling.

'Fantastic! It'll be take-away I'm afraid; I'm blonde, pregnant, and a Kiwi, so I'm not cooking anything,' she said with her best air-head look. 'Well, that's my excuse anyway. Here's a menu, if you guys could choose what you want and we'll make the order later. We'll get you to pick it up after the service.'

With that she returned to where she had been sitting and left them to spend a little time chatting before the service began, which Rob managed despite his discomfort. The presence of a man with Anne Le Bon did not go unnoticed, especially to that portion of the church's population who were of the kind of well-meaning soul who thought of singleness as about the worst affliction possible. She had begun attending the congregation the previous year, but any single males tended to give her a wide berth; and she was not altogether displeased about this. Anne could be downright scary if she wanted to be, which had come in handy a few times in her life when some less than desirable male company had tried to impose itself on her.

Pete had been doing a series of sermons through the Gospel of John, but for some of the older ladies in the congregation Rob's voice was the highlight of the service, as his strong tenor filled the building when they were singing.

'Where did you learn to sing like that?' trilled one cheerful old dear, as she talked to them both. Rob shrugged his shoulders.

'Most people sang where I came from,' he answered.

'Oooh, my grandfather was from England too,' said another, and Anne had to suppress laughter as she saw the pained expression on Rob's face. Evidently being mistaken for an Englishman did not please him at all.

'Actually, I'm not English,' he explained patiently. 'I'm from Wales.'

Anne then introduced Rob to several other people around their age, and she noted with some interest the interaction he had with two single ladies. The four of them stood talking together, and it soon became plain to Anne that both the women wanted to subtly ascertain Rob's availability. However, he was stunningly successful at avoiding the topic until one of them chose to ask him straight out.

'Are you married?' said Emily, a petite, attractive nurse who worked in the local hospital.

'No, I'm not,' he replied.

'Are you in a relationship?' she continued, and Rob shook his head.

'That's a surprise!' said the other lady, Rebekah, with a look of clear satisfaction. 'I thought it was impossible for a guy to go through Theological College and stay single!'

'Well, I managed it,' replied Rob with a disarming smile, 'and now I'm full time with the Army I plan on staying that way. It's a bit unfair on a lady to expect her to come following me around the country, and then spend so much time apart when I'm away on exercises and the like. I couldn't do that.'

The impact of this statement was immediately visible on the faces of the two women. Despite the friendly way in which Rob had spoken, there was something inescapably definitive about what he had said, that was obviously meant to deter any further inquiry. Anne was having difficulty not smiling; she had not met many men who could resist playing along with unsolicited attention from attractive women, but Rob was evidently one. Despite the unequivocal shut down they had received, the two ladies were not so easily deterred; so instead of pressing him more on relationships, Emily decided to use the indirect approach and invite him to the Bible study she attended.

'I think you'd really enjoy it; one of the elders leads the

study, and Anne comes along when she can!' said Emily, though she did not realise this would not entice him in the slightest.

'Thanks so much for thinking of me,' he said kindly, and both Emily and Rebekah brightened a little at these words; however, they were to be disappointed, 'but work'll mean I can't commit to anything like that very easily. As it is I'll only be here every second Sunday, if that.'

Anne thought for a moment that she might challenge him on attending the Bible study, however she decided against it; if Rob was an introvert, being social was the last thing he was going to want to do. What was more, he possibly tired of being cornered by single women. I know the feeling when it comes to men, Anne thought fairly.

At that moment Pete came up and rescued Emily and Rebekah from further disappointment at Rob's hands.

'Have you both got wheels?' he asked, looking at Rob and Anne. 'We haven't got any room in our car with the stuff that's in it at the moment.' Anne nodded, however Rob shook his head.

'My place is under a mile away,' he explained. 'I can go back and get my car.'

'What? In this heat! Anne could give you a lift, surely?' said Pete. 'That'd be all right wouldn't it?'

'I can do that,' said Anne.

'Great! Christine has already ordered what you wanted,' he said, and then went away to attend to a couple of things that needed doing before he left the church.

'So you don't like being mistaken for an Englishman, Padre?' she asked a little cheekily as they were seated in her car.

'Absolutely not,' he said, dark Celtic displeasure covering his face.

'Well, I'm French by birth, so you'll have no argument from me; the look on your face was almost like seeing Warrant Officer McIntosh called an Englishman.'

'A Welshman won't be happy at being called English, but with a Scotsman you may not survive!' said Rob, with some feeling, drawing a chuckle from Major Le Bon; so maybe he does have a sense of humour, she thought, he just doesn't let it out to play very often.

When they arrived at the restaurant, Rob went inside and collected the meals. The smell of the food as they drove to the Norman's place was pleasant and aromatic. It was not a long journey, and the two of them passed that time in virtual silence. Indeed, it seemed to Anne that Rob was almost willing himself into invisibility by taking refuge in the smell of the food. When they arrived they were ushered into the lounge room, and Christine told them to pull up a bean bag around the coffee table.

'Sorry for the informality, I just can't be bothered setting the table today; and from what I remember of you, Rob, you ate standing up half the the time anyway,' she said conversationally. 'But we wanted to have you over before you got your nose too far into work, otherwise we'll never see you.'

Rob seemed surprised at this remark; Anne merely raised her eyebrows and smiled as she thought that she might learn something about the Padre after all. Works hard, tends to avoid social interaction, she mused. So, I might be dealing with a workaholic here!

The early part of their time together was spent in light conversation about the goings on of the church, and friends from college, though before long Christine thought it would be polite to include Anne in the conversation.

'Where were you from originally Anne?' she asked, 'Every time I hear you speak I wonder if you've got an accent.'

'I was born in France, in Montpellier, and I lived there until I was ten; then Mum and Dad moved to Australia; to Ballina, in Northern New South Wales,' Anne explained. 'Papa is a marine engineer.'

'Nice! I love that part of the world,' commented Pete.

'One of the best; more soft and green that most of this country,' she said.

'Were you from a Catholic background?' asked Pete.

'No, we were Protestants; historically a lot of Huguenots came from Montpellier,' remarked Anne, 'though I didn't become serious about my faith until much later.'

'I can relate to that,' said Christine. 'I was a real wild child myself until my Dad died. It really made me think a lot.'

'Grief does that,' said Rob, and everyone seemed a little surprised when he spoke, as before that moment he had been doing a world class impersonation of empty space. They all then turned toward him, as if expecting further comment, but he was looking out a window and did not meet their gaze.

'I still regret the things I did; and it really gets to me sometimes; it makes me sad when I think about it, though sometimes I think I shouldn't feel that way,' said Christine.

'There's no script for grief, for the sadness of death, or regret, or broken relationships,' said Rob, looking back at the others, 'its experience is unique for everyone. But for me, grief is like the sea; sometimes the tide is high and we think we are drowning, other times the tide's low and we can see more clearly. Yet like the sea, the grief is always there, ebbing and flowing.'

'Do you think we ever get over things?' asked Anne, curious to hear his response. She had an intense dislike for the purveyors of platitudes, and was checking whether Chaplain Llewellyn was such a person.

'Well I don't think that "getting over it" is the most helpful way of thinking about grief ma'am,' said Rob, his grey eyes regarding her seriously. 'It's not a task we finish, and then move on; it becomes a part of us, though I think we reach a place where we're at peace with it, and can see that God has been at work in it for all its pain. But I don't think the pain ever leaves completely. Not in this life anyway.'

Anne looked at him for a moment, liking what she heard. Ideas like those did not come from a textbook, she thought, but were won from hard experience.

'That's a beautiful way of expressing it,' said Christine. Rob glanced over at her for a moment and smiled faintly, however he made no effort to continue that line of conversation, and his brief openness was again replaced by his characteristic reserve. Any awkwardness was saved by Pete choosing that moment to ask Anne a question.

'You been in the Army long?'

'Since I left high school; I went to the Defence Force Academy then Duntroon. I'm now here commanding one of the training companies,' Anne explained. 'People at home thought it was weird for a girl like me, an only child and all, joining the Army. But I really loved it.'

'Have you gone overseas?' asked Christine.

'Yes; Iraq, Afghanistan and East Timor,' Anne explained. 'Intelligence Corps gets deployed a lot.'

Anne then turn to Rob, and asked, 'So how about you? What's your story?'

'I'm from Wales, from a town called Ystradgynlais,' Rob explained, drawing a twisted facial expressions from Pete at the sound of the town name. 'Like you, my first language is not English, though I don't speak Welsh much right now, except to my family.'

'Have you travelled much?'

'Nowhere interesting.'

'You have some siblings though, don't you?' put in Christine.

'Sisters only; two older, one younger: Ceridwen, Rhiannon, and Catrin. They're all married. The oldest two live in Wales, but Catrin lives with her husband in Toronto.'

'Do you miss them, being over here by yourself?' asked Anne.

'Yes I do,' said Rob simply, looking down at his food as he did so.

'But you have your uncle in Sydney don't you?' asked Christine.

'That's correct,' said Rob.

'Aren't you lonely?' said Christine, and this time Anne could hear a degree of frustration in her voice when she asked the question. Even people who've known him before find him hard to fathom, she observed.

'Never thought about it really,' he said in a non-committal way.

Since Rob seemed to specialise in one phrase answers to questions, so she thought she would try and ask him something a little more open ended.

'So what brought you out to Australia?' she said.

'I wanted a change in life, so I came out here and I worked with my Uncle; my mother's brother, teaching music in Sydney,' Rob answered after a moment's reflection, though Anne could see from his body language that this was an area of life he did not like having probed. 'I'd already studied some theology in my own time back in the UK, but after a year of college here I became a candidate for ministry.'

'So how did you end up in Army Chaplaincy? We thought you'd be happy in that church in Sydney!' put in Christine.

'People suggested it because I like target shooting and keeping fit,' Rob replied, 'but I guess the plodding nature of Church life wasn't something I was enjoying that much. I wanted something with a bit more fizz, if you like.'

'You're being too modest there Rob,' said Pete, before turning to Anne. 'This dude is the last action hero! Crazy fit! Awesome at kick-boxing and shooting; as well as the arty things like playing the piano and singing. Didn't you teach martial arts as well while you were at College?'

'Yes I did.'

Rob's head drooped slightly as he said this, and Anne again smiled in a satisfied way.

'I learned about the kick-boxing this week,' she said. 'He's extremely good.'

'You're not so bad yourself ma'am,' said Rob, desperately trying to steer the conversation away from himself. However, it was not to be.

'And he was the most eligible and unattainable bachelor at college as well,' said Christine, and Rob gazed up at her with a look of blank despair. She seemed to be assuming that he and Major Le Bon knew each other well, or were at least friends, a misapprehension that Anne had no intention of correcting.

'Really Christine! Give the guy a break!' said Pete, coming to Rob's rescue.

'Will you ever go back to a church?' Anne asked of Rob, taking an opportunity to re-direct the conversation, whilst still suppressing her own laughter. Somewhere lurking behind her question was the thought that by being friendly when Rob felt under pressure, she might get him to talk more; it was a very old interrogator's ploy.

'I've no idea; I've learned not to say 'never' to God,' Rob said, looking slightly suspicious, 'he has a habit of turning things upside down when I do that.'

'I can relate to that too,' replied Anne. 'So what do you do to unwind after a week like this?'

'For me nothing beats music. To sit down at my piano, or to spend time singing, that's a great release,' Rob said quietly.

'Your voice sure got you attention at church; were you trained?'

'Yes, from a young age,' he admitted, 'though I've only started again in recent years.'

At that moment Rob's personal mobile phone went off, and he wiped his mouth. Seeing the number he stood up where he was.

'Excuse me, this may take a while,' he remarked, and he then rose and walked out of the room.

'*Shwmae*[2] Derek,' they heard Rob say as he left.

When he had gone, Pete turned to Christine.

'Did you really have to bring up Rob's love life? You know how much he hates it!' he remonstrated in a fierce whisper.

'Sorry! I just find it really sad,' said Christine, 'he's such a nice guy.'

'Not all nice guys need to be married,' said her husband.

'I suppose ...'

'And how many times did somebody try and set him up while we were at college?'

'Heaps,' answered Christine, with a hang-dog expression on her face.

'And how many of those attempts actually worked?' he said.

'None,' said Christine morosely.

'And how'd things go when Angela Baker threw herself at him?' continued Pete.

'Badly,' she replied, hanging her head a little further.

'Sorry Anne,' said Pete, turning to her, 'my wife's greatest regret ever since she got to know Rob was that he was single.'

'That's fine, no offence taken. I understand what drives somebody to stay single,' Anne replied, very pleased with the added insights she had gained so far that lunch time. Pete and Christine did not understand the peril of an unguarded tongue

---

2. Equivalent to "hi there" in the south Wales dialect of Welsh.

in front of a woman like her, and even as they spoke she eagerly added new pieces to the "puzzle of the Padre".

'To be fair, Angela Baker would make most guys want to stay bachelors,' said Christine sadly. 'She would hardly even talk to a man unless he was training for the ministry or the mission field, and even then she'd only give him the time of day if he followed her views on certain things.'

'But Rob was not up for her advances?' asked Anne.

'Not at all,' said Pete, 'he saw the way she treated people, so he kept out of her way ...'

'Then she started fawning over him,' said Christine, cutting in, 'I think it was because he didn't pay her any attention, and she was used to having power over people, so she wanted to get power over Rob too.'

'He just tried to be polite with her to start with,' put in Pete, 'but when she wouldn't take no for an answer, he gave her a public dressing down; right in the middle of a hallway after lectures.'

'What'd he say?' said Anne, curious to see how he dealt with women who annoyed him.

'He was really blunt,' said Christine, 'he told her that he wasn't interested in her at all, and that he was worried she wasn't really a Christian because she didn't show love to people, but treated them like dirt. He told her that she needed to repent.'

'Wow, I bet that went down well,' said Anne, quietly impressed. She made a mental note that it may not be a good idea to push Rob into a corner; the recruit who Rob yelled at probably had learned the same lesson. Anne did not realise how close she had come to this herself.

'And then she went mental at him,' said Pete, 'she screamed, but it didn't do any good. He just took her apart, verbally that is. It was a bit scary actually; I've never heard anyone yell so loud.'

'Sounds like she didn't like having her ego punctured,' said

Anne sourly, and Pete and Christine nodded their agreement. 'How did other people react to what he did?'

'A mixture of relief and fear I guess,' said Pete. 'They were used to him being so gentle that it came as a bit of a shock. A couple of people tried to challenge him about the way he spoke to Angela, but he called them out for being gutless and unwilling to take on a notorious bully like her. Rob can be terrifying when he wants to.'

'Why does he keep calling you ma'am instead of Anne?' asked Christine, looking for signs of Rob's approach.

'Because I outrank him; he actually works for me a lot of the time,' Anne explained. 'He's just being respectful.'

'Rob's a quiet guy ...' observed Pete.

'I've picked up that much ....'

'But when he decides to speak, it's always worth listening to,' he continued. 'There's something sad about him at times, though. You see it most when he's in a crowd; he just goes all quiet and withdrawn and looks like he's a million miles away.'

'But if I had a nervous breakdown he's the one person in the whole world I'd want around, apart from Pete,' said Christine. 'No stupid platitudes, no empty words, just ... well ...'

'Love, really ... not soppy, sentimental garbage, just real care,' added Pete.

At that moment they heard Rob's voice again, as he approached the lounge room, and he looked a little happier than he had been when he had walked out.

'*Hwyl am nawr*[3],' said Rob as he ended the call, and then looked up at the others. 'Sorry about that; it was news of my little sister Catrin. She's had her first baby; a little girl.'

After a general round of congratulations at Rob's sister's news, the conversation drifted in a more comfortable direction

---

3. Welsh equivalent of "Bye for now".

for him; mainly because he spent most of the time listening. However from time to time Rob would say something quite profound and helpful, or else make some quiet comment that brought laughter. Eventually he showed some signs of fatigue, so he asked if he could excuse himself, and Anne offered to take take him back to his house.

'It's been good to get to know you a little better Padre,' she said with a friendly smile as they drove away.

'And you too, ma'am,' he said reflexively, his face typically unreadable; though Anne was betting that he was not entirely happy with the way the conversation had gone that lunch time.

'I'm sorry you got embarrassed back there,' Anne said kindly, not seeing the point in ignoring the awkward interaction. 'I don't think Christine meant any harm.'

'She always thought me being single was a waste of a perfectly usable husband,' he said drily, and Anne laughed. A big part of her wanted to tease Rob at this point, especially given the fact that he had been so serious a lot of the time. There was also another part of her that was quick to spot a weakness and even quicker to exploit it; however she decided against it, as she was aware that her professional relationship with him may be damaged by careless words.

Anne only half-realised the degree of hostility he had for her, so hard was it to tell what he was thinking. However from her perspective, she had seen that there was a genuine depth to Rob, despite his quiet demeanour. In fact, Anne was beginning to feel that the chaplaincy of Charlie Company may be in good hands after all; even if he gave up personal information as willingly as a lion would give up its prey.

7

———

The work rhythm continued unabated for Rob and the other Chaplains, though a small change in the weekly routine came along in the form of the Yurali Patisserie run, which involved an early start just after sunrise. However there would not be much sun to enjoy, as it had begun to drizzle, and for most of the staff gathered to do the run, it was quite a cool morning. Rob however seemed to be in his element, and he made comments about it being a lovely summer's day, which drew a degree of derision and suggestions of madness. He was busy talking to a group of Corporals from Charlie Company when he heard a voice behind him.

'Morning Padre,' said Major Le Bon in greeting as she walked past. 'Ready to give Alpha Company a hiding?'

'I'll do my best ma'am,' he replied, coming to attention at the sound of her voice.

At this Anne raised her eyebrows at him and walked off with a rather off-putting smile on her face. As she walked away, Rob caught himself giving her body an appraising look. He had not really paid too much attention to her physique at church, or at lunch afterwards. Now however he found himself admiring her tall, athletic build; well shaped and not too thin, Rob thought. Pity about the personality, he added by way of warning. He was even more wary of her since the previous Sunday, because the added knowledge Rob assumed she had of him made it harder to maintain his polite but distant demeanour. Despite these feelings, he still found it difficult to withdraw his attention from her legs, and turn to the map of the route they were to take.

'She's got great legs I will admit, and her arse is a work of art! The rest isn't too bad either,' said Major O'Donnell patting him on the back; Sean had evidently noticed the visual attention Rob had been giving her. 'Better get a good look in now mate,' he continued, 'she can run like the wind, so it's not going to be easy to keep eyes on!'

Rob looked a little flustered that his private musing on her body had been noticed.

'Relax man, didn't God make woman? So you should be all for it, right?' said Sean laughing. 'Besides, she was checking you out herself before she came past, you chiseled Welsh stud you.'

'If she was, she needs her eyes examined,' said Rob darkly, sub-consciously running his fingers over the scars on his left arm.

'Don't talk yourself down mate; chicks dig scars,' said Sean, pointing at the marks, before walking off laughing to himself.

Oh well, thought Rob, pretty soon the whole place was going to know he had looked at Major Le Bon's legs, even though he found precious little else about the woman attractive. However he did not have long to ponder this awkward thought, before one of the PTIs called everyone to the start line. Rob noticed that the other Padres had elected not to run that morning, but were instead walking wearing their combat webbing.

'I don't believe in running,' said Alan firmly, 'it panics the troops and embarrasses me. But I see Anne has persuaded you to run instead.'

'Yes she has, though I didn't feel like I had a lot of choice in the matter,' Rob admitted.

'It often feels like that when you deal with Anne,' remarked Steve Schwarz dryly, earning a nudge in the back from Pat.

'Go on then, better show us what you're made of Rob,' Pat remarked, 'but don't let people push you into being hyper-competitive; it's a bad look for a chaplain.'

'Easy for you to say Pat,' remonstrated Alan. 'First of all, you have the on-call phone, so you don't have to endure this cross-country exercise, second is, you're not working with Anne!'

Rob grinned at Alan's words, and then moved up the field slightly to get a look at the other competitors. He saw Anthony Jenkins, Anne's 2iC, up the front. Rob knew him to be an excellent runner, like so many people from the Royal Australian Corps of Signals. However, it was beating Major Le Bon that was uppermost in his mind. Giving that woman another lesson in humility was his chief objective.

The sound of the starting gun rang out, and Rob set off at a steady pace, and up the first rather slippery hill. He was not far behind Anne at this point, but the progress was slow as everyone tried to find a clear path through the press of bodies. Rob did not think of himself as an especially good middle distance runner, however he had a tremendous burst of speed when he needed it; and he decided to keep that in reserve until it was necessary. Up and over the hill they went, and then running down the other side, before some long flat stretches along un-sealed country roads.

Early on in the run Rob ran steadily past a rather surprised Sean O'Donnell.

'Holy shit Padre! What's the hurry?' was all he managed to say as Rob continued to advance through the pack of runners. Sean quickly realised he was never going to be able to catch Rob, and he observed that the Padre's running style was very even and powerful, though it certainly lacked the obvious class of Anthony Jenkins, or the easy grace shown by Anne. Instead it seemed as it Rob would go through a brick wall if he had sufficient run-up.

After they had covered about two kilometres, Rob saw Anne was fifty metres ahead of him, and Anthony was another seventy metres beyond her; so he gave a measured increase to his pace. The dislike he had for Major Le Bon fuelled a fire deep within him, and he was a passionately, though not obviously, competitive person. This tendency, like many others in Rob, operated at a level completely unseen by a casual observer.

Pretty soon he was passing some of the faster runners, many of whom looked singularly alarmed at having been overtaken by a Padre. A few of them tried to keep up with him once he drew level, however his remorseless stride made that very hard to do. Yet they were mainly young and fit people, so Rob drew after him a determined band of runners who did not want to let him out of their sight; but try as they might, one by one they dropped behind him as he powered on with apparent ease.

By the time he reached the three kilometre mark, he was only ten metres behind Anne, however she had not gained on Anthony, who was now a good one-hundred and twenty metres in front of her, his gangly form still eating up the ground at an astonishing rate. In front of Anthony there were only ten people, in a loose gaggle just twenty metres beyond him, and it looked like he would soon run them down.

The rain was steadier now, and everyone had become thoroughly wet. Major Le Bon ventured a quick glance over her shoulder and for the first time it seemed she noticed Rob behind her. However he made no effort to make eye-contact. Rather he stared straight ahead, with a look on his face that would have preceded a violent death to an invading English host had he lived nine centuries before.

He gradually drew level with her, and spared Anne a brief glance before he increased speed slightly and started to draw ahead. They had now reached a stretch of bitumen, and Rob increased his stride length even further, though Anne was able to keep pace with him, preventing any extension of his slender lead. Anthony Jenkins was by now powering away, his light frame ideally suited to running any distance over five kilometres. For Rob however, the immediate goal was trying to draw further ahead of the OC of Charlie Company; but this was much easier said than done, for even as he tried to brake away she stayed on his shoulder, her stride quickening and showing no signs of flagging.

Again Rob tried for a surge of speed which was sooner matched by Major Le Bon, and as they came into the out-skirts of the town of Yurali, the two of them were running neck and neck; however when they were two-hundred metres from the finish line, she put on a tremendous burst that caught Rob by surprise, and try as he might, he was not able to run her down. Rob had to content himself with having finished only two metres behind the fleet-footed Major.

'Way to go Padre,' said one of the PTIs as the Rob came across the line. 'Major Le Bon is a very hard lady to catch.'

The two of them slowed down and turned off from the route of the run. Anne began walking in wide circles and taking in very big breaths, trying to stand up straight to give her lungs as much room as possible to inflate.

'Good run,' she said to Rob in between breaths, holding out her hand for him to shake. Rob grasped it briefly, though he did not smile as he did so.

'You keep yourself in pretty good shape you know,' Anne continued.

'Thank you,' was all he said in response as he tried to catch his breath, though he did manage a slight smile as he said this.

'You're very fast yourself,' he added eventually, 'I thought I had you back there but I couldn't quite do it in the end.'

'C'mon, let's get across the road and have a brew and something to eat,' Anne said, patting him on the back. 'I think Charlie Company could do pretty well this morning.'

'Looks like it,' replied Rob. 'Anthony has an unbelievable pace in cross country.'

'He sure does, but then again, cross-country running is an obsession with Sigs.'

The warm interior of the patisserie-cum-coffee shop was most welcome, as was the smell. Started by an enterprising Frenchman, hoping too cash in on passing highway traffic, the little outpost of France amongst the fields of wheat and canola had become quite successful, and was very popular with the staff of the nearby Army base. As soon as they entered, Major Le Bon began an animated conversation in French with the proprietor, and Anthony beckoned Rob over to the table where he was sitting.

'The OC said to me that she had told you to show us what you're made of; well done,' he said smiling smugly as Rob came over and sat down opposite him. 'Good to see you're not holding yourself back and playing the grey man.'

'Just following orders,' said Rob.

'You didn't run that fast when you were at Duntroon,' said Anthony, in an almost accusing tone of voice.

'I didn't need to,' replied Rob simply.

'So what constitutes a need to run then Padre?' asked Anne, as she sat down with the pair of them.

'Following orders ma'am,' said Rob blankly.

'Good answer,' shot back Anne, but then her gaze seemed to be caught by something, and it didn't take Rob too long to figure out that she was looking at his left arm. For a moment he too looked down; there they were, a profusion of scars, which where normally hidden by the sleeve of his uniform. Some of them were small, but others were much bigger, rather like he had been hit by pellets from an enormous shotgun. Rob self-consciously though pointlessly moved his right hand to cover some of the more obvious marks. However, before she could ask anything about the scars, they were joined by Sean O'Donnell, who immediately began enthusing about Rob's running.

'With that turn of speed you must be a devastating flanker Padre,' he said clapping Rob hard on the back.

'I do all right, sir,' said Rob noncommittally, and he was relieved when Anne drew the conversation back to the run.

'Looks like Charlie Company's getting very much the better of things,' she said. Sean just shook his head.

'Well, it's a bit hard when you, Anthony and Rob come so high in the placings. Only the top fifty are counting, so I might as well concede now!'

Whilst Sean and Anne sparred with each other, Rob ate and drank the hot things with alacrity after the coolness of the run. He was happy to let the conversation flow around him once they were joined by some more people, and as ever he listened carefully to what people said, and spoke sparingly himself. Eventually he excused himself from the table and went outside into the fresh air. The atmosphere in the Patisserie had become a little too close for his liking, perhaps in more ways than one. So he stepped outside and spent some time looking at the world around him.

Yurali like so many others in grain growing areas of New South Wales, lay alongside an important railway line, and had the usual features of wheat silos and the evidence of a more vibrant past. Rob looked at the way the streets ran, and was amusing himself estimating distances to various objects when a voice spoke to him.

'Looks like your preparing a fucking bank robbery or something Padre,' said F-Bomb, coming up alongside him. Corporal Nguyen, who had finished about three hundred metres behind Rob, had also found the close confines of the Patisserie were not to his liking.

'You were standing there casing the joint,' he continued. 'Problem is, there's fuck all here worth stealing.'

'Not at all, I just like to be familiar with my surroundings,' said Rob innocently.

'Yeah, my cousin said something like that before the cops arrested him,' said F-Bomb matter-of-factly.

'Really? What was he doing?' asked Rob.

'Ahh, he specialised in doing raids on ATMs,' said F-Bomb. 'But he got a bit to cocky for his own good and tried three raids in a week, and he was recognised by security cameras. He's still inside for that one.'

People with relatives in gaol were not new to Rob, so he nodded quite matter of factly at F-Bomb's description of his wider family.

'You got any relos in gaol Padre?'

'Got a couple who probably should be,' Rob remarked, thinking of two in particular who lived in Port Talbot, who had been in regular trouble with the law. 'Poverty, boredom and aimlessness aren't good for anyone. There was plenty of that around in Wales when I was growing up.'

'Yeah, and being a dickhead doesn't help either.'

'No, I don't think it does,' admitted Rob. 'Stupid can be very hard to teach as well.'

F-Bomb nodded philosophically.

'And when you're a stupid, arrogant, dickhead, you're pretty much fucked really,' he said, by way of summarising their conclusions, drawing laughter from Rob as they both watched another group of runners approach the finish line.

'How did you end up in the Army?' Rob asked.

'Well, my folks worked bloody hard to put us through school; my older brother did really well and is a doctor in Sydney,' said Corporal Nguyen. 'But I preferred a hands on approach. In fact, a hands on approach kept getting me in the shit at school.'

'When did you leave school?' Rob asked.

'When I was kicked out,' said F-Bomb in a casual but philosophical tone of voice. 'And I was kicked out because I gave a teacher a kicking.'

'Why'd you do that?' said Rob, with a smile that came from memories of his own.

'Well, the fuckwit's son was picking on my brother; calling him a geek and stuff, so I gave him a flogging; a good one too. And then I felt this hand grab my shoulder as I sank my boot into the prick, and who should be looking at me but this teacher who was the father of the fuckwit I was fucking kicking.'

F-Bomb recounted this in a light-hearted, descriptive fashion, rather as one would describe the memory of an amusing and innocuous incident during a childhood football game.

'So when I saw the look on the teacher's face,' Corporal Nguyen continued, 'I knocked his hand off my shoulder and I kicked him in the Jatz-crackers[1], then while his head was down I kicked that as well. I may have sunk in the boot in a few more times, just for artistic impression and stuff, but I won't say any more. It's rude to boast, so I'm told.'

'Well, that must have got you some attention,' said Rob grinning.

'Fucking oath it did; it was only that the Principal of the school knew what a dickhead the teacher's son was that I didn't end up getting charged by the cops,' he said. 'So I got expelled;

---

1. Jatz crackers = nackers = testicles. Jatz Cracker biscuits are a popular savoury cracker in Australia.

but then again, school's not for everyone, eh Padre? I joined the Army as soon as I could, and really enjoyed it. Better than where I could have ended up, that's for fucking sure.'

Rob nodded his agreement with F-Bomb on that comment; he had seen plenty of his school mates end up in trouble with the law, with drugs, or both. Corporal Nguyen was a fairly unsophisticated character in some ways, thought Rob, but he was very hard to fool and could spot a liar a mile away.

'So how did you end up with the nickname "F-Bomb"?' asked Rob, 'Was it because you swore a lot?'

'No, Padre; my given name is Phúc, P-H-U-C, and when my section commander saw it, he pronounced it the European way, and decided a name like that shouldn't go to waste! So I've been saddled with F-Bomb ever since.'

'That I can understand.'

'You don't seem put off by people swearing,' observed F-Bomb.

'Depends what they're saying actually; I don't like people blaspheming, but the rest is just over-using a few words, when there are perfectly good words loafing about doing nothing.'

'Like what?'

'Like "zounds", for instance.'

'Are you on fucking crack?'

'There you are, using the f-bomb as an emphasis, sort of an audible bold type,' Rob said grinning.

'What the fuck?' said F-Bomb.

'And now as a question mark!'

'Fuck me! Since when did you take the piss like this?' asked Corporal Nguyen.

'I'm full of surprises.'

'Fucking oath you are! Nancarrow won't forget in a hurry,' remarked F-Bomb. 'One thing I have to ask though, how the fuck did you stop yourself swearing at him? I wanted to kill the cunt.'

'I think it's scarier if you don't swear; like they don't know what's coming next. It makes them think you've got a lot more agro left to use, like.'

For a moment Corporal Nguyen just looked at Rob, before shaking his head, and continuing with another topic.

'If you've got some free time today Padre it'd be a good time to hang out with the platoon, we're just doing weapons lessons most of the day.'

'Hoofing!' said Rob. 'I'll see if I can come by.'

The Padre's turn of phrase drew a brief look of confusion from F-Bomb, however no sooner had the last group of those who had come on the patisserie run arrived, when the first bus arrived to take people back to base. Rob entered the vehicle and quickly took a seat up near the back, and started to stare out the window, lost in his own thoughts for a brief moment. He had enjoyed the run and the weather very much, and his mind was wandering off into recollections of past runs through a wet, though much colder landscape. Rob remembered his lungs burning as he moved rapidly across Dartmoor, mist over the River Exe as he ran through another more obscure but definitely memorable piece of Devon landscape, and the sense of exhaustion he had felt numerous times in the unforgiving Brecon Beacons in Wales.

However, his thoughts were interrupted by Major Le Bon sitting down near him, deep in conversation with one of the other Company OCs. Their talk was full of plans for staff college if they should be selected, with the two of them comparing notes on what jobs they'd like to do if they became Lieutenant-Colonels. Major Cliff Thomson, to whom Anne was talking, appeared to have some quite definite ideas on his approach to personnel management if he became the CO of a Regiment.

'I'm not going to give any oxygen to any malingering fuck-wits who want to claim they have PTSD[2] and shit like that,' he said emphatically. 'Most of it's faked for sympathy, and the genuine ones need to be kicked out because there's nothing that can help them!'

Rob could not see Major Le Bon's reaction to this, however his own was fairly strong.

'*Twll dy din di,*'[3] said Rob, muttering an old Welsh malediction, as he struggled with the urge to beat Major Thomson into a congealed pile of blood and phlegm. However the relative quiet on the bus meant that his words had caught Anne's attention. She turned around in her seat and saw Rob sitting there, looking over at them.

'Did you say something Padre?' she asked a little suspiciously.

'Just thinking aloud ma'am; sorry I was a million miles away,' said Rob, hoping this answer would satisfy her question.

'Really?' she said, patently not satisfied. 'So where was a million miles away?'

'Oh, just home,' replied Rob with partial truthfulness. 'The weather and the mud and running in the rain reminds me of it.'

'I'm sorry, but we don't have any snow to offer you here, for the extra-special homely effect,' said Anne, still looking skeptical, 'though sometimes you think it's going to snow, I can tell you.'

'Snow is only attractive for those who haven't had to sleep on it,' Rob remarked firmly, causing Anne to laugh.

'That sounds like the voice of experience there Padre,' she remarked, raising her eyebrows at him.

'Just a vivid imagination I'm sure,' replied Rob.

---

2. Post Traumatic Stress Disorder.
3. Arseholes to you!

With the look she had on her face, he thought Major Le Bon was about to begin interrogating him; however she seemed to think the better of it, and decided to change the tack of the conversation.

'So what's on the agenda for you today?' she asked. Rob was fervently wishing she would resume her conversation with Major Thomson, but it was not to be. She even seemed happy that she had an opportunity to talk to someone else.

'Well I'm going to swing by 23 and 24 platoons and see how they're getting on,' Rob explained. 'Corporal Nguyen said they were doing weapons lessons today, so I thought I'd use the opportunity to hang around.'

'Good,' she remarked simply, giving a nod of approval to this idea. 'Have you caught up with the news on Lieutenant Davies at all? He's due back today.'

'Is he now?' said Rob. 'Thanks for that, I'll catch up with him this afternoon.'

'Excellent!' she said. 'I'm going to give him to Battalion head-quarters to work there for a while before we try and stick him in a platoon again, but if you can keep an eye on him that'd be great.'

'Yes Ma'am,' he replied, thinking that whatever Major Thomson may think about people with PTSD, that Major Le Bon at least did not seem to share his views. Well, even a broken clock is right twice a day, he thought darkly, but a pang of conscience arrested the direction in which his mind was travelling.

They continued to talk over Charlie Company matters as the bus went down the road leading into the base, before it came through the gates and then deposited them all up near Battalion headquarters. Rob was relieved that Major Le Bon had not either tried to interrogate him or question his competence, which is what he felt she had done just about every time they had been together. When the bus stopped, they piled out and went to shower and change so that they could continue with the work that was waiting for them all.

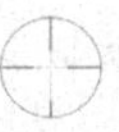

The weather did not improve as the day wore on, however Rob was hardly going to be deterred by a little rain, so he went in search of 23 and 24 Platoon, and he was soon circulating among them as they took breaks during their weapons lessons. He was also treated to the sight of Corporal Nguyen delivering a lesson; which was a precarious balance of wise experience and F-Bomb's unique brand of highly dubious humour.

'What're you doing Recruit?' he said, looking down at one individual going through weapons drills. 'Remove magazine first, otherwise you're going to end up doing an N-D.'[4]

The recruit muttered something about feeling rushed, which did nothing to help his case.

'Rushed?' F-Bomb fumed, 'What? What you're doing there is rushing yourself! Don't fucking do that man! Calm and methodical is how you've got to roll! Do you think the fucking Taliban sit back and drink tea while they wait when you've stuffed your weapons drills? "Terrible shame, infidel dog! We'll just halt our attack while you clear that stoppage".'

The recruit began to shake a bit, and Rob thought for a moment that Corporal Nguyen would simply turn the heat up, however he knelt down beside the young fellow and spoke more softly.

'Ease the fuck up, turbo! If you feel yourself getting shaky; remember, just slow down,' he said in the most reassuring voice Rob had ever heard him use. 'As soon as you feel yourself

---

4. Negligent discharge.

starting to get panicky, take some deep breaths. Remember: slow is smooth, and smooth is fast. Now run through the drills with me again now, and use the catchphrases, and build up your speed from there. Don't try and push the pedal to the metal when you've only got your L-Plates on.'

By the end of five minutes, that recruit had begun to show much more confidence. F-Bomb then moved along observing the others, one of whom Rob recognised as Nancarrow, the recalcitrant racist he had yelled at during 23 Platoon's first week. F-Bomb was evidently pleased with Nancarrow's progress.

'Recruit, you're all over it like a fat chick in a g-string.' At this remark a chorus of laughter broke out amongst the section, accompanied by various expressions of disgust. Nancarrow himself did a very passable impersonation of somebody vomiting.

'C'mon, what's the matter Nancarrow?' said F-Bomb. 'You know you want it! You just know you want to feel those rolls around you!'

'Is your girlfriend fat Corporal?' asked Nancarrow, before he could think better of saying anything. With a terrified look on his face, he seemed as if he sincerely wished he could wind those words back into his mouth. However, it was too late. Some of the section were expecting Corporal Nguyen to explode, but he simply stood there with an evil grin on his face.

'Words are like bullets Nancarrow; once fired they don't come back and they don't turn around,' said F-Bomb, enjoying watching him squirm. 'But fuck man, if soldiers were actually meant to have spouses, the Q-store would issue them. And since I have never found a NATO stock number for any such fucking thing as a girlfriend, boyfriend, wife, husband, partner, or whatever other fucking PC wank-word you want to use, I keep well away.'

When they took a break Rob came out from his vantage point to hang around with the recruits for a while.

'Loitering with intent there, Padre?' asked Corporal Nguyen as Rob came up.

'It's one of the core skills of a Chaplain,' he replied with a raise of his eyebrows.

As Rob had observed during the swim test, after their initial period of settling in, 23 and 24 Platoon had become fairly happy groups of people. This was due in large measure to the leadership provided by the staff in the Platoons, and the absence of particularly poisonous personalities amongst the recruits.

'I was a bit worried about Nancarrow to begin with,' admitted Corporal Nguyen, 'but I think you blew a new personality into him when you chewed him out. Now he's best mates with that really religious Chinese kid, Cheng. Never thought he'd pal up with an Asian.'

'I'm glad to see it.'

'I like to keep him a little nervous though, just in case,' F-Bomb continued, 'and he is scared fucking shitless of you.'

'I'm not sure that's a good thing,' said Rob.

'Padre, you really have to own your awesome! Besides, Nancarrow started a rumour that you're some fucking crazy ex-British special forces type who got religion; and by the time how fast you ran the cross-country gets around, it'll only fuel the fire. Fucking mad, eh?'

F-Bomb looked at Rob with a grin, but when he saw the look on Rob's face his smile faltered; for a moment it seemed that Padre Llewellyn went pale and stared off into the middle distance, before bringing himself back to the moment.

'You all right Padre?' he asked with an uncharacteristic degree of concern in his voice.

'Never better,' said Rob.

'So where were you from originally?' asked F-Bomb, eyeing him sceptically.

'I'm a Welshman; I lived in Britain until I came over here to teach music, and then I became a Pastor.'

'Oh, okay,' said F-Bomb.

'How's Lieutenant Weston going?' asked Rob, trying to change the subject.

Corporal Nguyen looked at him searchingly for an instant before giving an answer.

'I never thought I'd say this Padre, but he's been good; no random shit so far at any rate, though he's responsible for some of the nicknames the platoon has.'

'Nicknames?' asked Rob. 'Like what?'

'Well Nancarrow got Numpty.'

'Really? Why?'

'Well, Lieutenant Weston heard you call him that and thought it fitted fairly well,' explained F-Bomb.

Corporal Nguyen then told Rob of the names of the other recruits in his section. Piotr Horbaczewski got "wheelbarrow with a H", or simply "wheelbarrow". Albert Cheng had been given "Titanic" for the way he had sunk to the bottom during the swim test, and Joseph Pudubu got "Zeppelin" (short for Led Zeppelin) for a similar lack of buoyancy. Another recruit had been given the nickname "Tornado" because of the rotational speed he had achieved in his first attempt at an about-turn. However, this was not the only weather related name; Recruit Daniel Lucas, whom Rob had encountered very early in training when he had been a rather gloomy fellow, was referred to as "Cyclone", for being a slow-moving depression. About the only Recruit to escape without a nickname was the unfortunate Randy Alcock.

'And let's face it Padre, the poor bugger's suffered enough already,' said F-Bomb with apparent sympathy. 'I mean, who the fuck calls their kid "Randy" anyway? Let alone when their last name is Alcock. Parents like that deserve to be horse-whipped!'

'And I bet none of them mind the nicknames much either,' Rob remarked, grinning at F-Bombs remark.

'I wouldn't care if they did,' muttered F-Bomb, 'but you're right; these characters don't seem to take themselves too seriously.'

'Well that's a good thing,' said Rob. 'If you can't laugh at yourself then it all gets very sad and serious after a while.'

'The whole fucking world is too sad a serious these days; pay out on them for something dumb they've done, and they fold like Superman on wash day.'

Smiling again at F-Bomb's phraseology, Rob then went to circulate amongst the recruits for a few minutes.

'Say, Padre,' said Corporal Nguyen when the break was drawing to a close. 'Would you mind hanging around for a bit for the start of the next lesson. I just want to use you as a guinea pig for something.'

'Sure thing; but guinea pigs just eat, mate, quiver with fright, and die,' said Rob slyly. 'I hope you don't want me to demonstrate any of those things!'

F-Bomb burst out laughing, 'Padre, that's as funny as fuck, I'm gonna to use that line sometime.'

'Pardon me, but I have to ask,' said Rob, 'what exactly is funny about "fuck"?'

'All depends on what you're fucking, sir,' replied F-Bomb wisely.

'I should've known,' said Rob. 'What do you want me to do then?'

'I just want you to do a range estimation exercise with the recruits,' said Corporal Nguyen. 'Shouldn't take too long.'

'Sure thing,' Rob said, with a slightly twisted smile that caused F-Bomb to do a quick double take, before they went over to where the recruits were assembled, and Corporal Nguyen explained what was going to happen, in his inimitable fashion.

'Righty-o youse fuckers, gather round! Just for shits and giggles, Padre and I are going to demonstrate some stuff to do with estimating range to target,' he said. 'And because you've all played Call of Duty or some shit like that, I'm confident that you've got fuck-all idea how to tell how far it is from your beds to the fucking shitters in the lines, let alone that tree over there. Problem is, one day being able to estimate range without the aid of technology could be a life-saver. I have a laser range-finder here, that'll give me exact measurements, so I get the technology, you get to make idiots of yourselves. But after Padre has done a demo, I'll get youse all to have a crack and see what happens. Okay Padre, ya ready to rock?'

'Rock-on Corporal.'

'Okay, could you estimate range to the tree to the right of the shed, the tree with the yellow ribbon tied around it?'

'To within how many metres would you like it?'

'Fuck! I don't know. Twenty metres?' said F-Bomb, a little nonplussed.

'Okay,' said Rob and looked at the tree for a moment. He seemed to do some mental calculations, and then said with conviction. 'A bit over two hundred metres.'

'You sure Padre?' said F-Bomb, a little stunned at the speed and sureness of Rob's answer.

'Yeh, maybe about twenty metres more, but trees always seem further away than they actually are.'

Corporal Nguyen shook his head, and then used the laser range finder to measure the distance to the tree he had indicated.

'Shit!' he said under his breath. 'Two-hundred and twenty-three metres.'

There was a gasp from the recruits, before one of them piped up.

'You've set this up Corporal!' cried Recruit Alcock.

'Okay, Randy Alcock!' said F-Bomb, emphasising the recruit's name in the manner of someone announcing the name of a boxer before a title fight. 'You choose an object, and we'll do the test again and see, because I didn't set it up and I'm just as surprised as you are.'

'Righto Padre, could you tell me the distance to the top of the tower on the high-wire confidence course?' asked the sceptical recruit.

'Sure thing; hang on a moment.'

They watched as Rob's eyes went over the ground between him and the tower.

'About three hundred metres,' he said, 'but the mixture of trees and regular shaped objects makes it tricky.'

Corporal Nguyen then measured the range to the top of the tower and read it out.

'Two-hundred and ninety metres,' he said still stunned. 'That's fucking amazing Padre! Where did you pick up that party trick?'

'It's nothing really, I target shoot with a rifle all the time; from under fifty metres for small-bore, up to one-thousand for full-bore; so I'm used to what various ranges look like,' Rob said simply, causing F-Bomb to shake his head in disbelief.

A few more recruits tried their hand at picking objects for Rob to guess, and his estimation in most cases was close to the mark, though not quite as as scarily close as the first two. A general discussion then took place about techniques for esti-mating range, and the recruits all tried their hand at it, with varying degrees of success. However Corporal Nguyen was regarding the Chaplain with a degree of respect, and also a kind of suspicion; especially when he overheard Padre Llewellyn talking quietly to some especially keen recruits. F-Bomb heard him describing the nature of the target, the nature of the terrain, and ambient light conditions, as all being crucial factors in range estimation. That is skill developed over many years, thought F-Bomb, or my arse is a frying pan. And if he's only been a target-shooter, he continued, then I'm a white-man. He sounds like a hunter, but what would a Welshman hunt for fuck's sake? Savage sheep?

Later that day, three of the staff from 23 Platoon were gathered outside the platoon lines; namely Sergeant Maxwell, Corporal Nguyen, and Lieutenant Weston.

'I'm telling you, I know what I saw, and I think it fucking means something,' said F-Bomb insistently. 'As soon as I told him what Numpty Nancarrow had said about him; you know, being ex-pommie SF and stuff, he straight-away got this fucking thousand yard stare and turned white as a sheet. And this morning I could've sworn he was estimating range to target on the buildings of Yurali. And then he goes and estimates a series of ranges, with a fucking minuscule margin of error!'

Sergeant Maxwell had had his own suspicions about Padre Llewellyn ever since he had seen Rob yell at Nancarrow.

'He's pretty reggie[5] too,' he commented, 'nearly as much as Padre O'Neill, and he was a drop-short[6].'

Lieutenant Weston chose this moment to pose an obvious question.

---

5. Short for "Regimental". Refers to a person who has a very military bearing.
6. A drop short is a slang for a person in Artillery. It refers to dropping the shells short of their intended target, which is usually a bad thing. Artillery Corps has a reputation for being very Regimentally correct.

'Has it occurred to anyone to just flat out ask him?' he said. 'Surely he wouldn't lie about having past military experience?'

'It all depends on what you've got to hide, sir,' said Sergeant Maxwell. 'There are some things I've seen that I'd rather forget. I'd understand it if he had done some stuff in the past he didn't want to talk about, that he'd join the Army over here and leave his past behind.'

'Still, I don't think it'd hurt to ask; I mean just hit him up and see what he says,' reasoned Jar-Jar.

'If I were hiding something,' remarked Corporal Nguyen, 'I'd have already thought about how to fob-off that kind of question. Like when he was such a jet at range estimation, he just said some bullshit about being a target-shooter and left it at that. That Padre never walks around, thumb in bum, mind in neutral, like most other Chaplains I've known. He's switched[7] as.'

'Well he *is* a target shooter F-Bomb,' said Jar-Jar, 'and he may just be aware of his surroundings.'

At that remark F-Bomb just shook his head and walked away. In a few days he and the others had practically forgotten the speculations about the new Chaplain's past in the rushing torrent of work.

After the time spent with F-Bomb's section, Rob walked back to his office, lost in his own thoughts for a time. He had really begun to feel like he was relating well with the Charlie Company staff, though a couple of times he felt that his guard may have slipped more than was wise. Rob remained distrustful of Major Le Bon, and was still concerned about how much she

---

7.   Short for "switched on", i.e. aware of what is going on and very good and dealing with most situations.

may have learned about him during lunch at the Normans. As those thoughts wandered through his mind, there came from deep within him a resolve to lift his work-rate. For some years now, whenever he had felt threatened by another person, or vulnerable in any way, the first thing he tended to do was lose himself in his work. It was a sub-conscious, reflexive response to any sense of insecurity he might feel.

8

Over the following weeks Rob's already high work-rate rose sharply, and he went from coming to the mess for lunch at least three days a week, to only coming once every fortnight, if that. Rob's explanation when asked about this change was at least plausible; lunchtimes were an easy time to catch up with people he had been working with, so he was devoting time to them rather than the company of the mess. Anne also noted his absence from church; for even on Sundays when he did not have Chapel, Rob was not to be seen. When she asked Pete and Christine Norman if they had seen anything of their colleague from theological college, they both shook their heads; neither of them had talked to Rob at all since the Sunday he had come to lunch with Anne. Further, Rob took to giving Major Le Bon any updates about Charlie Company via email rather than in person, thereby minimising the possible interactions she could have with him. He had done this under the pretext of not wanting to waste her time, which Anne had certainly appreciated in her busy life. For her part, she also noted Rob's regimental formality with her had if anything stiffened. Most people as they got to know another person, became more relaxed, but not this guy it seemed. On the rare occasions when he spoke to her he was polite and business like as usual, though it was always plain that he wanted to get out of her presence as swiftly as possible.

In her more sarcastic moments Anne was beginning to have doubts that Chaplain Llewellyn was even human. However, the reports of his work performance from the Charlie Company staff had been universally positive, so there was no real point of concern she felt she needed to act upon. Anne considered calling him personally, but what was there to say? She had enough to do without chasing competent people; however she decided that she would have to try and pin down the elusive Padre for a chat.

Soon after Anne had made this resolution, 23 and 24 Platoon reached the stage of their training where they would attempting the bayonet assault course for the first time, and Rob decided to head down to observe those Platoons as they undertook that activity. When he arrived, Rob spent some time briefly with Recruit Tahlia Jefferson, who had grown enormously in confidence over the past few weeks, despite the doubts Rob and many others had had during her initial days of training.

'Now do you remember what I told you about going up this course?' asked Rob.

'You said to treat every target as if they were the person who'd hurt me most,' answered Tahlia quietly, but with an unmistakable intensity, 'and as if my use of force can stop him hurting others.'

'That's the way,' encouraged Rob. 'Controlled aggression is a good thing that can be used to protect others. It just needs the right focal point!'

With that advice she moved off with the rest of her section, and prepared to begin her assault. The course begins at the bottom of a hill, and the recruits first have to leap into a water-filled concrete enclosure known as the 'bear-pit', before running up hill through the rest of the obstacles. As he took a good vantage point, Rob could hear Bombardier Stewart addressing his section of recruits from 24 Platoon.

'I want to see aggression and determination,' he barked. 'The moment you start to feel yourself flagging is the moment you need to dig deep and find fire in the belly. Australia's enemies have long feared our skill with the bayonet and that tradition is not going to be broken with you!'

Soon afterwards the first pair of recruits started to run up the course, and as they leapt into the bear-pit the war-cries from the two males wavered and grew discernibly higher due to their bodies being immersed in the unexpectedly cold water. The entertainment value increased as the next two recruits ran up, with one of them stumbling and then falling into the pool.

'Get a move on recruit!' yelled Rob reflexively as the young man's head emerged spluttering from the water. 'The enemy won't stop just because you've got a nose full of water!'

'You heard the Padre!' said Bombardier Stewart with a grin, taking over Rob's harangue. 'Get that sorry wet arse of yours out of the water and moving up the course! Show some fucking determination!'

Rob recognised one of the next pair of recruits was going to be Tahlia Jefferson. As she began, the young lady ran at the bear-pit with a blood-curdling yell, hit the water, and moved through it at a fearful rate. She emerged on the other side and let loose another primal yell that in another age would have signified that death on two legs had just been unleashed, and proceeded to burn a path of destruction up the bayonet assault course.

Over the other side from where Rob was standing Major Le Bon and Warrant-Officer McIntosh were observing some of the recruits whilst they themselves waited their turn to do the course. Both of them were wearing camouflage cream, and carrying webbing and weapons, intent on doing the course themselves; Anne was a big believer in leading by example.

'O my word!' said Anne in wonder, as she observed Tahlia's measured violence. 'Look at her go!'

'That's young Jefferson, ma'am; the one Padre Llewellyn has spent so much time with,' observed the CSM.

'Well his investment has been worth it,' said Anne, and then spotted Rob lurking over the other side of the course.

'Jock, would you pass me your weapon and webbing please,' she asked.

'Why's that, ma'am?' he asked, looking at her quizzically.

'I want the Padre to do the assault course too,' she said, turning to her CSM. 'If he's been a soldier before, then he'll know what he's doing. And I also want to have a talk with him afterwards; he's been doing some really valuable work, and I want to tell him so.'

'Well, there's only problem with that plan, ma'am,' said Warrant Officer McIntosh.

'What's that?'

'He's just disappeared,' said Jock, nodding to where Chaplain Llewellyn had just been standing.

'Wha ...?' she said wheeling around and saw Jock was right; the Padre was nowhere to be seen. Anne made an exclamation of disappointment, and then stalked off to do the course with the recruits.

When everybody had finished, Anne sought out Recruit Jefferson, who was standing with friends, waiting for what would come next.

'That was great work Recruit! You really powered your way up there,' said Major Le Bon, coming up to her.

'Thanks ma'am,' said Tahlia in a strangely demure tone of voice given her recent ferocity.

'What Corps do you want to go to when you march-out?' Anne asked.

'I want to go to Artillery and fly UAVs Ma'am,' she replied.

'Excellent!' said Anne, beaming at the girl. 'And you've got some serious warrior skills too.'

'Thanks ma'am,' she replied modestly, and Major Le Bon and her CSM turned to go on their way.

'This is what I love about this place Jock,' said Anne, as they walked across to Charlie Company headquarters, 'watching somebody like that in action; a few weeks ago she was a civvie with no clue about military life, and now look at her!'

'It's quite a transformation she's made, that's for sure,' replied the CSM.

'I really need to tell Padre Llewellyn that I appreciate his work with Jefferson,' she continued, 'but I'm starting to think he's deliberately avoiding me.'

'Why's that?'

'Well, I haven't seen him at church since his first Sunday there.'

'Not sure what you can do about that one, ma'am, apart from ringing him and telling him to come to your office,' said Jock plainly.

Anne thought about this for a moment, but she was not sure.

'No, I'd rather not do that,' as she considered the option. 'I'll just watch and shoot and wait for an opportunity; if he is avoiding me he won't be able to do it forever.'

When a couple of days later Anne found some time to come up to the Chaplaincy Centre to talk to Rob, predictably, he was nowhere to be found, adding fuel to the impression Anne had formed that he was avoiding her.

'It's a relief to know people still seem to like him,' said Alan when Anne told him of how Rob was doing professionally.

'I was hoping he would be here actually,' said Anne, 'I haven't had any sort of conversation with him in a while.'

'He's probably out seeing one of the recruits, or a staff member,' said Alan, 'he's certainly filled up his diary pretty effectively.'

'Does he talk to any of you much?' she asked.

'Rob? Goodness no! Not beyond work anyway.'

Anne thought for a moment about asking Alan to tell Rob to come and see her, but again she decided against forcing an interaction; she would leave him alone for the present. However, Anne did mention that the Welshman had not been seen at church for a while; yet they both recalled that Rob had an Uncle in Sydney, and speculated that perhaps he had gone there over the weekends to see him.

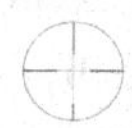

It was not long before Alan also became concerned about Rob, especially as it did not seem like he had deepened any kind of relationship with anyone, which to him was a far more worrying thing in the life of Padre Llewellyn. All he had seen was Rob going from busy to frantic, and now Anne's remarks added weight to that concern. Yet it was one thing for Alan to be worried, but pinning the elusive fellow down was another matter; he was the epitome of a moving target. The final impetus for Alan to act, in amongst everything else he had to do, came through seeing Pat walk in to the Chaplaincy Centre the morning after the first Rugby training session. The big man was evidently in pain, and walked gingerly to his office before finally coming back and collapsing in one of the chairs in the central area.

'What on earth has happened to you? Don't tell me! You've been cross country wrestling again!' said Alan, mildly amused by Pat's discomfort.

'Well if you must know, Mr Smarty Pants, it was Rob that happened to me,' said Pat, as he sat wincing in the chair.

'What? What do you mean?' asked Alan.

'Well, Sean O'Donnell got all the people trying out for this year's team to play a game of ten a side Rugby against each other, and Rob was on the opposite side to me,' explained Pat. 'Man he can hit hard. I tried to put some big hits on him in return, but it was like tackling a block of fucking concrete.'

'Why on earth did he do that to you?' asked Alan, a little alarmed.

'No idea mate, but that guy is a fucking maniac on the Rugby field. Sean told us to play hard, but not full bottle; well all I can say is I'd hate to be up against him if he was going all-out!' said Pat grimacing with pain. 'But what he did to me was nothing compared to what he did to Cliff Thomson. He marked out OC Delta Company for very special treatment.'

'What kind of special treatment?'

'Well, that wanker Thomson tried a squirrel grip[1] on Rob; I saw it happen,' explained Pat, 'and before we could say or do a thing, Rob had punched Thomson three times, neat as you like; and while the idiot was laying on the ground moaning and bleeding and everybody else was standing around like stunned mullets, Rob tells Thomson that if he tried it again that he'd give him a proper beating — and Sean just stood there, not knowing what to say. Rob's an animal; the sheer aggression he's got is bloody frightening.'

At that moment Rob walked in, without the same signs of physical distress, his face its usual unreadable self.

---

1. To grab a handful of nuts; i.e. the testicles.

'Morning everyone,' said Rob quietly, before dropping his bag in his office, and heading out again, after briefly explaining that he had an appointment with a recruit.

After he had left, Alan sat down with Pat, his face a picture of concern.

'To tell you the truth, I'm rather worried about Rob,' said Alan blandly.

'Rob be buggered, how about me?' protested Pat, as he moved uncomfortably again.

'No, I mean it Pat; he's working himself into the ground, and he's gone from quiet to downright uncommunicative,' argued Alan.

'He still talks about all the business things that he has to, and Anne still thinks his work has been great,' said Pat matter of factly. 'I don't think he's that interested in being anyone's bosom buddy, but I can't force him to do that.'

'Aren't you even a little bit concerned?' said Alan. 'I've not heard him talk about anything other than work for about a month now. I think he'll burn out before the end of the year at the rate he's going!'

'After last year I'm happy to have someone who works hard and isn't making waves,' said Pat emphatically, 'but if you're worried, please try and talk to him. I have enough to think about at the moment; and it's just as well he's working as hard as he is, otherwise not having a fifth chaplain here would be killing us.'

Pat then rose from the chair and ambled uncomfortably into his office.

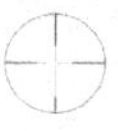

It was later in that day that Alan actually had an opportunity to talk to Rob, who had characteristically spent the whole time dealing with pastoral issues. He had returned to the office by

1500, and sat down to work at his computer; Pat and Steve were elsewhere on other duties, so Alan chose this moment to approach quietly and knock on the door.

'Hi there Rob; mind if I come in?' he asked from the doorway. Rob turned around and looked at him, before nodding.

'I'll be with you in a minute. I'm just about to punch out an email,' Rob explained, 'do you have something in particular on your mind?'

'Yes I do in fact; I have you on my mind,' said Alan, looking evenly at him.

'Why? What've I done?' asked Rob. He had now ceased typing and spun around in his chair to face Alan.

The older man did not answer immediately, but he walked in and sat down, and looked at Rob again for a moment before he spoke.

'I'm worried about you my friend,' said Alan seriously, 'for about a month now you've been working at an astonishing rate, and you've hardly spoken to any of us beyond greetings and work related matters. We've seldom seen you come to the mess, and when you do, you almost never associate with us. What's more, Major Le Bon has told me that you haven't come to church in a while, and that the pastor hasn't seen you either.'

'I've been very busy,' said Rob simply, 'and I decided to attend the other church of my denomination.'

Alan sat there for a moment evaluating those words. The idea of trying to be subtle with Rob drifted idly across his mind before he dismissed it and settled on the direct approach. Attempted subtlety was frequently wasted energy, Alan reminded himself.

'Is there something that one of us has done that has offended you in some way?' he asked calmly. 'Is there some reason why you'd choose to become a workaholic? I'd like a straight-forward answer please.'

Rob seemed to be taken by surprise at the directness of Alan's question.

'Alan, it's not anything that anybody's done,' Rob said slowly. 'I just decided that I should throw myself into my work.'

'Really? You were working pretty hard already,' commented Alan, at which Rob gave a noncommittal shrug.

'Well I'm not married or anything; I don't have a life, and I'm not that interested in getting one either,' he said. 'They're wildly overrated.'

'How are you getting on with Major Le Bon?' he asked, ignoring the sarcasm. Alan was surprised to see that Rob was uncomfortable at that question.

'I survive my relationship with that woman,' said Rob coldly. 'But don't expect me to ever like her.'

Alan looked away from the defiant grey eyes and sighed. Alan cared very deeply for Anne, and thought that Rob was probably misjudging her; so he decided to speak in her defence.

'Anne can come across as prickly, but you have to realise she's been through a lot,' he explained. 'She has very high standards, she's very passionate about what she does; and she's been scarred.'

'Really?' said Rob in a hard tone. 'Well if she's been scarred, I'd have thought she'd be more considerate. Major Le Bon is not the only one with scars.'

Alan was amazed by the venom apparent in Rob's response. Between Anne's opinion of Rob, and Rob's opinion of Anne there was a gigantic disconnect, and that fact bothered Alan immensely; as much because he could not understand the strength of Padre Llewellyn's negative feelings. He had no idea about the conversations with Major Le Bon that had caused Rob to dislike her so deeply.

'She respects you and your work, Rob. You might actually know that if you stopped still long enough for her, or even one of us, to have a chance to talk to you properly,' said Alan steadily. Of all the things he had said to Rob in this discussion, this seemed to unsettle the man more than any other. He just looked blankly at Alan for a moment, and it did not appear as if he had anything to say in response.

'Is there something you're running from my friend?' Alan then asked gently, in a moment of "pastoral inspiration".

At this the Welshman again stared blankly at Alan, who in turn gazed at Rob with a look of benign goodwill.

'Why would you say that?' asked Rob.

'I've been doing this job for a while now; I've developed a bit of an instinct for things shall we say,' observed Alan seriously. 'I don't mean to pry, but I do mean to care, so I'll leave you with a thought; we need friendships to really know ourselves, and to grow and heal. Without them we shrink. Have a nice day!'

With that remark Alan left Rob's office, and went about the rest of his work.

Once the heat of his own feelings had subsided a bit, Rob spent a while in quiet reflection, and try as he might, he could not shake off the feeling that there was more than a grain of truth in Alan's observations. Self-suspicion about his own motives was a trait that he had cultivated over the years, and after a short time he concluded that his colleague's comments had in fact been alarmingly close to the mark. As to whether he should do anything about those observations, he was not sure. There were risks involved in developing friendships; but Rob reminded himself that risk was a constant in all of life. However the question of the who and how of expanding his relational circle was a difficult one.

'How long is it since I made a new friend; a real friend?' Rob asked himself aloud. Not since your best friend died, came the answer in his mind; and probably long before that too. Moving countries had not helped either, and changing employment a couple of times was yet another factor. Church was too infrequent, and work relationships were too incidental to be easy places in which to try and expand his connections; and only one person moved in both those circles, and that was Major Le Bon. Someone like her was definitely out of the question. He was hardly going to try and befriend a superior, even if he did not dislike her so profoundly; though perhaps Alan's implication that he was being unfair on her was correct. As he thought things through, Rob realised he had not had an overly trying interaction with her for over a month, though he had hardly given her the chance to exercise his patience, so terse had been his interpersonal communication.

For about an hour afterwards Rob's mind went through a downward spiral as he wondered if there would be any success in making new friendships, even if he tried. It was so much easier the way he was, he thought sadly; the shallow teflon coated life, where nothing penetrates beyond the surface, and all the dirt is easily washed off afterwards. It was just as well that he was a workaholic; it stopped him thinking too much. These days he spent most of the time thinking about others and their problems, but every now and then his own sadness caught up with him, and washed over him like the waves of the sea. It was then that Rob felt his isolation the most, the lack of other people to gently or bluntly remind him of all he believed to be true. But for the moment, in the midst of the shades of blue whirling round him, he could not see how those kinds of relationships could ever happen again.

'There's too much to explain, too much that people won't understand; and what am I really?' he muttered. 'Nothing but

layers of grief and stale reminiscences playing a tune that no-
one wants to hear.'

Sleep did not come easily that night.

The questions Alan had raised were no closer to resolution
when all too soon the time for Rob's next stint as on-call Chaplain came around. It proved to be just as eventful as the last, and
he was very grateful to get home before 2200 on the last night of
his duty period. However Rob had barely been home five
minutes when the phone's strident ring cut short his thoughts of
relaxation. Muttering under his breath, Rob took the phone out
of his pocket and answered the call. However, instead of the
usual harassed Corporal ringing about a recruit, he found
himself talking to the CO of 2 RTB.

'Sadly Padre, one of the Psychologists at Murruwa has a
brother who has just been killed in Afghanistan,' Lieutenant-
Colonel Ramsay explained. 'I want you to come in to 2 RTB
Headquarters and you'll meet up with the duty field officer.
From there you are going to help deliver the FATALCAS[2] notification. Just come in DPCU as I'm guessing you're still wearing
it; we need to move as quickly as possible.'

'Yes sir,' he replied, and promptly got into his car and went
back into work.

When Rob arrived he discovered to his mild displeasure that
the duty field officer was Major Le Bon. Working with somebody
like her on a stressful thing like a notification was not what he
needed at the end of a tiring week; and he felt that the potential
for them clashing would be high. However he was serious
enough about his duty to not let these feelings show. He nodded

---

2. Fatal casualty notification.

to Anne as he entered the CO's office, and the CO then asked them both to be seated, as he explained the situation in more detail.

Rob swallowed hard; he had got to know Amanda through the sheer number of recruits he had talked to who had ended up needing to see a psychologist. She was a friendly, bright, and understanding person, who often spoke very fondly of her crazy, Combat Engineer brother.

As the CO spoke, Major Le Bon carefully wrote down the known facts, and prepared a short message in order to communicate the news effectively. In such circumstances mistakes and unclear language could result in dire problems.

'Captain Ainsley is the primary point of contact,' explained the CO, 'and she lives on the South side of town with her partner. The address is on the signal I gave to you, Anne. You both need to get moving as soon as possible.'

'Yes sir,' said Anne.

With that he left Rob and Major Le Bon to finish their preparations.

'Have you done one of these before, Padre?' she asked tersely, still looking through the information she had to communicate.

'Yes ma'am,' said Rob, 'I did a FATALCAS last year in Sydney.'

'Any pointers?' she asked looking up at him.

'Expect anything,' he replied seriously, turning his grey eyes toward her, 'people can do some wild things when they're in the midst of grief.'

'That's not very comforting,' she said in an almost accusing tone of voice.

'It wasn't meant to be ma'am,' he said; and the look in his face was enough to tell her that he was far from new to the shock of sudden loss himself.

Before long they were on their way, and it did not take much time to cover the short distance to where Amanda lived with her partner Jill Dyson, who was one of the platoon commanders with Delta Company. After a brief time of final preparation, Rob and Anne exited the car and walked up to the house, and Anne knocked on the front door. It was Jill who answered it.

'Hello, I'm Major Anne Le Bon, and this is Chaplain Rob Llewellyn. Is this the residence of Amanda Ainsley?' she asked, as she saw Lieutenant Dyson at the door. Jill did not answer immediately; however when it sank in that there were two people in uniform at the door, she ran into the main part of the house.

'Let's hope she's going to find her,' Anne remarked. After a brief moment, Jill returned with Amanda, who was looking wide-eyed. When she saw Rob and Anne, she froze to the spot, her hand over her mouth. A Chaplain and a Major at the door never meant good news for a Defence family.

'May we come in?' asked Rob, moving forward, sensing that some momentum needed to be restored to the situation.

'Yes Padre,' said Amanda in a small voice.

'Are you Amanda Ainsley?' asked Anne, moving in alongside Rob. They were both now standing near the lounge room.

'Yes ma'am,' said Amanda, in the same small voice.

'Is your brother Sapper Brian Ainsley?' continued Anne.

'Yes ma'am.'

'Would you mind taking a seat, I have some very important news to communicate,' said Anne, indicating the lounge chairs. Amanda complied automatically, deference to rank briefly overcoming her anxiety.

'It's my sad duty to inform you that your brother was killed in an IED blast today in Afghanistan,' explained Anne baldly. She continued for a brief time with the communication of the known facts, but the rest of it was lost on Amanda. The moment the news sank in, the young Captain doubled over and let out a long keening scream, a primal sound of grief that cannot easily be described, but is instantly recognisable to all who have heard it. Anne looked a little shocked and helpless, whilst Jill sat down next to her partner, her arm tight around her shoulders. Amanda continued to scream, pausing only to draw deep, ragged breaths, as the agony of grief washed over her in waves. Whilst she screamed, she slid slowly onto the floor, and lay there face down crying out, until she was unable to make any more noise.

Rob got up from where he was and sat on the floor alongside her, and motioned that Jill should do likewise. They sat there for several minutes, as Amanda continued to sob uncontrollably. At one point Jill seemed about to try and speak, but Rob caught her eye and shook his head, indicating that they should just let Amanda continue. It was about ten minutes later that Captain Ainsley was able to sit up; she sat there wiping her eyes, and looking a little sheepish.

'I'm sorry,' she said, though she spoke between sobs.

'Nothing to be sorry for,' said Rob, in a calm and gentle tone of voice.

'It hurts,' she managed to say, and then she lay her head on her knees again.

'Yeh, I bet it does,' said Rob looking at Amanda kindly, 'grief and pain; very similar they are.'

Major Le Bon sat unobtrusively to one side as Rob and Jill comforted Amanda. Anne's main part in this terrible drama was over, and so for what seemed like an age she just sat there, watching, and listening to Rob at work. His voice had a relaxing quality to it, almost like he was singing a quiet song as he spoke, and he radiated calm in a way that Anne had never seen before in any person, male or female. She observed that, as ever, Rob spoke sparingly, using words with a patient precision that reminded Anne of the care with which a sniper would use bullets. But he spent far more time listening, and it was as much the times he chose not to speak that brought calm into the situation, as when he used carefully chosen words to support the distraught young lady. All he said seemed to be directed towards helping Amanda know that she was not alone, and would not be left alone in the midst of the whole dreadful loss she had suffered. Occasionally Anne also thought she saw an effort on Rob's part to master his own emotions, especially when at one point his voice almost faltered, but he covered it up with a cough that was just a little forced, and moved on with what he had been saying.

Eventually, when Amanda could manage to sit up on the lounge again, she was in a position to ask some questions about what would happen with her brother's body, when she could expect that he would be returned to Australia, and what would happen afterwards. At that point Rob and Jill headed off to the kitchen to make a cup of tea, whilst Amanda asked Anne questions of detail. About an hour and a few phone calls later, Rob and Anne took their leave of the couple, and headed back toward Murruwa.

'Padre, that is the worst thing I've ever done in my entire Army career,' Anne said flatly as they drove away. 'I've been rocketed, shot at, and sworn at; but I feel like I murdered a person tonight.'

'And this is only the beginning of her pain,' said Rob. 'But you had to bring the hammer blow; that's a horrible duty. Notifications are really bad; I spoke to another Padre once who has PTSD because he was involved in six of them in two years.'

'Yikes! Six notifications! Well I can understand why he's got PTSD; but I've got to say, you were very good in there,' said Anne, 'you really know your stuff.'

'Thanks ma'am,' he said quietly. 'We're well taught I think.'

Anne had to stop herself from snorting sceptically at that statement. More than well taught, she thought, familiar with suffering more like it! Anne's well trained instincts told her that in some hours of anguish, trauma had etched itself like acid on Rob's soul; and that his compassion and wisdom were not just driven by a depth of faith or excellence in training, but they had been distilled in some dreadful bath of bitter tears. Rob's skills spoke of a person who ministered out the midst of their own deep pain. Yet Anne did not feel like she was in a position where she could explore such intimate and intrusive questions. Another gap in the puzzle, she thought, and sub-consciously re-arranged what she knew about Rob in her continuing effort to make a coherent picture.

In his time so far at Murruwa, he had more than measured up to the expectations she had of a Chaplain; he had exceeded them. Anne knew she had tried his patience at times. Alan Deakin had recently taken the trouble to say that he thought she might be pissing Rob off, though she was largely unrepentant. If he could not handle an environment where he had to deal with people who were hard to please, then the Army was no place for him.

'Where to from here with caring for Amanda?' Anne asked as she mulled over those thoughts.

'Well, I'll do follow up visits, and keep an eye on her, especially after the funeral,' he said, and Anne thought she saw him choke up a little.

'Why after the funeral?'

'Well, that's when people get forgotten; in the weeks and months that follow,' Rob replied. 'Everybody's normally all sympathy until the funeral, then they get on with their lives and leave the people grieving to their grief. People can make some really bad decisions when they're re-building their broken world all alone.'

'Seen it before have you?'

'Once or twice, yeah.'

'So how long will you keep in regular contact?' she asked.

'Depends really; after a while my face won't be such a welcome sight for those two,' he said. 'It'll be forever associated with one of the worst days of her life. So I'll just pray for wisdom, and that I'll be able to bring true hope and healing; beyond that all I can do is care.'

They were silent for a moment as Anne digested what Rob had just said, and wondered at the pastoral wisdom he had for such a young Chaplain.

'How're you going to wind down from this?' Anne asked.

'Probably on my piano,' said Rob.

'What sort of tune will you play?'

At this question he raised his eyebrows, and she wondered if he internally dismissing her as some kind of musical Philistine.

'I will just sit down and start playing, and I will keep going until the tune matches my mood,' said Rob, 'then I kind of just follow the mood through.'

'That's a real gift; I wish I could do something like that,' she said. 'When I've had a hard day, I just lay in bed and read usually. But it seems to work.'

'Reading helps to redirect the mind,' commented Rob, 'kind of the same thing really; just one involves the ears and fingers, the other the eyes.'

Their journey back to Murruwa was soon finished, and the two of them then briefed the CO on the notification, and what was going to happen from that point onwards; which took some time to do. When that was eventually completed, they then readied themselves to go their respective homes.

'Good evening, ma'am,' said Rob quietly, as they left the headquarters building, and then he turned to go up toward the Chaplaincy Centre.

'Not so fast, Padre,' said Anne in a commanding tone of voice, and Rob stopped dead in his tracks, and slowly turned around.

'Yes, what is it, Ma'am?' he asked, with obvious displeasure.

She stopped for a moment when she saw the perilous expression on Rob's face. However it was soon replaced by a look of blank confusion.

'I just wanted to thank you for the work you've done so far this year,' Anne said. 'You've been doing a fantastic job. I would've told you sooner, but I couldn't pin you down.'

Rob did not answer her immediately; instead he looked as if he could not quite believe what he was hearing.

'Thanks ma'am. That means a lot, coming from you,' he said.

'You're welcome,' she said firmly. 'And in future I want you to deliver any updates you have in person, unless you've got no other choice. Some things are better discussed face to face. I value your input and I'll make time to hear you.'

'Yes ma'am,' said Rob, still looking like he was having trouble comprehending what was being said to him. Anne then looked at her watch and realised the lateness of the hour.

'Drive safely now,' she said, 'we don't want any more casualties this evening.'

'No ma'am,' he replied, and with a salute he walked away with many things on his mind.

9

____

Taff sat at home, and stared dumbly at Johnno's photo, where it sat beside his bed.

'Nearly a year now, my old mate; I'm glad you knew I was back in uniform at least,' he said to the photo. There was Johnno, a giant of a man with his arm around Taff, a row of white teeth bright against the dark of his skin. 'I don't know why you had to die. Why mate? You had a wife and kids, and I had nothing; and you go and get blown to bits, not me. It doesn't seem fair, but that's the way it worked out. I know I can't change it, but it guts me just to think about it.'

Taff then picked up the photo, held it tight, and cried himself to sleep.

As ANZAC Day and its solemnity approached, summer had well a truly began to fade into autumn, with the leaves on many trees starting to turn from green and fade into yellows and browns. The days were contracting noticeably, and the smell in the air changed, as subtly the strident light of summer softened, and the texture of the air grew cooler on the skin. However the ceaseless rhythm of Murruwa had no regard for the passing of the seasons.

The coming of autumn also saw an increase in the number

of training sessions for Rugby, which came as a welcome diversion in the midst of the frenetic training program. Major Sean O'Donnell's love of Rugby was legendary even amongst the Rugby mad people of the Army, and he had busily recruited for his team well before even the prospect of the first game was on the horizon. Many, including his wife Tania, thought that Sean's love of Rugby pushed the bounds of sanity; though others would have said that he pushed the bounds of sanity in any case.

However, in the lead-up to the first game of the season, the normally ebullient Sean seemed to be quite grim. The game was not going to be played against any of the local Rugby teams, but another Army team from Canberra; and it seemed to Rob as if Sean was preparing the team to play against the All Blacks, rather than a trial game before the real season began. He was especially emphasising the number eight and the fly-half from the Canberra side, as being people that needed to be watched, and Sean also provided the team with some training that was specifically directed against common on-field ploys made by those two personalities.

'Morgs, who are these guys that we need to do this?' Rob asked Scott Morgan, as he sucked in great lungs full of air after they had done a series of sprints during training. Pat could be heard dry-retching a few metres away.

'Two of the biggest egos in Army rugby, Padre,' Morgs remarked. 'They're good, but they're also dirty. Sean wants us to shut them down big time; if we shut them down, their whole team'll fold.'

'What?' exclaimed Rob. 'Can't anybody else on their team play the game?'

'They can; it's just that their coach favours these two crackers and makes them the team centre of gravity,' explained Morgs. 'If we smash 'em they won't have many moves left.'

At that moment Sean O'Donnell yelled out in a clear voice,

'Okay everyone, time for warm-down; all the forwards over here now.'

As they began to stretch their aching limbs, Sean started asking each of them about their particular tasks for that week-end's game.

'Okay Rob, in your own words, what are you meant to do?'

'I need to hit their fly-half so hard that he never wants to touch the ball again,' said Rob with an uncharacteristic degree of relish, causing a wave of laughter to run through the others.

'Shit hot!' said Sean. 'Morgs, how about you?'

'Similar, but do it to the number eight instead,' he rumbled.

'Dang straight!' said Sean. 'The rest of you I want to focus on your normal games, though if you get a chance to pole-axe either of those two players, well and good; but Rob and Morgs, I want you to take every opportunity you can to get in their face and mess with their chi. In fact, I want their chi so fucked-up by the end of the game that they have to go and see a zen master in Tibet to re-learn how to tie their bloody shoelaces!'

With that imperative, they continued their warm down, and then departed for their homes. Friday was free from incident for Pat and Rob, due in large measure to the fact that Alan had agreed to take the on-call phone, which gave the latter a convenient excuse to leave the game; he was not that fond of "cross country wrestling" in any case.

That afternoon Rob went out for his usual run, though it was going to be lighter than normal in deference to the rugby game the next day. He took a route that gave him an easy five kilometre jog. Rob never ran with headphones, because he did not like to have his awareness of the world around him impeded by anything at all; so as he came around a corner, he saw down the road ahead of him a man and woman, and he could hear that they were having a rather animated and probably unpleasant discussion. Rob started to slow his pace, so that he could cross the road and give the pair a wide berth, however he then noticed that the woman was Major Le Bon, and she was arguing with a male, who was a little bit shorter than her. By the time Rob eased to a walk their words were clearly audible, though they did not seem to have noticed him.

'Why did you even bother coming here Paul!' heard Anne say, her arms crossed and glaring at the interloper.

'Well, a dog returns to his vomit,' replied the stranger with a sneer, 'that's in the Bible isn't it? Now that you're all religious you should know that. What a hypocrite you are! But don't worry, you're always going to be Bang Bang Le Bon to me.'

At that remark Anne looked like she was going to hit the man, however Rob chose that moment to speak up.

'Is there a problem here, ma'am?' he asked in a firm tone of voice, a calm and open expression on his face.

'Fuck off champ,' said the male dismissively, 'if she's ma'am to you, then I'm sir; so get lost!'

'I wasn't speaking to you, and I won't call you sir until I see the rank slide,' barked Rob, in an aggressive and authoritative tone of voice, taking both Anne and the man with whom she was arguing completely by surprise.

'Is there a problem, ma'am?' Rob asked again.

'Yes there is Padre,' said Anne with a sigh, looking at the one she had called Paul with deepest loathing.

'You're a fucking what? A Padre? Do you know who you're speaking to, dickhead?' said the stranger, squaring up to Rob, evidently unimpressed at being challenged by a Chaplain.

'No, but I'm sure if we find a doctor from the hospital you

escaped from, she'd be happy to tell you,' said Rob with a pleasant smile, and Anne's eyes widened in surprise.

'For the last time fuck off, smart mouth! This is none of your business,' said Paul taking a step toward Rob.

'It's become my business now, little man,' he said, still smiling. 'Take a swing at me if you like, and see what happens. You might actually be good enough to land a punch, but how would it look for a hero like you to get flattened by a Padre?'

'Rob, please ...'

'You wouldn't stand up for her if you knew what she's done,' said Paul nastily, getting into Rob's face. 'Or is she giving you some? I guess you need a change from choir boys. You're bloody lucky, because I hear she prefers girls these days.'

This was too much for the Padre, and before Anne knew what was happening he had thrown Paul to the ground, and pushed his arm up painfully behind his back. Rob then lent over and spoke in the interloper's ear.

'You're in way over your head with me, sunshine,' he growled. 'You can charge me if you like, but with the abuse I've heard, I think I've got enough evidence to kill your career; and if you come near this lady again, death will stalk you, I promise.'

Rob then released the struggling man, who got up and glaring and shaking, his face contorted in rage.

'You're fucked!' Paul yelled.

'Sorry, I don't think you're my type,' said Rob with an eerily pleasant expression on his face. Paul stood for a moment, fuming in the bitterness of his injured pride, before turning on his heel and storming off.

Once the threat receded, the tension gradually seemed to unwind from Rob's body, and he then turned to Anne and spoke.

'Are you okay ma'am?' he asked formally, sub-consciously

standing to attention. 'I hope you don't mind me barging in like that, I wasn't implying you couldn't handle him yourself.'

Anne did not answer him immediately, but she stood staring at Rob in amazement, unable to comprehend what she had just seen.

'What's wrong?' he asked, as he saw the look on her face.

'Nothing Padre; and I didn't take what you did as patronising,' said Anne eventually, coming out of shock. 'You've just had the pleasure of meeting my ex, Paul Veenenboer.'

'Charming fellow, I'm sure,' he said, and then added with a wry smile, 'I thought you were going to hit him. I would've enjoyed it if you had.'

'Hitting him was the last thing I wanted to do,' said Anne, 'but it was definitely on my list.'

'Are you going to make a complaint?' he asked.

'Not sure,' admitted Anne, 'it'd be hard to prove, and you didn't hear the whole thing. I gave him both barrels before you arrived. But if he tries to make trouble for you, let me know. I'll back you to the hilt.'

'Thanks,' said Rob, cringing inwardly at what it would have been like to get both barrels from Major Le Bon. 'What brought him here, if I may ask?'

'The rugby game tomorrow,' she said. 'But he decided to drop by just to be "friendly"; the jerk. By friendly he means reminding me of everything that he thinks I've ever done wrong.'

'Do you know what position he plays?' asked Rob, a trace of satisfaction on his face.

'In Rugby? Fly-half I think, but I don't know for sure,' said Anne.

'Hoofing!' said Rob quietly, the trace of satisfaction growing into a look of open pleasure. 'You have a good evening ma'am. Are you sure you'll be okay?'

'Yeah, I'll be fine,' said Anne. Rob turned to go, but she spoke again.

'Hey Rob,' she said.

'Yes?'

'Thanks for not walking past.'

'If I love my neighbour, then I must defend my neighbour,' Rob said, after looking at Anne for a moment. Then he bowed his head in farewell and broke into a run again, before disappearing around a corner.

Anne watched him leave, wondering at the different side to Rob she had just experienced. Instead of a formal or gentle manner and steady tone of voice, he had been confrontational, antagonistic, and aggressive; with an obvious confidence in his ability to handle matters if they happened to become violent. Rob definitely had a dangerous edge, that had been hinted at when she had experienced him kick-boxing, but for the moment she was too stunned to ponder what it all meant, and how it fitted in with the "puzzle of the Padre".

'And what on earth does *hoofing* mean?' she muttered as she went back inside her front door.

That evening it began to rain in a steady drizzle, and when Rob awoke the next morning the weather had not changed; nor did it change by the time the game was due to start. Rob was happy with this, it was more like home conditions for him. When he arrived at the Rugby oval on base, he noticed that a reasonable crowd had come to watch the spectacle, despite the unpleasant conditions. Rob was a little preoccupied as he prepared, though he noticed that Major Le Bon, Alan, Jar-Jar and Steve Schwarz were all in attendance.

Before they ran on the field, Sean discreetly took Rob and Morgs aside and pointed out their respective targets. To Rob's immense satisfaction he had confirmation that his main focal point was going to be Major Le Bon's ex-partner. So by the time the game started he was focussed firmly on making that man's life a misery.

The Murruwa side received the ball from the kick-off, but unfortunately the player to whom it came dropped the ball forwards, and conceded a scrum. So began a full ten minutes of immense pressure on the Murruwa line, with the Canberra team threatening to score a try on a number of occasions. The grim determination, size and power of their defence proved to be a formidable obstacle; however they could not avoid conceding a penalty goal, which took the score to 3-0 in favour of the visitors.

From the very first it was a bruising encounter, and it did not take long for the size and skill of the 2 RTB forwards to start having an impact on the opposition. A rampaging run from the Canberra number eight threatened to come through the Murruwa defence; however his progress was blocked by the form of Scott Morgan, who grabbed him around the waist and started to drive him backwards. However the Canberra player broke free of the tackle and started to move forward again, but just as he found some open ground, Rob added his weight to the defence, and drove his shoulder at high speed right into the bottom of the number eight's rib cage. The sound of the hit was audible from the side line in the form of a sickening fleshy thud, generating a cry of appreciation from the Murruwa supporters. The Canberra number eight collapsed, crying out in pain from the blow, causing the referee to stop play.

'Was that Rob?' asked Alan on the sideline, in an almost despairing tone of voice. 'I wondered where he channeled all the agro.'

'Yep, it was him all right,' said Anne, smiling grimly from under her umbrella. 'The swine he just hit is as big a jerk as Paul, only taller.'

'Is your ex out there too?' asked Alan.

'Yeah,' she said, 'and I hope the same thing happens to him.'

Alan only raised his eyebrows at this; Anne could be forgiven for wanting to see a man who had treated her so appallingly get ground into the mud.

'Well ma'am, Padre Llewellyn might be a Christian,' said Jar-Jar, who was standing nearby, 'but he hits like the hammer of Thor. I thought the Bible said "Blessed are the meek"?'

'Meek doesn't mean weak, Mr Weston,' said Alan mildly. 'It means humility before God, not being an eternal door-mat!'

'Well somebody's going to learn about humility out there Padre,' said Jar-Jar, 'but I don't think it's going to be Rob!'

Having made that remark, he went through the crowd of Murruwa supporters, and encouraged them to take up the cry of "Thor!" every time Rob made a big tackle. The classicist in Alan wanted to enlighten Lieutenant Weston by informing him that Mjölnir was the hammer of Thor, so strictly speaking they should call Rob by that name instead, but Padre Deakin decided to keep his peace. Besides, Thor rolled off the tongue a lot more easily, and few people cared about precision with mythology the way Alan did.

As the number eight was taken from the field and replaced by one of the reserves, Paul Veenenboer began an animated discussion with the referee, trying to convince him that a penalty should be awarded. Sean had warned the Murruwa players that this man would harangue the referee at every opportunity, and so it proved to be. However the person officiating in the game was not moved in this instance.

Not long afterwards the Canberra team tried a slick move out through their backline, however this went awry when one of their number went flying backwards with a Murruwa player attached to him. The cry of "Thor!" from the crowd told the tale of who had made the hit. Rob did not stop with the tackle either, because he had knocked the ball out of the opposition player's arms with the force of the impact. The resulting attack that he led culminated in a try for the home team, putting the score at 5-3. Rob's successful conversion of the try then pushed the score to 7-3.

With the removal of their number eight, the visitor's offence lacked some its previous rolling power, but a penalty against Murruwa late in the first half of the game left the score 7-6; a bare lead for the home side to defend coming into the second part of the game. The continuing rain was going to make it hard for either side to keep hold of the ball.

'Simple skills, nothing fancy,' Sean said to his team during the half-time break, though wet-weather rugby was not his preference. Like a true cavalryman, the gleeful chaos of open, running play was what Sean liked best; not the dour struggle of maintaining field position and grinding forward in set pieces. However this latter form of rugby was very much to Rob's liking, and he resolved to attempt a field goal if he had opportunity.

'Sean, I'd like to go for a drop goal,' he said, using first-name terms instead of rank, as is customary during sport in the army.

'Really? In this weather?' said Sean, surprised.

'Sure! The ground isn't that wet; not wet for a Welshman anyway,' said Rob with a grin. 'If I can get within forty metres, I'll give it a crack.'

'Mate, if you get one from that distance, I'm going to kiss you!'

With that dubious encouragement, the team went back out onto the field for the second half. Paul Veenenboer had proved elusive for Rob, he had only been able to put in one decent hit on the guy; however Rob was very patient and he would wait for the right opportunity to present itself. In any case he had achieved Sean's objective of reducing the effect the Canberra fly-half could have on the game.

The opportunity to score a field goal occurred sooner than Rob had hoped. Murruwa was driving the ball forward, and Rob saw that they were within the Canberra half of the field. He put his hand on the scrum half's back, and having a quick word to him, Rob positioned himself about ten metres behind and to the left. When the ball emerged from the ruck, it was deftly passed to Rob, who obliged by drop-kicking the ball over the posts for a field goal, taking the score to 10-6. This seemed to enrage Veenenboer, who castigated his players for not having realised what was going on. Even though they had seen that Rob had taken the conversion for the try, it had not entered the visiting team's mind that a flanker like him was also going to kick a field goal.

When the Canberra side received the ball at the kick-off from the re-start of play, they started to show a bit more adventurous spirit. Trying to out-muscle the locals had been failing badly for them, so they decided to run the ball instead, and all the while Paul pushed his team to keep things moving. However, a moment's inattention on his part as he looked up when a pass came in a little high, meant that he did not see the speeding form of Rob lining up to deliver a fearsome hit. In the resulting collision, Paul flew backwards with Rob still attached, but somehow managed to maintain control of the ball. The massive blow elicited another spirited cry of "Thor!" from the sidelines.

'Yes!' said Anne passionately, as her ex hit the ground with Rob attached, and Alan groaned slightly. However no one was prepared for what came next.

As the two landed together, in a moment of sheer devilment Rob said clearly, 'Doesn't go so well for you when you mix it with the boys, does it now?'

In that instant Paul recognised the voice and form of the man who had intervened in his argument with Anne, and he flew into a rage, fuelled by his growing frustration at how the game was going. Standing up, Veenenboer started throwing punches wildly at Rob. However the latter blocked them very effectively before landing a stunning open-handed slap to Veenenboer's cheek that brought him to his knees. The sound of it was audible from the sideline.

'That wasn't so very meek,' said Alan quietly.

'No, but it was fucking awesome!' said Jar-Jar with elation.

'Bitch-slapping for bitches,' Rob said grinning wickedly as Paul got to his feet. 'Come on hero, or did Anne rip your balls off when you broke up?'

At this Paul again flew at him; but Rob stepped neatly aside and tripped the fly-half as he came rushing in. By this time the referee was blowing his whistle and called the two of them out from among the players. Immediately Paul began ranting at the referee about what Rob had done.

'This fuckwit slapped me; he needs to be sent off!'

'Oh, go and play soccer with the other cry-babies,' said Rob, leaning past the referee who was trying to stand between them.

Almost out of his mind with rage, Veenenboer hurled further abuse at Rob, but the referee blew his whistle repeatedly until there was order, and told the two men to be quiet and go back to their places.

'Every time you touch the ball sunshine!' yelled Rob, pointing at Paul. This was too much for the referee, who called Rob back, along with Sean as the team Captain.

'Listen mate, I told you to get back to your place!' he growled at Rob. 'I'm going to have to penalise you now, and if you do that again, I'll send you off! Bloody hell! I know for a fact that there are two Padres on your team, show a bit of restraint for their sake man!'

'I *am* a Padre,' said Rob with a deadly gleam in his eyes, and then turned to go, leaving the referee momentarily speechless.

'What the fuck are you doing man?' said Sean, not quite sure what to make of this uncharacteristic behaviour from Rob. Sean had seen him be aggressive, but not a stirrer.

'I'm winding Veenenboer up,' said Rob, 'he's not going to be able to think clearly at all.'

'You evil bastard!' said Sean, who was nonetheless impressed. 'You're lucky you weren't sent off!'

'It's all right, I've done this before,' said Rob, and patted Sean on the arm before taking his place on the field again.

Paul Veenenboer was the Canberra goal kicker, so it was him who lined up to take the penalty kick. By virtue of where the incident had occurred, he was within easy ear-shot of the Murruwa supporters. So Jar-Jar chose this moment to introduce his own brand of humour into the game; in particular, through his skill at heckling.

'Ahh, ladies and gentlemen,' he said a loud, clear voice as Paul placed the ball in preparation for the kick, 'the question this afternoon is whether or not the Canberra kicker is going to stuff it, flop it and fuck it. The weather's wetter than a Collins class submarine, and the ball's as slippery as a politician's promise, so I think he's pretty much going to screw the pooch!'

A small wave of laughter went through the supporters, encouraging Jar-Jar still more.

'He's trying to look cool and composed ladies and gentlemen, but he's shattered, he's off like a frog in a sock. His concentration's disappeared like a fart in a fan factory; his knees are like jelly, and his pecker is uncomfortable. He's going to stuff it like a Christmas turkey!' he went on, as Paul stood still, lining up the posts.

'He's been shattered by the hammer of Thor! He's fuck, fuck, fuckity, fucking going to stuff it!' Jar-Jar said quickly as Paul ran toward the ball, and the attempted penalty kick did not even make it to the goal posts.

'Oh no! He's stuffed it!' Jar-Jar concluded triumphantly, and the Murruwa crowd cheered appreciatively.

Veenenboer did not have time to turn around and glower at Jar-Jar, because the Murruwa full-back had caught the ball and kicked it back toward the visitors. After this the Canberra team tried to make an attacking play; and it went well for them for a few phases. Yet just as Veenenboer looked like breaking through the Murruwa line, he found himself face to face with Rob, who picked him up with the force of his tackle, and drove him backwards out of the field of play before finally slamming him into the ground, and bringing a gratified cry of "Thor" from the sidelines. As Veenenboer rose from the ground Rob stood there pointing at him, with a deadly gleam in his eye.

'Every time you touch the ball!' he shouted triumphantly, and his opponent could not manage anything in return.

In the resulting line-out Murruwa drove forward with the ball, and their fly-half passed it to Rob as he sped around the edge of the maul, and then powered straight over the top of Veenenboer. Somehow the studs of Rob's boot connected with the head of the prostrate Canberra Captain as he ran onwards, before a deft pass to one of the Murruwa centres saw another try for the home side. Rob's conversion took the score to 17-6.

At the urging of their now-bloodied Captain, the Canberra forwards tried put in big hits on Rob whenever he had the ball, however they discovered that the powerful Welshman was a hard man to put down, and could absorb immense punishment. In fact, as often as he could, Rob tried to run into his would-be tacklers rather than avoid them, and in one case actually picked up the tackler and ran forward with him on one shoulder before being brought to the ground. More than one Canberra player ended up in a crumpled heap for their pains. True to his word, Rob continued to stalk Veenenboer around the field, waiting for a chance to pounce again, which meant that the latter completely lost his ability to coordinate play and impose himself on the game; with the result that the Canberra side became rudderless and ineffective.

In the end it was Pat and Morgs who administered the final coup de grace on Veenenboer, hitting him with such a powerful tackle that he had to be stretchered off the field. By the end of the game, Murruwa ran out victors 31-6. The Canberra team returned home with some significant bruises and one set of cracked ribs, courtesy of the brutal defence meted out by the locals, though no other lasting wounds resulted. The injuries sustained by Paul Veenenboer and the Canberra number eight meant they were not present at the post match function, where the two teams mixed in a relatively friendly fashion, despite the ferocity on the field. Rob sat in a mixed group together with Pat and Morgs, and Sean soon joined them; and he promptly fulfilled his promise of kissing Rob, as his 'reward' for having kicked the field goal.

'Fellas, that was one of the most punishing displays of Rugby I've seen in many years; I reckon we're going to see a couple of our guys asked to try out for the Army team,' said Sean, beaming ebulliently, 'in fact, they already asked me about you two,' he continued, indicating Rob and Morgs. Scott looked reasonably happy at the prospect, however Rob simply shook his head.

'Count me out Sean,' he remarked, 'I'm too old, and I'm needed here.'

Sean looked slightly crest-fallen at this, but Pat looked over at Rob with a degree of appreciation.

'Thanks mate,' he said, slapping Rob on the back, 'I don't think you're too old, but we do need you here.'

Surprisingly Sean just shrugged philosophically, as though he had been expecting Rob would say something like that in any case.

'Oh well,' he said with his characteristic manic smile, 'I've lived to see the day a Padre bitch-slapped Paul Veenenboer, and it's going to take more than a zen master to teach them to tie their shoelaces again.'

To his slight discomfiture, from that time on Rob was known as Thor to the other Rugby players and younger officers; but he knew that the nickname meant he was well and truly accepted by those with whom he worked.

10

_____

Even though he had not felt too bad after the game, the next morning at church Rob was moving in a way that betrayed a significant amount of discomfort. With Alan's words about isolation in mind, he was back at the church Major Le Bon attended, despite the reservations he had had. After much wrestling, Rob had decided that he needed to keep relating to her, rather than retreat just because he found her difficult. Their recent work together on the casualty notification had also helped Rob to see her differently, but his habit of keeping women at a distance still meant it was not going to be easy to move to a deeper friendship.

However, the main thing on his mind that morning was not avoiding women, but rather the amount of physical discomfort he was suffering. Rob had not played such an intense game of Rugby in many years, and it had taken quite a toll on his body.

'Well you will go and run into people for fun!' Anne remarked with a smile. 'I think you should stick to shooting, it's less dangerous.'

After the service, Rob looked over at her and he saw her gazing at him with one of her characteristic quizzical looks.

'What's the matter, ma'am?' he asked.

'Question for you Padre,' she said. 'Would you have a panic attack if I asked you out to lunch?'

'I guess not,' said Rob, though his face gamely tried to tell a different story, and internally he was alarmed that she seemed to be well aware of his continued discomfort in her presence.

'I want to talk to you about some stuff,' Anne explained. 'In confidence if that's okay?'

'Sure, that'd be fine,' he replied, relaxing a little when the thought of it being a discussion that employed his professional skills pushed past his reluctance to spend time alone with Major Le Bon.

For their lunch venue, Anne chose the Indian restaurant from which they had purchased take-away for their meal at the Norman's when Rob had been new to Murruwa. Indian food was a safe option for him, and he was quite willing to allow Anne to exploit his well-developed addiction to curry.

'How was last week for you?' he asked conversationally a little after they were seated, knowing that having her ex around must have been hard for her.

'It was fine until Paul arrived on the scene,' she admitted, 'I could've done without that.'

Anne then began to describe to Rob in some detail the history of her relationship with Paul, and how it had gradually gone sour. She was in tears by the time she was finished, and Rob sat listening to her, soberly absorbing the story she told.

'I sure learnt from what happened, but by the time I woke up to myself he was trying to control everything I did,' Anne continued. 'I was just glad I had friends I could turn to .... who took me seriously. But he had me convinced I was the worst one in the world. It was only the fact that a friend had the guts to tell me that he was cheating on me that caused me to snap out of it.'

'Abusive people try and define the very reality people live,' Rob said thoughtfully, 'but it can happen gradually, and sometimes it's barely possible to notice the cage closing around you. It usually takes a shock to break the cycle.'

'It was a shock all right, to find out he was cheating on me,' Anne admitted. 'Just seeing him brought it all back; the betrayal, and the pain of realising he was controlling everything I did. I thought I should talk to you about this. He said some cruel and untrue things about me after we broke up, and I wanted you to hear my side first hand.'

'It's all right ma'am, I saw what kind of guy he was by the way he treated his team mates; let alone how he acted when I saw you both on the street,' said Rob darkly. 'When a narcissist can no longer control you, they'll try and control how others see you instead.'

At this remark Anne nodded emphatically in agreement.

'After we broke up he tried to do just that; and when he heard I'd found my faith again, he started spreading the rumour that I'd gone gay, that I didn't shave my armpits, and a lot of other things besides! But, you know what the really galling thing is?' she said. 'My father warned me about him before we moved in together. Papa had never liked the look of him, and I didn't listen, and I regret it to this day.'

Anne looked outside for a moment as she re-gathered herself. Rob gazed at her gently, and as she met his eyes Anne gave him a watery smile.

'I became a lot stronger out of it all, but the strength came at a cost,' she explained. 'So ever since then I've been a bit prickly around men I don't know well.'

'That's not hard to understand,' Rob said, internally repenting of the bad attitude he had had toward her when they were first getting to know each other. An ounce of under-standing saves a pound of bitterness, he thought with regret.

'What's the matter?' Anne asked. 'What's that look for?'

'Nothing, I'm fine,' lied Rob, not wanting to try and explain to her what was really going through his mind.

Anne briefly narrowed her eyes at him before gazing out the window of the restaurant again, into the fading colours of autumn. The wind was blowing fallen leaves around on the paths outside, and occasionally they would be taken up in a brief whirlwind, and a vortex of brown and gold would fly through the air.

'Thanks for letting me unload on you,' she said as her eyes were drawn back inside. 'I needed someone to talk to.'

'I'm happy to help,' Rob said seriously. 'Life's like that; some days are grey even though the sun is shining. But I guess I'm beginning to think it's better if we have people to share those grey days, as well as the bright and happy times.'

Anne regarded him intently for a moment, and Rob felt like she was looking right through him.

'I've never met anyone like you ever in my life; you can be really gentle and kind and serious, but then this monster leaps out and you're all attitude,' she said. 'You're a strange padre.'

'It's better to be a warrior in a garden, than a gardener in a war,' said Rob.

'What? What's that supposed to mean?' asked Anne.

'I guess for me it means I'd rather be friends with people,' he replied, 'but I learned long ago that I had to be good at being an enemy as well.'

Anne looked up at him and smiled, amazed at his words, but Rob was staring out the window himself, lost in memory. However he soon came back from whatever avenue of the past he had been wandering, and he looked at her again.

'What? What is it?' asked Rob, seeing a concerned expression on her face, and slowly realising he had zoned out for a few moments.

'I was just remembering something; something that I've been meaning to ask you for ages,' she said.

'What would that be?'

'Rob, you do an awful lot of listening to other people,' Anne observed, 'but who listens to you? Who do you talk to on "grey days"?'

Rob looked at her blankly, utterly unable to think what to say next. She had caught him out in a glaring gap between the advice he would give to others, and what he actually did himself. At that moment there came a slight hardening on Anne's face, as if she was warning him not to try deflecting her concerns.

'I guess there's the other chaplains,' Rob said unconvincingly.

'But you don't really share much with them do you?' she remarked, pressing home her attack. Rob was wise enough to realise that Anne probably knew he was a bit of a mystery to the other three members of the Padre team.

'Your spies are everywhere, ma'am.' said Rob, raising his eyebrows at her, trying to deflect the question.

'Nice try buddy, but you're not getting away with a generalised non-answer to a personal question!' Anne said in a warning tone, and he squirmed visibly. 'I'm a professional questioner, so don't even try it! You just told me yourself it was better if you had others around. So do you have anyone here you can turn to?'

'Not really, no. I've never even thought about it to be honest,' said Rob eventually. 'I could try Alan I guess. He's really easy to talk to.'

'Yes, and he's wise as well,' she observed. 'But I want you to know that if you need someone to talk to, I'm available. Even if you just want to download and don't actually need an answer to your problem, my door is open.'

'Thank you, I may well take you up on that,' said Rob unconvincingly.

'Do you mean that? Or are you saying it just to get me off your case?' said Anne, looking at him defiantly. 'I'm serious you know; I don't joke about this sort of thing.'

'I wasn't saying you did,' said Rob looking at her intently with his grey eyes. 'You have my word that if I need someone to talk to that I'll seek you out. Thanks for offering.'

'That's fine,' she said with a smile, 'it's the least I could do for the man who bitch slapped Paul Veenenboer. I never knew you had so much attitude! It makes we wish you had joined as a warfighter, not a Padre.'

'Thanks, but I'm happy where I am,' he said.

'Where did you learn counselling?' Anne asked. 'You're really good at knowing what to say and when to shut up.'

'We were taught a little, and I read a lot more, but I guess I've always chosen my words carefully,' he reflected. 'It's a lot like marksmanship actually.'

'Counselling? Like marksmanship?' she asked.

'Well, yes, actually. A marksman tries to only shoot at a clear target, rather than spraying bullets everywhere,' he answered. 'One shot on target is what counts. It's the same with words; careless words will cost, carefully chosen and accurate words can do far more. To heal, correct or encourage.'

'You certainly know the dynamics of abuse well,' she observed, 'have you been through something like that?'

'Not exactly; not like yours anyway. But I've seen it a bit,' he answered, 'and it's such a common thing that I thought I should be across it. I've always liked trying to understand the sad and hard things in life. I'm weird like that.'

'I like that kind of weird,' said Anne with a cheeky smile.

'Really? I think most people find me a bit too serious actually,' he said, unable to determine whether what she said amounted to a compliment.

'Surprise me,' said Anne smiling more broadly, and he looked at her with a bewildered facial expression. That look hung there for a moment, before he caught up with the fact that she was probably teasing him, and then slowly, for about the first time either of them could recall since they had met, he smiled at her with a simple, friendly smile.

Their conversation then continued to move in a less intense direction, though neither of them had great stocks of triviality to draw upon once the topics of family and friends had been exhausted. However, since they did not know each other that well, there was still much to learn. To his own amazement, Rob began to relax in Anne's company. Perhaps it had been because she made herself vulnerable to him, but Rob found that his well-developed defences were lowering, just a little, for the first time in many years. Major Le Bon was starting to see inside him, it was the first time in many years he had allowed a woman inside the first circle of his defences.

It was not the fact that she asked questions that he found unsettling, thought Rob as he walked home after they had parted. It was that she often asked two or more at a time, which made it much harder to cast a carefully crafted equivocation in her direction; and he was only too aware that she would not tolerate the kind of trite answers he usually employed with people who were trying to get past his guard.

As Rob got nearer to his house he was in a bit of a daze; and by the time he arrived and went inside he was feeling dizzy. After closing the door, Rob collapsed on the lounge, and sat staring into space for a time. How long it was he remained there, he could not remember. I am going to have to tell her eventually, and everyone else, Rob thought. He had come to Australia to escape, but in hiding his past from others he had also succeeded in digging a moat around himself.

'Sooner or later I'm going to want to open up again,' he said out loud. Somehow, saying what was on his mind helped, but he could not understand why he was thinking such a thing. Rob had been so used to remaining unnoticed; indeed for a very important part of his life, he had spent a lot of time being deliberately inconspicuous. Even when he had had an up-front leadership role in a church or in other walks of life, he had been able to hide behind a persona. Few people really knew much about him; what he had done, and where he had been. He had been content that this be the case too; until now. But as uncomfortable as it was, he found there was a degree of pleasure in being known, if only in part.

'But why her?' he asked himself incredulously. It was not as if they had hit it off in their first few interactions.

'Am I falling in love or something mad?' he asked himself, as the tempest of emotions inside him began to build. However he immediately reprimanded himself, as the terminally cynical part of him supposed that Anne could just have been using her openness and offer of friendship as a means to get past his defences.

'I am *not* going there again,' he said, though he could not dispel the thought that he was saying that more to try and convince himself of that idea, than to express any certainty about forever avoiding romance.

He had learned the techniques of interrogators long ago, and this had fed his distrust of Major Le Bon; but his icy attitude had begun to thaw. I'm probably still churning because of what happened with Evan Davies, he thought, and that was a little too close to home as well. He went to and fro in his mind like this for a few minutes until he gave up in disgust and went over and sat down at the piano. Whatever it was that was going on inside him, it hurt, and he was starting to reach the "paralysis of analysis" that was an occasional struggle he had; the reverse side of his great ability to observe and analyse the world around him.

So he sat and played his piano, using music to clear his head, and as usual it worked to uncoil the knot of neurones that seemed to have formed. I've been running and hiding, keeping people at a distance, he mused when he took a brief break from playing. I've been hiding behind work and social formality, and I've become very good at it; but one woman comes along, and instead of skirting around with the usual social niceties she just punches straight through my defences and wants to know me. Absent-mindedly he ran his hand down the scars on his left arm. And I've got more scars than these, he thought bitterly, as he looked at the multitude of marks. He wore long sleeves as often as he could to deflect awkward questions.

'I'm always deflecting questions,' he said moodily. The scars on the left side of his face he usually dismissed as being from a vehicle accident. Well, that's part of the truth, but maybe it's time to start living the whole truth about myself, even if it does hurt! It seemed to Rob at that moment that he could hear the echoes of his past drifting on the autumn wind that was blowing outside.

'What a blind fool I've been, Lord,' he prayed, 'but how I am now going to stop being a fool?' and with those words he turned to his piano again, and played his heart in music.

Rob spent the rest of that afternoon in thought. He had allowed Anne inside his guard, or rather she had kicked and elbowed her way in, and now she had somehow touched a part of him that he had not allowed anyone near in a very long time. Just that simple offer of a friendly, listening ear had knocked him completely off balance. Well not really an offer, thought

Rob, laughing to himself; more of a demand with menaces, but one that seemed to be motivated by genuine care.

It had been so easy to keep girls away. Friendly, but never too familiar, had been his rule in dealing with the opposite sex, after one quite disastrous relationship that had hurt him to the very core; and it had been a successful strategy too. Of course, it had also succeeded in insulating him from all that was good in romance, however he had considered that this was a price worth paying; especially given the chaos he had seen in the love life of some of his friends. Rob's work life had not exactly been friendly for relationships either.

However, Major Le Bon was proving to be unlike any other woman he had ever known. For a start, relating to her was so different to relating to the civilian ladies at church, who he internally regarded as either too prim or too frivolous for his liking. Anne by contrast was tough, realistic, and had a direct manner that was actually refreshing; though he could do without her tendency to want to keep others off balance. Yet, now he knew her better, he could understand why she acted that way, and it was that same provocative nature that drove her boldness in asking if he had anyone to whom he could turn. Without it she would have been content to let Rob sit behind his fence in other than splendid isolation.

As he sat there he tried to think about the last time he had actually made a new friend; somebody whom he could really trust. Of all the things that Major Le Bon had done that had unsettled him it was her offer of a listening ear that was now causing the most consternation, and that simply because it made him realise how long it had been since he had had a friend he could confide him; someone he could trust.

'Trust?' he asked himself aloud. There was a scar that for him was deeper than those that were visible. A broken relationship, a long time of hard work and harder experience, then a move to the other side of the world — followed soon afterwards by the sudden death of his best friend, meant that he had become a very isolated person. That was it, he thought; friendship. He had forgotten what a great thing it was in the past four years, where he had lived an increasingly lonely life, even though he had moved among crowds of people. The kind of shallow, incidental friendship that was no deeper than clicking "like" on somebody's Facebook post was not the kind of thing he was missing; rather it was the kind of friend to whom he could pour out his heart, and be safe. In reality, it was now just him, and the intermittent interactions he had with his family. Using social media to reconnect with people from his past had not occurred to him; things like that seldom did. Instead Rob got his head down and concentrated on the life around him, disregarding the whispers of loneliness that from time to time tried to grab his attention. Up till now, that is.

Alan had said that people needed others to really know themselves, and that they needed to know themselves to be able to seek the healing they needed to live. At that moment the grief he was carrying, and the cost of his self-imposed exile seemed to hit him like a wave, and he wept; but when his emotions were spent, Rob felt a sense of resolve rising in him like he had not felt in several years.

'I have to stop hiding,' he muttered, 'the problem is, it's been a habit for so long that it'll be very hard to break.'

Anne, for her part, had welcomed seeing a little more than the professional front that Rob wore so well. He was a man with backbone, and a depth of faith and feeling; though with an undertone of sadness she could not explain. Rob's transition into the Regular Army had been nothing short of seamless. In all of Anne's experience in the Army, competence drew few questions and raised few comments. It was only incompetence that tended to attract attention. Briefly Anne's mind wondered at how many people in the Army did great but unheralded things, whilst the headlines went to those who did wrong, before she wrenched her mind back to Rob's sadness. Pete and Christine had mentioned it, and now she was sure she had seen it too; it was there in his eyes, where somehow memories still lingered after the events themselves had passed, and the grey shape of pain would from time to time cover his features. However, there were also some deeply attractive things about Rob. He was sensitive, insightful, and considerate, as well as having a very hard edge when needed; and there was no denying it, she did find him attractive. Yet Anne knew that she had barely scraped the surface with the guy. Still, Rob had revealed a little, and he had not shut her off; but whenever their conversation had wandered beyond the safe bounds of things like the quirks of his family and teaching music, it seemed to her that he flinched like a wounded animal. For once in her life, Anne decided that she should not push her way in, not any further anyway. Rob might have hurts and history that were under lock and key, she thought, but with time and trust, he might just let me unlock them for him.

In the week that followed, the time came when 23 and 24 Platoon reached the end of their basic training, culminating in a long activity, known as the 'Challenge', that assessed all their military skills to that point. After this the two platoons prepared for the greatest rite of passage at Murruwa, that was simply known as the March-out parade. They rehearsed in the week leading up to the day, going over, again and again all the drill movements required to pull off the spectacle.

When the day of the parade came they performed flawlessly, under the watchful eye of Warrant Officer 'Jock' McIntosh. Jock was noted for the thoroughness of his drill instruction, and he demanded high standards from the Charlie Company staff. Rob watched the parade with interest, from a vantage point just behind the Adjutant of 2 RTB, thinking all the time about the change he had seen since they had arrived only eighty days ago. After it was all over, with its ritual of drill, inspections and speeches, Rob went up the hill to where the march-out function was to be held, in the hope of being able to personally congratulate some of the recruits he had known well; however he was not sure that he wanted to meet the parents of the newly graduated Trooper[1] Nancarrow. On the other hand Rob was especially keen to see Tahlia Jefferson, who was now Gunner[2] Tahlia Jefferson, and would soon be training to operate Unmanned Aerial Vehicles (UAVs).

As he arrived at the Soldier's club, he was struck by the variety of dress people had worn for the occasion; some of which pushed the boundaries of what Rob's mother would have called good-taste. Indeed, had his mother been there, her commentary on the dress sense of the young ladies would have been laden with pungent irony. Evidently F-Bomb was having similar doubts.

'Padre, what's the bet that half the beauty parlours in town ran out of spray tan yesterday?' he said, noting the unnatural glow on some of the women, before nodding in the direction of a woman wearing an extremely short skirt. 'And check that out; if that chick over there leans over I'll be able to see her fucking

---

1. The equivalent rank of Private in the Royal Australian Armoured Corps.
2. The equivalent rank of Private in the Royal Australian Artillery.

breakfast, not just .... oh fuck!' F-Bomb said, almost in shock. 'She's wearing a g-string. Padre, that cannot be unseen! That's not underwear, that's butt-floss! I wonder if she brushes as well as flosses? Minty fresh d'ya reckon?'

Rob was having to stifle laughter at F-Bomb's commentary, and eventually he shook his head, like somebody trying to get water out of one ear.

'Lost for words, eh Padre?' said Corporal Nguyen sympathetically. 'I'm told the effect of seeing that sort of thing can take a while to wear off. But you'll probably return to normal .... whatever the fuck that is.'

F-Bomb was patently enjoying himself, and was about to launch into a description on what appeared to be the imminent structural failure of a dress that was trying gamely to contain more than its designer ever contemplated, when a male of about fifty years of age raced out of the club and down the road.

'Was it something we said?' called Corporal Nguyen after him, but the man was long gone.

'If he's caught wandering the MPs[3] will have him,' said Rob.

'If *I* find him, he'll have a lot more to worry about than the MPs,' said a menacing voice behind them; and Rob and F-Bomb turned to see Bombardier Ian Stewart, his face laden with displeasure.

'Why's that mate?' asked Rob, curious and concerned in equal measure about what had drawn this reaction from Ian Stewart.

'Do you remember young Jefferson peeing herself, Padre?'

'I'm not going to forget it in a hurry.' said Rob fervently.

'Well that cunt who just ran down the road was her step-father,' said Bombardier Stewart, 'and he was the one who abused her; and the poor kid's dopey fucking mother somehow

---

3. Military Police.

secured a ticket for that piece of shit to come to the march-out. Fuck me! Some people are as dumb as dog shit!'

'Ahh,' said Rob, 'and I take it he's been persuaded to procreate distantly, or he will be terminally disadvantaged?'

'If you mean that I said "fuck off or I will kill you", then yes,' said Ian, still bristling with anger.

'Love your work,' said Rob quietly.

'I hope you gave the piece of shit an incentive to not come near her again?' asked F-Bomb, in the tone of voice he would use on a recruit whom he hoped had completed an assigned task properly.

'I did,' said Bombardier Stewart. 'I also told him a little story about a Salami and shoving it where the sun don't shine.'

'Fucking artillery,' said F-Bomb, 'you guys were always sick bastards.'

'Least I don't have half an emu's arse sticking out of my KFF,'[4] came the Bombardier's smart reply. 'You do know that emus are only that big so that all that dumb can be fitted in?'

'Well at least being dumb isn't a core skill in my corps,' returned F-Bomb with a nasty smile.

Rob was relieved when the sniping between the two instructors was interrupted by Tahlia Jefferson running up to him, saluting smartly, and then hugging him tightly; much to Rob's embarrassment and the amusement of Ian and F-Bomb.

'Thank you so much Padre, for everything,' she said through tears. 'I could never have made it through without you!'

'You might be grateful Gunner Jefferson,' said Bombardier Stewart with a grin, 'but don't squeeze the Padre like that, who knows what kind of shit'll come out!'

---

4. Acronym standing for Khaki, Fur, Felt; the official Army designation of the distinctive Australian slouch hat. Armoured Corps soldiers and officers wear emu plumes in their hats as well.

After their laughter from that remark subsided, the four of them stood talking for a while, before Tahlia moved off to chat to some of the others. A steady stream of those whom Rob had known best amongst the one hundred and ten newly minted soldiers thanked him for his help and friendship. However one face he did not expect to approach him was that of Trooper Adam Nancarrow, who Rob had so radically re-aligned in his early weeks of training.

'Hi Padre,' rumbled Nancarrow, extending his hand. He had what looked like his father and grandfather standing with him. 'I just wanted to thank you for kicking me in the arse in my first week.'

'Pleasure,' said Rob, cautiously eyeing the senior Nancarrows.

'Yeh, thanks for making the young fella wake up to himself,' said the most senior, who Rob noticed was missing the lower half of his left leg. 'I told him that just because he had a fucking Viet for a section commander ...'

'Careful how you speak, Dad,' interjected the middle Nancarrow.

'I don't give a fuck! I don't mean no harm by it!' retorted the senior, before turning back to Rob. 'Anyways, as I was saying, having a Viet for a secco[5] wasn't any reason to get pissed off. I mean it wasn't his fault I lost me leg to a Vietcong landmine. Sorry, I'm not very politically correct, Father, but from what young Adam says, neither are you, and nor is that Corporal Nguyen! Young Adam's best mate is a Chinese lad too. Not a bad thing either. We're all better together if you ask me.'

'You were in the Vietnam war?' said Rob.

'Yeah mate,' continued the eldest Nancarrow, 'I was a combat

---

5. Section commander.

engineer. Bloody tunnels and bloody landmines, till one blew me bloody leg orf!'

'My uncle was a combat engineer in Vietnam,' said Rob.

'What? But you're a bloody pom!'

'I'm Welsh, yes, but my mother and her brother are Australian by birth,' explained Rob.

'What was his name?' asked the senior Nancarrow.

'Gareth Thomas,' said Rob. 'People called him Gaz.'

'Big fella? Got wounded pretty bad?' the older man asked.

'Yeh, that's him,' said Rob.

'Well I'll be fucked! I know him all right! How's the mad bastard going?'

'He does all right. Teaches music in Sydney nowadays,' explained Rob.

'Well, I'm happy for him. Real religious bugger, but could fight like a fucking thrashing machine! I was very sorry when he got hurt. Bloody jumping-jack got him fair in the ... well I guess you know. You tell him Wagon-Pole Nancarrow says hello,' the veteran said. 'Pete's me real name, but .... well, he'll understand. Heck of a sapper your uncle, heck of a sapper. If I'd've known that young Adam had pissed orf Gaz Thomas's nephew, I'd've kicked him in the arse myself, even if I've only got one leg. You and that mad Asian did a top job on the young fella, but I'm not sure about him deciding to become a bucket-head[6].'

'It's the plumes I think; they're very fetching,' said Rob cheekily, bringing a roar of laughter and momentary unsteadiness from the senior Nancarrow, before moving on farewell some more newly trained soldiers.

Soon Rob excused himself from the lunch, and walked back down to the Chaplaincy centre. He had seen two platoons in the process of going from arrival to march-out; and now life contin-

---

6. An old term for an Armoured Corps soldier.

ued, in its cycle of new arrivals and crises, with the ground note of the relentless training program playing in the background.

Not long later, Rob found himself yet again as on-call Chaplain. A few days later he was in the mess having dinner before going to another evening appointment. Thankfully, the next day he would be handing the phone over to Steve, so he felt light hearted with the anticipated relief of not having the presence of impending chaos lurking in his pocket for a few weeks.

There seemed to him to be much hilarity coming from the gang of young officers in the mess that evening, and he heard another a great peal of laughter come up as he ordered his meal. Much of the humour centred on a new Psych Officer by the name of Miriam Tolkovsky, who had just arrived at Murruwa, fresh from her SSO course. The crowd of Lieutenants were explaining some facts of military life to her, as she had spent barely three months in uniform. Jar-Jar in particular was in full-flight, trying to explain to her the concept of the Good Idea Fairy, and its effect on military policy.

'The Good Idea Fairy ...' Jar-Jar began.

'... or GIF for short,' said Tash Driscoll.

' ... yeah, GIF and shit; is legendary in the military, and every nation has a local incarnation; it's kind of like a franchise business in the fairy world,' Jar-Jar went on in the voice of a wildlife documentary presenter. 'However, the core business of every Good Idea Fairy is the same the world over. That is, to form apparently harmless ideas in isolation from the people who will have to live with their implications. These ideas are then passed on to the next mythical creature down the line, known as the Process Monkey, a dumb but industrious creature, who uncritically forms these lofty and misty notions into policy, and joyfully imposes them on the rest of the organisation, secure in the knowledge that even though the idea will cause untold chaos and unnecessary man-hours to implement, that it's for the Army's own good, and they should just shut up and get on with it.'

'Fuck, Jar-Jar! You forgot the most important bit!' rebuked Scott Morgan. 'The idea is delivered to the rest of the Army in the form of a pineapple, which the Process Monkey then shoves up the arse of the nearest Brigadier, who then passes on the pineapple to his or her subordinates.'

'And the only true all-corps skill in the Army is .....?' said Tash, waiting for the refrain.

'Taking a pineapple up the arse!' chorused all those present.

'When the Good Idea Fairy farts, the whole Army gets covered in shit!' put in Jar-Jar to general laughter.

'Okay, okay, I get the picture,' protested Miriam. 'And here I was expecting the Army to be organised!'

Looks of dumb horror crossed the faces of the others, but Rob spoke before they made any response.

'When you join the military you must embrace chaos. Warfare is an inherently chaotic business, and any war-fighting organisation must be able to adapt to new challenges, otherwise it'll perish on the field of battle.'

'Holy crap, Thor,' said Scott Morgan, 'have you been reading doctrine at bed-time again?'

'No, but it does rub off on you after a while,' Rob answered.

'I always thought it stuck, like shit on a blanket,' said Jar-Jar with a knowing look.

'That too,' said Rob.

'Hey Thor,' said Jar-Jar in a jocular voice, turning his eyes on the lurking Chaplain, 'it's my birthday this Friday night, and a bunch of us are going out. You interested in coming?'

'Sure,' said Rob with a grin, trying to force himself into a position of being social, though he considered that a night out with Jar-Jar may be the messiest night he had witnessed in quite a few years. Oh well, I know how to handle a messy night out, he thought later with a smile; at least this time people will probably keep their clothes on! Probably ...

11

The evening out for Jar-Jar's birthday started well for Rob, and he found it a pleasant diversion to spend time with his work mates. It was usually hard for him to relax in a pub, even after he had had a couple of beers. However, at this point he was contentedly absorbed in a discussion about Rugby, though unusually for Rob it was in the form of Rugby League. He was attracting a good deal of adverse attention from Scott Morgan and Tash Driscoll, because he had decided to support New South Wales in that year's State of Origin.

'I can't believe you're supporting the Cockroaches, Thor,' said Scott. 'I thought you were a good bloke!'

'New South *Wales*, now boyo,' protested Rob, 'and a man from my home town is obliged to support any team that calls itself the "Blues".'

Enjoyable as things were, as the evening wore on, he found himself a little distracted by Jar-Jar, who seemed to be becoming more and more morose; not exactly what Rob was expecting from someone celebrating a birthday, and certainly not from a guy like Lieutenant Weston, who was usually quite up-beat.

Rob usually tended to be a light drinker, especially when he was with a bunch of people he did not know especially well. Lieutenant Weston on the other hand seemed to be following a time honoured but patchily effective tactic when feeling down whilst out on the town: that is, drink more and see if you can shake off the blues. This Rob watched with growing concern, but Jar-Jar's plan seemed to be working, as by 2100 he was somewhat more cheerful than he had been. Several drinks later, a call of nature came to the birthday boy, and he went off in an attempt to find the toilet.

The normally vigilant Rob was at that moment engrossed in a conversation with Tash, and so did not notice him leaving their company. He was engrossed mainly because it was trickling through to his normally less than acute romantic senses that the single Tash was trying to see if she could tempt the single Padre. Welsh words cursing the disinhibiting effect of alcohol moved through his mind.

'So what do you do by yourself every night?' she asked, as she crossed her legs, and stroked her long, blonde hair.

Rob looked about him for a moment, feeling cornered. All the others were all engrossed in other conversations, so for the moment the attractive young Lieutenant had Rob to herself. He muttered something about reading and playing music, and realised he had just left himself wide open. Two beers and the guard is lowered, he thought ruefully, and how is this going to end?

'How about for fun? Do you ever just let your hair down and let go?' she asked, twinkling at him. 'Surely you did some wild stuff when you were a teenager?'

'Yeh, but only on the Rugby field,' he answered in as jaunty and cheerful a way as he could manage, trying to give a general impression of "I'm just a boring chaplain, nothing to see here, move along."

'Rugby players are normally more wild off the field than on,' said Tash, definitely not accepting the image he was trying to project. 'Didn't you ever wake up in bed with someone and wonder how you got there?'

'No, I never drank enough to do that,' said Rob. 'I spent more time keeping my mates out of trouble ....'

'I think it's time you found some trouble of your own, don't you?' she purred, fixing him with her pale blue eyes.

Rob grasped helplessly for an answer that was an answer that did not answer anything, however he was saved further exertion by Scott Morgan's voice breaking into every conversation around the table.

'Hey! Where the hell is Jar-Jar?'

Lieutenant Weston meanwhile, who had become disoriented on the way to the toilet, had then left the pub and ambled unsteadily down the road, largely ignored by the other Friday night revellers and a passing patrol of mounted police. His desire to empty his bladder was half-forgotten in the pleasant alcohol induced haze. However, it did not take long for this feeling to re-assert itself with some urgency.

'Got to siphon the python,' he muttered to himself. 'Hello, bladder calling, empty me or I explode!' he continued, as he wandered aimlessly down a small alley, before stopping and urinating at length against a convenient wheelie bin.

'Ah, wheelie, you'll be my friend,' he said as he lent against the bin, feeling the exquisite sensation of his swollen bladder returning to natural size, and thinking at that moment that plastic was the most comfortable surface in all the world. Thus comforted by the texture of the bin, and the relief that he felt, he thought it only fair that he should take the bin for a walk.

'Lonely life, left there by yourself,' mumbled Jar-Jar, pushing the bin before him, 'you come with me wheelie, and we'll fuck some shit up.'

As he started off he looked down at the path, Jar-Jar wondered if an earthquake warning should have been issued, as the concrete seemed to be rising and falling in an alarming manner, though with the bin in front of him, he had the extra balance he needed. Jar-Jar then made his way out of the alley, but instead of turning back toward where the others had been, he wandered off in an entirely different direction. The dark melancholy that had come on him earlier in the evening was now returning. It often seemed to be that way when he got drunk; eventually he became a ball of sorrow, rage or mischief, as every suppressed sense of abandonment or angst he felt seemed to flood back into him. Jar-Jar wept and raged as he walked along, with the wheelie bin in front of him, pouring out his heart to his plastic companion.

'This world's full of fucked up people, wheelie,' muttered Jar-Jar, becoming more and more agitated, until eventually he came face to face with a group of people who had been approaching from the opposite direction. For some reason that made sense to his clouded judgement, he began a largely unintelligible tirade against them. One of the group thought it might be fun to try and remove the bin from his grasp, however Jar-Jar screamed at them.

'Don't touch wheelie!' he yelled, and the group decided that a person who had such a strong attachment to a bin was best left alone; so they went on their way, giving him as wide a berth as possible, with Jar-Jar yelling obscenities after them. Feeling thus vindicated in his defence of the garbage bin, he continued his erratic path, having forgotten entirely his companions from earlier in the evening.

Alerted by the yelling, the mounted police patrol turned around and came back down the street at a trot, slowing to walking pace as they drew level with Jar-Jar, who seemed now to be trying to dance with the bin.

'Busting out some pretty crazy moves there mate,' said one of the police officers, as she regarded him with the well-honed caution of one who knows full well how suddenly drunks can turn nasty. Jar-Jar made no attempt at a response; he was now looking mutely up at the two officers seated on the rather large horses.

'Where're your mates?' said the other policeman, shifting in his saddle. Again Jar-Jar did not answer, but this time slowly sat down on the ground and put his arms around the bin.

'Oh great, a psycho with a wheelie bin fixation,' he continued in the resigned voice of a person who could do without seeing something new in the way of mental waywardness.

'Might need to take this one in,' said the other, 'who knows what old matey has been taking.'

Jar-Jar however had imbibed nothing but alcohol, which combined with his rather eccentric nature could produce quite enough chaos without adding drugs to his system.

Rob roundly cursed himself for not having been his usual vigilant self, and allowing the conversation with Tash to distract him. However after a quick search of the Pub revealed nothing they all spilled out onto the street in search of their wayward friend. Tash promptly unlocked her iPhone and looked up an app that had a means of tracking friends; or at least their phones.

'His phone is down the street this way,' she said, and they all moved off in the direction she indicated.

'At least one of us is switched on,' Rob muttered.

'Hey Padre! I'm a sig, I'm all over this technology shit,' said

Tash, 'and when you have a friend like Jar-Jar, you need every edge you can get!'

They all then went down the street toward where the signal from Jar-Jar's phone had come. By the time they found him, he had just sunk to the ground, clutching the bin as he looked up at the two police officers. To the mild surprise of the rest of the group, Rob walked forward confidently toward their errant colleague.

'Hey ho my friend, up a dando now,' said Rob, extending a hand to the wheelie bin hugging Lieutenant Weston. Jar-Jar took Rob's hand, stood up for a moment, but then began to sink to the ground again. Rob grabbed him around the waist to steady him, and Scott Morgan came in on the other side.

'Wheelie!' said Jar-Jar weakly, as the two others supported him.

'Was he with you lot?' asked the second of the police officers suspiciously.

'That's right, yeah,' said Rob, looking up pleasantly at the two mounted officers, and radiating responsible sobriety. 'We lost track of him just now. It's his birthday and he's full as a boot.'

'What's he been taking?' asked the first.

'Nothing apart from alcohol,' said Rob, 'the rest is just the bizarre fella we know and love.'

At that point Jar-Jar decided that the next item on the agenda was to be violently ill, whereupon he vomited copiously, which drew a number of responses of disgust from the crowd that was starting to gather nearby.

'Wheelie!' said Jar-Jar again, looking forlornly at the bin. 'I want wheelie.'

'Might be an idea if you take him home,' suggested the first police officer kindly.

'Yes officer, we'll do that right away,' said Rob, and with a word to the others, he and Morgs dragged Jar-Jar back toward where they had parked their cars.

'Wheelie!' Jar-Jar managed to say again, as he tried to drag himself away.

'Shut the fuck up man!' said Morgs impatiently.

'Let's bundle him in your car, and take him back to my place,' said Rob to Morgs, 'I don't think he should be left alone tonight.'

'Are you sure about that Padre?' asked Tash. 'He'll be right to just sleep it off won't he?'

However Rob was not be dissuaded; and he also had not forgotten the concerted attention Tash had been paying earlier in the evening.

'The mood he's in, he needs someone to watch him,' he explained, 'drunk people in dark moods are not great to leave alone.'

'Up to you mate,' Morgs rumbled, 'but if he says "wheelie" one more time, I'm going to stuff him head first in one and see if he likes it!'

When they arrived at Rob's house, it took some effort to drag Jar-Jar inside, however once they had succeeded, they sat him down on the lounge, and Morgs and Tash left to return to Murruwa. Rob sat there for some time afterwards, listening carefully to Jar-Jar's semi-coherent muttering, until finally sleep took the angry young man. Rob then laid Jar-Jar in a position that would prevent him choking on his own vomit, should he be sick in the night. Then after grinning about the irony of Jar-Jar rescuing him from Tash's attentions, Rob went to bed himself, having been careful to make sure the curtains were tightly drawn so that the errant young Lieutenant would not be woken up too early.

However when Rob rose the following morning, he made absolutely no effort to tone down the light or the noise of his morning routine. Rob briskly threw open the curtains, and moved into the kitchen; and after 'accidentally' dropping a couple of large pans on the floor, set about cooking bacon, eggs and hash browns for breakfast. Added to this was the noise of an electric juicer, and his rather impressive cappuccino maker. As the smell of cooking food and coffee spread throughout the house, and the cacophony of sound shattered the morning calm, Jar-Jar quite unwillingly began to stir.

'Morning sleeping beauty,' said Rob in an ostentatiously loud and cheerful tone of voice. The only response he got was a groan as Jar-Jar blearily tried to orientate himself.

'Where the fuck am I?' he asked eventually.

'You are "the fuck" in the Padre's house,' said Rob helpfully, a manic smile on his face, 'and you're here because last night you were absolutely snobbled, and in love with a wheelie bin.'

'What?'

'It's a bit much to wrap your head around, I know,' said Rob, 'but work with me now. Do you want some breakfast? Coffee maybe?'

'Yeah, something,' said Jar-Jar, staggering to his feet. He did a brief post night-on-the-town shake down of himself to make sure he still had his wallet and other essential items. Having established the presence of these things, he looked resentfully at the sunlight streaming in through the windows, before turning a rather interesting shade of green.

'Toilet's just down there,' said Rob, correctly diagnosing the problem, and Jar-Jar moved as quickly as he could. The sound of retching came quite clearly to the kitchen, however Rob drowned it out with the noise of making frothed milk. Jar-Jar returned looking a little better, and was greeted by the maddening sight of the Padre still beaming happily at him.

'That's the spirit Mr Weston, better out than in,' said Rob

bracingly, 'please take a seat over there at the table, breakfast'll be ready soon.'

Jar-Jar complied, and was soon seated in front of a large plate of food, a cappuccino, fruit juice, and most mercifully, a large jug of water.

'Here's some yaffling spanners for you,' said Rob, passing Jar-Jar a knife and fork, and then sat himself down opposite the dishevelled young officer.

The two of them ate and drank for some time in relative silence, and slowly some life and colour began to return to Jar-Jar's face. Rob eyed him suspiciously for a moment, before asking him a question.

'How well do you get on with your family mate?'

Jar-Jar looked at him, somewhat shocked.

'How did you ....'

'I listen my friend, and that makes me very dangerous,' said Rob slyly.

Jar-Jar toyed with telling Rob to mind his own business, however from some recess of his foggy mind he recalled the sheer aggression he had seen the Padre use on a couple of occasions. He eventually decided that fobbing off Thor of the rugby field would be an even worse idea than pissing off Major Le Bon.

'I never talk to them,' Jar admitted unwillingly. 'They packed me off to a boarding school when I was six, and I've been living an institutional life ever since. They always gave me presents on my birthday, but never any kind of relationship.'

Rob looked up at him after he said that, raised his eyebrows, and then took a long sip of coffee.

'My friend, ever since I first met you I've been wondering a lot about some stuff,' Rob began quietly, 'And it seems to me that your whole life is one big attempt at saying "screw you" to the world at large, and authority figures in particular.'

'Are you a psych as well, Padre?'

'No, just really experienced at watching people destroy themselves,' said Rob with a bite to his voice. 'Don't get me wrong now, I think we need jesters, people to show us how ridiculous things are, but I've learned some things about jesters, see.'

'What's that then?'

'Just this: If you want to find the saddest person in the room, you only need to look for the clown.'

Jar-Jar gazed at Rob, looking as stunned as a new recruit. To have somebody see through him so completely was a shock to his rather shattered system.

'I had a mate like you once; life of the party, a joker,' said Rob reflectively, 'and his story sounded a lot like yours. Rich parents who couldn't give a toss about him when it counted, so he spent his whole time doing crazy stuff to piss them off, and everyone else for that matter. It was like he was looking for attention or something; I don't know.'

'What happened to him?' asked Jar-Jar, seeing the pained expression on Rob's face. The Padre looked up at Lieutenant Weston, his grey eyes momentarily glinting like steel blades.

'He hung himself; got himself into trouble at work, he did, and hung himself,' answered Rob, and Jar-Jar stared at him in horror.

'Don't like your birthday much do you now?' said Rob.

'No I don't,' said Jar-Jar sadly, 'just another day when my folks don't give a shit about me.'

'Well, I won't get too Freudian on you or anything, but destroying yourself because you're pissed off with your parents doesn't seem like a good idea to me. There's no sense living in the bitterness of what your parents never gave you,' said Rob. 'If you really want to thumb your nose at them and the world, then be a different kind of friend, and father if it comes to that; and use that mind of yours for something other than nihilistic brain snaps. There's a lot more I'd like to say, but that'll do for now. And stay away from wheelie bins too! I don't think he was your type.'

'He? That bin was a she!' argued Jar-Jar.

'No mate; definitely a he,' retorted Rob, 'I'm not a very judgemental person, so it's up to you what gender of wheelie bin you want to fall in love with, but it just shows how pissed you really were that you couldn't tell the difference.'

The two of them bantered back and forth like that for a few minutes before starting a more serious conversation, about life, work and motivation. They talked for a long time about Jar-Jar's bitter and lonely past, and how that was shaping the decisions of his present life. By the time he left with Rob to go back to his room on base, Jar-Jar felt like he had gained a better insight into himself than he had ever had before.

Over the next few weeks, Anne started to detect a real change in Jar-Jar. It was not seen so much in what he did, but in the manner in which he did things. However the change was noticeable enough to come to the attention of Major Le Bon, who had been waiting patiently for Jar-Jar's next atrocity, and had been quite surprised at the delay in its coming. What was more, 23 and 24 platoon had also been put in the unenviable position where they had very little break in between platoons of trainees; no sooner had they marched out their first lot of recruits for the year, when another lot had marched in. This put a lot of strain on the staff, however Jar-Jar seemed to be doing a very good job of keeping everything moving along well.

'So what's he been doing?' Major Le Bon asked her CSM, Jock McIntosh, who had just been telling her how happy the staff of 23 Platoon had been, despite the fatigue they were feeling.

'Well ma'am, not only's all his admin been done on time, but he's been doing random things like pizza and coffee runs for his RI's, and he's even been tutoring F-Bomb in maths!' said the CSM.

'Tutoring who? In what?' she said incredulously. 'F-Bomb never struck me as the academic type!'

'Apparently his brother is a doctor, and he's decided it's time to up-skill himself,' Jock explained. 'And Mr Weston is bloody good at maths by all accounts.'

'Well I just hope he can avoid doing something random and crazy for a while longer,' said Major Le Bon, still a little wary of what Jar-Jar might do in an unguarded moment.

'Well ma'am,' said Jock, 'between you and I, I heard tell there was nearly an incident a little while back when they went out for Mr Weston's birthday; he was drunk as a skunk but apparently Padre Llewellyn stepped in and took him back to his place, and Jar-Jar spent the night there. I think the Padre must've got in his ear then, because apparently he's been different ever since.'

Anne stored this information away in her head. So the Padre crops up again, she thought. What took place between Rob and Jar-Jar was not her concern, however the good effects of that conversation were something she was benefiting from, so she decided if possible to add weight to the momentum for change. Her opportunity was not long in coming, though it was through a means that she had not anticipated.

A few weeks before, Pat had decided to give Rob the responsibility for presenting the Chaplain's brief on the Recruit Instructor's course, where he had to explain to the trainee instructors the peculiarities of Chaplaincy at Morshead Barracks. During this lessons Rob found himself getting a little worried about one of the Corporals, whose surname was De Blasio. It may just be that he is sick of PowerPoint slides, Rob reminded himself, however some other instincts and memories inside him told him to keep a close eye on that individual.

It turned out that Corporal De Blasio was going to be assigned to 23 Platoon to shadow F-Bomb as a section commander and recruit instructor. However F-Bomb was far from happy about the newcomer.

'It's not that he's a fuckwit,' explained Corporal Nguyen to Lieutenant Weston one day, 'but I think he's a fucking bomb waiting to go off. It might be worth finding out more about him.'

However Jar-Jar's attempts at doing this in a formal interview met with no real response. Corporal De Blasio did not highlight any personal issues during that time, though he did appear sullen. When Jar-Jar mentioned it to Rob in passing, the same general impression of the guy came across. If the Padre, F-Bomb and myself are all have the same feeling, then there is probably an issue, reasoned Lieutenant Weston. However, nothing prepared him for what came next.

One morning after a fairly intense PT session, the platoon was going through its ritual of showering and changing. Rob had been called to see a recruit with some ongoing home issues, and had just walked into the foyer when he saw a sight that horrified him. Corporal De Blasio, who had been supervising the movement of the recruits through the foyer, suddenly flew across the area and started screaming at one individual.

'You useless piece of shit!' he raved. 'How many weeks have you been here? Well?'

The recruit however, who was in his third week, was too stunned to answer, completely shocked at this sudden assault from a strange instructor. De Blasio looked set to continue his rant, but Rob's ringing voice intervened as the other Corporals and Jar-Jar came running into the foyer.

'Corporal De Blasio, come here now!' said Rob urgently, and the Padre's words were soon followed by the hands of F-Bomb and Erica Schulz being laid on him and he was dragged away from the recruit.

'Recruit, wait in the brew room for me! Is that clear?' said Rob to the nervous lad who was still standing on the spot he had been occupying when he had been released from De Blasio's grasp.

'Yes Padre.'

'Good man, I shan't be long.'

Corporal De Blasio was taken into Jar-Jar's office, and F-Bomb shut the door after Rob entered with Lieutenant Weston.

'How long have you been back from ops[1]?' asked Rob as soon as the door was closed. However Corporal De Blasio just looked at Rob as if he had been struck dumb, and both Jar-Jar and F-Bomb likewise looked puzzled. 'Please answer the question!' said Rob in deadly earnest.

'About a month before I arrived here, sir,' answered Corporal De Blasio morosely. Rob's eyes widened.

'Well that's fucked up right there,' said F-Bomb, in the tone of one who was all too familiar with such things happening. 'Who thought that was a good idea?'

'The same one who thought it was a good idea I come here after I'd lost mates in Afghan, and my wife'd left me a month before I came home,' said De Blasio, his eyes flashing with a bitter light.

To everyone's surprise, Rob yelled and punched the door at that point.

'Shit, Padre!' said F-Bomb, staring at him in shock.

---

1. Contraction of 'operations', referring to an overseas deployment.

'Of all the ...' Rob began, but his train of speech faltered and he put his hands in his hair, shaking his head at the same time. 'Is this Army so short of Corporals that they have to do this?' Rob asked of no one in particular, before he walked toward the door. 'I'd better go and speak to old mate in the brew room,' he said as he went out in an enraged mood.

'Fuck! Padre's a bit wound up,' muttered F-Bomb.

'Yeah, hasn't been that cranky since he ripped Nancarrow a new one,' mused Jar-Jar. 'Actually I think he's more angry than he was then, cause he hasn't calmed down yet.'

'That Padre ripped someone a new arsehole?' asked Corporal De Blasio.

'Yep,' said F-Bomb.

'What was he before becoming a Padre?'

'Fucked if I know,' said F-Bomb.

'But now Corporal De Blasio, we need to think about how we're going to un-fuck your situation,' said Jar-Jar.

Meanwhile Rob had gone over to the brew room. Thankfully the recruit was only a bit shaken and confused.

'Are you sure you're going to be okay,' asked Rob as they concluded their conversation.

'Yeah Padre, I'll be fine,' said the young man, 'but that guy needs help. Corporal Nguyen can be cranky, but that dude's off his rocker.'

'I think stressed to the point of breaking is closer to the truth,' said Rob sadly, and with that sent the recruit on his way, but with a resolution to catch up with him again in the near future.

Slow wheels began to turn endeavouring to deal with the incident appropriately, and alternative employment had to be found for Corporal De Blasio; employment that was away from recruits until he had time to work through his issues. So it was that Jar-Jar came to Major Le Bon with a plan that he and Rob had worked on. He knew it was usually best to present a solution to commanders, rather than just a problem; however he had formed the impression that with his Company Commander doing that was a matter of survival.

Anne listened, quietly impressed at the series of options Jar-Jar had come up with so that the troubled Corporal could be better managed, and have appropriate time and space to work through his problems. Lieutenant Weston had already tried to see if he could be posted back to the infantry battalion he had come from, however there seemed to be no possibility of that. Instead Jar-Jar had found a position in Battalion Headquarters, as well as a couple of other possibilities. When he had finished talking Anne eyed him appraisingly.

'Well done Mr Weston!' she said. 'Creative thinking, well applied to a difficult situation. Is there anything else?'

This last phrase she uttered with the thought that Jar-Jar would probably have nothing further to say. However, in that she was mistaken.

'Well ma'am, I'm actually a bit worried about Padre Llewellyn,' Jar-Jar blurted out suddenly, 'the stuff that happened with Corporal De Blasio really seemed to get under his skin. I wouldn't normally say anything, but he's been a real mate, and I think there's something eating at him.'

Anne cocked her head on one side for a moment as she took this in, her eyes boring into the young lieutenant as she did so.

Jar-Jar did not tell her that Rob had punched a door, as despite his concern, he had an inner reluctance to expose the Padre to too much scrutiny from Major Le Bon.

'Thanks for that Mr Weston, I'll have a word to him about it if I can, but don't hesitate to raise it with him yourself,' she said. With that statement, Major Le Bon dismissed him. As Anne considered what Jar-Jar had said to her about Rob, she could think of nothing that she had observed in him that especially troubled her. Rob seemed to be his normal self; that is, he was polite and reserved, with an undertone of something else. Perhaps I just needed to be there, she thought, and filed away Jar-Jar's observation for future reference. However, events were soon to push any concern she might have for Rob to one side.

12

———

'Taff, get down here quick!' he heard Johnno's voice say on the other end of his mobile phone, 'it's Dizzy.'
'Why? What's the matter?' asked Taff, dragging himself out of a chair.
'He's gone and necked himself, that's what!' said Johnno, and then hung up.
Taff ran and ran, the bitter sleet stinging his face, as the sound of sirens wailed in the cold air, their banshee shriek a herald of death and woe. As he ran around the corner down into the street where Dizzy lived, he could hear another terrible, haunted cry; and then he saw her, Dizzy's wife, standing in the middle of the street, screaming at the top of her lungs.
'He's dead, he's dead,' she shrieked, over and over again in between her shuddering sobs; and then she started throwing anything she could reach, her face now red with grief and anger. Taff ran up to her, and when he came within reach, she beat her arms against him in the hot agony she felt. And as he looked over her shoulder he could see the body on the ground, with two fellow Marines trying to revive it; but Dizzy was gone, he knew it in his heart. Taff let out a long cry of rage and grief himself ..... and then he woke with a start.
Sitting up in bed; another time now, and a different place. He tried

*again to steady his breathing, and tried to adjust his disoriented mind
to the present. Taff's heart felt like it was in his ears. Another dream,
he thought. Grasping hold of the small cross by his bed, again he
began to run his fingers over it, trying to anchor himself in time and
space; to ground himself in the present. It had been nearly eight years
since Dizzy had hung himself, Taff thought as he lay there, his heart
still pounding in his chest. Dizzy the happy joker, the life of the party,
the bearer of many unsaid sorrows.*

*'Only another dream,' Taff said aloud, before laughing bitterly. 'Only
a dream.' This is starting to happen a bit too much to be called 'only',
he thought wearily. Taff then laid down again, and tried to get back to
sleep.*

A couple of weeks later Rob was two days into his next stint as
on-call chaplain. This particular evening, he had managed the
small triumph of getting away from work early, and was sitting
at home enjoying playing his piano. As he was just starting to
lose himself in the music, the jarring noise of the on-call phone
shattered his musical focus.

'*Ach y fi!*'[1] he exclaimed in disgust before answering the call.

'On-call Chaplain speaking,' he said, fully expecting it to be
a call from one of the Recruit platoons.

'Uhhh, hello,' said the voice at the other end, a lady's voice.
This was not what Rob was expecting at all; normally there was
no uncertainty involved in calling a Chaplain at Murruwa. Well
at least this could be different, he thought to himself.

'How can I help you?' Rob asked.

'Umm, I'm not sure,' replied the woman. At this point Rob
could feel frustration and curiosity engaging in a sort of competition inside him.

---

1.   Expression of disgust, with no exact translation.

'Are you wanting to speak to an Army Chaplain?' Rob said, hoping to clarify the uncertainty.

'Yes, I am,' said the voice, 'this is the Murruwa Chaplain number isn't it?'

'Yes it is.'

'Well I have something I want to talk about,' she said, 'a couple of things actually.'

'Are you on base?' asked Rob.

'No, I'm AWOL[2] from a unit in Brisbane. I'm sitting in the McDonalds near the Caltex servo in town, and I really need to speak to a Chaplain.'

'Okay, I'll be right there.' said Rob, suddenly much more alert with the mention of the term AWOL.

'Thanks Padre,' she said, 'I'm the blonde in the maroon jumper.'

Rob was thankful that he had not changed out of his uniform as yet. It was not far from his house to McDonalds, though he avoided eating there if he could; even the smell of one of the restaurants turned his otherwise iron stomach. He drove the short distance, and met the girl in the main eating area.

'Hi, I'm Padre Llewellyn. What's your name?' he asked, as he approached the young lady, who had waved when he entered in uniform.

'Sylvia Dunford,' she said, rising and shaking Rob by the hand. 'Thanks for coming out to see me sir.'

'That's fine, but why on earth have you done a runner?' Rob said as he sat down.

Sylvia did not immediately answer his question, but sat there for a moment in thought as she considered what to say. Whilst she appeared somewhat upset, Sylvia was well dressed

---

2. Absent without leave.

and neat in her appearance. Whatever it was that had happened to her, Rob mused, it had obviously not affected her self-discipline.

'Sir, I work in a Q-store[3] in Brisbane,' she explained. 'And some things happened that really freaked me out. The area where I work started out as a great place to be, and I was enjoying it, but after a while I started to feel as if something was wrong, but I didn't quite know what it was. Then a couple of weeks back a Corporal and a couple of others asked to speak to me in private, and so I met them in the Q-store at lunch. They said they'd been watching me at work and decided I was clever, and that they should include me in the business they were running on the side.'

At this every possible alarm bell went off in Rob's head. People in a Q-store running a business on the side could not mean anything good, and he readied his mind for what he thought would be coming next.

'And what sort of business might that be?' asked Rob, his voice overflowing with displeasure.

'A couple of things,' said Sylvia, growing more agitated as she described what had been going on. 'They have access to a lot of special equipment that they said has some excellent customers on the outside, and they also supply designer drugs to the party scene.'

Rob gave a low whistle; drugs and stolen goods; and I bet that's not all, he thought, as he looked at the tears forming in her eyes.

'And they said, if I didn't get involved, that they'd make me have an accident,' said Sylvia, beginning to sob.

'What did you do then?'

'Well I went along with it for a few days,' she said. 'I thought

---

3.   A Q-Store is a place where military stores and equipment are held.

it would've been too obvious if I'd just disappeared; and they were watching me too. My Corporal also showed me a clip from a video of me having sex with a guy. I didn't know it'd been taken, or how he'd got hold of it. That really freaked me out. He said that if I even looked like causing any trouble he was going to post it on social media.'

Rob felt disgust and anger boiling inside, though his exterior was not showing it. Instead he channeled as much emotional energy as he could into concentrating on her story. These were extraordinarily serious allegations that needed to investigated, and there were two people he knew who would be a great help. Sylvia could see him thinking and assumed his silence meant that he was somehow disgusted with her.

'I'm sorry sir, you must think I'm some sort of stupid slapper.'

'Far from it,' he replied. 'But some of Christ's followers could be called slappers, so I should be the last one to criticise you in any case.'

She looked at him in a startled way when he said this. However, it was plain that the pressing question on her mind was what was the next step she should take.

'What am I going to do? I know they were serious about killing me.'

'We'll doing everything we can to keep you safe,' Rob re-assured her. 'How long have you been AWOL?'

'Just today; I drove straight here; I left at 0400,' she said. 'I'd always liked coming to Chapel at Murruwa, so talking to one of you guys was the first thing I thought about doing. I got the phone number from work before I left.'

'Is there somewhere that your work-place will've assumed you've gone?' asked Rob.

'Probably the Sunshine Coast, where my folks live; but I decided to head the opposite direction.'

Rob looked at her, wondering at the sense of desperation that would have driven her decision to drive so far.

'Right, what I want you to do is to come with me out to the base,' he said to her, 'then just follow me up the hill to the Chaplaincy centre. I'm going to ask two other people to meet us there, and then we'll talk about this some more.'

'Okay sir; but would you mind if I got another coffee first?'

'No, I think that'd be a good idea; this could be a long night.'

While Sylvia ordered her coffee, Rob rang Major Le Bon and Steve Schwarz. Having them involved would be vital; and it was most likely going to be a long night. As Rob drove out to the base with Sylvia Dunford following behind, his mind was naturally full of the human tragedy that had just been described to him. Whilst he was too cynical to assume anyone was being truthful, he had not really picked up anything about the girl that indicated she was lying. Nevertheless, having Steve and Anne involved not only gave him a measure of protection; it also meant that two people who were professional questioners would be involved. Besides that, between them their knowledge of ADF and civilian law was encyclopaedic.

When Rob arrived, closely followed by Sylvia, he was relieved to find the other two had both got there before him; they were standing in the car-park talking to each other, and waved as Rob approached.

'What's happened? You look like you want to murder someone,' remarked Anne as she took in the look on Rob's face.'

'I'm pretty angry, that's true.'

'That seems a bit of an understatement to me; you look like you're in that realm where rage shapes action,' she observed. 'You've normally got an unreadable face, or else you look gentle and receptive; the only time I've seen you like this is when you were playing rugby.'

Rob shrugged.

'Let's go inside,' he said. 'There is going to be a fair bit to explain here.'

'Hi, I'm Major Le Bon,' said Anne as she looked at Sylvia. 'You marched out of her with Charlie Company last year, didn't you?'

'That's right, ma'am.'

They all sat down in the central area of the Chaplaincy Centre and Sylvia, at Rob's instigation, began to explain again her situation. Steve sat there, taking copious notes, whilst Anne asked questions of detail; including the names of those involved, and the places and times when things had occurred.

'Was the sex you had whilst being filmed consensual?' asked Anne, continuing in the dispassionate tone she had been using all along.

'Yes it was,' answered Sylvia.

'Did you consent to being filmed?' said Anne.

'No I didn't, I had no idea. We met at a pub off base, and he bought me a drink. He seemed really nice.'

'And do you remember the name of the guy?'

'He was a Major from Canberra up in Brisbane on project work. He didn't say his last name, but I saw his ID,' said Sylvia. 'He had an unusual surname that just stuck in my mind. Veenenboer? Paul Veenenboer; that's it.'

At this Anne froze for a moment, and Rob looked over at her in horror.

'Padre, could you come with me please?' she asked Rob, turning to him with a similarly stricken look on her face.

'Sure thing ma'am,' he answered, knowing already what was coming next, and they stepped inside Rob's office.

'Rob,' she began, taking in deep, deliberate breaths. 'I'm certain that the guy she had sex with, and who filmed her, is my ex. It won't be appropriate for me to keep talking to her. People could say that I've shaped her into making an accusation out of spite.'

'Yes ma'am, I understand.'

'I think he's probably got videos of me too Rob,' she said looking directly at him, her voice quavering as angry tears started to form in her eyes. 'I did some pretty wild things when I was with him. If he filmed this girl, I think it's a safe bet he did it to me,' she continued, her voice shot through with anger and betrayal. 'And those videos could be all over the internet.'

Rob did not answer immediately; his well-honed instincts told him that a misplaced, pious platitude could be fatal. Instead he just nodded in acknowledgement, and waited for Anne's emotions to subside a little.

'Ma'am, that doesn't change the respect I have for you one bit,' he said after a while. 'No matter what you've done, or who you've done it with.'

Anne looked up at him with some degree of wonder at what he said.

'It means a lot to hear you say that,' she said gratefully. 'But I wonder what you'd think if you knew everything about me?'

'You've already been declared not guilty by the King of Kings. Who am I to think differently?' he said kindly.

Rob then sat again in silence, showing his care for her by simply being. Weep with those who weep Jesus said, he reminded himself, though weeping with Major Le Bon was actually a bit of a problem for him at that point. He was sorely tempted to go hunting that night, and rabbits would not have been his quarry.

'*Myfi piau dial, myfi a dalaf an ôl, medd yr Arglwydd*[4],' he said, reminding himself quietly of a Bible verse he had learned long ago, though with no great delight.

---

4. Vengeance is mine, I will repay, says the Lord.

'What was that?' asked Anne, looking up at him.

'Just jogging my memory, ma'am,' he replied, mastering his own feelings. 'Why don't you go home now? Steve and I can finish up here.'

'I don't want to drive at the moment,' said Anne with a shake of her head, and Rob looked at her with renewed concern. He had never seen her composure so utterly shattered. He was used to a feisty, authoritative, and persistent woman; not the brittle person who was now in his office.

'You could go down to the Chapel and wait there; I'll come down in a minute,' Rob suggested. Anne nodded in agreement without meeting his eyes, and then left his office and went out of the building.

Steve looked at her in confusion as she walked away; and Rob called him out of the central meeting area over to where he was standing. He quietly gave him a sanitised version of the reason for her leaving early. Steve's eyes narrowed briefly.

'It's all right mate, I've got this,' said Steve. 'With what young Sylvia's told me, I think a raid could be organised that'd nail these bastards well and truly.'

'You think she's telling the truth then?' asked Rob, though there was no real doubt in his own mind.

'Yeah I do; it follows a classic pattern of criminal behaviour,' replied Steve grimly. 'I've seen stuff like this heaps of times. Blackmail some poor young chick into being in the operation and pretty soon she is jumping through any hoop they want; and when I say any hoop, I mean any hoop.'

'Right, I'll just have a quick word with Sylvia, and then I need to go and talk to Major Le Bon.'

'That's fine Rob; I'm going to ring the CO. This is going to be on the Chief-of-Army's desk by morning. Then let the games begin!'

Rob then walked down to the Chapel where he found Anne

sitting quietly, and pulling up a chair he sat down opposite her. She gave him a watery smile as he looked at her. Rob would have willingly sat there and been silent with her for as long as she wished, and he did so for some time while the flood tide of emotions kept washing over Anne. What he found most difficult was to restrain his inclination to put a reassuring arm around her shoulders; it was the first time in many years that he had wanted to touch a woman who was not a member of his immediate family. A depth of compassion was moved in him at her plight, that made him even more remorseful over the attitude he had had toward her a bare few weeks before. Rob's thoughts then drifted onto how thankful he was that his job helped take his mind of his own problems, when Anne looked up at him and spoke.

'Padre, would you mind playing the piano for me?' she asked.

'Absolutely! Anything in particular?'

'No, just do your thing ... follow your mood through, or whatever it was you said you did.'

Rob nodded in acknowledgement, and then walked over to the piano, and beckoned Anne to follow him. After he had sat down, he bowed his head briefly, his hands on his legs, before he began playing a gentle, melancholy melody, his fingers gliding over the keys with a mesmerising familiarity and ease. Rob's hands were deep in conversation with the instrument, and his eyes were closed in concentration, as he willed the piano to express what was on his mind. He could not know precisely Anne's thoughts and emotions, but using every last fibre of imagination and empathy he had, Rob drew from familiar chords, and searched the keys for some blend of tones that would somehow capture her turmoil and hold it fast. Briefly he wondered at the strength of his desire to minister to Anne, then somewhere inside he felt the resonation of music and emotion he had been seeking, and followed the thread of music through.

Looking over at her briefly, Rob saw a path of glistening tears down her cheeks; but he played on for a minute or so before he began to sing, the song growing out of the tune that he had been playing, shifting seamlessly between the melodies. The words he sang spoke of hope and love in the midst of betrayal, that he hoped would give her courage beyond the pain she felt. When he had finished he turned around and he saw her eyes boring into him. As Rob looked at her, it slowly began to dawn on him that what he had done that evening had touched her very deeply.

'I have no words to take away your pain, but can I pray for you, ma'am?' he asked, and she nodded tearfully. When he had finished she looked at him with her dark eyes reddened by tears.

'Thank you Rob; I wish I'd had a pen and paper ready for that prayer; you made me feel like heaven came into this room,' she said, reaching out and grasping his hand in gratitude; and a brief, hot thrill coursed through him at the feeling of her skin on his.

'That could not have been my doing, ma'am,' he replied seriously.

They sat in silence for a while, before rejoining Steve back in the Chaplaincy Centre. In their absence he had spoken to the CO of 2 RTB, and the Chaplain and CO from Sylvia's unit, and had arranged for her to be accommodated at Murruwa.

'Have you two been down at the Chapel this whole time?' Steve asked in wonder, but when he saw the look on Anne's face he stopped short of asking anything further. Anne gathered up her hand-bag from a table and left.

'Thanks again Rob, for listening,' she said with a smile and wave as she left. He turned to Steve, who raised his eyebrows for a moment, but again thought better of saying anything. It was plainly not a night for smart-arsed remarks.

Rob woke the next day wondering if the previous night had been a dream of some kind, however the flurry of activity at work that came in the wake of those events left no doubt in his mind that it had been all too real.

'Well, it looks like we've unleashed a category five shit-storm here people,' Steve said, as he briefed the CO, with Rob and Anne the next morning. 'The Military Police want to have a yarn with Sylvia too. But the question is, what should we do with her in meantime?'

'Sir, I suggest we keep her here,' said Anne decisively, her resolution had evidently returned after the fragility of the previous night; and it was back to a calm and decisive Major Le Bon. 'She can work out of the spare office at the Chaplaincy Centre and be an admin assistant for the Padres until this is all cleared up; that way she won't easily be seen by anyone connected to her old workplace.'

'Great thinking Anne,' said the CO. 'But from now on, we're just going to have to wait for the slow wheels of justice to roll.'

His assessment was quite correct, for as well as the usual flow of recruits and staff members coming to the Chaplaincy Centre, serious looking men and women in suits came to talk with the 'admin assistant' who was temporarily assigned to the Chaplains. Her knowledge of the illegal sale of defence assets, of drug dealing, and illicit filming of sex was carefully recorded; and with patient thoroughness the various aspects of the investigation were coordinated.

'I think the ADFIS[5] guys are concerned there may be a nexus between the Q-store and officer from Canberra,' said Steve a few days later. 'That's what'd be worrying me; if there is some kind of Hydra of crime in the Army then the media are going to go off their tits about it. Let's hope that the connection is only on the lines of transmission of home-made sex videos. That's bad enough.'

'Where do you get your information?' asked Rob.

'Mate, when you were in the policing game as long as me, you just know these things from snatches of conversation; but let's just say I still have my sources,' said Steve. 'But I'll never stop looking at the world this way. It's too heavily ingrained in my head.'

At that remark Rob became unusually thoughtful, but whatever it was that was on his mind he did not reveal to anyone at that moment. Later that week Steve found out that a series of raids had been conducted by Federal Police, confirming the accusations that Sylvia had made to the last detail. That lunch time a quiet group discussed the latest developments. Rob, Anne, Sean, the CO and the other Chaplains sat around a table eating together. The usual banter was noticeably subdued, even Sean O'Donnell was not his effusive self.

There was no real pleasure expressed in the apprehension of any of the perpetrators of the crimes, for they all felt as if it reflected badly on them as members of the Army. Anne especially was in a dark mood; her ex-partner had been arrested as well. Apparently the police search of his computers had revealed some very unedifying things, that constituted a crime against children; though beyond pornographic material there did not appear to be any link between the Corporal in Brisbane and the Major from Canberra.

---

5. Australian Defence Force Investigative Service.

'Well, some people are going to be going to gaol for a good stretch,' said Steve.

'It shits me to tears that I serve in same Army as those people,' growled Sean.

Pat looked at him in surprise. It was not often anybody heard anything out of Sean that was not said with a smile. Pat however agreed entirely with the sentiments.

'When I first joined, c-nuts like that would have been lucky to live if they'd been found out,' he said venomously. 'Then the Army got all sensitive about bullying.'

'Actually, in the past many bullies got away with it too,' said Alan sadly, reflecting on his own past experience, 'their victims did not always have someone to defend them; still don't sometimes. In many ways, that exactly what we are dealing with in this case; bullies who abuse others for their own ends.'

Rob meanwhile looked like he was a million miles away, preoccupied by his own thoughts.

'What's going through your mind there Rob,' asked Anne, aware that they had lost him somewhere along the way.

'Any armed force is a reflection of its home culture; the triumphs and tragedies of Australian society walk living in our ranks,' he said, almost as if he was speaking to himself. 'None of us who join come in as a blank sheet of paper. We all have writing on the page already, inscribed by the life we've led, and the beliefs that drive the choices of our hearts. All of us here try to write things on the pages of the recruits, trying to instil in them values and beliefs beyond the material and the self. But whether the story we want to tell becomes part of their story is another matter; and sometimes there are those who'll be an embarrassment to the uniform, and there's not one thing we could've taught them that'll make any difference at all. There's no silver bullet of compulsory training that'll slay the werewolves in our midst; and it's only a fool who'd pretend otherwise. Real evil exists, and it's very resistant to re-education; just as real good resisted the re-education camps of the Soviets. This intractability in our wills is one of the things that makes us human. It's a thing that's beautiful, ... and dangerous.'

'Dude,' said Sean after the others had spent a moment digesting this. 'Where the fuck does that stuff come from? Why aren't you lecturing philosophy to a bunch of long-haired wankers at a University somewhere?'

'Because the short haired wankers in the Army need to hear it too; and Rob's philosophy is too realistic for a University,' said Pat drily. 'You should have been a Jesuit, not a Protestant!'

'Beware Rob,' said Alan, 'coming from Pat, I'm not sure that amounts to a compliment!'

Rob just smiled quietly, though most people were still trying to think through what he said.

'What worries me in this is what kind of knee-jerk dot com response might come out of Army Headquarters,' said Sean. At this they all nodded; the reaction from Canberra was often the worst part of a scandal in the Army.

'Yes, there's always the danger of Higher Command doing what they think will please or appease the ruling classes, rather than what will fix the problem,' said Rob cynically, his eyes flashing with a rather revolutionary light. 'The best we can do is empower people to stand against wrong, and back them up when they take action. Even if it's kinetic.'

'Spoken like an old soldier there mate,' said the CO, but Alan then brought their minds back to Sylvia Dunford.

'What will happen to our young friend who reported all this?' he asked.

'The RSM is hearing her charge for AWOL this afternoon,' replied the CO.

'She's still going to be charged? After all this, sir?' asked Pat in amazement and a degree of annoyance.

'Absolutely; she went AWOL,' said the CO calmly. 'However, she'll be dealt with fairly. You can count on that with the RSM. I'd like Padre Llewellyn to be there too. It won't take long to hear the matter.'

'Yes sir,' said Rob.

'I'll be having a chat to you about this later, sir,' said Pat ominously to the CO, his sense of justice still offended. Pat could be a raging bull of a man if he thought somebody was being treated unfairly. He had absolutely no fear of rank, and enormous moral courage.

'There'll be no need for that Pat,' said the CO mildly. 'Just have a yarn to Rob before you come knocking on my door.'

The rest of the lunch time conversation moved away from the events of the previous few weeks, and into the other goings-on at Murruwa, though Pat could not help shooting suspicious glances at the CO, who chose to ignore them. Private Sylvia Dunford's charge was due to be heard at 1330, so after lunch Rob made his way down to the Battalion Headquarters building, and was met there by Warrant Officer Peter Costigan, the RSM of 2 RTB.

'Come down the hall here Padre,' he said as Rob entered the building. 'I am going to hear the charge in this room. Come in and take a seat.'

Rob passed Sylvia in the hallway, she was sitting with the formidable Warrant Officer McIntosh, CSM of Charlie Company. It looked like he had been appointed as her defending officer. They certainly have not gone for the cuddly option there, thought Rob; though a more passionate advocate would have been hard to find.

As Rob entered the room he saw everything laid out as was customary on such occasions. The prosecuting officer was already in the room; the CSM of Alpha Company, Warrant Officer Anagnostopoulos.

'Hi Padre,' he said as Rob walked in. 'We shouldn't take too long today.'

'Is that a good thing or bad thing?' asked Rob.

'No idea sir,' said the CSM of Alpha Company, trying and failing to sound innocent. Rob eyed him suspiciously for a moment, before he was distracted by the arrival of the RSM, who promptly took his seat, and called for the accused to be brought in. Private Dunford marched in with her defending officer. The RSM read out the charge against her; that of being absent without leave.

'How do you plead?' he asked.

'Guilty, sir,' she replied.

The RSM looked at the papers in front of him for a moment before lifting his head and looking Sylvia in the eye.

'You're not going to go AWOL again are you?' he asked simply

'No sir.'

'Excellent, just the answer I was hoping for,' he said. Warrant Officer Costigan then stood up with all the paper work relating to the charge, walked over to a shredder, and quietly humming to himself, he unceremoniously fed in all of the documentation. He then turned around and resumed his seat, looking at the slightly stunned Private Dunford.

'Private Dunford, thank you for the moral courage you have shown,' said the RSM. 'You were put in a bloody difficult and dangerous position, and you did the only thing you could think of. You also took the earliest opportunity to tell others about serious criminal acts that were taking place. Myself and the other two Warrant-Officers here discussed your circumstances, and we agreed on two things. One is that we wouldn't have known what to do, but the second is that we would've wanted to do something similar, if we'd been in your shoes. I hope you're never faced with a choice like this again; but if you are, just call me, and I'll come and personally sort out the bastards responsible. Your posting has been altered at your request, and you will now work in the Charlie Company Q-store here at Murruwa. I'm sorry we had to go through this little charade. You are going to be on guard duty for a week, and you're to tell people that you were charged with being AWOL and appropriately punished, so it won't be screamingly obvious who dropped the perpetrators in the shit. What happened to that charge stays strictly in this room. Is that clear Private Dunford?'

'Yes sir.'

'I believe that you have a long and fruitful career ahead of you in the Army if you want it,' concluded the RSM.

When she had left, Warrant Officer Costigan turned to Rob, who was grinning widely.

'A nice balance of justice, mercy, and wisdom, Sarn't Major,' said Rob.

'That girl's got more balls than most males I know,' he said with conviction. 'And she's only eighteen! Given a couple of years I think she may be officer material. She's sure got a lot more officerly qualities than one of the dominos that fell after she gave the whole rotten pile a shove.'

'Indeed,' said Rob, and after shaking the RSM's hand, he left and went back to the Chaplaincy centre, where he assured Pat that Sylvia had not been unfairly dealt with, without revealing what had transpired when the charge had been heard.

'So what actually happened?' asked Pat.

'The RSM asked that nothing about what happened leave that room,' said Rob flatly.

A look of dawning comprehension crossed Pat's face, and he nodded in an understanding way.

'Well it looks like I won't be having an exciting conversation with the CO after all,' he said happily.

'Exciting for whom I wonder?' asked Alan slyly, immediately earning a scathing side-long glance from Pat.

That Sunday Anne again invited Rob to lunch at the Indian restaurant, after he had taken Chapel. Already the news media was full of stories of a scandal that had engulfed somebody whom they chose to describe as a senior army officer.

'I can't believe they described a Major as a senior Army officer,' she said contemptuously.

'Oh you know the media,' replied Rob. 'Their formula is celebrities, death, disaster, or deviance; and if they can somehow combine or accentuate different parts of the formula, so much the better.'

This extracted a laugh out of Anne, even though she was not at her most animated. She began to chew thoughtfully on some naan that she had just dipped in her Murgh Masala.

'I always thought I'd feel great if my ex ever got himself into a situation like this,' she said, 'but now that it's happened, I just feel sad. A little relieved as well, I guess, but mainly just sad.'

'Sad that the Rottweiler of consequences has bitten him on the backside?' said Rob.

'No, not really; more sad that he ever got himself into this situation. It doesn't surprise me though; not one bit.'

'The most scary people in the world, are those who no longer hear the voice of their own conscience,' said Rob, 'or those who perpetrate their evil with the burning conviction that they're in the right. With either kind of person there is no limit to what they'll do in the pursuit of their desires.'

The next day, Major Paul Veenenboer was found dead in his

apartment. Police believed that there were no suspicious circum-stances. For a short time after the news became common knowl-edge, Anne again was noticeably subdued. In the same way as she took no pleasure in the downfall of one who had caused her so much pain, Anne also felt no elation or satisfaction at his death. She just felt sad at the disregard of life and dignity that her ex-lover had had; for others, and ultimately for himself.

13

A troop of Royal Marines advanced carefully toward an apparently abandoned compound, in Sangin, Afghanistan. The robust form of now Colour Sergeant Jonathan Blakeney was second from the front. He and a fellow Royal Marine with a sniper rifle set up, and went down on one knee, while the rest of the patrol fanned out. Taff followed behind, unarmed and inexplicably wearing civilian clothes. 'Don't go in there mate, I don't like the look of it,' said Taff urgently, but try as he might, he could not make himself heard, and Johnno and the sniper entered the compound. However they did not get far; an explosion tore through the air, leaving only the shattered remains of humans where once whole men had stood.

'Johnno!' Taff called out, but as he reached out to intervene, the scene dissolved in a confusion of light, rocks and sand.

He then felt like he was free-falling, falling into oblivion, but soon seemed to land and the mental scene faded to an incongruously beautiful summers day, and people gathered round as what was left of Johnno was lowered into the ground in the solemnity of a military funeral. As the volleys fired in salute rang out, Taff turned to look at Johnno's wife and children; and saw their anguished faces staring

*back at him. He felt like a hot knife was being driven into his breast.
And then he screamed.*

*Reaching for the cross by his bed, he tried desperately to bring his
mind into the present, and his breathing under control. His normally
steady heart was thumping in his chest, and his pulse pounded deaf-
eningly in his ears as he flailed around, trying to find the reassuring
solidity of the cross. Slowly, very slowly, his terror and distress
subsided, but sleep did not return. He lay there for an hour or so before
deciding it would be better to fill his mind with something, rather than
try to get back to sleep with those memories lurking in the background, waiting for a chance to strike.*

*'Life's getting complicated enough without this as well,' Taff said, and
very grumpily rolled out of bed.*

A couple of weeks after the events surrounding Sylvia Dunford,
Anne sat enjoying the winter sun in her lounge room, jour-
naling about the tumultuous time she had just experienced.
Surprisingly, the tragedy of Paul's life and death, and her own
relationship with him, was not the main theme of her musings.
Instead an altogether more pleasant, though far from simple
matter was preoccupying her formidable mind; the matter of the
attraction she felt towards Chaplain Rob Llewellyn. It had been
lurking for a little while, in the background hum of life, but was
now bursting into unexpected colour.

Staring out the window, Anne watched a couple of birds flit-
ting around the small garden at the front of her town house,
apparently engaging in some kind of courtship behaviour. Their
twittering was punctuated at intervals by a frantic whir of wings,
as they darted to and fro among the bushes; and Anne felt as if
her mind was doing the same thing. At times she thought that
she should ignore her feelings, and just carry on a purely professional relationship; but now when even the sound of his voice
caused her a degree of excitement, she thought that could be an

exercise in futility. Lurking in the back of her mind was the observation that Rob was really one in a million. There were not many guys with his character and beliefs getting around who were currently single. However, Anne knew from experience that managing a relationship with another member of the military could be rather complicated. So how to proceed? As she mulled over this thought, the two birds seemed to reach the conclusion that they should abandon their chase and get down to business. As Anne watched them consummate their dance, she smiled to herself, and began to lay out a plan in her mind.

Rob was certainly a man she could respect, possessing a very alluring balance of courage and compassion; but it had been the latter that had well and truly melted her heart. He had seen her at her most vulnerable, and his response had been one of grace, discretion, and care, rather than judgement, condescension or contempt. This realisation comforted her deeply, reassuring the part of her that watched the character of males like a hawk. On the other hand, it was not easy to tell whether Rob in any way reciprocated her feelings. However, Anne Le Bon was not a person who ever wasted time wondering. Instead, she took action.

As Anne considered the options for where to go next, she eventually concluded that the logical step would be to invite Rob out on a kind of date by stealth, where she could get to know him a bit better without the intensity of being alone with him the whole time. Anne had shared lunch with Rob a couple of times, however on both those occasions she had declared a need to talk to him about struggles she was having. What she wanted now was to get him to open up about himself; to see the Rob behind the wall.

'How on earth am I going to get that to happen?' she said, once again staring out the window. Well I sure can't make him do it, she thought, he'll have to trust me first. Does he trust me?

Now there's a question! This took her back at her starting point; spending time with him was about the only way she could get him to trust her. Was it worth the time and effort if he just stayed behind the wall? Well, that was a risk she would have to take.

She knew Rob well enough to realise that if he felt pressured or isolated then he would be less likely to open up, so uncharacteristically Anne resolved to take an indirect approach. Rob likes most sports, she reasoned, time he did something a little different. With that thought in mind she decided to invite him to come fencing with her; and to her own mild surprise, Rob accepted willingly when she gave the invitation the following week.

'I think you'll like this,' she said. 'You ever tried it before?'

'Never. I've done boxing, karate and Kendo,' he said, stifling a yawn, 'but I've never done fencing.'

'Oh well, just take it easy, it's a bit more subtle than the other martial arts,' she explained, speaking from her own long experience in the sport. 'It's more about balance, economy of movement, and timing, than brute force. I'll pick you up tomorrow at five.'

'Sure, sounds like fun Ma'am,' said Rob, this not succeeding in his efforts to avoid yawning.

'You're looking pretty tired? Are you sure you're right to come?' she asked with a laugh.

'I'll be fine, I just haven't been sleeping to well lately,' he replied, and then the two parted. Anne would later wish she had pressed him as to the source of his fatigue.

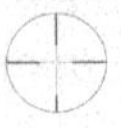

The following evening, Rob spent the early part of his first fencing lesson getting a grounding in the basics of the sport, and he discovered that the subtlety of movement required was tricky to master. He also found it very hard to keep his non-dominant hand out of the way, as everything else he had done in his life required the use of both hands; martial arts especially.

'It seems a shame to have it just hanging there,' he said to Jet Horikoshi, who was the main instructor. Jet regarded the ominous presence of Rob's other arm with a discernible degree of apprehension.

'One false move on my part, and you will try and remove my head!' said Jet, as he watched the balance and strength of the newcomer's movements.

'Sorry; old habits die hard.'

'Yes, but it'll benefit your mind to imprint new neural pathways,' said Jet mystically, and Rob did not feel inclined to disagree. He liked to try new things in any case, however frustrating they may be to start with.

In the meantime the Padre was attracting attention from others as well.

'Is he somebody from work?' asked a lady called Jen, nodding toward Rob as she was preparing to fence Anne. Jen was a stunning blonde, who worked as a physiotherapist.

'Yes, that's right,' Anne replied.

'He's really hot!' commented Jen appreciatively. 'Is he single?'

'Yes,' replied Anne. That's just what I need, she thought; take the guy out without it being an offical date and then every single woman I know is going to start hitting on him!

'About the most defiantly single male I've ever known,' added Anne, feeling a little bit guilty about this last remark, even though she had seen first hand how good Rob could be at deflecting female interest. The last thing she wanted was Jen chasing him.

'Oh! Is he gay?' Jen asked.

'No. I wondered that myself,' said Anne, 'but no; he's just single.'

'Well, you just make sure you introduce me later!' said Jen with a grin. 'A build like that is wasted on a single male.'

Anne was quietly glad that she had her mask on by the time Jen said that last phrase, because the look on her face was pure murder.

Eventually it came time in the evening for Rob to try free fencing, and Jet partnered him with Anne, though she had made sure she was hanging around when the time came. Graciously, Anne held herself back enough for it to be something other than a massacre, but nonetheless she defeated him with consummate ease. Time after time she would end up hitting him just over the heart with the tip of her foil, though with every hit she made, Anne took the time to explain to him some matter of technique so that he could continue to improve. What Rob could not see was the triumphant smile on her face every time she scored a point on him, as her mouth and eyes were hidden by the mask. Her intensely competitive nature could not help taking a degree of pleasure in being able to get the better of Rob in something.

After they finished for the evening, Anne succeeded in getting him out of the building without Jen noticing; and as they drove away Rob enthused about the sport. He seemed patently unconcerned about having been beaten by Anne, which was something she noted with great pleasure. Another piece in the puzzle, she thought delightedly as she turned it over in her mind; a male whose ego was not threatened by being bested by a woman!

Before they parted, arrangements were made for Anne to pick him up at the same time the following week, and as Rob sat at his piano that night, he meditated on the events of the evening again and again in his head. Even though he had a reputation amongst his friends in the UK for being a bit 'thick' when it came to women, he was beginning to think that Major Le Bon had more than a passing interest in his company.

Anne was actually proving to be pretty attractive in ways well beyond the physical, especially once you got past her tendency to try and keep people mentally off balance. He smiled to himself at that thought, his fingers playing a light, reflective melody. Thought provoking, fun, and refreshing were all words he was beginning to use of a woman he had not long ago heartily disliked. Further, what had once been a vague notion was now plain to him; he was falling in love with her, with an inexorable momentum. Romance and its attendant hazards were a place he had never wanted to go again, but now he was there he did not feel there was any way he could turn back. He just wished it was not happening now; there was an anniversary coming up that had been playing on his mind for about a month. Oh well, he thought with a sigh, since when had timing in anything been ideal?

Rob played on, as he considered that day, and the feelings he had for Anne that were now intersecting awkwardly with the other things on his mind. Well if I feel this way, he mused, I'd better tell her everything about me; not just the comfortable bits. With calculated resolution, and some nerves as a result, he decided he had better talk to her after the next time they went fencing. Time to give her another surprise, he thought with a smile, and then shifted into an up tempo tune in an effort to make the butterflies in his stomach fly somewhere else. However, Anne was to have several surprises next time they went fencing, and not all of them were to be pleasant.

When Anne arrived to pick Rob up the following week, the darkness in her car did not allow her to see his face very well, but she could tell he was a bit subdued. However her own preoccupation meant that she did no enquire as to the cause. At the venue, it looked like it was going to be a smaller group that evening, which Anne seemed to think was a good thing; though when she looked around she saw a person there who caused her to bite down on her bottom lip in concern.

'What's the matter?' asked Rob, picking up on her demeanour.

'Ahh, Lorenzo is here,' she said.

'Is that a bad thing?'

'Sometimes it is,' said Anne. 'He's a bit precious and full of himself, and he used to try and proposition me.'

'Really,' said Rob, in what Anne would later discover was a dangerously neutral and calm tone of voice.

'It's all right,' she said, not picking up on the ominous signs in Rob. 'I said if he didn't stop I'd kick him in the groin so hard his nuts would come out his ears.'

Rob grinned in a satisfied way and felt himself very attracted to Anne at that point; and he did not doubt that she would have had the capability of doing what she had threatened. Anne was a tall and very athletic woman, whereas Lorenzo was a shortish and lightly built individual; though Rob did not make the mistake of doubting the guy's fencing ability. Never underestimating an opponent, or potential opponent, was an ancient maxim of war.

After having been kitted out by Anne, Rob again experienced the feeling that he thought of as being like a turtle with tunnel vision. The view through the mask he found especially annoying, as he did not have the field of view that he liked to have. After warming up, Anne spent some time fencing with other people, whilst Rob was again taken aside again by Jet Horikoshi.

On the other side of the room, Lorenzo came over to where Anne was standing, as she took a break between bouts.

'Who's your friend?' he said in an oily, superior voice.

'A friend,' said Anne, attempting to hide her dislike as much as she could. Lorenzo had resented being constantly refused and finally threatened by her, but at least he had left her alone since.

'Really?' he said. 'I thought you never went near men.'

Anne ignored the remark; it seemed that some men lacked the social discernment to pick up on the fact that some women just were not interested in having a relationship with them, still less in having sex. Lorenzo was not the first she had met.

'He's a bit clumsy,' said Lorenzo, continuing resolutely in his social cluelessness.

'It's only his second time here,' said Anne.

Lorenzo looked like he was about to make some lewd remark, however a look from Anne communicated very clearly that her patience had completely expired, and even from within the bounds of his considerable conceit he was able to see that further conversation would be risky in the extreme.

After drilling Rob for an hour in the same basic techniques as he had learned the first week, Jet decided it was time for Rob to again try fencing with an opponent. To Anne's alarm, Lorenzo immediately volunteered for the task. You bastard, she thought. However she did not see the look in Rob's eyes, which were invisible behind the mask, as he recognised his antagonist. They were possessed of the same cold light he had had when he had faced down Anne's ex; however Rob had reconciled himself to the fact that he was going to lose this bout. He knew he had no hope of winning with his lack of experience.

After saluting the referee, and then each other, the two immediately clashed blades. However it was not long before Lorenzo's foil found its mark, and a point was awarded to him. Jet, who was refereeing, tried at this point to encourage Lorenzo to go a bit easier on Rob, and teach him some moves. However, the little man's ego was too awakened to consider anything other than trying to humiliate his opponent, and to harangue him for his clumsiness.

Rob was regretting his agreeing to the match going to fifteen points, for it was fairly soon seven-nil in his opponent's favour. However, a moment of over confidence cost Lorenzo, for Rob then executed a perfect parry-riposte, scoring a point, and drawing applause from some on-lookers. His ego stung, Lorenzo muttered so that only Rob could hear.

'So have you got between her legs yet?' said Lorenzo slyly. 'Or is she as frigid with you as she is with everyone else?'

It took a second or two before the full import of those words got through to Rob, however when they did a terrible resolve came over him, and when the bout began again, he launched a ferocious and unexpected attack.

It was a sight to behold, and it drew some remarks from the onlookers, for it possessed a lethal energy regardless of its lack of subtlety. Rob was using his sheer power and fitness to over-power the smaller man, and it took Lorenzo some time before he could recover the situation, however as he went to lunge at Rob, the powerful Welshman deflected Lorenzo's sword upwards, and then thrust his arm back as well, before quickly bringing an elbow into Lorenzo's face mask; a stunning blow that knocked the shorter man to the floor. The other fencers who had been idly watching the new-comer's skills were all stricken with amazement.

'Well, that was awesome,' said Jen, evidently much impressed, but Anne did not look so happy. Her ex had often threatened men on her behalf if they gave her a difficult time, he had wanted to keep that prerogative to himself. I'll be having words to to you about this, Anne resolved. The habit of violence is not something she wanted to see in a man, particularly a Chaplain.

'Oh, there's silly I am,' said Rob, taking his mask off and addressing Jet innocently. 'Old habits die hard.'

'Yes, it would seem so,' said Jet in a neutral, contemplative tone.

In the meantime, Rob went over, reached down and grabbed Lorenzo's hand. With a powerful and rather uncomfortable heave Rob brought his still dazed opponent upright, and then wrapped an arm around his shoulder.

'One more remark like that, and I may decide to permanently alter your facial geography,' said Rob quietly. 'I prefer to be friends with people, but I'm really good at the enemy thing as well, especially when people abuse women. Do we understand each other now boyo?'

Lorenzo moaned something in response. Some vengeful words had tried to form on his lips, however they retreated as he felt the strength of Rob's grip, and some primal sense of self-preservation told him that here was a man who never made threats, but who was remarkably faithful in carrying out his promises.

As Rob released the hapless Lorenzo, and helped him remove his mask, he glanced toward Anne briefly, before he then proceeded to help clean the abrasions around his opponent's face. Anne's face communicated nothing, which was not generally a good sign. The mask had been badly bent by the force of Rob's blow, and had been driven much further onto the face than it was ever designed to go. Rob then offered to continue the bout; however Lorenzo declined, and left soon afterwards.

The rest of the fencing class passed without incident. However, even without the provocation provided by Lorenzo, Rob continued to find it hard to restrain his left hand.

'I still think it seems a shame to have it just hanging there idle,' Rob complained again to Jet as they were fencing.

After they finished that bout, it was time to pack up the equipment and leave. As soon as Anne and Rob had sat down in her car to go home, she turned to him with a hard look in her eye.

'Did you iron out Lorenzo deliberately?' she asked in a voice that was a careful balance of severity and sarcasm. 'Or did your elbow swing like that by accident?'

Once his initial shock had worn off, he looked at Anne in some distress.

'Yes I did "iron him out" deliberately; he asked if I'd got between your legs,' he explained quietly, 'or whether you were just frigid, and after that ...'

'I can look after myself you know! I don't need you to attack every male who insults me! I wondered when I told you what he was like whether something like this would happen,' she said furiously. 'An officer and especially a Chaplain needs to be above that kind of thing; I don't need you to mark your territory by brutalising males who give me a hard time. Keep the brute force to the rugby field if you can help it! You showed more restraint with Paul!'

Rob's face became a picture of turmoil, though for once Anne was not really analysing what she was seeing. She was too preoccupied with her annoyance, and the nagging insecurity that came because of what Rob had done that night. Rob eventually recovered himself, and responded to Anne's challenge.

'I'm sorry for embarrassing you. I didn't mean to suggest that you're helpless or defenceless,' Rob said quietly. 'But don't think for one moment that I'll accept words like that from anyone. Now, if you'd please excuse me, I think I'd like to walk home.'

With that, he quickly got out of the vehicle and began to walk briskly across the car-park, before Anne could say another word. She sat back in her seat for a moment and closed her eyes; frustrated with Rob for walking away from an awkward situation, and frustrated with herself for having given him such a dressing down.

'I could've done that a little better I suppose,' she said aloud as she sat in the car. 'And Lorenzo has earned that and a lot more; it's just nobody's gone and done it before!'

However, by the time she opened her eyes again, Rob was nowhere to be seen. He probably broke into a run when he got out of the car-park, she thought. For a moment she considered getting out of the car and following him on foot, however she soon thought better of it; Rob would have moved too far too quickly, so she could not be sure of finding him in the streets. Instead Anne decided she would wait and then drive to his house.

'There's no way I'm going to let a spat ruin this friendship,' she said to herself as she drove off. Anne hoped that with a bit of exercise he would have calmed down enough to be able to talk things through. She was not going to think about the possibility that he might not have calmed down. As she drove, Anne tried to put herself in Rob's head for a moment, but all she could imagine was that Rob would be feeling some amalgam of stung pride, confusion, lurking sorrow, frustration and anger. Regret was probably there also; regret at his actions, and regret at ever having allowed this woman to get close to him inflict such pain.

Getting home and getting in front of his piano were probably now the only things on his mind, she reasoned. How well would he receive an interruption to that?

'Well, I guess I'm about to find out,' she said as pulled up outside his house. As she saw him come running up the foot-path, Anne got out of her car and walked toward his gate, intent on meeting him there, and coming inside if she could.

The expression on his face as he drew near was not exactly friendly; his posture was closed, and defensive as he slowed to a walk. As he looked at her, Rob did not seem capable of saying anything at all. He just stood there staring at her as she leant against his gate.

'Are you just going to just stand there looking at me like that, or can I come in and talk this over?' Anne asked tersely.

'Come in then,' he replied, without enthusiasm, and the two of them entered the house together. As they came into the lounge room, Anne immediately challenged him.

'Is that the way you always deal with awkward situations? By running away?' she demanded.

Anne almost instantly regretted having spoken those words. That wasn't the best way of getting him to trust you, said a small voice in her mind. Being a provocative person by nature sometimes meant that she spoke before she thought; and part of her was kicking herself for not having been more careful, because she could see that she had hurt him. It had taken such a long time to get Rob to open up that she did not want to cause him to close again by her own thoughtlessness.

'If you must know I got out of your car because I was angry and I didn't want to say things I'd regret,' he said. 'I didn't attack that guy without provocation. He wanted to humiliate both you and me.'

'There's a time and a place for force Rob,' she said as evenly as she could, not convinced he had seen her point.

'Is there now?' he challenged, and then he seemed to grow hard and cold.

'Yes there is!' she snapped in reply. 'I've seen combat, and people have died on my say so. I know a thing or two about it.'

'With respect, Ma'am,' said Rob in a slow, formal voice, 'I know a lot more about the use of force than you ever will.'

Anne did not know what to make of this challenge.

'Oh, come of it Rob! That's a pretty big call for an SSO to make, especially a Padre,' she said eyeing him sceptically. 'You might be good at shooting and martial arts but that isn't war-fighting!'

'Oh well,' said Rob in an oddly sad voice. 'I suppose now's as good a time as any.'

'As a good a time for what?' Anne asked impatiently.

Without answering her question, Rob then turned around and walked across his lounge room to a cupboard, that he then unlocked. Anne could see very little of what was inside, though her eyes were drawn to the incongruent sight of a stuffed toy sheep that had some kind of tag hanging around its neck. He took several items out of the cupboard before walking back toward her. He then threw them down on a table with a look of disgust on his face.

'What's this?' she asked. As she looked down she saw what seemed to be a military file of some sort, along with a few photos, and a green beret with a badge in the form of a globe surrounded by a laurel wreath.

'My dirty little secret, that is. I was actually going to tell you tonight because I trusted you. Now I'm just telling you cause I'm fed up; fed up with your patronising GSO crap,' he barked at her defiantly. 'That, Ma'am, is my personnel file and a few memories from when I was a Royal Marines Commando. I was a sniper during both tours I did to Iraq. Green slimers[1] like you sent people like me to do the dirty work. There are few people at Murruwa who can rival my combat experience, and you don't even come close!'

Anne stood rooted to the spot, staring at Rob stricken with amazement. There in a tidy file lay the missing jigsaw pieces she had been seeking.

'But you said you'd never been in the Army!'

---

1. "Green slime" is the nickname for Intelligence. Used more in Britain than Australia.

'Are you deaf?' he yelled. 'I said Marines! They're part of the Royal Navy, not the Army! Or don't you know that?'

'Oh, dear Lord, what have I done?' she muttered to herself.

'There are people in this world who are alive today because I know when not to use force,' he continued, addressing her as if she was a poorly performing recruit, 'and there was a kid of twelve or so in Iraq whose brains I blew out because he had a suicide vest on and more people would have died if I hadn't had the balls to pull the trigger. I live every day with that memory, but I had no choice. Don't you dare try to tell me that you know more about the use of force!'

Anne remained still, almost unable to move for the shock. So many things about Rob now made sense. No wonder he understood people like Evan Davies so well, she thought, as he looked at her with cold contempt.

'I'm sorry,' said Anne lamely, when she found words again. 'Why didn't you tell me this before?'

'Do you think I actually want people to know about my past?' he said. 'Do you think I want people to know that I've killed? Or that I've got a horror movie on instant replay in my mind? I wanted respect for my skills as a Chaplain, not some cheap notoriety from being a war-fighter! All people are going to want to know now is how many jihadis I've slotted!'

'But people do respect you as a Chaplain, Rob,' said Anne, her dark eyes looking at him with a mixture of concern and apprehension. 'Knowing you've been a war-fighter won't change that one bit.'

'Really? I'm not sure GSOs respect anything Chaplains do! Even when we're cleaning up the crap you lot produce,' said Rob harshly. 'Don't think I haven't heard the way you lot talk about chaplains! Sneering, superior pillocks the lot of you! I once heard that toss-pot Major Thomson saying that Padres had no place in the modern military ...'

'Don't you dare put me in the same category as Thomson!' she snapped back at him, her eyes wide with hurt, but Rob cut across her.

'He's lucky I didn't hospitalise him there and then! I still might if I get half a chance! Is he going to sit with people who're out of their mind with grief? Or are you? Chaplains are like the smelly garbage collectors of the Army, dealing with all the horrible personal stuff so high-flyers like you can get on with congratulating each other on how good you are. But I suppose it's not easy to get promoted when your work force is committing suicide on you, is it?'

Rob then picked up a photo he had taken out of the cupboard and held it up before her.

'Do you see this guy here? My mate Dizzy hung himself cause he got in the crap when he roughed up a recruit. We'd been back from ops for a month, and some git posts us to Lympstone to train nods[2], and who gets the blame for when it all goes arse up? Not the fucking idiot who insisted we go there!' Rob demanded, and Anne recoiled at his uncharacteristic obscenity. 'But if a Marine stuffs up and hits someone, or gets a bit carried away in the heat of battle, he'll go to gaol! And the stupid politicians who send us to these countries for no good reason, what happens to them? A nice pension, and never wanting for anything ever!'

And that explains his turmoil over Corporal De Blasio, she thought, as she looked at the photo of Rob with his arm around a smiling Royal Marine. Rob then turned around and picked up another photo, and stood there holding it with shaking hands.

'Or how about this fella? Dead because the *Intelligence* was wrong when he went into some manky village in Helmand! It was hard for me even seeing your Corps badge, remembering

---

2. Slang term for a Royal Marine Recruit; also noddy.

what had happened to him,' he growled in an accusing tone. Anne looked at the face of a big, dark-skinned Marine with twinkling eyes, as Rob momentarily lost his rage, and began to cry.

'My best mate he was,' he went on shakily, 'we went through Lympstone together, were snipers together, did two tours of Iraq together. Then some toss-pot gets his facts wrong and my best mate dies in the dirt like a dog!'

'I'm sorry ...'

'When I was recovering from being blown up,' he said through his tears, as he pointed at the scars on his face, 'I decided I was going lock up this part of my life and throw away the key. I wanted a future that didn't involve me being a killer! But I can tell you, ma'am, hardly a day goes by when I don't wish I'd stayed in the Marines and died in Afghan with Johnno! A year ago today I helped lower what was left of him into the ground! Do you know what's it like, sitting at your best mate's funeral? Do you know what it's like, looking his wife in the eye, wondering if I had been there whether I'd've seen something that would've saved his life? Or seeing his three kids, who were asking me why "Uncle Rob" wasn't with their dad, and saying he'd still be alive if I had been?'

'I'm so sorry,' said Anne softly.

'So am I!' he yelled. 'Sorry I ever came here! Sorry I ever joined the army! Take it all away with you! Read it! You'll learn all about me; and when you're finished, shred it! I never want to see it again!'

Rob said those last words with a dismissive contempt that Anne found distressing; more distressing than any of the personal attacks he had just made. She felt it was almost as if Rob was cutting himself as he angrily tried to cut himself off from what he had been. She picked up his file gently; even reverently, and held it close to her chest, subconsciously protecting it from Rob's anger and grief.

'Are you going to be okay, Rob?' she asked, as she looked at the now shaken man who was standing opposite her. Gone was his intensity; instead he looked somehow shrunken and diminished now that his anger had been expressed. But even in the aftermath of the storm the lightning was still visible, in the look of blended fury and grief that he gave her.

'I'll be fine ma'am,' he said with an effort, 'just go.'

'But Rob ..'

'Please! Just leave me alone!' he said commandingly, and then he turned his back on her. Anne looked at him for a moment, hovering on the verge of speech; but then she turned and left. There were tears in her eyes as she went.

Anne drove home in a heavy fog of emotion, and then she ran inside her town-house and flung herself down on her bed and wept in a way that she had not done since the aftermath of breaking up with Paul. She wept because of feeling like she had hurt a man who had been a real comfort to her in hard times. She wept because of Rob's turmoil and hurtful words, and the fact that he had not told her about his past until she had inadvertently backed him into a corner. She wept because she felt like the misunderstandings of one evening had destroyed a friendship that she was even daring to hope might become much more than that. However, when her emotions were spent, Anne did not allow herself to indulge any tendency toward self-pity, nor did she nurse any resentment. Instead, she got up from her bed, and went over to the personnel file she had taken from Rob's house. Then Anne started to read its contents with the practised eye of an intelligence officer, and an other-worldly sense of calm. Not long afterwards she took two diaries from a shelf in her study, and then read them in parallel to Rob's file, taking notes as she did so, exclaiming several times as she came across fragments of information that helped fill in the blanks of what she knew about the former Royal Marine. After about an hour she looked up from a growing pile of paper and stared at the wall, deep in thought.

'Yeah, I bet that's what you're going to try; but I won't let you do it!' she said aloud, and before another ten minutes were past, she had formed her plan of action.

14

———

When Rob arrived at work the next morning, it was on the back of an unpleasant night with little sleep. Alan saw his greyed features as he walked in and immediately asked what was troubling him, however Rob made no reply. Instead he asked the other Padres to gather in the central area of the Chaplaincy centre; and for the first time he spoke to them in some detail about his past. They all listened in silence as he described his previous life, the bomb blast that had led to his coming home early from Iraq, and his decision to leave the Royal Marines and train for the ministry. He omitted the death of his best friend, and the angry interaction he had had with Major Le Bon. He figured they would find out about the latter soon enough. The former was his business, and his alone. On one level the other Chaplains were not surprised at his military background, but on another they were stunned that he had kept it to himself for so long. However, their surprise at Rob for not wanting to reveal his past was nothing compared to what he had to say next.

'I also have to tell you gents,' said Rob formally and seriously, 'that I'm going to contact my denomination this morning, and ask them to withdraw my endorsement for military chaplaincy. I feel like now my past is out and known that it'll be too much of a distraction for people; and I don't think I want to spend the rest of my time in the Army being better known for having been a killer than being an effective Chaplain.'

At this Alan's eyes widened, and Steve Schwarz's narrowed; but it was Pat who spoke for them all.

'Like fucking hell you will!' he said; however the rest of the words that were forming a disorderly queue in his mouth were thwarted by the sound of the door of the Chaplaincy Centre being opened, and Anne Le Bon walking in. She sought out Rob's face, and addressed him firmly and directly.

'Chaplain Llewellyn,' she said, 'the CO wants to speak with you immediately. Get your hat and come now.'

It was now Rob's turn to be wide-eyed.

'Yes ma'am,' he said, but the look on his face was thunderous.

Rob got up, grabbed his hat and followed Anne out the door, while the others were too stunned to say a word.

'What's going on ma'am?' Rob demanded as they started to walk down hill toward the Headquarters building.

'As I said, the CO wants to talk to you,' she remarked, 'it doesn't get much simpler than that.'

'Any idea what about?' he asked.

'What do you think?' said Anne tartly.

'If this about our argument last night ...' he began, but Anne cut him off.

'Chill the heck out will you!' said Anne firmly. 'Just do what you're told and follow my lead. You can thank me later.'

With that remark the two of them entered HQ, and Anne knocked on the CO's door.

'Anne! Padre!' said the CO warmly, 'Come on in. Take a seat.'

This was not what Rob had been expecting. He had been thinking that he was in some sort of trouble, so to be invited to relax took him completely by surprise. He and Anne duly took a seat and waited for what was coming next.

'Now Rob,' the CO continued, 'Major Le Bon tells me that there's been a bit of a slip-up and that your service with the Royal Marines hasn't been recognised by the Army. Very modest of you not to blow your own trumpet.'

'Sir?' asked Rob in confusion, however the toe of Anne's boot impacted painfully on his ankle at that moment, and he was unable to do anything but look at her incredulously.

'As I said earlier sir, Rob showed me his record of service last night,' Anne explained with a dead-pan face, 'I was amazed that something so important had been overlooked, so he handed it over to me, and Captain Jenkins is working on the admin to fix the problem as we speak.'

The CO looked down at a sheet of paper on his desk. Rob made as if to talk, but another impact of the toe of Anne's boot stopped him short.

'Major Le Bon gave me a summary of your record of service, and I'm very impressed,' the CO began. 'Two tours of Iraq, a tour of Northern Ireland, a humanitarian rescue mission in the Congo, a qualified sniper and Mountain Leader, and a Queen's medal for marksmanship. To top it all off, you were rated very highly as an instructor. Impressive CV mate! Makes me wish you had decided to go to infantry instead!'

'Thanks sir,' said Rob in amazement.

'But while you're posted here I want to get as much out of you as possible,' the CO continued, 'so I'm going to ask Pat if he'd be willing to have you do remedial marksmanship coaching from time to time; when your other duties allow of course.'

'I'm not sure Pat's going to like that much,' said Rob, and lifted his boot just in time to avoid Anne kicking him again.

'You let me worry about what Pat will think; and I know

you're a target shooter, so you obviously don't think you're to holy to touch a rifle,' said the CO with a slight bite in his voice, 'and I'd also like you to do up a presentation for the officers on the ethics of killing. I'd like to hear how you worked those things out. Anne tells me you're quite the philosopher, so it should be right up your alley.'

'But sir,' said Rob, in an almost resigned tone of voice, and this time he was not successful in avoiding Anne's boot.

'Good, I'm glad we understand each other, mate,' concluded the CO, who rose from behind his desk and extended his hand to Rob. 'Now I suggest you two go off and see if you can understand each other as well. Thanks for taking the time to come down.'

With those cryptic words they were dismissed, so Rob and Anne walked out of the CO's office, and left the Headquarters building. For a brief time Rob walked in sullen silence, moving toward the Chapel instead of his office. Probably wants to play the piano, Anne surmised.

'What on earth did he mean "thanks for taking the time", he ordered me to do that!' Rob growled as they neared the Chapel, 'what happened in there was the biggest load of bollocks I've heard in a very long time.'

'Don't think of it as bollocks,' said Anne calmly. 'Think of it as necessary theatre.'

'What?' he squawked. 'What was necessary about it?'

'Right buddy!' said Anne, pulling Rob aside and marching him into the foyer of the Chapel.

'I have a couple of things to say to you,' she went on as she released him and he turned to face her. 'Firstly, it was necessary theatre because I needed to make sure you being a Royal Marine was recognised without you getting in the crap for not disclosing your past. It'll come out when you apply for a higher security clearance anyway! Look Rob, I'm very sorry for what happened last night; and I can tell you're still pissed off. I'm sorry I hurt you, and I'm sorry for the way I spoke to you, I'm sorry for the sorrow I dredged up; but really! You have to make yourself a bit easier to help! It's no good getting your knickers in a twist and feeling all misunderstood if you don't give people a chance to understand you in the first place!'

Rob did not answer her, but his face showed that Anne's words had found their mark.

'Do you know I was in Iraq when you shot that kid?' she demanded.

'I had no idea,' he said quietly. 'But it could've been anyone, it's not as if I was the only Marine who had to shoot a child.'

'It was during a mixed suicide bomber and VBIED[1] attack wasn't it?' said Anne, and Rob eyes widened in surprise. 'I spent my whole deployment briefing on the IED incidents that were occurring in country; I know which ones hit the Royal Marines!

'I remember when you got blown up too; the IED didn't detonate correctly, I figured it out when I read your service record. I knew a sniper pair had been wounded that day.'

'I never knew that,' Rob said, almost to himself, 'I always thought it was just a small bomb.'

'You have to stop running and hiding,' said Anne. 'I know you've got scars! Even before you showed me that file, I knew! I could see it in your eyes! Nobody could go through what you've gone through and come out unscathed, but hiding things away and pretending like they've never happened won't do you any good! You wouldn't tell anyone else to do that, so why do it yourself? Here, of all places, you're going to find people who understand!

'I don't mean to play the victim here, but if you think it'll be hard if people know your past, you just try being a woman in the

---

1. Vehicle borne IED.

army!' she continued, now trembling with emotion herself. 'When I slept around a bit all my achievements were put down to me being a slut, and when I left Paul after him being such a bastard they said I'd gone gay or frigid! At least you're going to get some cred for your history instead of people obsessing about what you do with your genitals!'

Anne's words hit like a slap in the face for Rob, and for a moment he looked at her sadly, as if all his follies had struck him in one moment.

'You're right. I'm sorry, I've been a fool,' he said eventually. He then brought himself to attention and looked her in the eye. 'I'm sorry for the way I spoke to you last night too. I was hurt and I attacked you, and I said some things that were untrue and unkind. That was very wrong. Please forgive me.'

Anne was slightly taken aback at hearing such a frank admission of fault, but then she smiled warmly at him.

'Stand easy, Padre, I forgive you. Don't think you have to be perfect,' she said. 'I respect you as you are. You hit out 'cos you've been hurting for a long time and you've never admitted it, not because you hated me.'

Rob then looked at her a little unsteadily, seemingly undone by her act of forgiveness and being known by he. Of all the things she had done to try and get past Rob's guard, none had been so effective. No longer did the dour armour of inscrutability cover him like a shield; instead raw, wounded, and unmasked he stood, revealed in unalloyed vulnerability. Rob wavered for a moment, and then fell to his knees weeping, unable to contain the emotion he felt. Anne took him gently by the arm, and ushered him into the Protestant wing of the Chapel, so that this moment of fraught indignity would be kept safe from passing eyes.

When his emotions subsided, Rob spent some time

breathing deeply to steady himself, as Anne sat opposite him, smiling kindly.

'I'm sorry, I'm so sorry,' he said, as she sat with an arm around him.

'What for? For being human?' she replied a little testily. 'You saw me in tears! Why shouldn't I do the same for you? You need to preach grace, peace, and forgiveness to yourself as well, you numpty!'

'You're right; thanks for being a real friend,' he said weakly.

'Pleasure.'

'You set up that whole thing with the CO didn't you?' Rob asked.

'You bet I did!' said Anne. 'I guessed you were going to try and leave Army, so I thought I'd outflank you. I don't want to lose you; all the grief you've endured means you really know how to help people. I've never seen anyone better than you at knowing what to say and what not to say when someone is hurting. The way you were able to just sit there when Amanda Ainsley was screaming I knew you'd been through hell, and had somehow managed to come out the other side. You've got a lot to offer the Army, but you need to listen to your own advice as well.'

'Of all the impossible, cantankerous, plain flat-out amazing women,' Rob said, 'you are the best!'

'That's quite a compliment! I may actually be blushing!' she said through laughter, and Rob smiled sheepishly. 'Do you realise, genius, that most of the staff of Charlie Company think you were British Special Forces? A few years of theological training won't remove the marks of ten years; you're not the only warfighter who's become a padre, you nong.'

'And another thing,' she went on with a mischievous smile, 'I want you to come fencing again next week.'

'Really?' he asked nervously.

'Yes, really. Jen called last night and she said everyone wants to buy you a beer for flattening Lorenzo, and so do I,' she said. 'You were only trying to be a friend, and I thanked you by chewing you out. I'm sorry. It's just that Paul used to be big on threatening guys who gave me a hard time; he wanted to reserve that for himself. I guess I wanted to make sure you weren't the same.'

'I know you can look after yourself ma'am, but I just saw red,' he explained, 'so I decided to stun him. If I'd done the job properly he'd have been in hospital; or worse. I'm sorry to have reminded you of your ex.'

'Well, now I actually know what you were, I can understand why you did it. And on the anniversary of burying your best mate! Anybody would be a bit touchy!' Anne replied. 'But when you make yourself such a man of mystery it can be a bit hard to figure out why you do the things you do. Though don't make a habit of belting people when they piss you off, it's not a good look.'

'Sorry.'

'That's fine Rob,' she said with a sigh. 'Will you forgive me for backing you into a corner?'

'I forgive you,' he said with utter sincerity. 'It'd make a mockery of everything I believe if I didn't.'

'Thanks. You're an amazing guy, you know,' said Anne. 'Can I pray for you Padre? I'm allowed to do that aren't I?'

'Yes, of course ma'am,' he said, mildly surprised at her offer, but grateful nonetheless. Anne then laid a hand on his shoulder and prayed for peace in the midst of his turmoil.

When she had finished, Anne gave him a hard, searching look.

'Rob, have you ever been assessed to see whether you have PTSD?' she asked.

'Yes ma'am, I have. But no, I wasn't diagnosed with that,' Rob said in reply. 'My uncle sent me to a psych when I'd been in Australia a year. He was a Combat Engineer in Vietnam, and could see I was struggling. But I wasn't diagnosed with it.

'It's not as if it's compulsory or anything!' he said, bristling slightly, as she looked at him doubtfully.

'No, not PTSD,' he continued mildly. 'But she did say I was wrestling with the compounded effects of grief. Grief upon grief; not just my best friend, but others as well. The sadness will always be there I think, ebbing and flowing.'

'I think the best healer of souls is one who has known the wounds,' she said reassuringly, and squeezed his hand. Anne then rose and smiled at him, her beautiful, dark eyes twinkling, before turning and walking out of the chapel. Rob sat there, and watched her go with a very different cyclone of emotions inside him.

Rob's return to the Chaplaincy centre produced a chorus of objections and argument before he stilled the clamour and explained his change of heart to them, including Major Le Bon's role in it all. Pat promptly told him to "bugger off home" for the rest of the day, as he looked very drained, and to everyone's surprise, he complied. By contrast, that evening Rob was surprised at how relaxed he felt as he lay in bed, given the events of the previous twenty-four hours. Reaching for the cross that he often used to ground himself in reality when he had bad dreams about the past, Rob ran his fingers over its metal surface, and described the texture to himself in his mind, at the same time wondering at God's sense of timing. Rob had been able to reveal his past, and remain friends with Anne despite the conflict of the previous evening, and his own clumsy attempts at protecting himself. He then rolled over and looked at the photo of him and his best mate Johnno, that sat beside his bed. Rob picked it up and read the words on the back of the frame for the first time in a couple of years:

To Taff, you Welsh git! No matter what you do in the future, don't ever forget what you've been. God bless. Your mate, Johnno.

'Wish I'd taken your advice to start with,' he said, talking to the picture, and he then he turned his head back and drifted off to sleep; a sleep tinged with sorrow that was yet blessed for having been shared.

As it happened, there was not much in the way of fall-out about the revelations about Rob's past, as it made sense to most people. In fact many treated the news as if it were not new at all; and Rob actually felt a great sense of release at no longer having that part of his life fenced off. He also found that his relationship with Anne became a lot more relaxed, and the next night of fencing proved to be quite entertaining. Evidently he had become something of a folk hero amongst the other participants, as Lorenzo was heartily disliked by all the females and most of the males in the club. So a brief visit was made to a local licensed cafe after they had finished, so the others could make good their promise to buy Rob a beer.

Jen, whose idea it had been to have an evening out to honour Rob's aggressive action, spent some time trying to communicate her interest in him, though to Anne's amusement Rob seemed completely unaware to Jen's efforts to get his attention. Polite, kind, and entirely oblivious was how he came across.

'Jen seemed pretty keen on you,' Anne ventured carefully as she drove him home later on. There was the merest trace of insecurity in her voice as she made the observation.

'Really?' said Rob, completely taken aback.

'Yes really! I'd've thought you'd have picked up on the way she smiled, and the fluttering eyelashes,' she said, enumerating the more obvious signs, amazed that someone as perceptive as Rob could have missed those cues.

He then grinned as if amused with old memories.

'What's going through that mind of yours?' asked Anne.

'My mates in the Royal Marines thought I should be sent back to the manufacturer for repairs when it came to women,' he admitted.

'I find that very hard to believe!' Anne said emphatically. 'You don't strike me as someone with low emotional intelligence!'

'When it comes to that sort of thing, I'm dumb,' Rob said flatly. 'The fellas in recce troop presented me with a toy sheep and suspected fault tag after one evening out.'

'Why? What'd you do?' asked Anne, remembering the sight of the sheep in Rob's cupboard.

'More what I didn't do. A nurse who was drinking with us one afternoon asked me if I wanted to go lingerie shopping with her and a friend.'

'And what did you say?' asked Anne, her eyes wide.

'Well, I told her that I was sorry, I didn't find clothes shopping that interesting.'

'No way!' she said, amazed.

'Yes way. The lads were too stunned to say anything at the time, though I think one of them actually dropped a glass in shock,' remarked Rob. 'So the next day they presented me with a toy sheep and the fault tag. I'll give you the email addresses of a couple of witnesses if you don't believe me!'

'A sheep?'

'Same joke as made of New Zealanders; the English call the Welsh sheep-shaggers,' Rob explained with a groan. 'It came in a box marked "Welsh sex toy". They thought I needed some practice with something more familiar.'

'And you kept it?' she asked, laughing.

'Yeh! They're my mates!' said Rob. This she could understand; within the military, mockery of that kind could often be the most sincere expression of friendship.

For a moment Anne was unsure what to make of this frank and embarrassing admission, but then it struck her that he was being entirely open, which was a change in itself. The guarded, careful speech was gone, instead Rob was letting her see right inside him. Now that's more like it, she thought. When they arrived at his house, the two of them stood talking outside for an age before Anne drove away, glowing in a satisfied way about how far their relationship had come. Her desire to get to know him better had been fulfilled, though her initial plan had gone completely awry. If no plan survives first contact with the enemy, she pondered, what happens to plans with a man with whom she had fallen in love?

When the revelations about Rob's past became widely known, questions were inevitably asked about the kinds of things he had done as a sniper; though thankfully these enquiries were not of the nature that just had a shallow interest in killing. People were more interested in the philosophical and ethical underpinnings of what he had done, and what influence it had all had on what he was doing now. It was Jar-Jar who spoke for many when he began asking Rob questions one evening in the mess when Rob was eating with a gang of Platoon Commanders.

'Hey Padre, not trying to be rude or anything,' Jar-Jar said, as they sat together, 'but did you leave the Royal Marines because you became a Christian, or were you one all along?'

'I have been a Christian for as long as I can remember,' Rob replied. 'And I'd wanted to be in the military all my life before joining the marines.'

'Why was that?'

'Well I think it was because I wanted to get out, see the world, and do things, and not just get stuck in a rut, or end up on unemployment benefits.'

'What'd your folks think?' asked Evan Davies.

Rob shook his head.

'They didn't like it at all,' he answered. 'Mam wanted me to be a music teacher; both my parents were teachers, see. Her brother had been in the Australian Army in the Vietnam War and came back scarred, so she was afraid. But I could never be a school teacher.'

'Nor could I,' Tash Driscoll said firmly, 'I'd kill the little shits.'

'Yeah, pretty much,' Rob agreed.

'How did you reconcile what you were doing as a sniper with being a Christian?' Jar-Jar asked. 'The two don't seem to go together very easily to me.'

'I knew somebody was going to ask this! I can see why you would, but I think that there are a few common misconceptions people have about the Bible and war,' replied Rob. 'For one thing, when it says in the Ten Commandments to not kill, it would have been better to translate that as murder; the Hebrew word refers to the taking of innocent life, or unlawful killing. Fair play now, if somebody says to me that they can't kill because the thought horrifies them, then they'll have my support, because it *is* horrifying, and anybody who thinks it's not is a bit of a worry if you ask me. But if someone says it's always wrong to kill, then I disagree very strongly.'

'How about when Jesus talks about turning the other cheek?' Jar-Jar asked.

'When Jesus said that, I understand him to be referring to personal vengeance, not right across the board for all circumstances at all times; and people forget that Jesus drove people out of the temple with a whip made of cords,' replied Rob. 'And the highest compliment Jesus paid anyone was to a centurion; not a pacifist by any means. He said that he had never seen faith like it. Also, the apostle Peter baptised a centurion in the book of Acts. In neither case were they told to stop being soldiers. The only advice given to soldiers in the New Testament is to be content with their pay rather than extorting money or treating people with undue harshness. But again, they're never told to stop being soldiers; also, in the book of Romans, the Apostle Paul says that the state wields the sword to be a terror to wrong-doers. I'd still kill if I had to, and I don't doubt I could, but I don't really want to be in the position again where it's my main job.'

'So how did that go when you were a sniper?' continued Jar-Jar. 'I mean, when you had to slot people and stuff. I don't mean to be a cock, but I am interested in how you work through this, because I don't think many people in Army have really thought about this sort of thing.'

'Well, I've had to kill for sure, though I took no great pleasure in it. I just focussed on getting the job done,' Rob admitted. 'To me it's a regrettable to have to go to war at all; but I think if you're not willing to go to war, far worse things can result.'

'Is that kind of a "just war theory" approach?' asked Tash.

'Within reason, I guess; though I must say I don't really look for a just war,' said Rob. 'I tried more to act justly in the middle of it all, whatever the cloudy motivations of the politicians.'

'But what about sniping?' put in Scott Morgan.

'I saw it as a life-saver,' he said carefully. 'If I'd not killed, then more death and destruction would have come to my mates and civilians too. A sniper team can create havoc and stop the escalation of a contact, or they can shorten it once it has started by taking out an enemy commander, machine gun, or the like.'

'Did you ever have doubts about anything you did?' asked Jar-Jar.

Rob considered this for a moment, struggling to express his thoughts.

'Yes I did; war can be a very doubtful thing,' he conceded, 'but one of the most important ways my faith works with warfare is when I have to deal with moral ambiguity. In any walk of life, I think you have to have a way of dealing either with the mistakes you've made, or the things that have happened that you hate; or even worse, the things that you do that are actually wrong.'

Evan Davies nodded emphatically at this point.

'Yeah, my time in Afghanistan felt like an eight-month tour of moral ambiguity,' he remarked, which drew noises of agreement.

'The biggest struggle I've had is when friends have died and I've not been there,' Rob continued. 'But when I was still a sniper, I'd sometimes look at the death and destruction I'd dealt out after I took shots, or once when I saw a car with a guy who charged a check point and there was no bomb, and struggle with the whole mindless destruction of what'd just happened. Most of all I've had a hard time with the whole Iraq war, and I've kept on struggling, because I think all we've done is swap one evil for another.'

'You got that right Padre,' said Evan. 'I mean what the hell were we thinking going in there like that? We've just fucked it for everyone.'

'I don't think I can disagree with you, though I wish I could,' said Rob. 'But I think we can only know and control so much before we go in to these countries. It's very hard to sort truth from lies if you're only some poor Marine or Digger. All we had to go on is what the media said.'

'Or the website of some crack-smoking conspiracy theorist,' said Tash glumly.

'I like conspiracy theories, I collect them!' interjected Jar-Jar, who was promptly hit by a flying bread-roll.

'So what made you stop being a Royal Marine when you did?' asked Tash. 'Why'd you go and do something else? Did you have a crisis of conscience or something?'

'I had no crisis of conscience,' said Rob sadly. 'I didn't think that being a sniper was wrong in and of itself; but I didn't want to kill people anymore. I wanted to bring life and hope instead of death. And being a pastor was the best means I could think of. God sort of shoved me into it really; it's a bit hard to explain.'

Jar-Jar looked at him in wonder at that point.

'I wish I had your faith sometimes Padre,' he said, 'but I just can't believe in God after what I've seen done in the name of religion.'

'Really?' replied Rob. 'I'm similar actually. I can't believe in humanism knowing what has been done in the name of scientific atheism by Communists; or by the Nazis who worshipped human power. I can't believe in humanity at all, because whatever the name in which people commit acts of barbarity, it's still people doing it. I guess you'd call me an a-humanist.'

'No faith in human nature then?' asked Jar-Jar.

'None whatsoever,' said Rob, 'just a deep cynicism about people's motivations; including my own.'

'Well, we agree on that much,' Jar-Jar replied, smiling grimly. 'I picked that up in the way you deal with recruits; but you still have compassion on people who fail. How does that work?'

'Well that's a longer story,' said Rob.

'And?' said the others in unison, evidently wanting Rob to continue; which he did, and at length.

Later that week, Alan Deakin was alone in his office just after lunch when a knock came at his door, interrupting a rare moment of relaxation.

'Come in,' he said, reluctantly putting down the latest issue of Model Railway Journal. Alan then looked up and saw Anne Le Bon standing in the room, his mild resentment at being disturbed evaporating when he saw her.

'Do you mind if I close the door?' she asked, at which Alan just shook his head, so she shut it, and sat down.

'To what do I owe this pleasure Anne?' he asked with a smile. 'Rob's out on a call at the moment, so if it's Charlie Company stuff, I suggest you wait till he's back.'

'No, it's ...,' Anne hesitated, itself a very unusual thing, 'well, it's personal; and it's not something I feel like I can talk to Rob about. Not yet anyway.'

Alan regarded her closely, not quite sure what was coming next.

'Is it something he's done?' he asked.

'Yes, I suppose it is in a way,' was her reply, but she said no more, still seemingly struggling to express herself.

Vagueness of this sort was entirely uncharacteristic of Anne, thought Alan, she normally said exactly what she was thinking without hesitation.

'Well you may need to be more specific here,' he said, 'I'm not picking up what you're putting down.'

'Alan; you and Jo have been like a second set of parents to

me, and I am so thankful for that,' she said, 'you've been such a blessing. And I just don't know what to say, this is so unexpected, and I am not absolutely sure what I'm thinking here. Well no, I'm sure all right, just not sure what to make of it or what to do with it.'

Slowly Alan's mental machinery clanked away, trying to discern the reason behind Anne's demeanour; such rambling by her could mean few things, and in this case it probably could only mean one. He lent forward and said, 'My dear lady, are you trying to tell me that you've fallen in love with him?'

At this she nodded, and to Alan's lasting surprise she started to cry.

'You know what I went through last time,' she said, blowing her nose on a tissue from a box that Alan had immediately proffered, 'but Rob's so different. I made him angry the other night, and it nearly broke my heart.'

At this she lifted her head again, and spoke more like the normal Anne.

'He's hard-working, and kind,' she declared, 'and perceptive.'

By now Alan was grinning broadly, and started to laugh, until Anne picked up the box of tissues and threw it at him.

'Ow!' he exclaimed, rubbing his nose where the edge of the box had hit him.

'Why are you laughing?' Anne demanded in between sniffles.

'Forgive my mirth,' he replied, 'but I just find it ironic. For so long we were worried about whether you two would get on, and now this!'

'Nobody's more surprised than me!'.

For a moment Alan looked at her thoughtfully.

'How much do you actually know about Rob?' he asked.

'A lot more now, he's opened up a fair bit since I found out about him being a Royal Marine. We also had lunch a couple of times after church on Sundays when I wanted to talk about personal stuff, but he didn't give away anything really. I hope now his past is out in the open he'll keep being transparent,' she replied. Anne then explained her side of the horrible interaction she and Rob had had that night after fencing. This went some way to explain to Alan why Rob had come into work the next day with the intention of leaving the army entirely.

'The dark horse! He's kept the Sunday lunch thing quiet!' said Alan, amazed. 'But then again he always keeps things quiet. He never blows his own trumpet, and he seems to go into anaphylaxis when people pay him attention.'

'Yep, that's him,' agreed Anne.

'One thing though,' he continued, 'if you're wanting to grow closer to him, make sure he also opens up to you; I mean really opens up. We've only just found out about one of the most important parts of his life. That speaks to me of someone who doesn't like people getting close to him, besides every other sign I've had!'

'Do you think he's trying to hide anything more?'

Alan thought for a moment, before shaking his head. 'I don't think he'd lie, but you can't ignore the fact that he didn't share something so fundamental until he was backed into a corner. Who knows what other hurts are lurking there.'

Anne nodded in response, 'And I have no real idea what has happened to him when it comes to relationships either.'

'Have you tried to probe him on that front?' asked Alan.

'Not really no; I was trying not to push too hard in case I scared him off,' she admitted somewhat bashfully.

'Are you feeling quite well?' Alan replied incredulously, 'I thought you were a big believer in scaring men?'

'That's usually very easy,' said Anne contemptuously, 'but

with Rob, no. Though it did take a while for him to drop his defences at all; he just tries to ask people questions about themselves so he doesn't get attention.'

'But I am guessing the barriers are still there?'

'I'm not sure, but I wish we'd found out about him being a Royal Marine a lot sooner,' she said.

'Yes, he caught on so quickly that it was screaming at us that he had a military past,' Alan reflected, 'but it was just such a relief that he didn't really need to be brought up to speed that we didn't bother with asking him.'

'Did Rob tell you that he face-ripped a recruit?' asked Anne.

'What do you think?' said Alan. 'Of course he didn't!'

'He didn't tell me either, but when I asked F-Bomb about it, he said it was the most freaky thing he'd ever seen,' she went on, 'he just flicked a switch and went off like a grenade.'

Alan shook his head for a moment, as he continued to mull over what he knew of Rob in his mind.

'Well there are lots of questions here,' he said eventually, 'I just hope he's willing to give you the answers. One question for you though: how's a relationship going to work for you where your career is going at the moment? I can't imagine that your going to be stuck with Major as your ceiling rank.'

'Alan, I'm not so wedded to this career that I can't think beyond it,' she said with conviction, 'and from everything I've seen of him, I think that if there's any male out there who has the humility to be with a woman who's going up the chain, then it's Rob.'

Anne and Alan continued their talk for another five minutes or so before she left, resolved in to find out about the remaining unknowns in the former Royal Marine's life. Alan for his part was both happy and concerned. He was happy that Anne had feelings for Rob, especially because they had a shared faith and Rob seemed to be a fundamentally decent fellow. However Alan was concerned as well; especially that when push came to shove, Rob may not be able to handle the intrusion into his hermetically sealed private world that romantic attachment would bring. Alan drove home to his wife that afternoon deep in thought, and resolved to pray about this new development.

15

The next day was somewhat dull, with the kind of sneaky cold that is characteristic of the winters in Murruwa. The Chaplaincy centre hummed with activity for a while, however both Pat and Steve were soon called away. Pat walked out muttering curses at the on-call phone that he had inherited from Steve earlier in the week. However, neither was Steve off the hook; a Bravo company recruit had got a rather nasty 'Dear John' text, and was in need of counsel. So the day reeled and rolled at a mad-cap pace, and it was not until later that Rob and Alan were able to draw breath, having both been called out on various tasks themselves. Neither Pat or Steve had yet returned.

Of all the times when he felt the death of his best friend the most, it was now. Just having someone to talk to about the feelings he had for Anne would have lifted the burden of the turmoil he felt; just to have Johnno laughing at the turmoil would have been enough to at least help him see things more clearly. But wishing could never bring people back from the dead. He had the beginnings of friendships with some people, but without a doubt his best friend was now Major Le Bon, and that made things decidedly awkward.

The rest of the day did not ease his sense of preoccupation, so he decided to go for a bit of a walk around the base to clear his head. Besides, he mused, walking around and loitering with intent was part of a Chaplain's job description, so he could at least look like he was doing something purposeful. Nonetheless, Rob was in a bit of a daze, and initially he stood near the sign for the Chaplaincy Centre, simply lost in his thoughts.

As he set off down the hill, Rob started to reason through how he was going to approach this conversation with Anne. He tossed various options back and forth, mentally evaluating each in turn. Initially he was leaning toward inviting her out for a fancy dinner; but then he wondered whether they should just have dinner at his place and not have the bother of going out. That was it, he thought, just tell her to come around, casual and comfortable, because he wanted to talk to her about some things. What he did not want was the possibility of Anne sending him off balance by wearing clothes that caused his head to whiz any more than it was already. Brilliant, he thought, ask her to come around in comfortable clothes and be prepared for a long conversation. He could declare his feelings, and Anne could see he was being transparent; after that, the ball was in her court.

As he walked, Rob was once again glad of a wind in his face, even though it had just started to rain. It was a very Welsh day for Australia, even more so than the day of the Rugby game, with light rain drifting gently in waves, and the surrounding hills obscured by the misty air. For a moment Rob stopped walking and closed his eyes, taking in big breaths in an effort to savour the moment and calm his mind; however a familiar voice interrupted his reverie.

'Fuck I hate this weather Padre,' said F-Bomb. 'But I guess a Pom like you'd love it! Fuck! I just wish it make up its bloody mind and just rain! But no! Instead we've got this shitty light stuff. Now Darwin rain, Padre, that's proper rain!'

Rob grinned and shook his head.

'I'm sure you're right,' said Rob.

'Say Padre; it's true what people are saying; that you used to be a Royal Marine and stuff?' asked F-Bomb as they set off walking down hill together.

'Yes it is.'

'How come you never said so sooner? We all thought you were something military, but you kept going on about that shit about being a target shooter!'

'I guess I never wanted to think about it again,' Rob admitted. 'Bit stupid I know. But it *is* true about me being a target shooter.'

'But Padre, that's like me saying I'm fucking awesome; it might be true but it doesn't even come close to the reality,' said F-Bomb, this time drawing laughter.

'I thought people knowing I was a sniper would be a distraction actually; that they wouldn't take my ministry seriously.'

'Fucking bullshit mate; it means people will take you much more seriously now; particularly if you're pissed off, armed, and have a clear line of sight!' said F-Bomb, with an evil grin. 'I knew as soon as you ripped Nancarrow that you'd been military, but I also knew you were a decent padre because you really helped the poor fucking crackers who needed it.'

'One of the dumbest things I ever did I think; but ... oh I don't know,' said Rob sadly.

'Who gives a fuck Padre? We all have our fucktard moments,' said F-Bomb kindly. 'On that note, I'll be taking a platoon through their first live fire serial soon. Do you wan't to come down to the range and help out?'

'Sure; I'm not on call again for a couple of weeks. Just give me the date and I'll lock it in.'

'Shit hot! Now no holding yourself back either! I want to see awesome!'

'You got it,' replied Rob, and turning away from the direction in which F-Bomb was travelling, walked down toward the high-wire confidence course.

Later that afternoon, Rob was sitting at his desk doing some quiet reading when the thought occurred to him that he should talk to Alan about his feelings for Anne; in the absence of any of his old friends, Alan was about the only person he thought he could confide in about his attraction for the OC of Charlie Company. Rob tried to talk himself out of it, however his growing anxiety gradually ate through his desire to keep his feelings for Anne private. So he rose, walked across the central area, and knocked at Alan's door.

Looking up from his work, gave him a strange, warped smile.

'How can I help you my friend?'

'Do you mind if I have a chat in private?' asked Rob.

'Not at all! Come in, close the door. I was wanting to have a talk to you in any case,' said Alan. 'What seems to be your main immediate problem?'

'I don't really know where to start actually,' said Rob, looking down at his feet for a moment, as if gathering his thoughts, before lifting his head again and sighing. 'The thing is Alan, I have been feeling a bit strange lately; well for a while now really.'

'Stranger than usual?' asked Alan, smiling playfully, but Rob did not rise to the bait; he seemed too intent on saying what was on his mind.

Finally he looked Alan square in the eye and asked, 'What do you do when you feel like you're falling in love with a superior officer?'

Alan looked at him for a moment, his eyes wide. Rob looked concerned 'What's the matter Alan, you look like a recruit on his first night in this place?'

Alan still stared blankly at him, before eventually finding his voice again.

'Are you telling me that you're falling in love with Anne Le Bon?'

Rob nodded, and Alan let out a low whistle.

'I know this is awkward!' Rob went on. 'If it's going to cause trouble I'll do what I can to stop my feelings growing.'

'You will do no such thing,' said Alan, his eyes flashing, with a note of anger in his voice that Rob had never heard before. 'Now you listen to me! C.S. Lewis said that the only place outside of heaven where you could be safe from the dangers of love is hell. Burying your feelings for her will only cause confusion and pain for you both, and I won't stand for it. Anne Le Bon is as dear to my wife Jo and I as if she were our own daughter. You must be open with her! You must tell her straight up what you feel, and not hide behind the mask of professional formality that you so often wear.

'You can't insulate and isolate yourself from pain in this world. Pain freely felt can be used by God to produce good things in you; pain avoided and buried will warp and destroy. Anne greatly respects you professionally, but also likes you as a person; you will do her and yourself no harm by expressing your feelings.'

Rob was silent for a while as he took in Alan's tirade; the sudden urgency of his words had caught Rob completely off-guard.

'I'm sorry,' he said finally, 'you're completely right. I've been hiding for a long time and it's become a habit. But she's been slowly melting me, ... it feels a bit strange actually.'

'I rather think that it's just you coming back to life,' said

Alan. Rob simply nodded again by way of answer, and sat there wondering how much Alan had already guessed about him.

'Thanks for talking to me, my friend, but really the only option you have is to tell her straight what you feel,' said Alan, breaking the silence, 'she doesn't like mucking about in any case.'

'Yeh, that much I've figured out,' said Rob, and then he left Alan's office an even more preoccupied man.

After Rob had left his office, Alan closed his eyes in silent prayer for a moment, then shook his head in wonder.

'I'm not sure I have enough personalities to deal with this!' he said, and then tried with some difficulty to get his mind back into the work he had been doing.

'You there Rob?', asked Alan later that afternoon, when they had both returned to their respective work tasks.

'Yes Alan.'

'For some reason a call came to my desk phone from 25 Platoon, Charlie Company. Can you take it please? I'm at periscope depth, and losing pressure in the main ballast tank,' he remarked.

'What's it about do you know?'

'Not sure exactly, though if they've just been given their phones it could be a romantic problem.'

'Oh, fantastic, I'll go down right now,' replied Rob, and then walked off toward Charlie Company.

When Rob arrived at 25 Platoon he was met by the recruit's section commander, Corporal Justine Martin, who explained to him that it indeed was something to do with the guy's love life. She had already spoken to Recruit Damien Thomas, but the young man had been adamant he wanted to see a Padre as well, and Rob found him waiting in the brew room.

'Hello-eh,' Rob said in a relaxed manner, lapsing into South Wales slang in his greeting, 'Damien Thomas is it?'

'Yeah, hi Sir,' he managed.

'Corporal Martin said you were having a love life issue,' said Rob.

'Yeah; I got dumped by my fiancé.'

'How'd she do that now?' said Rob, groaning inwardly, whilst gamely trying to sound sympathetic. When he had first arrived Pat and the others had warned him about recruits who were in the depths of despair after breaking up with their partner of two weeks; and he had met his fair share of them in his time so far at Murruwa. It could be very hard to show any sympathy under such circumstances.

'She did it by fucking text,' Damien said moodily, 'and now she's blocked my calls. She didn't have the guts to speak to me in person.'

'How long had you been going out?' asked Rob.

'Three years, since we were both 21; we got engaged two months before I came here,' he explained. 'Before I went away she was talking about how it was me and her forever, and that she'd wait for me no matter what I was doing; training, exercises, deployment — anything! Then she goes and texts me to say she's found someone else. Mum said she dropped the ring back at her place; that's something I guess. But why, Padre? Did she mean what she said? Why would she just say shit like that and not mean it?'

Rob exhaled and shook his head. So it was obviously not a two-week special this recruit was thinking about. It was a relationship that had had some serious time and effort spent on it.

'I can't answer your questions, but that's a big investment you've lost,' said Rob kindly, 'I'm sorry to hear it.'

'You reckon you are, Padre.'

Rob looked at Damien with sympathy, absorbed by memories of his own.

'I've been in your shoes,' he said quietly, 'some years ago now.'

'Why did that happen to you?' asked the Recruit, with a note of amazement.

'I'm not immune to it you know!' said Rob with slight exasperation. 'I find it hard to understand sometimes, even now years later; she dumped me by letter, even though we were living in the same town. But there was a lot more to it, other people interfering and stuff like that, and that made it really hard to take. She said she didn't want to see me again, and it was no use trying to talk it over. We'd been a couple for two years, not engaged yet mind; and that was all she could manage. It's more than a text though, I'll give you that.'

'It hurts Padre.'

'Yeh, I bet it does,' said Rob.

'Corporal Martin told me it was better to find out now than after we were married,' Damien managed to say, 'and then she said my ex was a fucking treacherous bitch who wasn't worth my time.'

Rob smiled slowly, remembering advice given to him by his own friends, 'A very wise woman is that Corporal Martin,' he said at last.

The two talked for a while longer, both reflecting on the sense of loss they had felt in the sudden death of their relationships; and the sun had set by the time they had finished their conversation. Of all the interactions with staff and recruits Rob had had about failed relationships, none had reminded him so much of his own; and with his feelings for

Anne having now grown to such an extent, past hurts were even more to the fore.

Rob toyed with going straight home, but after the memories that had been dredged up, he thought that he would go up to the Chapel again; to pray, play music, and sing. He had come to love that space, its deep silence, and all that it represented in the life of Murruwa. So with more painful memories having been reawakened, and his nerves about his next step with Anne, Rob was drawn to it in a deep and elemental way.

It did not feel as if Janet had broken up with him over a decade ago. Rob was a person who gave himself completely to anything he felt passionate about, and the failure of this relationship had so marked him that he had never wanted to go near women again. Being a Royal Marine had also provided plenty of time away, so it would have been hard to develop another romance in any case; but for Rob something inside him had died the day when Janet had sent him that wretched letter, with its words that not only rejected their relationship, but him as a person as well. Perhaps part of me did not die, Rob thought sadly, as he walked at an uncharacteristically slow pace; perhaps I tried to kill it.

'So many decisions in the bitterness of my heart,' he mused aloud.

After having taken that familiar path from Charlie Company to the Chapel, Rob walked in through the foyer intent on playing the piano, practically oblivious to all else around him. As he sat down he closed his eyes and breathed deeply for about a minute, willing the complexity of emotion inside him to work its way out through his fingers and onto the keyboard. When he began to play it was a soft and sad tune that he had composed himself some time ago, and that he knew by heart. The sound drifted through the chapel, leaving a hush upon the place; and when he finished it seemed that the notes still lingered in the air.

After a moment's pause Rob started playing an improvised tune, and he steadily increased his tempo. As ever, his fingers searched for notes that would express what was inside his heart, so that his feelings could distill and drive the music like thermal currents beneath the wings of a soaring bird. Eventually he slowed his playing again, and he felt drawn to sing a ballad of love lost, but in English this time, rather than Welsh. Despite all the Welsh songs he knew that were about romantic angst, this song was the one he most wanted to sing, as it seemed to captured the particular regret and lost joy he felt better than any other song he knew. Through his voice and the piano, Rob drew a picture of living sound that filled the space with an echo of the pain that he had once felt; and it seemed, felt still. The turmoil of his growing feelings for Anne, and the fear and uncertainty that they caused were a ground note beneath it all. When he had finished, he bowed his head, momentarily spent, and his tears fell like rain on the keyboard; but yet he was also relieved to have given voice to what he felt. All this time spent protecting myself and the only result was sorrow unresolved, he thought regretfully, but today is a new day! However, as all these emotions coursed through him, Rob heard the sound of a woman's voice speaking behind him.

'Who was she?' it asked.

Rob turned in surprise, and he saw Major Le Bon sitting in a seat, her dark eyes gazing at him searchingly. He was momentarily annoyed at having discovered his private reverie had not been private at all, and also wondering how she knew he was singing about a woman. Rob was not quite sure what to say by way of reply. Well this might change the idea of having dinner with her, he thought wryly.

'A girlfriend; my only real girlfriend in fact,' he said, quite ashamed of his admission.

'She really hurt you,' said Anne with a degree of certainty, as she rose and then moved to sit down beside him.

'Oh, she hurt me all right,' he said grimly.

'I'm sorry if I'm intruding,' she said, 'I was here enjoying the silence when you came in, and I thought I'd stay for the show. I'll leave if you want.'

'That's fine, please stay,' he said, marvelling slightly at hearing himself say it, 'talking to a Recruit this evening brought back the memories, so I thought I'd better go and work the feelings out a bit.'

'How long ago did this happen?' she asked.

'About twelve years I think,' he said, counting for a moment. 'Yes, twelve years.'

'Seriously?' said Anne. 'Have you had a relationship since?'

'Not one; I've never even tried,' said Rob. 'Quite the opposite in fact. A bit silly I know.'

'Not silly at all! Pain drives decisions, and sometimes those decisions have a valid reason at the time,' said Anne, looking hard at him again. 'I made some pretty desperate resolutions when I broke up with Paul, and I haven't had a serious relationship since it happened.'

Rob digested her words for a moment. She was doing for him what he often did for others; helping them feel normal. Somehow hearing her say that made him feel less isolated and strange, and more like an ordinary human being.

'Ma'am, do you remember saying that if I needed somebody to talk to about things, you'd be happy to be that person?' he asked, hardly daring to believe she might actually hear his story.

'Of course I do, and I meant it!'

'Well now would be one of those times, see.'

'Okay, I'm listening.'

Rob then began the tale, that he had told to no one in its entirety, not even to Johnno and his other mates in the Marines; those friends who had been closest to him at the time when the events had occurred.

'Janet and I met at church in Taunton when I was fairly new to 40 Commando. We got on really well, and we both ended up in one of the music teams. We started going out not long afterwards. Things were going fine for a while, but eventually a few problems emerged. The difference in our backgrounds was one,' Rob said. 'Her parents attended the church too, and they started to show disapproval, their little girl going out with a common Marine and all. But it was one of the Pastors who really tipped it over the edge. He started criticising me for not being of good enough leadership materiel to go out with a girl of her "gifting".'

At this Anne's eyes widened in surprise.

'Are you serious? How could he say something like that?' she asked incredulously. 'I'm a pretty critical person and I haven't even begun to think that!'

A dire look came across Rob's face, shot through with injured pride.

'It all started when I said I wouldn't sign a form saying I'd submit to his authority when we went on a ministry retreat. What that form really meant was that we had to do whatever he said, no matter what. I told him I'd keep my own mind, and search the Bible for myself to see if the things he said were true. I didn't trust him; he cared more about controlling people than pastoring them. For him maturity and having leadership potential meant being a clone.'

'That church sounds like a cult!' exclaimed Anne.

'Oh, it was heading that way for sure; now that I'm older and wiser I see it,' he said smiling ruefully. 'But I was young and full of dreams and ideals, and so was she. But this guy decided that because I wouldn't submit to him without question, I wasn't good leadership material. So he and her parents used that to drive a wedge between us, and she ended the relationship with a letter. Then she told the elders of the church some personal stuff I'd shared with her; struggles and doubts I'd had, and they tried to use it against me. I've never felt so betrayed. I'm just glad I was strong enough in my own faith to fight them off.'

'Did they kick you out of the church?'

'I left before they could; if the elders hadn't been a bit scared of me then they would have tried to do more,' he explained. 'They were used to pushing civilians around, not a Marine who'd fight back. I may have also told that pastor that if I ever saw him again I'd punch his teeth out the other side of his neck.'

'You threatened him?'

'No; I made a promise!'

'Tell me something surprises me!' Anne quipped, and Rob smiled in response.

'Did you see her again?' she asked.

'To my surprise, I did. She'd said she didn't want to see me again, so I made no effort to find her,' Rob said. 'But one day, Janet saw me on the street, and came up to me. Thankfully I wasn't alone at the time. She tried to talk to me, but I told her to save her words, because I thought she was without courage or honour; and that her church had perverted the gospel, which was far more serious.'

'Was she trying to make amends do you think?' asked Anne.

'Perhaps she was, because she seemed very hurt when I cut her off and then cut her down,' Rob said sadly, 'but I was so angry; to dump me then tell people who wanted power over me all the struggles I had within myself. It took me a long time before I forgave her, but I began to realise how deeply wrong it was to hold a grudge like that; and how harmful. It's like poison in the soul.'

'And you swore off relationships because of what she'd done to you?' she said.

'Yes I did,' admitted Rob, 'I never again wanted to let a woman know me well enough to hurt me, and from that time on I seldom looked at the opposite sex with any interest. From then on I just threw myself into being a Marine like it was the only thing in the world. My best mate Johnno said I was the most Corps-pissed[1] bootneck[2] in 40 Commando. Ever since then whenever I feel threatened I tend to hide myself in busyness, or I use politeness as a kind of fog to conceal my feelings.'

'Well this explains a lot about you, and the way you've acted over the past few months!' said Anne. 'But I have to ask, did everything that happened affect your faith? I struggled for a long time after the break-up with Paul.'

'I suppose it did for a while, but I ended up going back to Wales on weekends when I could, to a church that actually believed in grace, not in some stupid slick image,' said Rob.

'Are you still committed to being single?' asked Anne with a smile. The question pierced him like a spear. Rob paused and looked hard at her for a moment; and then he shook his head, aware that his heart was beating much more quickly than normal.

'Not really, no,' said Rob, with evident effort.

'Have you fallen for anybody since then?' she asked, and the point of the spear drove in a little more deeply.

'Up till now I've never given myself the chance. I've always been too busy and distant from people,' he conceded, forcing himself to be open; but at the same time he could not shake the habit of deflecting a personal question. 'After a long time keeping your guard up it can be quite hard to drop it.'

---

1. In love with the Royal Marines.
2. Slang term for a Royal Marine.

'You're not doing too badly at the moment,' said Anne, her dark eyes twinkling, and the atmosphere in the air between them seemed to crackle with unseen energy.

'It helps when you trust someone,' said Rob, looking at her carefully. 'How do you go with trust after everything you went through?'

'I have my moments,' said Anne smiling broadly now, 'but I guess I realise that you have to know a person well before you get too closely entangled with them.'

Rob nodded in agreement and then caught himself; he knew in his heart that she had guessed the feelings he had for her. I *have* to tell her now, he thought, but Anne spoke before he could re-muster his thoughts.

'Up till now you said? Does that mean you *have* fallen for somebody?' she asked, using one of her imperious stares, though she was still smiling as she did so.

'Yes it does ma'am,' he admitted, feeling very small and vulnerable for one who was capable of such great courage. He then looked at her with teary eyes and said, 'I've fallen for you.'

With those words the two of them stared intently at one another; and just as Rob was beginning to question the wisdom of making his feelings known, Anne took him by the hand, and Rob looked over at her smiling face. For a moment they just sat there; but then some tender gravity drew them inexorably together, and before Rob knew what was happening his lips and Anne's met, and with a delicate passion they kissed. When eventually they drew apart he looked up, and saw her dark eyes looking at him hungrily.

'I've fallen for you too Rob,' she said, a little breathlessly, 'I thought you might've guessed by now!'

Tears flowed down Rob's cheeks again, so Anne took his face in her hands, running her fingers down the scars, and then kissed the saline paths the tears had made. Then they sat and talked to each other in flowing torrents; not as Major and Chaplain, but as lovers who had known the scars of violence, and the injustice of the world; and the pain of their own follies.

'You know, I faced all of the stuff in Iraq without flinching at all, but it was in romance I've always struggled the most,' said Rob. 'It all comes down to fear really. When I have a weapon in my hands, even though there are lots of other things going on; things that might kill me even, I still have my training and experience to give me some illusion of control.'

Rob then paused and shook his head. As things became more personal, his accent became a little more pronounced.

'But with romance I am at the mercy of another; and after what happened with Janet I just decided it would be better if I shut myself off,' he confessed. 'The problem is that I think it became a habit that slowly reached into the rest of my life as well. So when things happened in Iraq, I found it hard to say what was on my mind; and I just bottled it up and said very little. Then when Johnno got killed ....'

Again he paused, searching for words for what he wanted to say next, as Anne sat listening intently to his story. It took Rob a little while to talk, as he wrestled gamely with blended grief and memory.

'I kind of collapsed really; but Uncle Gareth had been a Combat Engineer in Vietnam, and knew I was in trouble,' said Rob sadly. 'Though he got me help so I could live again, I guess I knew that the scars would remain, but I also learned I could use my scars to help others. I learned again what it meant that weakness could be strength. But the big thing I've missed is just plain old friendship; really since I left the Marines, but since Johnno died I've felt it the most. He was my last strong link to a time when I had a tight gang of mates.'

'But when we had lunch together alone after church; the day after the first Rugby game, when you said that I could talk to you if I needed someone to confide in, and you made me promise and everything,' he said, shaking his head in wonder, 'that nearly undid me, that did.'

'Pleasure; I've always liked interfering with people's equilibrium,' said Anne cheekily. Rob was caught by her smile, and it was a moment before he was able to resume his line of thinking.

'You invited me to be vulnerable! I can't tell you how much that means to me. I realised then how long it had been since I'd been vulnerable to anyone; or even had a real friend I could talk to. And when you forgave my bitter words the other day, that broke me, in all my pride; you made me remember that to admit vulnerability requires a grasp of the truth and the willingness to live by it. I preached grace but never practised it with myself! But vulnerability is not weakness, it's an act of courage in a world that values seeming over substance.'

'You really should be teaching philosophy!' she said, still digesting his last couple of sentences, but Rob continued to speak in a mighty flow, like a dam that had been breached.

'I joined up when I was seventeen,' he said, switching to a more historical rather than philosophical train of thought. 'It was a bit of a disappointment for my family, to say nothing of me getting kicked out of school for beating up a teacher.'

'Beating up a teacher!' exclaimed Anne.

'Yep, the sleaze tried to sexually assault my little sister,' he explained. 'So I thought I'd return the favour by hitting on him in a different way.'

'I'm seeing a pattern here,' said Anne drily.

However Rob ignored her smart remark and ploughed on with his life story.

'I always wanted to do something outdoors and active, to really test myself, but after that happened, one thing led to another and I joined the Royal Marines when I was seventeen. When I enlisted, the main operation was Northern Ireland; but then the world started going sour again, and then Iraq and Afghanistan. I never did a tour of Afghan though, I left before 40 Commando went.'

'How'd you find Theological College after ten years as a Royal Marine?' Anne asked.

'Well, I enjoyed the study, and some of the people were great; but most of their lives had never really been touched by hardship,' Rob explained, 'I think a lot of them found me a bit grim actually.'

'Can't think why,' said Anne smiling at him innocently, and then Rob started to laugh; for joy and relief, and at the absurdity of his own insecurities.

'You know that's the first time I've ever heard you laugh properly?'

'Really?'

'Yes, really!' she said. 'It seemed to me sometimes that you were afraid of laughing in case people saw too far inside you.'

At that remark, Rob looked at her in surprise, and tears welled in his eyes. Anne then grasped his hand.

'I'm sorry, I just don't know when the shut-up sometimes!'

'That's okay, I think you're right,' said Rob. 'Thanks for being pushy, feisty, and everything else you are. I'm grateful for it!'

'You're welcome! I don't really know how to be anything else these days,' Anne confessed resignedly. 'One thing though, now that we're an item, if you call me ma'am when it's just us two, I'm going to slap you. My name is Anne, and I want to hear you say it.'

'And you think I'm violent!'

'I thought you were thankful for me being pushy?' she challenged, and Rob laughed again. 'Go on now! Call me Anne! I dare you!'

'I love you Anne,' he said seriously, and she beamed at him.

'Much better!' she replied, and leant over and kissed him again.

As they left the Chapel they paused in the foyer. The light of a full moon was shining through the Rising Sun badge that was formed in the stained glass over the entrance, bathing the foyer area in a complex silver and gold glow.

'Good night *cariad*,' said Rob softly, as they stood there holding hands.

'*Cariad*? What's that mean?' she asked.

'It's Welsh for "love"; or it can be used for "darling" as well,' he explained. 'I haven't called anyone that for years. Hope you don't mind!'

'Mind? I love it!' Anne exclaimed, grabbing him by the collar and pulling him close. 'Words like that could make me do some very rash things!'

Rob dropped his head slightly, with a rather giddy smile on his face, and they kissed again, before walking together up to where his car was parked. There they parted, and Rob went home the happiest he had ever been in his life.

16

The following day Rob arrived at work early, and the first thing he did was to speak urgently but briefly with Alan, and the two emerged from Alan's office grinning broadly. Pat and Rob then left for a meeting with the CO of 2 RTB, whilst Alan and Steve left for character training at the Chapel. Soon afterwards Anne, Rob, and Pat, were sitting in the CO's office. Pat wasn't quite sure why Anne was there, but Rob had explained that Anne wanted a meeting with him and the CO, so he had agreed to come.

'Anne tells me that she wants to have a talk about how Padre Llewellyn is employed within the battalion,' said the CO to Pat.

'Why's that?' asked Pat, looking wary and confused.

'I can't have Padre Llewellyn as the Chaplain for Charlie Company any longer,' she explained.

'What the bloody hell has he done?' said Pat, clearly thinking his worst fears were about to be realised.

'It's nothing bad,' she said looking at Rob with a gleam in her eye, 'he and I are now romantically involved, and it's not appropriate for him to keep working so closely with me in Charlie Company. So I ask that from next week he be allocated elsewhere, and that one of the other Padres be assigned to Charlie

Company. He can use the rest of this week for handover/takeover.'

Pat looked at Rob, blankly. 'Well I'll be fucked,' he said eventually, shaking his head in disbelief.

'Not you mate, you're a Catholic Priest,' commented the CO with a grin. 'But in time it may apply to others in this room.'

Pat ignored the remark from the CO, and looked at Rob and Anne despairingly, 'I'm absolutely stoked for you two, but no more bloody surprises please. I've had enough for the moment,' he said, before adding, 'I'll allocate Rob to Alpha Company with a fellow Rugby tragic, and Alan can come over to Charlie.'

The CO at this point started to chuckle, which then grew into full-blown laughter.

'Sean O'Donnell'll be ecstatic,' he said eventually. 'Though I don't think making him even more ecstatic is a great plan!'

He then turned to Rob and Anne and said, 'I hope things work out well for you both. But we've got a Mixed Dining-In this Friday; I wonder if I could get you Rob to wear mess dress with the decorations you earned in the Royal Marines, and Anne to wear civvies, and that you come as a couple. That should really mess with some heads around here. We could do with cheering up after some of the shit that's gone down this year.'

So it was that Rob was allocated to Alpha Company, whilst Alan would change over to Charlie. OC of Alpha Company, Major Sean O'Donnell, greeted this news with the boundless delight that had been anticipated by the CO, though in reality his delight in anything he liked was boundless.

'You and Anne being an item just blows my mind,' he enthused as Rob sat in his office, 'that's the best news I've had since whenever the hell it was the Wallabies last won the Bledisloe Cup!'

'I'd appreciate it if you kept it under your hat until the mixed dining in on Friday night though sir; we want to give people a surprise.'

'No wuckers[1] mate,' he said, 'I can't wait to see their faces, I'll have a camera and microphone ready to record people's reactions. The Padre has thawed the Ice-Queen! Yeah!'

'I think actually that she may have been the one who thawed me,' Rob admitted.

'Whoah! French temptress melts Padre's heart? That's wilder than the wildest thing in a bag full of wild things! So when are you selling the movie rights to this romance? It's got it all!' said Sean, who then began trying to sound like a voice-over from a movie trailer, 'Steely eyed ex-sniper Chaplain is awoken to love by charming Intelligence Corps Major. Did she use duct-tape and cable ties, or was this an affair of the mind?'

'There is a lot of mind in it Sir, but also heart. No duct-tape though!'

Rob was trying to maintain composure whilst being torn between embarrassment, and helpless laughter. But Sean O'Donnell's enthusiasm remained unbridled.

'Okay, no duct tape; I'll take the cable ties as a given; but from what I've heard about Royal Marines, that's fairly typical. Wow! It's Fifty Shades of holy fuck, it really is!' he said, 'But you guys wouldn't have done it yet would you? Won't your balls drop off or something if you do it before you get married?'

'No,' said Rob weakly, under the onslaught of Major O'Donnell. The fact that he was being teased so mercilessly in such a ribald fashion was a good sign. It meant people liked him. The Royal Marines had not been any different.

'Well, it's going be to awesome working with you mate, and the reason why you are coming to work with me is even more awesome,' Sean said, 'Anne's a top chick and I hope you guys

---

1.   Short for no 'wucking forries". Spoonerise the words and you'll get the idea.

end up really happy with each other. Though I have to ask the question, does she really have hairy armpits?'

'I have no idea; I've never even seen her armpits,' Rob replied, a look of confusion on his face.

'Wow,' came Sean's wide-eyed reply, evidently impressed that Rob's knowledge of Anne's body did not even extend to her armpits, 'I guess you never know what'll happen when you see a woman's armpits; it might even lead to pole-dancing! But you two are pretty fit, so you should be all over that one!'

Rob collapsed with laughter again, which Sean found impressive.

'Dude, I have not seen you laugh so much ever!' he said, 'Did she blow a different personality into when you kissed? Please tell me you have kissed!'

'Yes, and yes I think,' Rob replied.

'What? Do you mean you think she kissed you, or you think she blew a different personality into you? Mate, if you can't remember if a woman as hot as Anne Le Bon has kissed you then you have problems that are way above my pay grade.'

'We did kiss, and I think she may have blown the frost off my personality.'

'That's so beautiful! But don't get too deep on me, otherwise I'll cry,' said Sean, the slightly manic grin still in place, 'I'm a very emotional man you know.'

Their conversation eventually moved onto more business-like issues, which mainly centred on the new recruits who would be arriving at Alpha Company in a fortnight. Rob emerged from Sean's office reeling slightly. Talking to Major O'Donnell was like conversing with a person who was having a prolonged but benign manic episode. Behind the boundless enthusiasm was an almost perfect extrovert who delighted in any challenge put in front of him. There was nothing feigned about Sean at all, though for some that could be the really scary part of dealing with him.

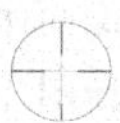

The mad rhythm of Murruwa stopped for no-one, not even for people in love, and so it proved for Rob for the rest of that week. A cursory glance at his diary would have revealed a fairly packed schedule, though in between times he would catch himself grinning for no particular reason.

Of all the other Chaplains, Steve Schwarz was the only one unaware of Rob's relationship with Anne, but he had noticed a clear change in Padre Llewellyn. Rob had just left the Chaplaincy centre uttering a great peel of laughter at some remark Pat had made, whilst Steve and Alan had been in conversation.

'It seems like our Welsh mate's learning to lighten up a bit,' said Steve to Alan, a note of suspicion in his voice. Any change in a person's behaviour tended to spark his interest, but then again he had spent many years looking at patterns in people's behaviour, and certain features tended to stand out after a while.

'Yes indeed, I think a ray of sunshine may have broken in,' replied Alan, 'though I will grant you that up till now his personality has been as dark and brooding as the land from which he came.'

'So what's happened?'

'No idea,' replied Alan with utter untruthfulness.

'You're a hopeless liar you know!' warned Steve. 'When you try, you look as guilty as a room full of Collingwood supporters.'

'I daresay all will become plain,' said Alan cryptically, 'but I think that having people know his past has helped him be more at ease with the present.'

As that Friday evening came around Rob found himself getting more and more nervous. He had a natural, and highly trained aversion to attracting attention. He had scored very highly on camouflage and concealment during his selection course for being a sniper in the Royal Marines; but not only that, he had a reputation amongst his fellow Marines for being able to fade into the background. As he dressed he remembered with blended sadness and amusement, the evening he had worn a hot pink suit in an English Pub and was hardly noticed. This was helped of course by the fact that the other costumes worn by Reconnaissance troop had been even more outlandish, including Johnno wearing a camel costume, and the Troop Sergeant sporting a rather racy leather mini-skirt with fish-net stockings. However tonight he would be bound to attract attention; not because of himself, but because of the woman he had with him. It was their first public outing as a couple, and even if he was not always easy to notice the same could not be said of Anne. Her tall, athletic build drew attention whenever she wore anything other than DPCU.

Rob finished his preparations for the dining-in night, pinned his miniature medals to his mess-jacket, and then carried it on a hanger out to his car.

He took the brief drive to Anne's town-house, and walked to her front door. Already he could feel his heart racing a bit, and that which occurred next did not contribute to any efforts he was making to calm his aroused senses. Anne appeared at the door in a knee-length, wine-red evening dress, with matching bolero to which was pinned her sizeable rack of medals; her shoulder length hair hung free, and her dark eyes appeared to flare as she saw him. Rob was so used to the sight of her in uniform that he was completely unprepared for the vision before his eyes; nothing she had worn to church had been quite so arresting to the senses. Anne stayed in the doorway briefly, as if she was savouring Rob's enjoyment, before walking down the two stairs, and lightly kissing him on the lips. There was an understated class about the way she was dressed that made her seem that much more beautiful to Rob's eyes.

'You look amazing!' he said, when he eventually found his voice.

'Just amazing?' she asked, raising her eyebrows at him.

'Okay then; rwyt ti'n hardd! Rwy'n dy garu di!'[2] said Rob.

'That's better,' she replied, drawing him closer to herself and kissing him again, a little less lightly this time.

'But you wouldn't have understood a word I said!'

'I got your drift by the way you said it,' Anne answered, smiling.

Hand in hand they walked to Rob's car, and he held the door open for her.

'I have something for you by the way,' he said and fumbled briefly in his left pocket and presented to her a small blue box. When she opened it Anne saw a gold Celtic Cross on a fine chain. There were no gems set within it, just the scrolling that was characteristic of Celtic artwork.

'It's beautiful,' Anne said, evidently very pleased. 'May I wear it now?'

'Of course,' he replied. 'I have been waiting a long time to give that to somebody; never thought I would, to be honest, but I liked it and bought it just in case. No matter what happens between us, I want you to keep it.'

Rob was on the verge of speech again; however the intensity and complexity of his feelings were beginning to cause a traffic-

---

2. You're beautiful! I love you!

jam of thoughts, words, and emotions. However Anne hushed him.

'Just enjoy the moment, you don't have to try and explain it as well,' she said. 'I love this kind of jewellery. *Maman* brought me up to have classic tastes.'

They clasped hands briefly, before Rob walked around the other side of the car, and got in. Anne could tell that he was feeling nervous, because of the look of hard concentration on his face. It was a look that would have been indiscernible from the face he wore going into combat.

'Chill the heck out will you,' said Anne as they drove away. 'Anybody'd think you were getting ready to kill someone.'

'Sorry,' he said. 'I'm nervous about what people'll say; I don't really like being noticed that much!'

'Right! I make you this solemn promise,' said Anne. 'Every time you look nervous or edgy tonight, I'm going to kiss you - in front of everyone! You got it!'

Rob exhaled briefly before glancing over at Anne who was regarding him with an air of Gallic defiance, almost daring him to contradict her.

'I love you!'

'I love you too,' she replied, 'so just relax!'

Rob bowed his head for a moment and then looked over at her. He had faced death, grief and disappointment with a dour and unbendable courage, but joy was undoing him; joy that somehow reawakened every sorrow and fear he had been hiding or holding back. Anne took him by the hand and gave him a reassuring look.

'I'm sorry; you've had a lot to deal with this year. I don't really care if you're uptight or not; I love you anyway,' she said. 'You've held in so much for so long, so you might be a bit unhinged for a while, but that doesn't change what I feel for you. And I'm still serious about kissing you if you look nervous!'

The skies outside the car were grey, and there was a chill in the air that seeped into the bones, but for the two of them it was as if the sun shone on a brighter day, despite Rob's initial nerves. They passed the rest of the journey out to the base in silence. Anne could tell Rob was focussing on breathing deeply to ground himself, so she laid a hand reassuringly on his leg, and left him to his mental discipline. Once they were parked she could tell he was much calmer, and then Rob turned to Anne and gave her a wink.

'Well, shall we go and give people something to talk about?' he said, with a fire in his eyes.

'Now that's more like it,' said Anne beaming at him. They walked toward the main entrance to the mess, clasping hands eagerly, oblivious to the wondering looks they were getting from some of the others who were arriving at that time.

Winter Mess dress gives more colour to an Army Dining-in night, with each Corps having a distinct colour to their main jacket or its facings. With the addition of the wives and partners in civilian clothes, there was a festive brightness to the occasion that defied the grey skies and cold temperatures. A gathering of people near the glass doors that led into the building saw Rob walking in hand in hand with a lady; a stunning brunette with dark eyes, who was regarding him with a look of unmistakable affection.

'Crikey! Who's the glamazon Rob's got hanging off his arm?' said Steve in awe at the sight of the woman, watching the two of them walking in together. Whoever she was, thought Steve, she is dang tall, because with heels on she was had a clear inch on Rob.

'Hang on a minute,' he continued, looking past the elegance to a face he recognised. 'It can't be! That's not Anne is it?'

Alan and Jo Deakin, who were standing talking to Steve and his wife Beth, caught sight of the couple as well, and Jo let out a small squeal as she recognised the sight of Anne without her hair in a bun.

'Oh. My. Word,' was all Steve could say, before turning to Alan, his eyes dark with suspicion.

'You knew, didn't you?' he demanded.

Beth, Jo and Steve all looked at Alan, who suddenly felt very exposed.

'I may have been privy to certain information,' said Alan, 'but the demands of propriety, confidentiality and discretion were such that full disclosure could not be made until the proper alignment of all relevant celestial bodies.'

'Does that flimflam amount to a confession of guilt?' demanded Steve, at which Alan tried his best to give a vacant smile.

'Well there's certainly one celestial body out there,' said Jo Deakin. 'And she's definitely aligned with another.' She then turned to her husband and raised her eyebrows.

'And I'll deal with you later!' she said haughtily.

'Goody!' said Alan, at which Jo slapped him sharply on the backside.

A number of other heads had been turned by their arrival. As they entered through the glass doors, Rob put his arm around Anne's waist, and she turned and kissed him quickly on the lips. A voice in the background said, 'Oh yeah, Padre!' It was Sean O'Donnell, who soon afterwards was rubbing his arm where his wife Tania had just thumped him.

'Just leave them alone Sean, I think it's beautiful!' she remonstrated with him.

'It *is* beautiful,' he said taking her by the hand. 'But there's no way I'm leaving them alone. Come on over and say hi.'

Sean then turned and saw Alan and Jo Deakin embracing Anne, and Rob continuing to smile in a somewhat giddy fashion.

'I better get the Padre a beer, Tania, he needs something to settle his nerves,' Sean said merrily. 'Would you like something as well?'

'A G&T would be nice,' she said.

'I'm all over it,' he said as he went to the bar; from where he procured drinks, whilst Tania went over to where Rob and Anne were standing.

'Hi, I'm Tania O'Donnell,' she said extending her hand to Rob.

'Good evening ma'am, pleased to meet you,' he said formally, his nerves still lurking in the background.

Tania then embraced Anne, whom she had known for some time.

'I'm so glad this has happened,' she said quietly as Rob became engaged in conversation with Sean who had presented him with a beer, 'I hope it works out well for you both.'

'Thanks! Not what I was expecting at the beginning of the year, that's for sure,' replied Anne.

The fact that they were a couple was received with a lot of goodwill, though Rob found it a little overwhelming.

'Anybody'd think we'd just got engaged,' he said as they filed into the dining room behind the CO, who was the dining President for the evening.

'Why? You got a ring handy?' Anne said saucily, and she laughed aloud as Rob turned bright red.

'Just you remember what I said about you looking edgy and embarrassed,' she said as they got to their seats, that had conveniently been placed together, 'because right now I want to kiss you very hard.'

'Would it be all right if I got embarrassed later on when we have some privacy?' said Rob innocently.

'I'll think about it!' she said, looking at him with her eyes wide, caught off guard by his flirtatious retort.

That evening was forever etched in Rob's memory, and a sense of love and community flowed over him that he had not known in a very long time.

Not long afterwards, Rob and Anne spent an evening with Rob's younger sister Catrin (nicknamed Bear) and her husband Derek, who had come over to Australia with their young daughter. They, along with Rob's Uncle Gareth, had come out to Murruwa to visit.

When the news had got out in the Llewellyn family that Rob had a love interest, Catrin and Derek had decided to mix an opportunity for a holiday with an opportunity to check out Anne. The Llewellyn's were a tight knit family, who were anxious to meet this new lady in Rob's life. However it was an enjoyable time for Anne, and in the space of one evening with them at Rob's place, she discovered most of the remaining pieces to the puzzle that had been Padre Llewellyn.

'It was so hard on Bear for me to leave,' reflected Rob, when he and Anne were enjoying an evening walk together a couple of days later. 'I think she had in her mind that I would always be around, looking out for her. But even without getting kicked out of school, I found living in the valleys hard; I always had an eye for far horizons, and the idea of becoming a teacher was something that revolted me. That's why my mother and I clashed eventually; I guess she never really understood me, because I never wanted what she thought was logical and respectable for my life. The last straw was when I flattened the music teacher at school, and I went to the Marines.'

'You're a very protective person you know,' said Anne.

'Noticed have you?'

'Yeah, once or twice,' she said and gave him a friendly punch on the arm. 'Though I think you would have made a good teacher. The stuff in your personnel file said you were rated *very* highly as an instructor.'

'Teaching soldiers is one thing, cariad, but teaching school children is quite another; trust me I've done both,' said Rob with a groan. 'But in my mother's mind I've always been this wild creature that's been off doing its own thing; somebody who needed taming, but who refused the bridle. She thought after I broke up with the girl in Taunton that I would come to my senses, leave the Marines, and settle down. But it didn't happen; then came both my trips to Iraq.'

Rob's voice trailed off for a moment, as he thought of the awkwardness between him and his family, and the sound of his mother crying when she saw him after the IED blast. Anne reached out and took his hand in hers, and they walked silently for a while, as Rob distilled his thoughts.

'After getting hit by the IED, it took a while to recover from my wounds,' said Rob eventually, 'and I chose to discharge, and come out here and help Uncle Gareth teach music.

'I think Mam got a glimmer of hope then; and she'd always liked the idea of me being a pastor, almost as much as being a teacher. My training for the ministry was another bonus if you like, even though I was living so far away,' Rob went on. 'But then I went and re-joined the military didn't I?'

'Was she angry?' asked Anne.

'I think she must have been,' commented Rob, 'though she never said so; but Ceridwen sure did. She said that I must be crazy to go and endanger my life again. I've never heard her so mad at me.'

'Sooner or later they'll have to realise that they can't run your life,' said Anne, 'and besides, your act of rebellion in joining the Australia Army is how we ended up meeting.'

'Ceri only said it because she loves me, and didn't want to see me get hurt again,' said Rob fairly, before adding with a small smile, 'but I did remind her that running my life wasn't one of her responsibilities.'

'It's funny you know,' said Anne, 'I find it hard to think of you as a rebel. You've always seemed to me to be so kind and faithful. If they'd wanted a rebel they just needed to see me in my teens.'

'We're both rebels, just in our own ways. A lot of people are scared of that big bad world out there, cariad,' said Rob reflectively. 'They think that by not doing risky things that they can avoid dark days coming too soon.

'Don't get me wrong now, my family are great people; kind and hard-working,' he continued. 'But this strange world of bullets, blood and bombs that we inhabit is beyond their reckoning. And many people are afraid, but what they really dread is not the darkness of sorrow, but the piercing shafts of light that shine between the clouds, for in that fearful glare the fragility of their peace and prosperity can be seen; that there is no way of managing risk out of existence, that they are only a heart beat from eternity, that all they treasure is but one moment of madness away from destruction.'

Anne regarded him intently for a moment, and drawing Rob close they stood for a while in comfortable silence, contemplating the unusual life they led; its joys, perils and annoyances.

'Do you think it's a waste of your talents being in the Army?' asked Anne eventually. 'When I first heard you sing it really made we wonder why on earth you'd choose the Army with a voice like that.'

'Not at all a waste,' Rob said emphatically. 'Gifts in art, music, and poetry are very important in the military. Virtually every culture in days past has tried to instil in warriors skills beyond the sword. But in our current age people seem to think it's only brutes and beasts that are fit for combat.'

'I have known some brutes and beasts in my time,' said Anne

with feeling. 'But I do think you could've taken your skill with music a long way. Could still, if you wanted.'

Rob ran his fingers gently through Anne's hair, gazing intently at the woman he loved, enjoying the light of the moon that was by now riding in the sky above them. He had not been stung by what she had just said, but he did think it deserved a considered response. Eventually he asked her a question.

'Have you ever spent much time talking to the guys in the band at Murruwa?'

'No I haven't, only the occasional word with their OC,' Anne replied. 'Why's that?'

'Well, every single one of them has a lot of talent as a musician, I mean serious skills. I've listened to them practice and heard their stories,' said Rob. 'But they've almost all chosen to pursue music in the Army because it's a way of being a full-time musician and actually having money for food! I'm good at singing and piano, but succeeding in music takes more than talent. It takes determination, ambition; even self-obsession. And it takes luck, if you know what I mean; knowing the right people and being in the right place at the right time, like.'

'And you don't like the limelight do you?' observed Anne.

'No, I much prefer the moonlight with you,' he replied, kissing her gently.

'Well, there is one thing for sure, lover,' said Anne a little giddily, 'I'm not going to try and tame you. I like a walk on the wild side myself.'

17

One consequence of Rob's admission of having been a sniper was his periodic presence on the range, but the recent conversation with Corporal Nguyen meant that a new and promising double act had their first public outing. Rob's skill with a weapon and F-Bomb's way with words certainly meant that it was going to be a memorable time for the recruits. Especially for the occasion, Anne, the CO, Pat, and Sean O'Donnell were also there to watch.

'Above all you've got to be comfortable,' F-Bomb explained as Rob lay prone on the firing line, 'it's no good being all hunched up like a dog trying to shag a tennis ball. Just relax, breathe easy and build your position slowly. Padre Llewellyn used to be a sniper in the Royal Marines, and he can shoot off a bee's dick at a thousand metres. He's here to demonstrate building the basic shooting position, and a couple of other things you might try depending on your body type and so on.'

So Rob lay on the ground demonstrating good technique, as well as some common faults, while F-Bomb rattled off a seamless patter of long remembered lines as the recruits watched and then tried to build their own shooting positions accordingly.

Eventually the time came for live firing to commence, but first Corporal Nguyen asked Rob to show everyone how it was done.

'Go and fill two magazines Padre,' he said, 'first I'll get you to check zero on the rifle, and then we'll go for a really small group. If we have some time then we'll use the second magazine to demonstrate some common faults.'

'Okay then.'

As he filled his magazines he watched Pat moving amongst some recruits who were going to be firing on the next range over from where he was. Rob grinned as he saw the big Catholic priest sharing some raucous joke with those who were waiting their turn to fire. Pat certainly had a knack for making people laugh, Rob thought, though he was close enough to observe that there was one fellow who did not seem to be joining in the hilarity. For a moment he stood and looked at the young man, trying to gauge his mood. Long years of experience made Rob very watchful around people on a rifle range, however a quick call from F-Bomb meant that his attention was taken off the recruit.

As he came to the firing line Rob lay down, and fired two serials of five rounds to check the zero on the telescopic sight, which required very little adjustment. The experienced military members who were watching could not help but wonder at the unhurried, smooth, but utterly deadly grace he brought to shooting.

'Padre will now demonstrate a 20 round, bolt-adjust serial,' Rob heard F-Bomb say through the electronic hearing protection he was wearing. 'Here he will be trying to fire the rounds into as small a group as possible. He'll rest after each five rounds, and at the end we will measure all four five round groups, and determine the average size.' F-Bomb then turned to Rob and said, 'Four, five round groups, in your own time, go on.'

Rob fired away; his shooting position, breath control, and trigger pull were all textbook perfect. Shooter and rifle seemed to be in a seamless and comfortable relationship, and it was no surprise when the average group turned out to be just over thirty millimetres. Rob changed out the magazine, and readied for what Corporal Nguyen wanted to do next.

However, at that moment a commotion on the range to their immediate right interrupted F-Bomb's instruction. For a moment there was a lot of yelling, but then a shot rang out, but from the sound it was evident to Rob that the barrel was not pointing down range toward the targets.

'What the fuck?' said F-Bomb as a Corporal from Bravo Company came racing toward them.

'Get everyone out of the way, we've got one who's gone postal and wants to shoot people!' she yelled as she ran past.

The staff rapidly began to shepherd the recruits toward any cover they could find, whilst a short distance away a man in some distress could be seen, and he was screaming at the top of his lungs. As the crowd cleared only one other figure was evident on centre-stage of the developing drama; that of Chaplain Pat O'Neill gesticulating as if he was trying to calm down the disturbed individual.

'I'm gonna kill 'em!' the young man raged, 'Stop following me!'

'C'mon Padre,' said F-Bomb in Rob's ear, 'take that weapon and let's get a better view of this.'

Without thinking Rob complied, in an automatic reaction to the situation, and the two of them found a place where they had clear line of sight on the recruit without being in a position where they could be easily seen themselves.

'Looks like that's Padre O'Neill trying to calm him down,' commented F-Bomb looking through a spotting scope that he had grabbed from the firing line, 'I knew he had balls of steel.'

'Too right he does,' muttered Rob, but then added as he sized up the situation. 'If the Recruit aims his weapon, I'm going to fire.'

'Roger,' replied F-Bomb. 'Shoot for centre-of-mass; nothing fucking artistic like a head shot.'

'Agreed,' said Rob clinically, calmly bringing the sight on to the young fellow's chest, and waiting to see how the deadly drama would unfold. Though he had not been a sniper for some years, the skills remained, and with the patient artistry distilled from long training, Rob calmed his breathing after the initial exertion and excitement, rapidly clearing his mind, until all that remained was a crystalline clarity of purpose. Though the lens of the telescopic sight did not have significant magnification, Rob recognised the sombre recruit he had seen earlier in the group that had been near Pat.

Pat in the meantime was unaware of the two patient, deadly men watching the drama he was acting out with the recruit in front of him. He had come down to the range that day to watch Rob shoot, but no sooner had he arrived than Anne had asked him to talk to a recruit who seemed to be oddly confused. The guy had always been a bit strange apparently, but this sudden jump in behaviour was not expected. Pat had spent some time observing him, as he laughed and joked with the other recruits in the fellow's section, but had been as surprised as anyone when the recruit had stood up and started yelling, before firing off a round that had thankfully missed all those near its path.

'C'mon now mate, it's all right, we'll keep you safe,' said Pat, trying to adopt a relaxed posture. He was trying to distract the guy as long as possible so all other staff and recruits could be brought to safety. Tears streaked the face of the young man and he breathed in great heaves through clenched teeth, his face contorted in a horrible mixture of rage and anguish.

'Keep away!' the young man shouted, 'They're after me!'

Pat took a step backwards before leaning up against one of the posts that supported the shelter over the firing line.

'So what'd'ya like doing when you're not in this hole, mate?' asked Pat, no stress apparent in his voice. However the recruit gave no answer, but stared into space, both hands still on his rifle.

F-Bomb was watching the whole drama playing out through a spotting scope he had taken from the firing line.

'Well I'll be fucked, the Padre's as cool as a cucumber,' he muttered in respect for Pat's courage, before a voice behind them spoke urgently.

'F-Bomb, a couple of RIs are going to try and work around behind him while the Padre's got his attention.'

'Ack; but if he aims that rifle we're going to slot him; let 'em know that.'

'Roger; I have radio comms with them,' came the reply from the Corporal, 'I'm going to hang just here and keep you aware of their location.'

'Roger that,' replied F-Bomb simply, his eyes focused on the drama before them.

The recruit now began to look at Pat, and for a moment he relaxed; but then it seemed as if he focussed in on the crosses on Pat's collar, and then the troubled young man's face contorted in rage again, and he then began to rave in a frightening manner.

'The second thief on the cross, no forgiveness for me! I am the destroyer!' the young man screamed, and for the first time Pat began to feel seriously afraid.

'I am the destroyer!' he shouted again.

'Holy shit, I think we're going to have to shoot this one,' said F-Bomb in an agitated tone, as he watched the drama.

'Roger,' said Rob clinically, settling to take a shot.

Pat began to pray under his breath as the young man became more agitated.

'I am the destroyer,' the recruit screamed again and he looked as if he was going to shoulder the rifle.

'*Bydd drugarog wrthyf, O Dduw, yn ôl dy fyddlondeb,*'[1] Rob prayed, the cross-hairs still resting on the upper part of the recruit's chest.

However at that moment Ian Stewart and Lydia Timoshenko appeared, ready to jump the recruit from behind.

'Stop, stop, stop!' said the Corporal behind them, and Rob automatically removed his finger from the trigger, and then he saw the two Charlie Company instructors grab the young man. Pat then drove forward, hitting him with a rib-crushing tackle, and very soon he was disarmed and restrained.

'Fuck me,' remarked F-Bomb as he got up from where he

---

1.   Have mercy on me O God, according to your lovingkindness.

had been lying, 'I thought we were going to have to slot him for sure!'

'Very nearly did,' said Rob as he stood, and then stared with a pained expression as the recruit was restrained and led away.

'You right there Padre?' asked F-Bomb when he saw the look on Rob's face.

'Just wondering what will become of him,' he muttered in reply.'Not much we can do about it mate,' said Corporal Nguyen.

'But it still makes me sad,' reflected Rob. 'What little kindness there is in the world seldom gets shown to people with a mental illness. When he's discharged from the army he'll go out into the community where who know's what will happen to him.'

'What the actual fuck Padre? Are you on crack?' said F-Bomb in surprise. 'You were just about to equip old mate over there with an extra hole in his body! And now you're all sympathy!'

'Just because I was willing to kill him doesn't mean I stopped viewing him as a person,' said Rob calmly, as he calmly unloaded the rifle, and for a moment F-Bomb stared at him, amazed. However the cutting remark that was forming in his mind was cut short by the thought that perhaps the Padre took as little harm from all the killing he had done, because when the heat of battle had passed, he never forgot the humanity of those he had shot. Or maybe that is why he had been able to walk away when he did.

Slowly the commotion died away, and people came over to Pat, expressing in various ways their relief at everyone still being alive. Despite the calm demeanour he had shown during the whole ordeal, Pat was now visibly shaken.

'I thought I was had it there fellas,' said Pat coming up to Rob and F-Bomb, his hands trembling as he spoke. 'It was a balls effort from Lydia and Ian to jump him like that, and somebody told me you two were going to shoot him!'

'Yeh, that's right,' said Rob, and Pat looked at him and just shook his head.

'I don't want to think what'd be happening now if you'd killed that bloke.'

'Well, thank the Lord I didn't,' said Rob quietly.

'Padre O'Neill, you look like you could do with a stiff drink there,' observed F-Bomb.

'Too right, and I'm going to do that first opportunity I get,' said Pat wiping his brow, before turning away and walking off in the direction of his vehicle.

A few minutes later, as Rob stood meticulously cleaning the rifle, Anne came over, her face showing a professional front over a depth of concern she could not quite hide.

'I've just heard what happened,' she said. 'I was shepherding recruits out of the way. Pat told me you were ready to shoot.'

'Yes, I was,' said Rob, with a small smile. They looked at each other for a moment, before Anne patted him gently on the arm.

'Are you okay?'

Rob shrugged.

'It could've been a lot worse.'

'That doesn't answer my question!'

'I'm okay; well, I haven't had time to think about it yet.'

'Righto, I'll ask you later then. I need to go back to Charlie Company Headquarters,' she said, 'but I'll come up after 1600, okay?'

'Sure, that'd be great,' he replied, and calmly continued with the task of cleaning the rifle. Rob had always found the smell of the light machine oil soothing, as if the odour somehow signified that the battle was over, and what called itself normality could now continue, undisturbed by the siren call of chaos. As the texture of the oiled steel ran through his fingers, he mused that there would always be a part of him that was tightly wound and waiting should ever danger demand a deadly or daring response. It was making sure that he was not always living as if on the brink of urgent action that could be the tricky part.

'Better go on the piano before I leave then,' Rob said in response to that thought, and finished the re-assembly of the weapon.

When Rob had finished he went back to the Chaplaincy centre, and was met there by the CO of 2 RTB, who had come to thank Pat for his courage. Soon the incident would be known within the upper echelons of the Army, and the potential for interest in what had happened was significant, to say the least.

'The thing we have to remember sir, is that the seventeen to thirty year old age group is the key time for when people are likely to develop a mental illness,' explained Pat as they discussed what could be done to prevent further incidents like that in the future. 'Recruiting can screen these kids as much as they like, but we're still going to get troubled ones coming through the system. What we need is a robust drill for when it does happen.'

'Like what you did today?' asked the CO with raised eyebrows. 'Like having Rob here ready to shoot the poor bugger?'

'Hopefully not, but we sometimes have to be prepared to take life in order to save lives,' said Rob sadly. 'That's part of the premise on which we go to war.'

'That's true mate, and nobody's saying you've done anything wrong either; you were the best qualified person to be out there' said the CO, 'but I hate to think what'd be happening now if you'd taken a shot and killed that recruit.'

'Well let's just be thankful it didn't happen,' said Pat firmly. 'All I know is that I'm glad Rob and F-Bomb were ready to do the unthinkable; and doubly glad that Bombardier Stewart and Corporal Timoshenko got there first.'

The CO left soon afterwards, and Rob and Pat knew that there would be yet another investigation, though they were confident that its findings would be sane. What happened once the results of the investigation got passed up the chain of command could be another matter. Sometimes people sitting in the Canberra bubble see things in a different way, thought Pat darkly, as Rob walked down toward the chapel; it all comes of too much time looking at the arse ends of politicians, the shit clouds your vision after a while. As he completed that thought, he heard somebody enter the Chaplaincy centre, and it turned out to be Anne, who walked in wearing civilian clothes.

'He's gone down to the Chapel hasn't he?' she asked, and Pat nodded in response. 'You need to come out for a drink Pat, you look awful. It's past 1600 now, time to unwind don't you think? Or do you have that wretched on-call phone?'

'No, I don't,' said Pat, 'Alan took it off me.'

'Excellent!' said Anne. 'You need to come over to Rob's place as soon as you're changed. F-Bomb and Lydia are going to be there too.'

'Jeez you're bossy sometimes Anne,' said Pat in a slightly exasperated tone.

'I prefer to think of it as leadership, but I don't care anyway,' said Anne defiantly. 'I'm going to make sure you're looked after.'

With that Anne turned and walked out of the Chaplaincy centre, going down the stairs toward the Chapel. As she walked in, she was once again greeted by the sound of Rob's emotions coming off the keyboard in strident waves of sound. Sorrow made musical radiated from the instrument; the sorrow of a gentle man whose heart desired to live at peace, but whose hands had also been trained for war. Then slowly the music

began to change, with the sadness and a kind of resolve
blending into one, and then he began to sing a ballad:

Long ago and yesterday,
I lived another life,
Stalking in the shadows,
Of places rent with strife,
I dealt out fear and chaos,
And had it dealt to me,
Till my life was turned to blood and dust,
By the blast of an I-E-D.

The past is catching up with me
No matter where I run,
But I'm scared of others knowing
The kind of things I've done.
Lonely, living exiled,
Lost among my fears,
Running from the memories
That echo in the wind.

A broken man and battered,
I took another road,
Twisted by emotions,
That in fear I never showed,
I turned my mind to something else,
But written in today,
Is engraving from the life I've led,
Like letters from the grave.

The past is catching up with me
No matter where I run,

But I'm scared of others knowing
The kind of things I've done.
Lonely, living exiled,
Lost among my fears,
Running from the memories
That echo in the wind.

I stand alone and lonely,
Lost among the years,
Knowing what I need the most,
Is to face my greatest fears,
So I'll defy my demons
And self-pity's sins,
I'll turn my head and listen
To those echoes in the wind.

The wind is full of voices,
Memories made alive,
I can't escape their howling,
I cannot even hide.

The past is catching up with me
But I'll no longer run,
Though I'm scared of others knowing
The kind of things I've done.
Lonely, living exiled,
Lost among my fears,
I'll stand and face the memories
That echo in the wind.

He turned to her with a grin on his face and asked, 'So what do you think?'

'That was amazing! Did you write it yourself?' asked Anne.

'Yes; indeed I did; "Echoes in the Wind" I call it,' said Rob, 'I finished it a couple of days ago, though I'm still not quite happy with the music.'

'It sounded great to me! You're a genius,' she said shaking her head. Rob just smiled his usual gentle smile and looked intently at her.

'You and I are going to be social tonight,' Anne said, drifting over to him, rubbing his shoulders and kissing him on top of the head, 'no moping around and getting all dark and Welsh on me. I've invited a crowd over to your place.'

'Sounds like a plan,' he said, 'though I'm not feeling that bad; it was a relief that nobody died today.'

'Well, Pat needs a drink, even if you don't,' she said, 'why don't we just go over to the bottle-o and get something on the way home?'

'Sure thing *cariad*,' said Rob, squeezing her hand, and the two of them walked off together.

As the gathering at Rob's place got under way, Anne realised what a novelty it was for her to see Rob's house as a social hub rather than a place of retreat. However she then caught herself; it was still being a place of retreat, it was just that Rob was opening it up to others as well. The smell of food and the sound of laughter and friendship permeated the evening.

Those who have dealt out death, or who have walked with danger, share a special bond that heightens their relationships, thought Anne. Pat, F-Bomb, Lydia and Rob were causing each other to laugh hysterically with various tales, some of which involved Rob. For them, hearing the more chaotic side of the apparently respectable Chaplain was quite a revelation.

'No fucking way Padre! Pics or it didn't happen!' said F-Bomb, in response to one tale of a night out with his fellow Marines. At this Rob duly went inside and produced a photo album, and then showed all present a picture of him wearing a lycra dress.

'Holy shit; that can't be unseen!' was all F-Bomb could manage, at the sight of Rob and the rest of reconnaissance troop, 40 Commando, wearing a variety of highly questionable clothing.

'You're not telling stories about taking off your clothes are you?' asked Anne.

'Not until after 2100; but it eventually involved nudity!' explained Rob.

'Why 2100?' asked Anne.

'I don't know; it's just what we did!'

'Anne, you might think that Rob is a quiet, sensitive, serious man,' said Pat, 'but beneath that responsible exterior I think lays a maniac who every now and then likes to grab the world by the under-garments and set its jatz-crackers on fire.'

At this remark, Rob looked up at Anne and smiled sheepishly. However, just then, his personal mobile phone went off, and he went into the music room for what was a relatively brief conversation. When he joined the others again, Rob wore a somewhat puzzled expression.

'What's the matter Padre?' said F-Bomb, looking at his face. 'Another recruit gone postal or something?'

'No, it was Jar-Jar,' said Rob slowly.

'What's he done?' asked Anne, getting nervous at the mere mention of Lieutenant Weston's nickname, despite his better performance in recent months.

'Nothing actually,' replied Rob, still looking a little confused. 'He just told me he wants to get baptised.'

'He what?' exclaimed Pat.

'He wants to get baptised,' said Rob again, as much for his own benefit as for the others in the room.

'Well that's random,' said Pat.

'Does he want to get immersed, Padre?' asked F-Bomb, with an evil smile, 'because I'll give you fifty bucks if you hold him under!'

Rob and Anne continued talking together long after the others had left, going over the events of the day, but also talking about the future.

'I spoke to my career manager today,' said Anne in a leading sort of tone, causing Rob's stomach to do a quick back-flip. In a matter of months Anne would be coming to the end of two years at Murruwa, which usually meant she would be posting out. Rob was still coming to terms with having a romantic attachment, and he had been trying to push aside the thought that they may be parted all too soon.

'Okay then,' he managed by way of reply.

'I've been recommended for Staff College,' she continued, and Rob's heart sank a little further. Anne was a great officer, who would be bound to go higher, he thought morosely.

'Where do they do that?' Rob asked.

'In Canberra,' Anne explained, and then paused for a moment, as if reluctant to say what was on her mind.

Rob's stomach now felt like lead; not what he was wanting at the end of a stressful day. However he forced himself to think about Anne instead.

'You seem a bit unsure of something there,' he asked.

'Well, I am bit unsure about something actually,' she said, and then looked over at him with a faint smile. 'I told my career manager that I didn't want to go to staff college; not yet anyway.'

'You what?' he said, shocked. 'What's caused that?'

'One of the reasons is sitting next to me at the moment!' Anne said, and Rob turned bright red.

'Are you doing that just for me?' Rob asked. 'I couldn't live with myself if I thought I'd held you back.'

'Calm your farm you Welsh lunatic!' she replied, punching him on the arm. 'It's not just you! But you're a priority in my life now, so get used to it! There's no need to go and get all guilt ridden on me. If I wasn't prepared to make you a priority I wouldn't have been in for this romance in the first place.'

'So what else has lead to this?' asked Rob, still reeling slightly from Anne's onslaught.

'Life experience! I don't want to have my sense of self so wrapped up in the military that I can't walk away from the Green[2] without having some sort of identity crisis,' she said emphatically. 'And no matter how much you give, Army will always be willing to take a little more; and after you're gone nobody will remember who you are for very long. I want to explore other dreams too, so I told my career manager I'd like another year here. He said there were plenty of jobs for Majors lying around at Murruwa, while I decide whether or not to go to Staff College.'

Rob had suspected that Anne was not quite the typical career driven Army officer; she had too curious and provocative a mind to accept a conventional trajectory for her life. So he decided to move the conversation away from talk of careers.

'Do you have any other life goals?' he asked. 'Having a family or that sort of thing?'

Anne thought about this for a moment, though Rob could tell instantly that some part of the question he had asked was causing her discomfort.

---

2. "The green" is a term used to refer the Army as an institution.

'I knew this'd come up sooner or later,' said Anne, leaning back and closing her eyes for a moment.

'What's the matter?' said Rob, taking her hand, his fingers intertwining with hers.

'Argh! How do I explain this? No point in putting it off either,' she said to no-one in particular, and then turned toward Rob and looked him squarely in the eye. 'Because of my wild younger days, I ended up with a bad STI that means it'll be very hard for me to conceive. The infection was treated and cured ages ago, but its mark remains, if you get my drift.'

Rob nodded in acknowledgement, and then spoke before Anne could say another word.

'Anne Le Bon,' he said, very firmly, 'don't think for one moment that I want to be with you any less if you can't conceive children! I'm in love with you for you, not for your potential for breeding. You're the woman I love, not some prize cow.'

'Moo!'

'No. I'm serious!' replied Rob earnestly.

'I know you are, and it means a lot to hear you say that,' she said, as she gripped his hand more firmly.

'I mean every word,' he said, with a smile. 'Besides, my sisters have already produced seven grandchildren as it is! And if you want to go to Staff College eventually I'll back you as well. You're a gifted woman who has a lot to offer.'

'Thank you. Are you sure you're okay after today?' she asked.

'Yeh, I'm fine actually; I didn't just stop being a sniper because it was becoming hard for me,' he admitted. 'I hate to admit it, but if I'm honest with myself, one of the things that made me want to walk away from sniping was that I could see it was becoming too easy; killing that boy was not hard at all, and that scared me. Nietzsche said that if you gaze long into the abyss, the abyss gazes into you. I wanted to take my eyes off the abyss before I became one with it; I wanted to lift my eyes beyond it, and spend my days thinking of a time when the abyss would be no more.'

Anne ran her hand gently over the scars on his arm; she was becoming used to these philosophic bursts that would occasionally shoot out from Rob's mind. He glanced down at the marks, enjoying the gentle sensation of her touch.

'Scars,' he reflected, 'and I've got more than just these.'

'So have we both,' said Anne, and he pulled her close and kissed her on the head.

'I know; scars of memory in particular,' he remarked. 'From my first week here I have been hounded by them. Evan gets sick and I had a dream about shooting that boy; Alan has a go at me about my isolation, and how much I miss Johnno hits me between the eyes, like I'd been trying to deny it for years. Corporal De Blasio loses it, and I dream about Dizzy hanging himself. I fall for you and I realise I have been running from love for the past twelve years.'

'Well you'd better stop running, because I'm quicker than you!' she said, digging him in the ribs.

'I'm not going anywhere my lady,' said Rob, 'the hounds of heaven were running me down anyway. I feel more whole than I've felt for years.'

'You know something I love about you?' Anne said, looking at him with her dark eyes glinting, a sure sign that a smart remark was coming his way.

'I expect I'm about to find out,' Rob said, a little resignedly.

'You're deep, you're perceptive, and you have better intuition than most women I know,' she observed, her eyes still alive with premeditated mirth.

'Why thank you,' he said, 'where's the catch then?'

'Why must there be a catch?'

'There is, just by looking at you, I can tell you want to be cheeky but you're trying to rein it in,' he said, and Anne laughed.

'The catch is, my love, that you can be incredibly melancholic and over-analyse the crap out of everything,' she continued.

'Right you are, cariad,' he said. 'I don't think I can change that either.'

'I don't want you to; besides, I can be a pushy cow sometimes, so we make a good team,' she said with a smile, and the two of then leant companionably against each, and talked on into the night.

Hours later, as Anne was driving home, her mind was contemplating many things; and chief among them was what Rob had said to her after she confessed the difficulty she would have in conceiving children. Those words had meant more to her than she could explain, and from that moment on Anne was sure in her heart that she wanted to marry him. It was a sure sign to her of something she had already sensed — that for Rob the word love was not just a feeling, but also what he would do for her every day, whether he felt like it or not.

OTHER BOOKS IN 'THE SHEPHERD'S WATCH' SERIES

A Wind of Bitter Tears

The Devil in the Downdraft

Angel of Wrath (still to come)

ABOUT THE AUTHOR

Roger Marsh is the author of *The Shepherd's Overwatch* series of novels, which are drawn from his own service as a Padre in the Australian Army during the War on Terror. Serving alongside frontline troops in Afghanistan, Roger witnessed the brutal realities of modern conflict — not only its physical toll, but its deep psychological and spiritual wounds.

The son of a Korean War veteran, Roger was raised in rural Australia, where he developed a love for the outdoors, martial arts, and the quiet resilience of country life. Before joining the Army, Roger attended the University of Queensland, where he gained a Bachelor of Arts with specialisation in Biblical languages and political sociology, and also worked in the security sector. These experiences combined to further shape his understanding of human complexity, and of hazards that can come in the line of duty. In time, he also completed theological studies, and went into the ministry.

Roger lives with his wife and family in rural Queensland. He is also an avid scale modeller, archer, and marksman, as well as being a Welsh speaker. Not currently in paid ministry, Roger divides his time between writing, mentoring, cooking, walking dogs, and hanging around with his family.

Printed and bound by CPI Group (UK) Ltd, Croydon, CR0 4YY

21/04/2026

02094655-0001